ANDY McDERMOTT

THE RESURRECTION KEY

HEADLINE

First published in 2019 by
HEADLINE PUBLISHING GROUP

First published in paperback in 2020 by
HEADLINE PUBLISHING GROUP

1

Cataloguing in Publication Data is available from the British Library

ISBN 978 1 4722 3694 4

Typeset in Aldine 401BT by Avon DataSet Ltd,
Bidford-on-Avon, Warwickshire

Printed and bound in Great Britain by Clays Ltd, Elcograf S.p.A.

HEADLINE PUBLISHING GROUP
An Hachette UK Company
Carmelite House
50 Victoria Embankment
London EC4Y 0DZ

www.headline.co.uk
www.hachette.co.uk

For Kat and Sebastian

Prologue

The Southern Ocean

A frigid wind bit Arnold Bekker's cheeks as he gazed at the ragged white peaks rising from the grey waters ahead. After six days at sea, the prospect of standing on solid ground was a blessed relief.

But the terrain ahead was not land.

The stark vista was an iceberg, a two-mile-long slab that had calved away from Antarctica. The research vessel *Dionysius* was on a mission that to most people sounded crazy; even those behind it, Bekker included, occasionally questioned their own sanity.

Their objective was to chart the berg officially known as D43 and test the feasibility of towing the entire colossal mass the three thousand miles to Cape Town in South Africa. If it could be done, it would provide the parched country with billions of gallons of pure, fresh water.

Crazy indeed. But if the plan paid off, it would not only save a nation from thirst, but make its backers a fortune. *No risk, no reward*, as Bekker's fiancée liked to say. He agreed with the sentiment, but at the same time it drew a wry smile. He was the one freezing his balls off, while Imka oversaw the operation from a climate-controlled office back home . . .

He retreated into the relative warmth of the ship's bridge. A plotting table was laid out with a large blow-up of D43's most recent satellite photograph, two weeks old. The first task was to circumnavigate the iceberg to check for any more recent changes; a section breaking away, for instance, or a fault line developing. 'Are we ready to start?' Bekker asked.

The *Dionysius*'s skipper, Botild Havman, tapped at the picture's edge. 'We're here. We'll go around it clockwise, a kilometre out.'

'Won't that be too far to see anything?'

'We'll see enough. And we'll be clear of most of the bergy bits and growlers.'

Bekker hid his amusement at hearing the terms for smaller ice fragments pronounced in a strong Swedish accent, and went to the windows. The iceberg filled his view, its various strata standing out clearly. The deepest submerged parts were at least a million years old, prehistoric snow compacted into ultra-dense blue ice. D43's visible bulk was only about a tenth that age, but still ancient. If the plan worked, the residents of Cape Town could be drinking water from ice older than the whole of human civilisation.

Havman issued orders, then brought the *Dionysius* on a course paralleling the iceberg's western flank. Bekker watched the great mass slide past. This close, second thoughts rose about the whole project. Would even a couple of repurposed supertankers, the only vessels theoretically powerful enough to tow such a colossal object, be enough?

He considered calling Imka over the satellite video link to voice his doubts, but held off. They had already spoken an hour ago, when the iceberg was first sighted, and the bandwidth was not cheap. Better to wait until he had something specific to report.

The ship continued around the berg. In places, surface snow had been washed away to leave a surreal landscape of glassy ice. D43 had partially rolled as it tore free of the ice cap, exposing strata of cyan and turquoise and deep blue. No photograph could have prepared him for the sheer beauty of the sight. Maybe Imka would regret staying in the warmth after all . . .

His entrancement was disturbed by a discussion between Havman and a crewman. 'What is it?' asked the South African.

'Something odd on the radar,' the captain replied. 'Inside the ice.'

Bekker came to see. On the screen, the iceberg showed up as a ragged, fuzzy line to the right of the central dot marking the *Dionysius*'s position. The ice's varying density accounted for the radar return's diffuse appearance – but within it was a sharply defined shape. 'What's that?'

'Don't know,' said Havman. 'It's solid, though. Rock – or metal.'

'How could it be metal?'

'Meteor, perhaps. Or a ship or plane.'

'That deep in the ice?' Bekker looked back at the swathes of blue – the product of time, far older than the couple of centuries since humans started to build their ships from metal rather than wood. But the shape on the radar screen seemed too symmetrical to be a mere rock, even one that had fallen from space. So what could it be? He let out a brief, involuntary laugh.

'What?' asked Havman.

'I just wondered if it was a UFO. A spaceship,' he clarified. 'But that's ridiculous. Isn't it?'

Havman's studiously blank expression spoke volumes. He regarded the radar screen again. 'We might be able to see it soon. There's an opening in the ice.' He pointed out an indentation in the fuzzy line.

Bekker went to the windows – and saw it for real. 'It's a cave!'

Havman followed his gaze with binoculars. 'A big one.'

'We could probably fit the whole ship inside.'

Chuckles from the bridge crew. 'I don't think that would be wise,' said the captain. 'We could send in the boat, though. If that's what you want to do. It will cost us time.'

Bekker took his point. But the cave was tantalisingly close . . . 'We need to see what it is,' he decided. 'We *are* doing a survey, after all. How long would it take?'

'Thirty minutes, perhaps.' Havman checked the water. 'Not too much floating ice. We can bring the ship closer.'

Bekker tried not to sound too childishly enthusiastic. 'Okay. Let's do it. If it's nothing, we'll carry on with the survey.'

'As you wish.' The Swede adjusted the *Dionysius*'s course.

The ship soon drew level with the opening. Bekker tried to see inside, but all he could make out were twilight-blue walls of ice. He went back to the radar. The object should have been in line with the entrance. 'I can't see it.'

Havman rechecked the screen. 'It must be embedded higher up.'

'We'll definitely have to take the boat in. Maybe we can climb up to it.'

The captain cocked an eyebrow. 'We? Mr Bekker, do you have any experience in ice climbing?'

'No, but—'

'You're my client, but you're also my passenger, so your safety is my responsibility. You hired people who know what they're doing. Let them go.'

'I suppose you're right,' Bekker reluctantly agreed.

The *Dionysius* heaved to, crewmen preparing its boat for launch while Havman and Bekker spoke to the man and woman who would make the trip. Wim Stapper was a blond Dutchman with the wiry build of an extreme sports enthusiast, while the Finnish Sanna Onvaan had short, fiery red hair and the strong upper body of someone who spent much time dangling from high places. Both were in their late twenties and expert ice climbers. They were as enthusiastic as Bekker about the unexpected side mission. 'If it is a UFO,' said Onvaan, grinning, 'maybe we get to take selfies with space aliens!'

'We don't know if it's a UFO,' said Bekker. 'If it's just a big rock, then we'll carry on with the survey. But,' a smile, 'if it *is* a spaceship . . . get lots of pictures!'

Havman shook his head. 'You have all seen too many movies. Don't get too excited – that is when you make mistakes.'

'We will be okay,' Stapper assured him as he zipped up his red coat. 'We know what we are doing.'

'Good. Then don't take any risks, and stay safe.'

'Risk is our business – and our hobby!' said Onvaan cheerily.

The captain was unimpressed, but kept any further comments to himself. Instead he led the way to the ship's tender, a bright orange thirty-foot rigid inflatable boat. Onvaan and Stapper boarded, then the RIB was lowered into the water and the pair set out, Onvaan at the tiller.

Bekker looked towards the cave. The waters were dotted with growlers, relatively small hunks of ice that nevertheless could weigh as much as a car. As with all icebergs, most of their mass was hidden beneath the surface, seemingly innocuous pieces becoming potentially shipwrecking obstacles. 'Watch out for the ice, okay?' he said into a walkie-talkie.

The retreating Stapper made a show of scanning the sea. 'Ice? Ice? Oh, *that* ice,' he said, gasping at the berg.

'Funny. Okay, see what's in there.'

Bekker watched the boat weave around the bobbing growlers towards the cave mouth, then he and Havman returned to the bridge. 'What's it like?' the South African asked as the RIB slipped into the shadows.

The reply was surprisingly distorted considering the short range, a crackle behind Stapper's words. 'Everything is blue, very beautiful.'

'Can you see the thing in the ice?'

'A bad choice of words if you have seen the movies I have!' The Dutchman laughed. 'We are coming out of the entrance tunnel . . .'

A long silence. 'Wim? Are you still there?' asked Bekker, concerned.

The reply was prefaced by another laugh – but one of nervous disbelief rather than humour. 'Yes, yes, we are here. And so is, ah . . . You know we were joking about a UFO?'

'Yes?'

'I think . . . that is what we have found.'

The silence this time was on Bekker's part. 'Are you joking?' he finally managed.

'No, no, I'm not! It's inside the ice, stuck in the cave wall. It is metal, and . . . *big*. As big as a plane. I am not kidding you,' Stapper added, pre-emptively.

'It really does look like a UFO,' Onvaan added in the background.

'It's hard to tell exactly, but I'd say about . . . a third of it is out of the ice?' Stapper went on. 'It's at an angle. There are windows near the front. They look like eyes.'

Bekker practically heard the shiver in the other man's voice as he realised what he had just said. 'Can you get to it?'

'Yeah, yeah. The cliff climb looks easy— Oh!'

Both Havman and Bekker flinched. 'What is it?' demanded the captain.

'I see a way in! There is a hatch in the side.'

'We can reach it, no problem,' said Onvaan.

'I don't know,' Bekker said, misgivings growing. Assuming this wasn't some dumb joke by the climbers – and he didn't think their acting ability was up to it – then they had found something unknown. And the unknown could be dangerous. 'Take pictures, then come back. We need to see what we're dealing with.'

'No, no, it will take two minutes to climb to the door,' replied Stapper. 'We can't come this far and not look inside!'

Frustrated, Bekker looked to Havman for support. 'If they were my crew, I would order them back,' said the captain. 'You are their boss.'

'Yeah.' He spoke into the radio again. 'No, get back here. Or . . .' He halted, aware there wasn't anything he could threaten them with short of being fired, and then the expedition would be over before it even began. 'Just get back to the ship.'

The lack of a response meant the pair were either ignoring him, or already climbing the ice wall. '*Pielkop!*' he muttered.

The walkie-talkie remained silent for a few fraught minutes, then crackled to life. 'We are at the door,' said Stapper at last. The distortion was worse than before. 'It's big, nearly three metres high. It opened when Sanna touched a round thing on it. We're going in.'

Bekker sighed in resignation: they were entering with or without his permission. 'If there's any danger, get out and come back to the ship.'

'We will. But the ice is solid. I don't think—'

The Dutchman was abruptly cut off by a harsh caw of static. 'Wim?' said Bekker. 'Wim, can you hear me? Wim!' No answer. 'Shit!'

Havman marched to the helm. 'I will bring the ship closer. If they are in trouble, we can reach them faster.'

'Good, okay,' Bekker replied, before trying the radio again.

There was still no response.

'Why did you let them go in?' demanded Imka Joubert over the satellite link. The video quality was low and glitchy, the computers at each end straining to make the most of the parsimonious bandwidth.

'I told them not to!' said Bekker. Thirty minutes had passed since his last contact with the explorers; he had called his fiancée as much to vent about the situation as report on it. 'This is what happens when you hire thrill-seekers – they go seeking thrills!'

'When *I* hired them?'

'Okay, when *we* hired them! But we lost contact when they went inside this thing, and still haven't heard anything from them.'

'What *is* this thing?' Imka asked. 'What did you find?'

'I don't want to say on an open channel. Let's call it an . . . old ship.'

'What, like a sailing ship?'

'I'll tell you more when I can set up an encrypted link.'

A disbelieving laugh. 'You really think anyone is eaves-dropping?'

'I don't want to take any chances. Trust me, Imka.'

'I do. Otherwise I wouldn't have let you go down to the bottom of the world, would I?'

He chuckled. 'You want to swap places? You're the one who knows all about ships . . .'

'I'm fine here, thanks. Did I mention it's twenty-two Celsius today?'

'No, and I wish you hadn't. But the *Dionysius* isn't equipped for salvage work, so we'd have to—'

He stopped at a sudden rasp from the radio. Havman snatched it up. 'Hello, hello!' he said. 'Are you all right?'

An ear-shredding screech of static – then a voice pierced the distortion. '*Het heeft haar gedood! Het heeft haar gedood! Mijn God, help me!*'

'It's Wim!' said Bekker, jumping up in alarm. His native Afrikaans was very similar to Dutch, and he knew exactly what Stapper was saying: *It killed her! It killed her! My God, help me!* 'Wim, what happened? *What* killed her – what happened to Sanna?'

The crew reacted in shock.

'Help me! Help!' came the panicked reply. 'Oh God, it's coming after me!'

'*What* is?'

'*De demon!* Sanna woke it up! It—'

Stapper's words were cut off, not by static but a loud thump, followed by banging sounds. He had slipped, skidding down an icy slope – then came a pained shout as he hit something. But it was not the only shout. In the background was another voice, with a strange, throaty echo to it that barely sounded human.

Then the channel fell silent.

'Wim!' yelled Bekker. 'Wim, can you hear me? Wim!' He turned to Havman. 'We've got to help him! We need to get into the cave. If you launch the lifeboat—'

'Are you mad?' said the Swede. 'There's a murderer running around!' He hesitated, then with clear trepidation issued orders to the crew. 'We'll take the whole ship inside,' he told Bekker. 'We'll be protected while we look for him.'

The *Dionysius*'s engines came to life. Bekker stared fearfully at the shadowy cave mouth, then belatedly realised that someone was calling his name. 'Arnold! Arnold, what's going on?' said Imka over the satellite link.

'Imka, something's happened,' he replied. 'Wim and Sanna are in trouble.'

'What kind of trouble? What—'

'I'm sorry, I have to go. I'll call you back as soon as we've found them. I love you.'

'I love you too. But—'

He ended the call and rushed to the windows. The ship quickly closed on the iceberg. Dull thunks echoed through the hull as the prow struck bobbing growlers. The entrance loomed ahead. 'Will we fit?'

'We'll fit,' said Havman grimly. 'Try to get him on the radio.'

Bekker called Stapper, to no avail. The captain slowed, bringing the *Dionysius* into line with the cave's tall but relatively narrow mouth. The South African watched – then suddenly remembered something. 'He said "it" . . .'

Havman didn't divert his gaze from the icy passage. 'What?'

'Wim said "it" killed Sanna, not "he".'

'He was panicking. People say the wrong words when they panic.'

'But he said it several times. "It" killed her, "it" was coming after him. And there was something else. He called it *"de demon"* . . . the demon.'

The temperature on the bridge seemed to drop as its occupants exchanged worried looks. Havman was the first to speak, standing straight and resolute. 'It doesn't matter. All that *does* matter is that we rescue him.' He eased the *Dionysius* into the gap.

Bekker tensed, but Havman guided the ship cleanly through the cave mouth. The change in lighting from the stark whites and blues outside to sapphire-tinted gloom rendered him momentarily blind; he blinked, trying to take in his new surroundings as the four-hundred-tonne survey vessel slipped into the mysterious cave.

Shadows swallowed it.

'There! I see something, five degrees to port!'

Ulus Cansel, captain of the freighter *Fortune Mist*, stared intently through his binoculars. The ship had been halfway through its voyage between New Zealand and Cape Town with a cargo of frozen lamb when it received a weak distress call. A nine-hour diversion at full speed had brought it to the source, but now the signal, from the RV *Dionysius*, had fallen silent. Cansel had been a mariner for almost thirty years; he knew all too well that that was a bad sign. The *Dionysius* had almost certainly sunk.

But that didn't mean there weren't survivors. A spot of colour against the grey sea had caught his eye: a man in a red coat, huddled on a chunk of floating ice. 'Man overboard! Mr Figueroa, Mr Krämer, launch a lifeboat.' The crewmen hurried from the bridge.

The Cypriot surveyed the surrounding waters. There was a large iceberg a few kilometres distant. The glossy sheen of raw, snow-free ice over much of its surface told him it had recently rolled; had the *Dionysius* been crushed by it?

He wouldn't know until they completed a wider search, but the priority was recovering the survivor. An order, and the *Fortune Mist*'s horn sounded. At first the figure didn't move, leading Cansel to fear he was dead, but then he shifted slightly. 'He's still alive!' the captain called out. 'Get him aboard, quick!'

The lifeboat reached the floating ice.

Jakob Krämer regarded the stranded man warily. The floe was only small, and the lean German was sure it would pitch over if he climbed onto it. 'Hey! Can you hear me?' he shouted in English.

No response. He asked the same in his native language, but the man remained still. 'Hold us steady,' he told Figueroa. 'I'll pull him closer.'

He manoeuvred a boat hook to snag the man's coat. Straining, he pulled him across the ice until he was almost within reach. The floe rocked, bumping the lifeboat. Krämer cursed, then stretched out as far as he dared. His gloved fingers caught fabric; he clutched it tightly and hauled the unconscious man to the boat's side.

The ice tipped again, sending a freezing splash over the man's legs. He flinched, but his rescuer now had a firm hold. Figueroa joined in, and they brought the limp figure aboard.

Krämer examined him. The man was young, his face pale

from the cold. If he had spent much longer exposed to the elements, he would be dead. 'Get us back to the ship, fast,' the German said. Figueroa returned to the outboard and brought the boat around. 'We got you,' Krämer said, trying to reassure the survivor. 'You are safe.'

The man's eyes snapped open. The sailor felt a sudden unease; he was looking *through* rather than at him, the gaze almost manic in its terrified intensity. 'Demon . . .'

Krämer blinked at the feeble whisper. 'What?'

'Demon . . .' the man in red repeated. His accent sounded Dutch. 'In the ice. Sanna woke it . . . it killed her! We took the key. We took the key!'

Krämer realised his passenger was clutching something tightly to his chest. He looked more closely – and saw a glint of metal.

Gold.

'We woke the demon,' the young man went on. His breathing quickened. 'It killed Sanna – killed everyone!'

Krämer was more interested in what he held than his words. Demons? His near-death had obviously driven him mad. He shifted to block Figueroa's line of sight with his body, then started to prise the man's fingers open.

'No, no!' gasped the Dutchman. 'The key – don't give it the key!'

'We will be at the ship soon,' said Krämer loudly, trying to drown out his voice. He finally forced the young man's hands apart and tugged the object free. 'It's okay.'

'No!' he cried again. 'They killed, they . . .' He slumped in exhaustion.

'It's okay,' Krämer said again, giving Figueroa a surreptitious glance before examining his prize.

What it was, he had no idea. It certainly didn't look like a key. A plate-sized metal disc, its central hub inlaid with a circle of polished purple stone, into which was set a large crystal. At first he had thought the object was gold, but now he saw it wasn't quite the right colour, with a distinctly reddish tinge. Writing was inscribed in its surface, but he didn't recognise the language.

He turned it over. Both the stone and the crystal continued all the way through its centre. More unknown words ran around them.

One symbol was unmistakable, though.

A skull.

It faced to the left, jaw open as if shouting. It was oddly deformed, the back of the head elongated. Something about it unsettled Krämer. Maybe the survivor's ravings about demons had got to him . . .

He shook off the thought and hid the object inside his coat. Even if the gold wasn't pure, its weight told him it was still worth a lot of money. And the only other person who knew about it was a madman, in shock from his ordeal. He wouldn't be believed. *No, you didn't have anything when we found you. You must have lost it in the water. Sorry.*

The German pulled his zipper back up. He felt no guilt about what he had just done: the man was still alive, wasn't he? That was worth more than any piece of treasure. And it gave Krämer the chance to escape from the drudgery of life aboard a freighter. He knew of places online where such salvage could be sold, with no awkward questions asked. A few months from now, his life could change for ever.

He smiled at the thought – then looked down in alarm as the man stirred. 'We're at the ship,' he said hastily. 'You're safe.'

'No, not . . . safe,' came the weak reply. 'More demons. Sleeping in . . . the ice.' His hands searched for the object with growing desperation. 'The key! Where is it?'

'I don't know,' replied the German. 'You must have lost it in the water.'

'No, I had it! Listen!' He suddenly clawed at Krämer's coat, pulling the startled crewman closer. 'The key – it wakes them. Sanna woke one. It . . . it killed her, killed everyone on the ship! If they wake, they'll kill us all!' His voice rose to a shout. 'The demons will kill us all!'

1

New York City

Four months later

Professor Nina Wilde paused for dramatic effect as she regarded her students, then spoke. 'My first rule of archaeology: no find is worth risking your, or anyone else's, life over.'

That aroused surprise from her audience. 'Yes, I know that may sound weird, from someone with my track record,' she went on. 'But I'm speaking from experience – very, *very* painful experience. I've lost count of how often I've almost been killed out in the field, and a couple of times in my own home. But I've forced myself to keep a very good count of the people who actually *were* killed because of my discoveries. And it's too many. Which is why I'm talking to you in a lecture hall rather than chasing around the world after legends.'

'But you've found so many,' said a young woman. This early in their first semester, Nina hadn't yet memorised all her students' names. Madison?

'Yes, I have – but I wanted to leave some for you to find as well.' Some laughter at the joke, which was a relief. It was only the redhead's second year in her academic role, and she still found balancing research and teaching hard. 'I hope I'll inspire

15

you to make your own discoveries. But I also want you to learn from my mistakes.'

'What mistakes?' asked a man – a *boy*; God, they were all so *young*! – she was fairly sure was called Aiden.

'I used to think it was my job, my *duty*, to bring lost wonders back to the world,' Nina told him. 'Which I did. Atlantis, the tomb of Hercules, El Dorado, Valhalla, the Ark of the Covenant . . . and more besides.'

'It's a very impressive list.' She remembered this youth's name: Hui Cheng, a student from China. Her concern that he had won admission to the university based solely on his wealthy parents' bank balance had already been assuaged by his work, breadth of knowledge and drive.

'Thank you. But it came at a price. It seems like every discovery I made had some madman, or occasionally madwoman, after it for nefarious ends. And I don't just mean tomb raiding for money. I've faced people trying to start wars, take over countries, nuke cities . . .'

'You didn't talk about this in your books,' said Aiden dubiously.

'My books are about the actual archaeology. If you want explosions and gunfights and car chases, you can always watch the ridiculous movies based on them!' More laughter. She let it subside, then continued, more sombrely: 'But the antimatter explosion in the Persian Gulf three years ago? That was caused by something I found. When Big Ben in London collapsed? Again, caused by one of my discoveries. The religious cult gassed in the Caribbean, the skyscraper destroyed in Tokyo – all ultimately my responsibility.'

'But you weren't *personally* responsible,' said Cheng. 'The incident in Antigua, you'd been kidnapped! You didn't have a choice.'

'They wouldn't have happened if I hadn't been involved,' Nina insisted. 'My thought process at the time was: I *can* find these things, so I *must* find these things. I never considered whether I *should* find these things.'

'So . . . you wish you *hadn't* found them?' Madison asked. 'You think your whole career's been a mistake?'

'No, but I think I've *made* mistakes. The lesson they've taught me is actually my *second* rule: think before you dig. Before you put the tip of your trowel into the ground, ask yourself some very big questions. Am I the right person to make this discovery? Am I doing so for the right reasons? And most of all, do I have the ability to protect this discovery? If you can't truthfully answer yes to all three, then you should hold off. Always remember that your actions will make you a part of history too – and you want it to look favourably upon you.' She cast her gaze across her students, one by one. 'What I've come to realise is that you need great wisdom to know if you should return an ancient wonder to the world. Even after everything I've experienced, I'm still not sure I have that wisdom.' A pause, then, with dark humour: 'And I'm damn sure none of you do.'

She knew that would not go down well. Most of the young men and women limited their affronted responses to facial expressions, unwilling to challenge a professor, but there were inevitably a few vocal objections. 'I don't think that's fair,' said Aiden. 'You don't know us.'

'No,' Nina replied, 'not as individuals, but I'm forty-five, and by now I know *people*. You're all, what? Eighteen, nineteen, twenty? That's an age where in many ways I envy you – the whole world's just opened up, and you can do anything. You can even bend down without your back hurting! Damn, I miss those days.'

The humour helped ease the tension. 'But,' she continued, 'while you've got limitless energy and enthusiasm, you don't have *experience*. And I can tell you, ironically enough from experience, that when you're young, if someone tries to give you the benefit of *their* experience, you're all like "yeah, whatever, grandma". I was the same! And unfortunately, that got me into trouble – trouble that affected other people. If I'd realised what I was getting into, I would have done things differently. Or possibly not at all.'

'But then everything you've discovered would have remained lost,' said Cheng. 'Our knowledge of ancient history would be incomplete. It would be *wrong*.'

'It would, yes. But that goes back to my first rule – is that knowledge worth the lives lost to uncover it? All of you, take a look at each other.' Nina waited for them to do so. 'Now, if you thought you were on the verge of making an amazing discovery, but you knew that in doing so you'd be directly responsible for the deaths of some of your classmates . . . would you still do it?'

The question aroused discussion. Cheng was first to reply. 'But that's a flawed premise, Professor.'

She arched an eyebrow. 'Is it now?'

'It assumes we have accurate foreknowledge of the future, which we don't. You can only make decisions based on the information you have at the time. We *can't* know that any of us will die.'

'Experience helps you with risk assessment, though. Crossing the street? You're probably safe. Going into a region of the Congo jungle controlled by warlords? Not so much. And that wasn't a hypothetical. I did it – and it was a mistake, a terrible one. I hope none of you ever do the same.'

The room fell silent for a moment. Again Cheng spoke first. 'I have a hypothetical I'd like to put to you, Professor.'

She nodded. 'Go on.'

'Suppose you believed you had evidence of a civilisation millennia older than anything currently known. The evidence isn't yet definitive enough to convince mainstream archaeologists, but you're certain you'll confirm it if you're given the chance to mount an expedition.'

Nina grinned. 'That sounds familiar.'

'That was how you found Atlantis, wasn't it?' said Madison.

'Yeah. Extra credit for reading my first book!'

Cheng waited for the laughter to subside. 'This isn't about Atlantis, though. What if it was a completely unknown civilisation? The product of an extinct race, related to but separate from humans. A discovery like that would shatter the foundations of almost every religion, especially the Abrahamic ones where the Book of Genesis is regarded as the literal truth.' The round-faced young man regarded her intently through his glasses. 'Would you still try to find it?'

Nina became uncomfortable. He was describing, with unnerving accuracy, a situation she had already experienced, and she was still not sure her eventual solution had been the right one. 'I would have to give that a great deal of thought,' she said, trying not to sound defensive. 'It would be possibly the most groundbreaking discovery in archaeological history. But on the other hand, it would be telling over three billion Christians, Jews and Muslims that the entire basis of their belief system is untrue – to say nothing of the non-Abrahamic religions it would impact. And some people get very angry if their beliefs are challenged. Wars have started over less. So in your hypothetical situation, I would be very, very careful about how I revealed what I'd found.'

She watched for any indication that he somehow knew the truth about events fourteen years earlier, but instead he cocked his head quizzically. 'So you *would* try to find it?'

Amusement ran around the room, the students enjoying that one of them had caught out a professor. 'As I said,' Nina replied, irked, 'I'd give it a lot of thought. At one time, I *would* have gone looking for it, yes. Now, I'd be a lot more cautious. Rushing into things gets people killed. And that's not a hypothetical answer.'

Her discomfiture at Cheng's question meant the end of class

soon afterwards came as a relief. 'So, Professor Wilde,' said Aiden, 'what're your other rules of archaeology?'

'There's only one more,' Nina replied, with a half-smile, 'and it's simple: try not to blow everything up.'

'You need a rule for that?' asked Madison.

'You'd be surprised.'

She gathered her belongings, noticing Cheng leaving in a hurry. She couldn't dispel her suspicion that he knew about her encounter with the religious organisation known as the Covenant of Genesis. But how could that be possible? She had – with great reluctance – agreed to keep her knowledge of the ancient race known as the Veteres a secret for exactly the reasons she had given. Not that it ultimately had mattered. All evidence of their existence had been destroyed, and every member of the Covenant itself was dead.

Coincidence, she decided as she headed out. There were already numerous theories about ancient precursor races on the kookier fringes of the archaeological world; Cheng had just come up with his own take. Nothing to be concerned about.

That thought lasted for as long as it took her to reach her office – outside which Cheng was waiting. 'Can I help you, Mr Hui?'

'Actually, yes, Professor,' the young man replied, almost twitching with eagerness. He glanced up and down the corridor. 'But in private?'

She decided to humour him. 'Come on in.'

Her office on the ninth floor of Columbia University's Schermerhorn Extension overlooked Amsterdam Avenue, traffic noise rising from the street below. A lifelong New Yorker, Nina had long ago tuned it out. She sat at her desk and gestured to a chair. 'So what have you got?'

'I didn't want to say anything in front of the others,' he said, sitting. 'Partly because I didn't want everyone to make fun of me, but also because if it's real, it could be an even bigger discovery than Atlantis. I think I've found what I was talking about in class. Evidence of a civilisation that existed before humans!'

She gave him a deliberately non-committal nod. 'I'm listening.'

He opened his laptop, a new, sleek and, she guessed, very expensive model. 'Okay, there are places on the dark web where people buy and sell stolen antiquities.'

'I know.' Certain corners of the internet were home to all manner of criminal activity, relying upon encryption, anonymity and obscurity to hide from law enforcement. Unlike the mainstream internet, it was impossible to find such sites using a search engine; access was by invitation only, buyers and sellers of looted items using near-untraceable cryptocurrencies to cover their financial tracks. 'It's a real problem.'

'I managed to get into one of the sites – I pretended to make friends with someone involved and bought a password,' Cheng explained. 'I was looking for stolen Chinese artefacts so I could tell the authorities. But instead . . . I found this.'

He turned the screen to show her. It was a picture of a metal object: a golden disc. At its centre was a circle of stone and crystal. Nina didn't recognise it – but she *did* recognise what was scribed into its surface.

She tried to conceal her alarm. The symbols looked very much like the written language of the Veteres. 'That's . . . an interesting piece. What is it?'

'I don't know. The seller, who's in Germany, called it a key, but didn't say much more. I don't think he *knows* much more. I suspect he stole it. But I've believed for a long time there was a much earlier civilisation than anything we currently know. I think *this* is proof.'

She raised an eyebrow. 'A long time? How old are you, Mr Hui?'

'Eighteen, Professor.'

'And you've been challenging the archaeological establishment since . . . puberty?' She immediately felt almost guilty at the jibe. It was the kind of dismissal she had faced early in her own career.

'I've always wanted to be an archaeologist, Professor,' said Cheng, not quite hiding a frown. 'Just because I'm young doesn't mean I haven't worked hard.'

'Of course not. My apologies. But if there's any evidence of a non-human precursor civilisation, I'm not aware of it.'

He gave her a probing look. 'I've studied the mythologies of the Hebrews, the Hindus, my own country. There are many common aspects, even when they describe fantastical things. Shared legends. And you've proved many times that legends can be based on reality. Atlantis, Hercules, King Arthur, the angels of the Book of Revelation – you found them all. I think this,' he indicated the item on the screen, 'is another one. And it'll prove my theory, when I obtain it.'

'Jumping the gun a little, aren't you?'

'No, I've been in contact with the seller. I'm going to Hamburg to buy it.'

'What?' said Nina, alarm returning for a different reason. 'Ethical considerations aside, that's insanely dangerous! People selling stolen artefacts on the dark web are by definition criminals. There's a good chance they'll take your money and give you nothing, but if you meet them in person they *might* give you something – a beating! How much does the seller want?'

'Fifty thousand euros.' The reply was matter-of-fact.

She was shocked, by both the amount and his insouciance. 'Fifty thou— And you're planning to *pay* it?'

'My family is rich.'

'You know what else rich families pay? Ransoms!'

'He seems trustworthy,' Cheng insisted.

'Con men always do, right up until they disappear with your money.' A grim thought. '*Please* tell me you're not planning to pay this guy in cash.' His hesitation was answer enough. 'You might as well go dressed as a lamb with a sign saying "Hello, wolves"!'

'But the artefact will prove my theory!' He indicated the symbols upon it. 'This language is completely unknown. It's valuable for that alone, but if it really did come from an ancient race, it could lead me to them!'

'Or you might be risking your own neck for nothing. Remember my first rule?'

'You took greater risks to find Atlantis.'

'Yeah, and as I said, a lot of them were mistakes.'

'But you still found Atlantis. Would you give that up?'

'What's done is done,' Nina told him. 'But now I want to keep other people from making the same mistakes. Or bigger ones.'

Cheng sat silently for a moment. 'I'm sorry, Professor Wilde, but . . . I really have to do this,' he said finally. 'I'd hoped you might even come with me, but I guess I'll have to go on my own.' He closed the laptop.

Exasperated, Nina shook her head. 'I can't stop you – but I can *seriously* advise against it.'

'If I don't go, the artefact will probably disappear into someone's private collection, or be melted down for the gold. The seller told me others are interested.'

'He's only saying that so he can jack up the price.'

'The price hasn't changed. I can fly to Germany to see him this weekend.' He gave her a pleading look. 'If the artefact is shown by testing to be older than Atlantis, would you be willing to hear my theory?'

'Mr Hui, if you make it to my class on *Monday*, I'll be willing to hear your theory,' she said. 'I think going to Hamburg alone, with fifty thousand euros in cash, to meet a criminal you contacted on the dark web is a spectacularly bad idea. Please, don't do it.'

'I'll be fine,' he insisted as he stood. 'Just because I'm young doesn't mean I'm naïve.' He smiled. 'I'll see you on Monday. And I'll have the artefact.' He took out a folded piece of paper and put it on her desk. 'The dark web address and password for the site where I found it. If you look, I hope you'll be convinced it's worth obtaining. Thank you for your time, Professor.'

He left. Nina blew out a frustrated breath. It was Wednesday now; knowing he was conscientious about attending lectures, she imagined Cheng would probably fly out on Friday night, arriving in Hamburg on Saturday . . . and then who knew what might happen? His protestations aside, everything about the chubby young Chinese screamed innocent abroad. Some criminal in a notorious port town was doubtless already licking his lips at the prospect of an extremely easy fifty thousand euros – at the very least.

At least leave him his kidneys, she silently willed the universe. Losing one of her students would not go down well with the university. But what could she do? Threaten him with bad grades, or expulsion? If his parents were as wealthy as she'd heard, that would only invite a lawsuit, which her bosses would take just as badly.

And Hui Cheng was an adult, responsible for his own actions. If he wanted to go, she couldn't stop him. Could she?

That thought kept rolling around her mind even as she headed home, distracting her from the big night to come.

2

'Happy birthday, Daddy!' trilled Macy Wilde Chase. The sentiment was echoed by the others around the restaurant's table.

Macy's father was considerably less enthused. 'Yeah, loads to be happy about,' groused Eddie Chase. 'My hair's gone, my eyesight's going, I'm half deaf . . . and the worst part is, I'll never feel this good again.' The guests at the birthday dinner laughed.

'Look at it this way, honey,' Nina told him. 'You've got all your body parts, you've got your friends, you've got your family – and you've got an amazing daughter. When I get to fifty, I'll feel pretty thankful to have all that.'

Eddie gave her a half-smile. 'Careful what you wish for. When you get to fifty, Macy'll be fifteen, and she'll hate you.'

'No I won't, Mom,' Macy insisted.

He looked to his sister for support. 'Sorry, Nina,' said Elizabeth Chase. 'I remember when Holly was fifteen, and oh, there's so much I'd rather forget.'

Holly Bennett, now twice that age, nodded. 'Afraid it's true.' Unlike her uncle, who had retained his gruff Yorkshire accent even after seventeen years in the United States, she had developed a transatlantic twang after only two years working in New York.

Nina pouted. 'Well, enough about me. Everyone can pile back onto Eddie now!'

Eddie's father, Larry Chase, clapped his hands. 'We can? Excellent!' His wife, Julie, jabbed him with an elbow.

'Tchah!' Eddie exclaimed, before standing. 'I didn't want to make a big deal of turning fifty, but Nina went behind my back to organise this do . . . and I'm glad she did. I'd no idea so many of you would come such a long-arse way just to say happy birthday to a bald bloke from Brighouse.' He gestured at his friends. 'I mean, we've got people from Israel, Russia, Brazil, the Congo, even bloody Australia! It's a real honour to see you all.'

'Our pleasure, mate,' said the Australian Matt Trulli, who was here with his husband Pat. 'I mean, you've saved the world a few times! Least we could do in return.'

'And you've saved me and Nina a few times, so thank you all. Cheers!' Eddie raised his glass, the other guests following suit. 'Now, enjoy the food. Should be good – it's costing enough!'

Everyone laughed.

'Yorkshiremen never change,' said Julie to Nina as Eddie sat. 'Short arms and long pockets, that's the saying, isn't it? At least that's what his father says about them.'

Larry, originally from Buckinghamshire in southern England, gave his northern-born son a mocking smile.

Nina grinned. 'Tell me about it.'

'I'm not wrong, though, am I?' said Eddie. He picked up a menu. 'I mean, 'ow much just for garlic bread . . . Oh, bloody hell.' He frowned, having to hold it almost at arm's length to read the words. 'See what I mean about getting old? Everything either stops working or starts hurting. Pain in the arse. Sometimes literally.'

Nina's grandmother, Olivia Wilde, tutted. 'Really, Eddie. Of all the things you might be, I've never thought of you as a whiner. I'm almost twice your age, and do you know what I've learned?'

'Never eat prunes after a curry?' suggested Eddie with a smirk.

'Something else I've never thought of you as is a comedian,' Olivia replied, unfazed. 'But age isn't important – it's attitude. How *well* you live matters more than simply how long. I spent the prime of my life focused on entirely the wrong things, and it wasn't until I met Nina and reconnected with my family a few years ago that I realised how empty that was. Now? I'm ninety-six, and certainly not expecting to make it to a hundred—'

'Don't say that, Grams,' Macy cut in.

'Well, it's true. But I'm happier than I was before, frailties be damned, and it's not as if I'm sitting around waiting to die. I don't worry that I've done everything I ever will; I look forward to what I'm still going to do. You should do the same.'

'She's right,' said Nina. 'You've done so much already; like Matt said, you've saved the world. Several times! But just because you've got nothing left to prove doesn't mean you've got nothing left to achieve.'

'You've certainly achieved a lot, Nina,' said Elizabeth. 'Congratulations on your professorship, if that's the right word.'

'Thanks. Yeah, I went full circle and ended up back at my alma mater.'

'It must be a change teaching instead of being out in the field.'

'It is. I don't know which is more scary – facing a bad guy with a gun, or fifty new students all staring at you!' Chuckles from around the table. 'I do prefer the quiet life, though.'

'You're not tempted to go back out on one last big adventure?' asked the Israeli Jared Zane.

'I'm not planning to, no. Research and teaching is a full-time job.'

Elizabeth turned to Macy. 'And I've heard you want to follow in your mum's footsteps and become an archaeologist too?'

The young redhead nodded. 'Yeah. Mom thinks she's found everything there is, but I know there's more out there. So I'm going to find it.'

'She wants to prove me wrong,' Nina sighed. 'Ten years old, and already she's out to torpedo my professional reputation!'

Macy narrowed her eyes. 'You *are* wrong, Mom. I know what happened with the trikan, even if you don't believe me.'

'The trikan?' asked Elizabeth.

'An Atlantean artefact,' Nina explained. 'Similar to a yo-yo. It's a weapon, although nobody's been able to figure out how it works. At least,' she added, 'until Macy claimed she got it to do all kinds of physics-defying tricks.'

'I *did* do it,' Macy said, glowering at her. 'I made it change direction in mid-air just by wanting it to.'

'That's what it does in the *movies*. Not real life.'

Her glare deepened. 'You always say that! But I can tell the difference between a movie and real life. I'm not *stupid*.'

'I don't think you'll have to wait until she's fifteen, love,' said Eddie, amused, before addressing his friends. 'Now I know what Nina must have been like as a kid. Macy's always reading about some ancient thing or other, or watching documentaries.'

'I wouldn't call them documentaries,' Nina said snippily. 'Anything involving UFOs or ancient astronauts or demons is junk science, nothing more.'

'Didn't people used to think that about Atlantis?' Nina gave him a stony look, which brought a broad grin in return. 'Anyway! Let's talk about something else before my wife and daughter get into a fight.'

'So, are *you* going to change your life now you are fifty?' asked the Congolese Fortune Bemba. 'Somehow I cannot imagine Eddie Chase spending the rest of his days relaxing in a hammock.'

'If we had a garden, I'd have a hammock in it already!' Eddie told him. 'Nah, as far as running around the world dodging bullets goes, I'm done. Don't want to tempt fate by looking for trouble again.'

Fortune nodded. 'Good luck with your quiet life, my friend!'

That was enough excuse for another toast. 'Good luck!' chorused Brazilian ex-cop Ana Rijo and her boyfriend, the hulking Russian mercenary Oleg Maximov. Everyone else followed suit.

Eddie and Nina clinked their own glasses. 'Sounds good to me,' he said. 'You?'

'Staying out of trouble?' she said. 'Absolutely. Here's to a quiet life!'

They both drank, then Nina eyed her husband's faintly pensive expression. 'What is it?'

'Can't help thinking I'm going to hear Ron Howard's voice saying, "They didn't get one."'

She laughed. 'A cultural reference from the twenty-first century? I'm impressed! But we don't need to worry. I mean, I'm not about to jet off around the world looking for some ancient artefact . . .'

'Honey,' said Nina a few hours later, 'you remember how I said I wasn't about to jet off around the world looking for some ancient artefact?'

'Yeah?' Eddie replied, followed by a more forceful: 'Oh, you're bloody *kidding* me!'

'I know, I *know*! But something's come up.'

He entered her study, giving her a stern look as he folded his arms. 'What?'

She turned from her laptop to face him. The mysterious artefact Cheng had shown her dominated the screen. After returning home, she'd found the paper he had given her in her purse. Out of a mixture of intrigue and concern for his welfare – and maybe with the encouragement of a few drinks – she had installed an anonymising Tor browser so she could access the dark web, then used the address and password to reach the seller's page.

What she found caught her interest, almost unwillingly. There was a more detailed description of the object in both German and English, the text hinting at its origin: *obtained near the South Pole*. The hidden redoubt of the Veteres had been in the Antarctic. There had to be a connection.

Then there were the crystal and the purple stone at the disc's centre. They appeared to be the same materials as ones she had found in an Atlantean vault buried in Turkey: materials that, in conjunction with the earth's natural energy fields, produced strange, even dangerous, effects. She knew from unpleasant experience that the Veteres, like their distant descendants from Atlantis, could harness these powers.

A key, the seller called it. But to what?

'This is something one of my students found on the dark web,' she explained. 'It's almost certainly a Veteres artefact.'

'I thought everything of theirs was destroyed.'

'So did I, but it seems history always finds a way to resurface.' She indicated part of the picture. 'This text looks like the same script from the Veteres records in Antarctica.'

'What about that?' He nodded at a smaller image. 'Badly drawn pirates?'

The second photo showed a highly stylised skull. 'I don't know what it represents – but the text around it is in a different language. It almost looks Atlantean.'

'This thing's from Atlantis?'

'I don't know. The characters don't quite match, and some of them I don't even recognise. It could be an earlier form; proto-Atlantean.'

'Can you read any of it?'

She nodded. 'This word . . . if it were written in Atlantean, I'd say it was "rebirth" – or "resurrection". I can't translate anything else, though. Maybe if I saw the real thing . . .'

'Which is where?'

'Germany. Somebody's trying to sell it on the black market.'

He peered at the screen. 'Fifty grand? Jesus! Who'd pay that much?'

'My student, unfortunately! A Chinese kid called Cheng, with a wealthy family. He wanted me to go with him to buy it.'

'Why you?'

'I'm his professor – and I have a track record of finding lost civilisations, remember? But when I said no, he decided he was going anyway. And I think he's going to be played for a sucker to the tune of fifty thousand euros at best, and end up face-down in the River Elbe at worst.'

'You don't think it's genuine?'

'No, I *do*, and that's the problem. If some kid can find it on the dark web, so can other people.' She pointed out the stone and crystal. 'These are the same kind of things we saw in Turkey. Remember how somebody stole the entire vault from under the noses of the Turkish government and the IHA?'

'Hard to forget. The thing probably weighed twenty tons.'

'Any group that could do that would have to be big, well connected – *somebody* in Turkey must have turned a blind eye – and rich. It was a huge job, but they did it literally overnight without leaving a single clue. An organisation like that won't let a nerdy eighteen-year-old beat them to the punch.'

'What kind of organisation, though?' he asked. 'Everybody in the Covenant of Genesis is dead, and they were the only ones who knew all about the Veteres. And the vault in Turkey was from Atlantis, not the Veteres.'

'But they're linked – both civilisations could channel earth energy. We already know that's a power the American government would go to great lengths to obtain, never mind any other country.'

Eddie pursed his lips thoughtfully. 'And you said this kid is Chinese? There's a country that's trying pretty damn hard to get more power all around the world. Maybe he's working for the Chinese government.'

She gave him a mocking look. 'Cheng's eighteen, and I'd

guess the most physical training he's ever had was clicking a mouse. I *really* don't think he's a Chinese spy. I'm more worried about him going to Hamburg chasing this thing, and not returning.'

'So *you* want to chase after it instead?'

'I can't stop him going,' she said. 'But I can make sure he comes back.'

Eddie perched on the edge of her desk, then sighed. 'So much for the quiet life. That lasted, what, three hours?'

'I know,' she said. 'It wasn't what I planned at all. But if Cheng goes on his own, I have a horrible feeling he'll be sticking his head in a lion's mouth. He's clever, very smart, but . . . well, he's still a kid.'

He made a disapproving noise, then looked back at the screen. 'Hamburg, eh? I've been there. Long time back, when I was in the army, but I doubt it's changed much. Sort of place where you need to stay on your toes.'

'Any advice?'

'Don't go on your own. Especially in the rough part of town. Which is where I can guarantee the guy selling this thing will be.'

'Yeah, I'd already resigned myself to that,' she said with dark humour.

'When's he going?'

'This weekend.'

'And I already know I won't talk you out of going with him, 'cause you're back in full Nina mode . . .'

'Hmph!'

Eddie straightened. 'I'll come with you,' he said firmly.

Nina knew he would be as stubborn having made the decision as she, but still gave him a dubious look. 'What about Macy?'

'Holly or Olivia can look after her.'

'Macy'll be pissed at us both, you know.'

He grinned. 'You should be used to that by now.'

It was her turn to sigh. 'I know. Oh well. Better start thinking about how we're going to break this to her in the morning.'

'Think we'll have to work faster than that,' said Eddie as the study door opened.

Macy entered. 'Break *what* to me?'

'All yours, love,' the Yorkshireman said to Nina with a grin.

'Gee, thanks,' she replied, before taking a deep breath as she faced her daughter. 'Okay. Honey, this weekend, your dad and I have to go away for a couple of days.'

'Why?' Macy asked.

'Ah . . . some business came up at the university. I need to go to Germany to help collect an artefact.'

Her face lit up. 'Can I come?'

'Sorry, honey, but no. You'll have to stay here.'

Macy's smile turned instantly into a scowl. 'What? *Why?* Why does Dad get to go, but not me?'

Nina looked to Eddie for help, but he merely gave her an infuriating little smirk. She glared at him, then continued: 'The place we're probably going . . . it's not really suitable for a girl your age.'

A snort of outrage. 'Mom! I'm *ten*, not five!'

Eddie finally joined in. 'To be honest, love, I wouldn't be happy about you going there even if you were a grown-up.'

Macy's expression did not lighten. 'I can't *believe* you're going to Europe without me.'

'We'll be back as soon as we can,' Nina assured her. 'Olivia or Holly will look after you while we're gone.'

'But I don't *want* them to look after me!' she protested. 'I want to come with you!' She glanced at Nina's laptop. 'What's that?'

'That's the artefact we're going to collect.'

'That skull looks familiar. I think I've seen it in an archaeology video.'

'I doubt it, honey,' Nina said. 'This thing's only just been discovered.'

Macy's only reply was an irritable huff as she turned and stalked out. Her mother and father exchanged long-suffering glances, then followed her into the living room. 'It'll be okay, love,' said Eddie. 'It's only for two nights. And I'm sure Holly and Olivia'll do something fun with you.'

'Holly only ever offers to take me to the zoo, like I'm still six,' Macy complained. She picked up her toy trikan, based on the weapon from the movies rather than the real artefact, from the coffee table. 'And I love Olivia, but she's really old. She can't do anything fun.'

Nina sighed. 'My little girl's already turning into a teenager. And she's only ten!' she said to Eddie, before turning back to her daughter. 'So what *do* you want to do?'

A shrug. 'I dunno.'

'Yep, definitely sounds like a teenager,' Eddie said.

Macy pouted, spinning the trikan on a short length of its string like a yo-yo – then whirled towards Eddie and sent it flying at him. 'Hey, Malkovich! Think fast!'

It was a family joke from the film *Being John Malkovich*, warning that the other person should duck. Eddie did so – but not quickly enough. The toy deflected off the top of his head as he bobbed, hitting an ornament on a shelf. It fell to the floor and smashed.

Macy gasped in dismay. Eddie stared at the broken pieces, aghast. Nina, meanwhile, had to use every ounce of self-control not to whoop in delight. 'Oh . . . no,' she managed. 'That's a shame.'

The broken object was a pottery cigar-box holder in the caricatured shape of a beaming Fidel Castro, which had come with the Englishman when the couple first moved in together – and which Nina had long since abandoned hope of ever removing from their home. She tried not to smile about their daughter doing it for her.

Eddie regarded the debris for one last moment, then, with a heavy breath, crouched to collect the fragments. 'Oh Dad, no, I'm so sorry!' Macy cried, kneeling to help him. 'Can you fix it?'

'No, it's bust,' he said, shaking his head. 'Oh well. Guess it did its job.'

As far as Nina knew, it had never held a cigar in its life, and she was sure he didn't mean its everyday purpose of storing loose change. 'What do you mean?'

'Didn't I tell you where it came from?'

'I always kinda suspected Cuba, but no.'

'Hugo gave it me as a souvenir while we were doing a job in Cuba, yeah.' He nodded towards the framed pictures occupying part of one wall: Eddie's former comrades-in-arms, many of whom were now dead. Hugo Castille had been his closest friend during his time as an international troubleshooter. 'We actually met Castro, you know,' he added, almost as an afterthought.

Nina was surprised. Her husband had always been discreet about his military and mercenary past, but never mentioning *that*? 'You did?'

'Yeah, briefly. One of those "how the hell did I get into this situation?" moments. Didn't agree with his politics, but he was a funny guy.' He finished gathering the larger pieces and put them in the bin.

'I'll get the vacuum,' said Macy, hurrying to the hall cupboard.

'So Hugo bought me this,' Eddie went on, crouching again to collect the spilled coins, 'partly as a joke about meeting Fidel, and partly to say: "Hey, don't sit around moping about the past" – I'd just got divorced – "because you never know what's going to happen next." And that part was certainly true. After me and Sophia split up, I had a couple of years doing all sorts of crazy stuff . . . and then I met you.'

'And then things got *really* crazy,' she said with a smile.

'You're not bloody kidding,' he replied, grinning, as Macy returned with the vacuum cleaner. 'So maybe poor old Fidel's done everything he was meant to do. I've reached fifty, so that's one chapter of my life over, but there are new ones to come.'

'Lots and lots of them, hopefully.'

'That's the plan!' He deposited the coins on a countertop, then moved so Macy could vacuum up the remaining fragments. 'Can't believe I didn't duck in time.'

'Like you said, you've reached fifty,' Nina reminded him. 'You aren't as quick as when you were twenty.'

'Or forty-nine, apparently. Thanks, Macy.'

Macy switched off the vacuum cleaner. 'Dad, I'm sorry I broke it, I really am.'

'It's all right, love,' he said, squeezing her. 'It's just a thing. Nobody got hurt. So,' he went on, recognising an opportunity, 'do you think you'll be okay without us for a couple of days?'

'I suppose so, yeah—' Macy gave him a sidelong look, realising she had been guilt-tripped. '*Dad.*'

He grinned. 'You'll be fine. We'll call Holly and Olivia in the morning.'

'And I'll tell Cheng we're going with him,' added Nina.

Eddie let out a wry chuckle. 'Off to Germany at a moment's notice? Hugo was right. You never *do* know what's going to happen next.'

3

Hamburg, Germany

Cheng looked around as he, Nina and Eddie emerged from the S-Bahn station. 'So this is the famous Reeperbahn!'

'Infamous is more like it,' said Eddie. 'It doesn't look like much in daylight, but things'll kick off once it gets dark. And whatever you do, keep hold of that bloody bag.' As well as a backpack, the young Chinese carried a black nylon holdall; in it was fifty thousand euros in cash, which he had collected from a bank in central Hamburg.

Nina was already regretting her decision to come. The evening flight from JFK had been delayed, not taking off until the early hours of the morning, and when she'd called Macy on arriving in Germany, her daughter was still angry and petulant about being forced to stay at home. The knowledge that they still had to deal with the artefact's seller, who she was certain would try to pull some con, did not improve her own grumpy mood. 'Do I want to know what you were doing in Hamburg's red-light district?'

'Nothing I caught anything from, don't worry,' her husband replied with a grin. 'It's pretty much a squaddie rule when you're in Germany. Come to Hamburg, go to the Reeperbahn, drink too much, ogle people, try not to pass out in a gutter and wake up with all your money gone. Hey, I was young,' he added, seeing her disapproval.

'I didn't do anything like that when *I* was young.'

'Maybe you should have. Might have made you more . . . adventurous.' He waggled his eyebrows suggestively.

Nina felt her cheeks flush. 'Eddie, we have *company*.'

'He's not listening.' Cheng was consulting a map on his phone, only to become distracted as two young women wearing extremely short skirts and high heels trotted past. 'Hey, Cheng! Close your mouth, you're drooling.'

The Chinese student hurriedly snapped his jaw shut. 'I was not! I was, uh . . .'

'I'm guessing you haven't seen anything like this in China,' said Nina. The buildings along the Reeperbahn advertised their business with Teutonic bluntness. Most were dedicated to sex, all tastes and kinks and fetishes catered for, and the remainder provided sustenance and supplies to wide-eyed visitors.

'I have to admit, no, Professor,' said Cheng, forcing his eyes back to the phone.

'So where are we going?' Eddie asked.

'He told me to come to an apartment off a street called Grobe Freiheit at seven o'clock.'

The Yorkshireman laughed. 'That's *Große* Freiheit. Pronounced like "grocer".'

'You know it?' said Nina.

'Yeah. Lots of boozers and nightclubs and theatres.'

'Not the kind that do Shakespeare, I assume.'

'Topless Shakespeare, maybe.' He pointed west. 'It's along there.'

The trio started down the street. The Reeperbahn was switching from daytime mundanity to the excitement of the night – or the sleaze, depending on one's point of view. Nina definitely veered towards the latter. Packs of young male tourists were heading for the bars to drink up the courage they needed to enter somewhere more exotic, older men in ones and twos moving purposefully towards whichever establishment catered to their evening's desires. Female visitors were in the minority, and were either in groups for mutual reassurance, or tagging along uncomfortably with partners. The women who actually worked in the district, whatever their age and profession, all had similar expressions: a stony indifference that couldn't quite be masked even behind the brightest fake smile.

'Is it safe here?' she asked, moving closer to Eddie.

'Lots of cops about,' he replied. 'This is a big tourist attraction – they don't let anyone cause trouble.' She wasn't reassured.

They passed sex shops and porn cinemas and greasy-smelling fast-food joints, eventually coming to a circular plaza at an intersection. 'Oh, I've heard about this!' said Eddie with enthusiasm.

The metal outlines of five figures stood around the circle. All held musical instruments: four guitars and one set of drums.

'Who are they?' Nina asked.

'It's the Beatles! John, Paul, George and Ringo. They played in clubs here before they got famous.' He stood behind one of the guitarists, striking a matching pose with an air instrument.

She looked at the lonely fifth figure. 'So who's that?'

'Stuart Sutcliffe. Or Pete Best. One of the fifth Beatles.'

Cheng regarded the statues with curiosity. 'What are the Beatles?'

Eddie gave him an incredulous look. 'You've never heard of the Beatles?'

'No.'

'One of the most famous bands of all time?'

He shook his head. 'Sorry, Mr Chase. I don't know them.'

Nina laughed. 'Eddie, he was only born eighteen years ago. It'd be like expecting you to know the big names in pre-war jazz!'

'This is why I feel old,' the Englishman complained, before facing a street leading north. 'Anyway, that's the Große Freiheit. Where exactly are we going?'

Cheng examined his map again. 'Behind a theatre near the far end. There's an alley next to a bar.'

'A back alley in a red-light district? Yeah, that sounds safe,' said Nina as they set off again.

'I'll watch out for you both,' Eddie assured her.

They made their way up the Große Freiheit. The bustling street was even more open than the Reeperbahn about its trade. Neon blazed, flashing signs and loud music trying to entice punters into the bars and clubs and shows. The couple noticed with amusement that Cheng was trying desperately not to gawp at the more outré passers-by: thigh-booted women and transvestites, a bare-chested man in leather trousers and a bright pink pimp hat complete with peacock feather, a man and woman dressed head to foot in shiny black rubber and bondage harnesses.

'See anything you like?' Eddie joked.

'No, no,' Cheng mumbled, redirecting his gaze towards his feet.

'Where's this alley?' Nina asked.

He checked the phone. 'Next to a bar called Fausters.'

Eddie chuckled. 'Guess it's a gay bar, then.'

'Why?'

'*Faust* is German for fist. So it's literally called "Fisters".'

The young man was puzzled, then his eyes popped wide as he realised the meaning. 'Oh! But, but we don't need to go inside,' he stammered.

'You don't want to expand your horizons? And other things.'

'Eddie,' Nina chided, seeing Cheng's embarrassment deepen.

Her husband laughed again.

Fausters was not hard to find; its neon sign was in the shape of a clenched fist surrounded by a heart. A theatre across the alley beside it was emblazoned with posters for drag acts. 'This is it,' said Cheng.

Eddie looked down the narrow passage. A couple of theatre

employees were smoking outside a side entrance. 'Looks safe, but I'll go first anyway.'

He led the way. 'How do we find this guy?' Nina asked.

'There's an apartment block behind the theatre. He's in number five.'

They rounded a corner, entering a small courtyard. Nina crinkled her nose at the stench from a pile of garbage bags atop an overloaded dumpster. Cheng led them to a doorway beside it.

'Nice,' she said. 'I don't know how people could live here. Never mind the smell – listen to the noise!' Thudding basslines from the theatre and bar competed in volume.

'If you live here, you're probably working nights,' said Eddie. 'Or so desperate for a roof over your head that you don't care.'

'Or you're the kind of person who sells stolen artefacts over the dark web. Let's see if he's home.'

Cheng pushed an intercom button. A pause, then a curt '*Ja?*' came from the speaker.

'Hello?' he said. 'It's Hui Cheng.'

Someone peered down from a window, then the voice returned. 'Come in.' A lock released with a clack.

Eddie opened the door. A motion-activated light flicked on, revealing a cramped and grubby hall. He led them up the narrow staircase to the first landing. 'Here, number five.' He rapped on the door.

A man peered warily out before swinging it wider. 'In, in,' he said, gesturing impatiently.

They entered an untidy studio overlooking the courtyard, a single bed in one corner. The man, a weather-beaten thirty-something with a scruffy beard, regarded the trio suspiciously before turning to Cheng. 'You are Hui, yes?'

Cheng nodded. 'Yes.'

'The eyes gave it away.' He looked at Nina. 'And I can tell from the tits that you are Nina Wilde.'

41

Eddie glared at him. 'And you can tell from my fist that you'll have no teeth if you talk to my wife like that again.'

'Who are you?'

'Her husband, obviously.'

Nina thought the man was about to object to Eddie's presence, but then he turned back to Cheng, eyeing his bag. 'You have the money?'

'You have the artefact?' she countered.

'Of course. Show me the money, and you can see it.'

Nina exchanged a look with Eddie – neither of them remotely trusted their host – but Cheng unzipped the holdall, revealing bundles of two-hundred-euro notes. The man stared greedily at them, then smiled. 'Jakob Krämer. Good to meet you.'

'Likewise, I'm sure,' Nina replied sarcastically. 'You've seen what you want; now show us what you've got.'

Krämer gave the money another hungry look, then slid a canvas duffel bag from beneath the bed. He withdrew a tightly bound bundle of clothes, which he started to unwrap. 'I suppose you want to know where it came from.'

'It'd help, yeah.'

'I was crew on a cargo ship going from New Zealand to South Africa. We answered a distress call and found a man on an ice floe. He was carrying this.'

'You stole it?' said Nina, appalled. 'You rescued this guy, then robbed him?'

'The man is insane! He had no use for it. He was screaming about demons.'

'You said *is* insane,' Eddie noted. 'Present tense.'

'He's still alive?' Nina asked.

Krämer nodded. 'He is in a mental hospital in Holland. Still crazy.'

'What, you checked up on him to make sure he won't tell anyone about what you stole?'

The German ignored her, peeling away the last of the clothing. 'Here it is. The key.'

He held it up. The artefact was bigger than Nina had thought, about nine inches across. Even in the low light, she instantly knew from the metal's reddish gleam that it was the gold alloy the Atlanteans called orichalcum. 'The key to what?'

'He did not say.'

'What *did* he say?'

'Not much. As I told you, he is insane. He said a demon frozen in the ice woke up and killed his shipmates. His ship must have sunk, because we did not see it.'

Nina frowned. 'A demon?'

'That is what he said. So he must be crazy, *ja*? There is no such thing.' Krämer lowered the key. 'Now, it is time to talk business. You still want to buy it?'

'Yes,' said Cheng.

'Then you will surely be willing to pay a little extra money.'

Eddie rolled his eyes. 'Oh, here we go.'

The colour drained from Cheng's face. 'But . . . we had a deal.'

'There are others interested. But you were the first, so I will be fair and give you the chance to buy it now.'

Nina regarded him coldly. 'How much do you want?'

'One hundred thousand euros.'

Cheng blinked; Nina blanched; Eddie laughed. 'You're taking the piss!' exclaimed the Yorkshireman. 'That's twice what you were asking!'

'If the famous Nina Wilde is willing to come to Germany to see it, it must be more valuable than I thought. If you want it, you will pay what I ask.'

'I . . . I can get the money,' said Cheng, flustered. 'But I don't know how long it will take. I have to call China, talk to my – my family.'

Nina found herself saying words that surprised even her. 'I can pay the rest.'

'You *what*?' Eddie erupted.

'We can afford it. And this artefact looks genuine – which means it's worth every penny.'

Krämer looked at the key. 'Then perhaps I should ask for even more.'

'Perhaps you should ask for a boot up your arse,' the Englishman snapped. 'Nina, are you out of your bloody mind? Fifty grand! That's like giving him Macy's college fund!'

'I don't think you appreciate just how much an Ivy League education costs . . .' But she was already wavering. Eddie was right: without the financial backing of the university or her former employer, the International Heritage Agency, she would effectively be taking money from her family to indulge her archaeological curiosity.

The thought of Macy swayed her. 'No, you're right,' she admitted. 'That was a dumb idea. I think younger me took over for a moment. Sorry, Mr Krämer, but I've changed my mind.'

The sailor was taken aback. 'If you do not buy it now, I will sell it to someone else,' he insisted.

'And then you'll try to stiff them too? Dangerous business.'

'Yeah,' Eddie rumbled. 'You might try it on someone who isn't as nice as us.'

'I can get the money,' Cheng insisted. He raised his phone. 'I will call now—'

Nina put her hand over it. 'Cheng, no. We should leave.'

He looked at her in surprise. 'But the key – it could prove my theory!'

She had already had similar thoughts: the artefact could be new evidence of a civilisation that long pre-dated humanity. But that was a can of worms she was unsure she wanted to reopen – and besides, a little voice at the back of her mind

44

warned that Krämer was full of shit. 'It might, or it might not,' she told the Chinese youth. 'But this guy, this *thief*, is just out to rip you off. I don't believe there are any other buyers at all. Maybe *we* should set the price – and it'll be a damn sight less than fifty thousand euros.'

'Easy way to find out,' said Eddie. 'We'll go and see how long it takes him to call us back.'

'No, I can get the money,' said Cheng. 'I want to—'

'Mr Hui,' Nina said firmly. 'Do you want to pass my class?'

'Yes, but—'

'Then do what I tell you! Remember what I said about young people not listening to older people with the experience to know what the hell they're talking about? This is one of those times. Come on. We're going.'

He huffed, summoning the courage to challenge her. 'No, no. You can't make me!'

She almost laughed. 'Wow, it's like Macy came with us!'

'She might not be able to make you,' said Eddie. 'But I can.' While the Yorkshireman was fairly stocky, he was still taller than Cheng, and he moved closer to loom over him.

'Cheng,' said Nina, 'let's go. Now.' She closed his bag, then started for the door. The young man reluctantly followed, Eddie behind him.

Krämer scuttled to catch up. 'Okay, we can still make a deal! Eighty thousand? No, seventy-five, I will be generous.'

Nina ushered Cheng out. 'Forget it.'

'No, wait!' Desperation entered the German's voice. 'Okay, I will take the fifty thousand. A deal is a deal, *ja*?'

'Deal with this,' said Eddie, flipping him the bird as he closed the door.

They started down the stairs. 'We can't just walk away!' Cheng protested.

'Yeah, we can,' Nina replied. Below, three men entered the

hall and headed upwards. 'The guy was a total con man.'

'But he had the—' Cheng broke off as the first new arrival, a cold-faced blond, pushed rudely past him, his companions doing the same.

Nina and Eddie moved aside to let them through, but the stairway was so narrow they still brushed against each other. 'Oh, *excuse* me,' the Yorkshireman shot after them. The leader gave him a contemptuous look. 'Arseholes.'

'He had the key,' said Cheng, resuming his descent. 'It's genuine, you said so yourself! It could lead us to a lost civilisation. After everything you've discovered, how can you turn your back on that?'

They exited the building. 'Did you listen to a word I said in my lecture?' Nina demanded, stopping in the middle of the courtyard and facing him. 'Yes, I've made some amazing discoveries – *at a great cost*. This might be about money, not lives, but I want my students to learn from my mistakes, not repeat them!'

'But I have the original fifty thousand euros,' said Cheng, slapping the holdall. 'We could go back and pay him. Then we'd have the key!'

'He'll call you again, I guarantee it. And this time he'll want a lot less—'

She broke off at raised voices from above. Eddie looked up, seeing shifting shadows behind a window. 'Ay up. That's Krämer's flat.'

'Must be those guys who passed us on the stairs,' said Nina. 'Maybe he really *does* have other potential buy— *Aah!*'

They all leapt back in shock as Krämer was hurled through the window.

4

The screaming German landed with a bang on the overflowing dumpster. Nina whipped up her arms to shield herself from flying glass. 'Jesus!'

She looked up. The blond man glared back from the window, then shouted to his companions: 'Find the key!'

Krämer slid off the dumpster. Nina hurried to him. 'Oh my God! Are you okay?'

'*Ja*,' he gasped, squinting up at her – then slipping a hand out of his jacket. He still had the key. 'Help me . . .'

'Eddie!' she cried. 'We've gotta get him out of here!'

Her husband sighed. 'So much for staying out of trouble!'

Krämer's attacker had turned to watch the other men tear the squalid room apart – then he whipped back around as Nina and Eddie brought the German to his feet. 'He still has it!' he shouted. 'Get after him!'

'Time to go!' Eddie barked, shoving Krämer towards the alley.

Nina followed. 'Cheng, come on!'

The young Chinese was frozen in bewilderment. 'But what is—'

She pulled him after her. '*Run!*'

Eddie and Krämer hurried around the corner. Still towing Cheng, Nina glanced back – to see the blond man draw a suppressed pistol. 'Oh shit! *Gun!*'

She yanked Cheng into cover. The crack of a bullet striking brickwork just behind them almost drowned out the silenced weapon's flat *chack*.

Eddie and Krämer were a few metres ahead, but the sailor could only manage a loping run, one leg hurt in the fall. The alley stretched towards the glare and noise of the Große Freiheit. If they could reach it, they could lose themselves in the crowd, or even find some cops—

A loud crash from behind warned they wouldn't make it. The shooter had dropped down on to the dumpster. He would be able to take another shot before the fleeing group reached the street.

Eddie realised the same thing – and changed direction, shoving a startled smoker aside and pushing Krämer through the theatre's side entrance. 'In here!'

Nina swept Cheng inside as the theatre worker shouted after them. They were in the backstage area, loud music from the auditorium echoing through narrow passageways. 'Which way?'

'Dunno – try here!' Eddie rounded a corner, the others following. Doors marked with peeling stick-on stars greeted them. 'Dressing rooms; we must be near the stage.'

The smoker at the entrance shouted again, then cried out as he was clubbed down. 'He's coming!' said Nina. Running footsteps echoed behind them.

The corridor ended at two more doors, one a lavatory bearing a symbol of a male figure – wearing a huge beehive wig. The other was ajar, bright lights beyond. The Yorkshireman barrelled through. It was indeed a dressing room, illuminated mirrors along one wall and rack upon rack of showy female clothing against the other. A pink-haired drag queen gasped as the interlopers burst in. 'Sorry, 'scuse us,' said Eddie as he hurried past. 'Nice wig!'

There was an exit at the far end, but the pursuing footsteps were catching up fast. 'Go, go!' Nina shouted to Cheng as she halted. If she could jam the door with one of the racks . . .

Too late. The blond man was almost at the entrance—

She snatched up a large container of face powder and hurled it into the hallway.

The cardboard tub burst open like a smoke bomb, a dense cloud of flesh-toned powder erupting in front of her pursuer. He reflexively jumped back, coughing. Nina shoved a clothing rack at the doorway to block it, then ran after the others.

Eddie reached the exit. 'Keep going!' he barked, pushing Krämer and Cheng through before turning back to Nina. 'Come on, quick!'

'I'm coming, I'm coming!' The cloud was already thinning. The man appeared in the blocked doorway just as she reached the exit. Eddie propelled her through, following as the gun snapped up and fired. The round struck woodwork in his wake, splinters stabbing at the back of his bald head.

He shouted for the others to keep moving, but held position. The rattle of laden coat hangers told him the gunman was moving the clothing rack. He peeked around the door. The drag queen ducked fearfully under the countertop. Beyond her, the blond man grunted in annoyance as he forced the heavy rack aside. He still held the gun. The Yorkshireman looked for anything that could even the odds. All that was within his reach was clothing . . .

And shoes.

He snatched an item from the closest rack and withdrew as the gunman pushed into the room. It was Nina's turn to call for him to hurry. He waved for her to keep going, then looked back into the dressing room – using the mirrors to see without putting his head into the gunman's line of sight. He was taking a risk: if his opponent used the same trick to spot him, he could shoot him straight through the wooden wall . . .

But his pursuer's gaze was fixed on the exit as he rushed past the drag queen. Eddie tensed, waiting for him to get closer—

Then attacked.

The Yorkshireman spun out, swinging his weapon – a glossy black PVC thigh boot with a six-inch platform and a ten-inch stiletto heel. The towering sole weighed well over a kilogram, striking the blond's skull hard enough to send him reeling into the clothes racks. One of them toppled, burying him amongst its sequinned and feathered wardrobe.

Eddie hurled the boot at his head, drawing a yell of outraged pain. He looked for the gun. His adversary's right arm was pinned by the overturned rack. He threw clothing aside, trying to snatch the pistol from his hand—

Noises from the passageway. The downed man's comrades had caught up. Eddie instantly abandoned his search and ran through the exit.

Nina waited at the top of a flight of stairs, Krämer and the panting Cheng beyond. 'What happened?' she asked.

He vaulted up the steps. 'I gave him the boot.'

Her response to the feeble pun was a long-suffering sigh. Cheng's, on the other hand, was confusion. 'What do you mean?'

'I whacked his head with a kinky boot. That's nothing,' he added on seeing the student's befuddlement. 'I once broke someone's jaw with a foot-long dildo.'

'Not ours, I hasten to add,' said Nina as they hurried through some swing doors.

The music became louder. They were behind the stage, a couple of outrageously outfitted drag artists awaiting their cue. An illuminated green sign marked an emergency exit, but the way was blocked by a burly stagehand, who called to more men in the backstage area for support before running at them.

'We can't get out!' gasped Cheng.

'Yeah, we can,' Nina told him. 'You ever wanted to take to the stage?'

Eddie hurried to a large castored prop chest. 'I'll catch up!' he shouted, pushing the heavy box towards the stairwell.

Nina raced past the waiting drag queens onto the stage, Cheng and Krämer following. A trio of cross-dressing performers turned to usher them into their act, a blend of cabaret number and burlesque striptease, only to react with surprise when they saw the newcomers were not who they'd expected. The lead queen, clearly a seasoned professional well used to unexpected developments, immediately addressed them suggestively, arousing laughter from the audience.

'Ah, sorry, wrong turn!' Nina said, squinting into the spotlights to find an escape route. A central aisle was visible through the glare. 'This way!'

She jumped down, Krämer behind her. The German staggered on landing, his leg still hurt. Cheng didn't move, gawping transfixed at the performers; specifically, their very revealing cleavages. 'Oh for God's sake!' Nina shouted. 'They're not real! Get down here!' The young man blinked, then in a fluster hurried after her.

Eddie, meanwhile, had brought the chest to the top of the stairs – just as the blond man and his comrades rushed out of the dressing room. The leader's gun came up—

The Yorkshireman dropped on his back as a bullet cracked over him, then kicked the box hard over the top step. The pursuers frantically scrambled back as it cartwheeled to the floor and burst apart.

Eddie jumped up and ran after Nina. The first stagehand tried to block him, but even many years after resigning from service, the former SAS man was more than capable of defending himself. Barely two seconds later, the German was on the floor, gasping. The other stagehands suddenly slowed, not wanting to join their co-worker. Eddie nodded to thank them for their good sense and ran onto the stage.

His appearance drew a mocking introduction from the lead, something about liking bald men – he didn't understand the rest, but guessed it was rude – and more audience laughter. He gave her a bow, then leapt off the stage, seeing Nina and the others heading for the exit.

It took less time than he liked to catch up, Krämer's leg slowing him. 'Keep moving!' he shouted as they reached the doors. A look back. The blond pursuer rushed out from the wings. The drag queen began another sarcastic remark, only for concern, then fear, to course through the auditorium at the sight of the man's gun.

Eddie and Nina bustled their charges through the exit. They hurried across the lobby and out into the Große Freiheit. The street was busier than when they had arrived. 'You see any cops?' Nina asked.

'Nope,' Eddie replied. He gestured towards the Reeperbahn. 'Police station's that way.' He started into the crowd, the others in his wake.

Shouts and screams sounded from the theatre. 'They're coming!' cried Cheng.

Krämer grimaced. 'I – I cannot go faster. My leg!'

'You could hide and we'll take the key,' Nina suggested.

A humourless laugh. 'Do you think I am stupid?'

'Amongst other things, yeah! Looks like your other buyers decided to save themselves fifty thousand euros.'

'I do not know who they are,' Krämer protested as he hobbled behind Eddie. 'I lied to you – there *are* no other—'

The Yorkshireman suddenly slowed, the sailor almost stumbling into him. Several groups of drunken young men had converged on the same stretch of street, bringing movement to a crawl. 'Buggeration and fuckery! There's ten stag parties going on at the same time.' He searched for a quick route through the throng, found none, then simply barged into the crush.

The reaction was predictably hostile. Neither he nor Nina needed fluency in German to understand the insults flung in their wake. But more angry shouts rose along the Große Freiheit behind them – rapidly getting closer.

Their pursuers were catching up.

Eddie went faster, shoving people aside. A youth in a football shirt screamed slurred abuse after him, his similarly attired friends joining in – then Cheng yelled in shock as one yob knocked him to the ground. 'Hey!' Nina roared into the attacker's face as she interceded, reasoning – hoping – that he wouldn't hit a woman. 'Back off!'

She grabbed the shaken Cheng's arm and helped him up, pushing him onwards, only for him to stumble into one of several men with identical cropped haircuts. '*Hoy!*' barked the offended party. '*Verpiss dich, du Arschloch!*'

Eddie heard the commotion and stopped, turning to see Nina and Cheng between the two angry groups – and coming up fast behind them, a flash of blond hair amidst people being body-slammed out of the way. They were about to be caught in the middle of a fight—

He started it early.

Eddie delivered a brutal punch to one of the bellowing football fans, slamming him into his fellows, then whirled to drive an elbow into the back of someone whom he guessed from the haircut was a German sailor. The man reeled into a shipmate and knocked him down. A split second of stunned silence . . .

Then all hell broke loose.

Nina shrieked, hauling Cheng with her as the two drunken sides launched at each other, unsure who had started the trouble and not especially caring. Eddie had already pushed on, deliberately bowling a member of a stag party into the expanding brawl as he went. 'Move!' he yelled to Krämer.

'Shit!' Nina yelped as someone took a punch to the face and missed her by inches as he fell. 'Dammit, Eddie!'

But she knew why he had done it. The gunman and his

companions were almost on them – only to be caught in the swelling chaos. The blond man had just enough time to lock eyes with her before a drunk in a tracksuit hurled himself bodily at him. Both men fell, vanishing amongst flailing fists and feet.

She saw gaps opening as the non-belligerents in the surrounding crowd tried to get clear. 'Cheng, quick!' she shouted, following Eddie and Krämer. A whistle shrilled, followed by another; the police were already responding.

Cheng behind her, she caught up with her husband. 'Keep going,' Eddie ordered, angling towards the side of the street as the approaching cops ran down its centre. 'Once we're clear of the fight, they won't even look at us.'

'You're sure?' she asked.

'Do we look like a bunch of lads out on the piss?'

'Good point.'

They moved towards the Reeperbahn, policemen charging past with batons drawn, and reached the little plaza of the Beatles-Platz. A police car pulled up to disgorge more officers. Eddie veered well clear as the cops ran for the side street, leading the foursome past the other Fab Four. 'Over the road, quick!'

He led them across the Reeperbahn, ducking into the crowds outside the bars and heading for the first side street. 'Down here,' he said, looking back. If their pursuers had escaped the brawl, they hadn't yet made it to the Beatles-Platz. 'You know your way around here?' he asked Krämer.

The German nodded. 'There is a park along this road,' he said. 'We can go through it to the red-light district. There are always lots of people. We can lose them.'

They jogged down the side street, Krämer still hobbling. 'So you don't know who "they" are?' Nina asked.

'No,' he replied. 'I lied to you about the other buyers. I was trying to get more money.'

'But you must have spoken to someone. Otherwise how

would they have known where you were?'

'I spoke to no one!' Krämer insisted as they entered the park. 'I only gave my address to Mr Hui.' He glanced at Cheng. 'I never saw those men before – and I do not know how they found me.'

'They might be spooks,' Eddie suggested. Krämer didn't understand the slang. 'Intelligence services,' he clarified. 'Spies.'

'Spies?' The sailor looked unnerved. 'Working for who?'

'How would I know? The blond guy sounded Scandinavian, but I don't know why anyone from IKEA-land would want to take the key from you.'

'Speaking of the key,' said Nina, 'have you still got it?'

Krämer had kept the artefact inside his jacket. 'Yes. I have decided . . . it is too much trouble. You can have it. For the fifty thousand euros.'

The redhead laughed and shook her head. 'Can you believe this guy?'

They reached the park's far side. Eddie checked the street for potential threats, seeing none. 'Which way?' Krämer gestured left. 'Seeing as we just saved your life,' the Yorkshireman went on as he led the way, 'I think we should charge you a rescue fee. Something in the region of, I dunno, fifty thousand euros?'

Krämer was not amused. 'I was almost killed because of the key! I need money to get out of here safely. They could be waiting in my flat.'

'If we're talking money, that's up to Cheng.' Nina looked back at the young Chinese. 'How are you doing?'

He was still breathing heavily from the exertion – and fear – of the escape. 'I'm okay. But those men tried to kill us! And you and Mr Chase both seem so . . . unconcerned!'

'Oh, I'm *very* concerned, trust me,' Nina replied. 'But this is the kind of crap I didn't write about in my books. If I had, they'd be six hundred pages long, because it happened *all the goddamn time!*'

Krämer directed them right. Music from bars along the new street reached them. Nina turned back to the German. 'So, somebody wants the key badly enough to try to kill us. If you want to get out of here, now might be a good time to tell us more about it. Like *exactly* how you got hold of it, and from whom.'

He nodded reluctantly. 'I was on a ship called the *Fortune Mist*. We heard a distress call – this was four months ago – from another ship, the *Dionysius*. We did not find it, but we rescued the crazy man. His name is Wim Stapper. He is Dutch; he is now in the Henkeman hospital outside Rotterdam.'

Nina made mental notes of the names. 'And he had the key?'

'Yes. He was holding it to himself like it was the most important thing in the world.'

'And you stole it from him.'

'Yes, yes, I did,' he snapped in irritation. 'And look where that has got me!'

They reached a busy, noisy square. Eddie again checked for danger, then angled across it. 'So did this Stapper say anything else about the key?' Nina asked.

'He said . . . one of his friends, I forget the name, woke the demon,' Krämer said, following. 'It killed everyone else. It wanted the key, but Stapper got away with it.'

'Did he describe this demon?'

'No. He only said it was in the ice, and there were more of them. The key would wake them somehow. The only other thing he said,' the German went on ominously, 'was that if the demons woke up . . . they would kill us all.'

'Yeah, that's reassuring,' said Eddie. 'After everything else we've been through, now Beelzebub's got a devil put aside for me?'

'For me, for *meeee*,' Nina couldn't help singing in response. 'But there's no such thing as demons – I'm more worried about bullets than brimstone. That's everything he said?' she demanded of Krämer.

'That is all,' he replied. 'If you want to know anything else, you will have to speak to him in person. But I understand he is not very talkative. He has gone completely mad.'

They headed down another street, busy bars on both sides. The crowd grew thicker again, but now had a different feeling, contrasting with the out-for-a-good-time vibe of the Große Freiheit. While most of the men – and they were nearly all men here – moved with purpose, many kept their heads down almost furtively. 'The red-light district?' Nina asked disapprovingly.

'Yeah,' said Eddie, 'but don't worry, I didn't bring us here to go window-shopping. Reason I did is 'cause there are always cops around. They're probably not keen on the place, but prostitution's legal in Germany, so they're not here to bust the girls – but they *will* bust the heads of any punters who try anything funny. There's a street down here that's like hooker central, so *die Polizei*'ll be keeping an eye on things.'

'Do I even want to know how you're so well informed?'

'I told you, I was a twenty-year-old squaddie when I came here last! Anyway, it's just here.'

A side street had a tall barrier blocking its end, men going in and out through gates. Whatever was happening behind it was hidden from view, but from the lurid red lighting cast over the buildings beyond, Nina could take a pretty solid guess.

Krämer indicated a sign. 'You will not be able to go in,' he told Nina. 'Women are not allowed. Except for the whores.'

'I wasn't planning on visiting,' Eddie said impatiently, continuing past. 'See? Cops.' Several police officers were outside a nightclub ahead, two questioning a pair of worried-looking young men while the others stood in a loose cordon to deter onlookers from getting involved. 'If you've just run through a crowded theatre with a gun, you won't want to stroll right past a bunch of armed coppers who've probably got your description already.'

'They might have *our* descriptions as well,' said Cheng nervously.

'Maybe, but cheerful bald guy who bows to the drag queen when she takes the piss out of him? Not threatening. Ivan Drago-looking arsehole waving a gun? Threatening. Only one of 'em'll make people call one-one-zero.'

'Hope you're right,' said Nina as they approached. But to her relief, the cops gave them no more attention than any other passers-by. 'Okay,' she said to Krämer after they passed, 'what do you want to do with the key? As long as you've got it, those guys might keep coming after you. And don't use the word "fifty", or anything close to it,' she chided. 'Cheng, if you pay him that much, I'll give you an F for the semester right here and now!'

The German made an aggrieved noise. 'You have to give me *something*. I cannot go back to my room in case they are waiting for me!'

Cheng thought for a moment. 'What about . . . twenty-five thou—'

'Done,' Krämer snapped.

Cheng blinked.

Nina frowned, but the Chinese youth was already opening his bag. 'Jeez, at least keep it hidden,' she said. 'And get out of the cops' sight before you start handing out wads of banknotes. You'll get us arrested, or mugged, or both.'

'Down here,' said Eddie, rounding a corner and finding a darkened doorway. He stood guard, Nina partly watching the street and partly glaring in annoyance as Cheng handed the German half his money.

'Okay, now give him the key,' she said pointedly after Krämer tucked the notes away. He gave her a dirty look, but passed the artefact to Cheng. 'Right, you've got it – so put it away before anyone sees it.' Her student dropped it into the holdall and closed the zipper. She looked back at the sailor. 'Anything else you can tell us about the key or what Stapper said?'

Krämer shook his head. 'Not much. There was a big iceberg near where we found him, but that is all I can think of. Stapper's ship wasn't wrecked on it, though. We searched. The iceberg could have rolled over and crushed it into the water.'

'Okay. I guess we're done, then.'

'Thank you,' said Cheng as Krämer quickly departed.

'Don't thank him,' Eddie said. 'That thing might still land you in trouble.'

'We have to get out of Hamburg,' said Nina. 'Maybe those guys chasing us were arrested in the fight, but I don't want to bet my life on it.'

Eddie nodded. 'We should go to a different subway station. There's one at St Pauli.' He jabbed a thumb eastwards.

'Good idea.' They set off.

'So, we've got this thing. Where are we going? Home?'

'No,' said Nina. 'Well, not directly. There's someone we need to talk to first – Wim Stapper.'

'What, the guy from the ice? Why?'

She glanced at Cheng's bag. 'He found a Veteres artefact, somewhere off Antarctica. He's the only person who can tell us anything more about where it came from – and what he meant by "demons".'

'Demons, right,' said Eddie dismissively. 'Didn't Krämer say he was in a mental ward in Holland? Bit of a diversion, and we'll have to pay for new tickets home if we're not flying out of Hamburg.'

'Don't worry.' Nina turned to Cheng and put on an over-broad grin. 'I know someone with twenty-five thousand euros now going spare.'

'I . . . could pay for the flights, yes,' he agreed reluctantly.

'Macy'll be pissed off with us for coming back late,' Eddie warned.

'She's pissed at us for going at all. Or rather, for going without her. She'll be fine.'

'I'm sorry for putting you through this trouble,' said Cheng as Nina took out her phone.

'That's okay,' she replied, about to call her daughter – then giving him a curious look.

He was smart, and knowledgeable, and inquisitive. Yet she had accidentally mentioned the Veteres . . . and he hadn't asked who they were.

Krämer rounded a corner, then found his phone and dialled.

The reply was almost immediate. 'What happened?' snapped a woman in accented English.

'What do you mean, what happened?' Krämer replied angrily. 'Who were those men?'

'I do not know.'

'You didn't send them?'

'Of course not. Why would we interfere with our own plan?' A pause, then: 'Do Hui Cheng and Professor Wilde have the key?'

'Yes. So my part is over, *ja*? I want the rest of my money.'

'You will have it. Where are you now?'

'Walking towards Hans-Albers-Platz, near the Reeperbahn. Are you far away?'

'No. There is a park between Talstraße and Hein-Hoyer-Straße, behind a large white building on Simon-von-Utrecht-Straße. Do you know it?'

'I'll be able to find it.'

'Good. Meet me at the gate on Talstraße.'

'And you'll have my money?'

'I will.' The call ended sharply.

Krämer reached the bustling Hans-Albers-Platz. No sign of the men who had chased him, but he decided not to take any chances. Rather than heading directly for his rendezvous, he went east along Friedrichstraße, steering well clear of his escape route from the Große Freiheit.

Fifteen minutes later, paranoia having taken him on a circuitous path, he arrived at his destination.

Wu Shun was waiting, dressed in black jacket and tight jeans. The Chinese woman was attractive enough, Krämer thought, but there was something about her he didn't like, and he couldn't quite put his finger on what.

It didn't matter. He wasn't going to marry her, after all. He had completed his part in whatever she was doing, and now it was time to get his money and leave Hamburg – as quickly as possible. 'I'm here,' he said, checking their surroundings. She seemed to be alone.

'Good. Walk with me.' She started into the little park.

Krämer moved up beside her. 'Where is my money?'

She briefly opened a shoulder bag to reveal banknotes inside. 'Twenty-five thousand euros, as agreed. Did you get the money from Hui?'

'Not all of it. Only fifteen thousand,' he lied, hoping she might make up the difference. 'I wanted all fifty.'

'That is not my problem. You are fortunate I am willing to pay you at all.' Her voice was quiet and even, but there was an angry edge to it. 'Hui and Wilde were going to leave without the key because you doubled the price.'

'How did— You *bugged my flat*?' he yelped in realisation.

'Keep your voice down. And yes, of course we did. This is very important to us. Your greed could have ruined everything.'

'So could me being shot!' he snapped. 'I was thrown out of a window – your bugs didn't stop that, did they? And you have no idea who those men are?'

'No,' said Wu, 'but we will find out.' No doubt, just a statement of fact.

'Well, I wish you luck,' said the German impatiently, 'but now it is time for me to go. My money?'

She looked around. To their left, apartment buildings overlooked the park. The grassy area to the right was darker, trees blocking most of the nearby illumination. 'Over there.'

Krämer checked the shadows, but saw nobody lurking in wait. He angled with her off the path. They circled behind a tree, out of the light. 'Okay. The money.'

She slipped the bag from her shoulder, supporting it from beneath as she used her other hand to open it. 'Here.'

Krämer stepped closer. Even in the darkness, the bundles of clean, new banknotes stood out clearly. 'Good. I will—'

Her supporting arm suddenly moved – and a slender carbon-fibre blade sank deep into his stomach.

Krämer gasped, trying to draw back, but a fire spread through his body, incinerating his nerves and paralysing his muscles. 'You, you . . .' was all he managed to whisper before the hideous sensation reached his mouth. He convulsed, a strangled rasp forcing its way from his throat, then crumpled to the ground.

Wu gazed at him with no more emotion than if she had crushed a bug. A glance at the apartment buildings to make sure she was not being observed, then she crouched, checking his pulse.

She found the beat immediately, racing as terrified adrenalin flooded his system, but already beginning to slow. She kept her hand in place, feeling it become weaker, slower still.

And finally stop.

She searched him for Hui Cheng's money. He had lied; there were ten thousand euros more than he'd claimed. Wu was not surprised. She also took his phone, to conceal the electronic trail linking them. The poison on the knife was undetectable in a standard autopsy; with nothing left on his body to raise the eyebrows of the police, it would seem like nothing more than a mugging gone wrong, a down-on-his-luck merchant sailor taking a wrong turn.

Wu straightened. The German's dead eyes stared up at her. She returned the blade to the Kevlar pocket on the bag's underside and set off, without even a glance back at the man whose life she had just ended.

5

Rotterdam, Holland

'I don't think this is a good idea,' said Eddie, shifting uncomfortably as they waited in the reception area of the Henkeman psychiatric hospital. 'I mean, the guy's obviously got major problems if he's been locked up here for four months – and you want to show him the thing he's freaked out about.'

The key was now in Nina's bag. They had left Hamburg with no further trouble, and her fame as an archaeologist even got them through airport security with no awkward questions about the ancient artefact. 'He's the only person who can tell us anything about it,' she reminded her husband. 'He knows where it was found – and what happened there.'

'Krämer said he was ranting about demons! I don't think he's a reliable witness.'

'What will you do if he tells you where it came from?' asked Cheng, working on his laptop. He had already taken advantage of the wait at the airport and their overnight stay in Rotterdam to type up a record of events.

'I don't know. We might not get anything coherent from him – hell, they might not even let us see him.'

The wait lasted several more minutes. Finally a door opened and one of the facility's medical staff approached. 'Professor Wilde?' said Dr Eline Kuiper.

'Yes?' said Nina hopefully.

'We would not normally allow Wim to receive visitors who are not relatives. However, because of your standing, and because you may be able to help break through his catatonic state, we have decided to allow it.' The tightness of her lips suggested she disagreed with the decision.

'Thank you.'

'His health is the most important consideration, though. So your visit will have limits.'

She nodded. 'I understand. What are they?'

'Only you will be allowed to see him, in my company. You may try to speak to him for five minutes, no longer. If he becomes agitated, you will leave immediately. Is that understood?'

'Absolutely.' She gave the two men a glance. Eddie was relieved to avoid the encounter, though Cheng seemed disappointed. Kuiper gestured for Nina to follow her.

'Good luck,' said Eddie.

'Thanks,' Nina replied with trepidation.

The facility was a hospital, not a prison, but it still had strict security measures. Nina and Kuiper, accompanied by a male orderly, passed through two sets of entry-coded doors before reaching the accommodation section. While all the rooms were soundproofed, Nina still heard muffled sobs and shouts from some. Unsettled, she stayed close behind the doctor.

Kuiper stopped outside a door. 'I will check on Wim's condition.'

'Does he get violent?' Nina asked.

'No, but he sometimes becomes very frightened. Please wait.' An exchange with the orderly, then she went into the room. Nina remained outside, feeling the weight of the key in her bag.

A minute passed, then there was a gentle rap on the door. The orderly checked through a peephole and opened it. 'Professor Wilde, come in,' said Kuiper.

Nina took a pensive breath, then entered.

The room was small but light, a tall, thin window reinforced with fine wire mesh overlooking a leafy quadrangle. A small table was home to a pad of paper and felt-tip pens, but there was no indication they had been used.

It was easy to see why at the sight of the room's occupant. Wim Stapper was in his late twenties, but any youthful energy had been drained by his ordeal; his face was drawn, a body that had once been strong and wiry now merely thin. He did not react to the new arrival, gazing blankly from the bed at something beyond the ceiling.

The doctor spoke to him in gentle Dutch, but got no response. 'This is his normal state,' she whispered to Nina. 'A near-catatonia. He is aware of us but does not want to respond.'

'Why not?'

'Most probably fear. He suffered a traumatic experience before his rescue. The only way his mind can deal with it is by hiding from the world.'

Nina regarded him sadly, feeling a pre-emptive guilt. Something terrible had happened to the young Dutchman, but the only way to find out what would be to remind him of it. 'Does he speak English?'

'Yes. Fluently, according to his family.'

'Can I talk to him?'

Kuiper reluctantly nodded, then checked her watch. 'Five minutes.'

Nina stepped closer. 'Hello,' she said softly. 'My name's Nina. I'm an archaeologist – I look for lost things from the past. Things that have been buried.' She put a little emphasis on the last word. Stapper's eyes flicked towards her, but then looked back at the ceiling. 'I've found something – something stolen from you when you were rescued from the ice.'

No reaction for a moment . . . then almost inaudible words slipped from his lips. 'The ice?'

Nina looked at Kuiper, who was surprised. 'He does not usually react to strangers. But please be careful what you say next. The memory can upset him.'

'I'll try my best,' said Nina, not sure how to dance around the subject. 'Wim, I've got something I'd like to show you. Is that okay?'

This time, he didn't respond. She gave Kuiper another glance, then slowly took out the golden disc. 'I have the key.'

'The . . . key?' murmured Stapper. He turned his head towards her – and his eyes went wide as he saw what she was holding. 'The key! No, *no*! The demons – they want it! They want to kill us all!'

Kuiper hastily interposed herself between Nina and her patient. 'I'm sorry, but you need to leave now.'

'No, no, wait!' Nina begged. 'Wim, the key! Where did you find it? What happened to the *Dionysius*?'

The mention of the ship instantly changed his attitude, blind fright becoming a contemplative confusion as his brow furrowed in thought. 'It . . . it came to rescue us, came into the cave. But too late. Everything . . . turned over.' Kuiper backed away, startled by her patient's change of mood. 'The spaceship was . . . trying to move, it turned everything over.'

'The *what*?' exclaimed Nina. 'The *spaceship*?'

'In the ice,' Stapper went on. 'Buried inside D43. It was very old. Sanna and I, we found it in the cave.'

She had no idea what D43 might be, but Kuiper filled in another blank. 'Sanna Onvaan,' the doctor said quietly. 'One of the people on his ship.'

Nina made a mental note to investigate the *Dionysius* and its mission, but there were more important questions to be asked. 'And is that where you found the key too?'

Stapper's gaze returned to the orichalcum artefact, regarding it with a mixture of awe and fear. 'Yes, yes. In a room of gold and crystal. Sanna saw where it belonged and put it in.'

'Then what happened?'

'Nothing, at first. Later the spaceship started to light up, but by then . . .' His expression began to shift back towards fear. 'We had found the demons.'

'The demons,' Nina echoed. 'What can you tell me about them?'

'Dead, but alive,' was the contradictory reply. 'Giants, lots of them, in glass coffins. The key . . . Sanna used the key, and one of them woke up. It—' Sudden horror filled his eyes. 'We tried to talk to it, but – it killed her!' he shouted. 'It killed her, and tried to kill me! It – it wanted the key!'

'*Now* you need to leave,' Kuiper told Nina forcefully, rapping on the door to summon the orderly. 'He is terrified!'

'Wim, *where* did you find the key?' Nina asked as she backed away. 'Where is this – this spaceship?'

'D43!' the young man cried. The orderly hurried in, firmly ushering Nina through the exit. 'Inside D43, the ice cave! The *Dionysius* – it's still there!'

The door closed again, cutting him off. Nina stood still for a moment, then looked at the object in her hands.

A *spaceship*? She didn't believe for a moment that was what the Dutchman had found. Partly because it would mean accepting as fact the ridiculous pseudoscience Macy and Eddie enjoyed taunting her with, but also because of the obvious inconsistency with Stapper's other claims. Demons were as unacceptable to her as UFOs.

Besides, she already knew a secret truth that partially explained things. The lettering on the key appeared to be a product of the Veteres – and she had seen their ancient corpses in a tomb deep within the long-hidden Garden of Eden. Humanoid, but not human, resembling the Grey aliens of popular culture; she could easily imagine someone high on the adrenalin of discovery instantly assuming they were extraterrestrial in origin. In fact, the opposite was the case: the Veteres had existed on earth before humans, a different branch of the same evolutionary tree that had also produced *Homo neanderthalensis*, *denisova* and *floresiensis*, as well as *Homo sapiens* themselves.

But it was one hell of a leap of the imagination to think such a corpse had woken up and attacked. What did *that* mean?

She waited in the hallway until Kuiper and the orderly emerged. 'Is he okay?'

The doctor gave her a baleful look. 'He has calmed down. But he is very agitated – I should not have let you see him.'

'I'm sorry. Will he be all right?'

'In time, I hope. But you should leave. Now.'

'Okay. Thank you for letting me see him.'

Kuiper did not reply with anything more than another glower. The orderly escorted Nina back to the reception area.

'How did it go?' said Eddie.

'Well, he told me some things about how he found the key,' she said. 'But I don't know if any of them will be any use.'

'What did he say?' asked Cheng.

'A lot of it was crazy talk. More about demons, and . . .' She hesitated. 'A spaceship.'

A crooked grin spread slowly across Eddie's face. 'Sorry, what?'

She sighed. 'A spaceship.'

He cupped a hand to one ear. 'Don't think I heard you right. Can you say that again?'

She leaned closer, waiting for his smirk to widen – then snapped: 'Get bent, Eddie.'

He cackled. 'Oh, Macy'll be *so* happy when she hears that. Which she will, 'cause if you don't tell her, I'm going to!'

'Like I said,' Nina continued impatiently, 'there was a lot of crazy talk. But he did mention some things Krämer didn't know.

His ship, the *Dionysius*, went into a cave – and might still be inside.'

'I checked the name *Dionysius* on my laptop at Hamburg airport,' said Cheng. 'It's a research vessel, registered in South Africa. Or it was – it was listed on the Lloyd's Register as lost two months ago.'

'Wasn't Stapper found *four* months ago?' Eddie asked.

'It probably took that long before the insurance company was willing to pay out,' said Nina. 'And I'd hope the ship's owners at least tried to search for it, and its crew. But if it was inside this cave, nobody would have seen it.'

'How could it be in a cave? Krämer said they found Stapper in the middle of the sea.'

'He also said there was an iceberg nearby,' Cheng pointed out.

'The ship's *inside* the iceberg?' Eddie was understandably incredulous.

Nina thought back to the Dutchman's fragmented conversation. 'Stapper kept mentioning something called D43. Is there a naming convention for icebergs?'

'You're asking me? I can barely remember whether port or starboard is left!'

'There is,' said Cheng. They both looked at him. 'The letter, A to D, is the longitudinal quadrant where the iceberg was first sighted. The number is its position on the list of icebergs that have been tracked.'

'Thanks, Wiki,' said Eddie. 'When did you look *that* up?'

The young man looked abashed. 'I, ah . . . I like to learn. I read about all sorts of things. Not just archaeology.'

'That's a good attitude,' said Nina. 'The broader your experience, the better. And it's helped us, because if this iceberg is a big one, it won't have melted to nothing in just four months – some of them can drift for years. Which means it's still out there . . . and so is the ship!'

★ ★ ★

'Yeah, we'll be home soon, love,' Eddie assured Macy over his phone as he paced across the hotel room. 'No, I know we were supposed to come straight back, but something cropped up.' He listened to his daughter's angry protest. 'Yeah, I know! But your mum thought it was important.' He didn't need to add *even if I didn't* for it to be clear.

Nina shot him a glare, but she was in the middle of a phone call of her own. She and Cheng had used the young man's laptop to track down the owners of the *Dionysius* in Cape Town. After some phone tag – it was, after all, a Sunday – they'd eventually got hold of the company's boss, a man named Janco Vorster. The possibility that his lost ship might still be intact immediately caught Vorster's full attention. He explained it had been chartered to carry out a feasibility study about towing an iceberg to South Africa to alleviate its water shortages.

Now she was talking to one of the expedition's organisers, a woman called Imka Joubert. 'Is . . . is this a joke?' she said after Nina explained the situation, a hint of hope overlaid by a much greater fear that it was about to be dashed.

'No, I assure you it's not,' said Nina. 'I've spoken to Wim Stapper in Rotterdam, and—'

'Wim?' she cut in. 'How is he? Is he . . . better?'

'I'm afraid not. But he told me some things you deserve to know. Is D43 an iceberg?'

'Yes, yes,' Imka confirmed. 'It was the main candidate for the survey.'

'Wim said the *Dionysius* went *inside* it, into a cave, to rescue him and a woman called Sanna.'

'Sanna Onvaan, yes. Oh God, did he say what happened to her?'

Nina hesitated before answering. 'I'm sorry, but . . . Wim said she died.'

Silence for a long moment. 'Oh. Oh no.'

'I'm sorry,' she said again.

'Did he . . . did he tell you anything about the other people on the ship?'

'I'm afraid not. Something happened inside the iceberg. I don't know what, Wim wasn't making much sense, but I think the ship became trapped in the cave. Wim managed to get out, but he didn't say if anyone else did.'

Imka struggled to keep her emotions in check as she spoke. 'Something happened *before* the *Dionysius* went inside. I was talking to Arnold . . . my fiancé.' Her voice almost cracked. 'There was a lot of shouting, and they said Wim and Sanna were in trouble. I remember hearing the captain say he didn't want to launch a lifeboat, something about protecting the crew. Arnold told me he would call back as soon as he found them. He . . . he never called.' The last words emerged as a choked gasp of grief.

'If the iceberg's still intact, the ship might be too,' Nina said, wanting to give the distraught South African some thread to cling to. 'Would it have had enough provisions to support everyone for this long?'

Imka took a deep breath, trying to recover her composure. 'The survey was planned to last for two months, at the most,' she said. 'If everyone cut down to minimum rations . . . perhaps.' Then, almost pleading: 'If they're still alive, can you help me find them?'

'I honestly don't know,' said Nina. 'Maritime rescue isn't my area of expertise. I got involved because Wim found an archaeological relic inside the iceberg.'

'A relic? Nobody told me about this.'

'Nobody knew – one of the rescue ship's crew stole it from him. It could have come from something buried in the ice. Can you still track the iceberg?'

'The currents will have moved it, but . . . yes, I'm sure I can find it.' Urgency entered her voice. 'And if I can, then we can launch a rescue mission! Janco has another ship. We can use it to reach D43, and find Arnold and the others!'

Her sudden surge of desperate hopefulness alarmed Nina. Whatever had happened to Stapper and the crew of the *Dionysius* could still be a threat, waiting in the ice. 'I'm not sure that's a good idea.'

'But we have to try! If Arnold's still alive, I have to find him. And if . . .' She trailed off. 'I have to know,' she finally said, solemnly.

'I understand,' Nina told her. 'Look, let me give you my contact details. If you tell me what you're planning to do, I might be able to help.' She hesitated, aware that Eddie had broken off from his conversation with Macy to fix her with a warning look, but spoke anyway. 'If you find the iceberg, and there's an archaeological discovery inside it, I should be there.'

Eddie's expression changed to anger. Nina looked away. 'I'll call you again soon, okay? Please don't do anything without letting me know.' She gave Imka her contact information, then disconnected.

Her husband concluded his own call, saying goodbye to Macy before rounding on his wife. '*What?* You want to go looking for this thing?'

'Oh, come on, Eddie,' she replied. 'You *know* I'm going to. People have already died because of whatever Wim Stapper found.'

'And it never occurred to you that he might have killed them himself and pretended to go crazy ape bonkers to cover it up?'

'If he's faking, there'll be an Oscar heading his way for Best Actor. And why would he come up with such an insane story when he could have just kept it simple and said his ship hit the iceberg and everyone else drowned?' She paused, thinking. 'I'm *certain* the text on one side of the key is in the Veteres language.

Their existence is a secret I promised to keep; we *both* did. Because if the truth gets out, it could throw half the world into turmoil – as if things weren't bad enough already! If there really is some kind of Veteres outpost frozen in the ice, I need to see it.'

'So you can decide what to do with it.' It was not a question but a statement, annoyed at her assumption of authority.

'If I have to. You'd rather someone else did?'

'If it means we don't have to leave our daughter behind for a week while we traipse around on a fucking iceberg, yeah.'

'There's something else,' Nina went on. 'I wasn't sure before, because the photo on the dark web wasn't good enough to show all the details. But now that I've seen the key in person . . .' She stood and headed for the door. 'Come on.'

'Where to?'

'Cheng's room. I want to show you something.'

He reluctantly accompanied her to the neighbouring room. She knocked.

'Uh – wait, please! Wait, please!' the young man responded from within. A pause, long enough for the couple to give each other quizzical looks, then the door opened. Cheng blinked at them. 'Oh! Professor, Mr Chase. Hi. Er . . . can I help you?'

'Hi, Cheng,' said Nina. 'Is it okay if I look at the key?'

'Yes, yes, of course. It's right here.' He led them to a desk. His laptop was closed on it, but she noticed that some LEDs set into the case were alight and the fan was still going, as if it were in the process of entering sleep mode.

Eddie realised the same thing. 'Catch you watching porn, did we?'

'What? No, no!' Cheng stammered.

'Eddie!' chided Nina. 'Excuse my husband, please. He has a . . . *youthful* sense of humour.'

'That's okay,' the Chinese replied hastily. 'No problem.' The key was next to the computer; he presented it to her. 'Here.'

The side with the Veteres text was face-up. Nina looked at it for a moment, paying close attention to the edges of each character, then flipped it over.

'It's a different alphabet, isn't it?' said Cheng. 'It looks a lot like Atlantean. At least, to me,' he added, looking to her for validation.

'My thoughts exactly,' she said, holding the key up to the light. To her annoyance, she couldn't quite focus on the fine details. 'Damn it. I need my reading glasses! Back in a second.' She handed the key to Cheng and hurried out, leaving the two men standing alone.

'So, uh . . . Mr Chase,' Cheng said awkwardly after a moment. 'I, ah . . . I didn't say thank you for getting me out of trouble earlier. So . . . thank you.'

'No problem,' Eddie replied. Another uncomfortable pause, then: 'Your English is really good. You done a lot of travelling?'

Cheng shook his head. 'No. The first time I left China was to come to New York! I learned English from, ah . . .' He glanced at the door as if worried Nina might overhear. 'From Marvel movies and *Friends*.' A nervous giggle. 'Could I *be* any more lame?'

Eddie's silent stare in response told him that he probably could not. Luckily for the student, Nina chose that moment to return. 'Okay,' she said, taking back the key and donning her glasses, 'this is what I thought. It's definitely a different alphabet from the obverse, as you said, Cheng.' The young man beamed. 'Proto-Atlantean, for want of a better term. But if you look closely, you can see another difference between it and the text on the other side.'

She flipped the key over so they could make a comparison. 'The text on one side is cast into it,' Cheng said, almost immediately. 'And so's the skull. They were part of the original design.'

Nina nodded. 'But the words on the skull side weren't. They were engraved rather than cast – even carved, looking at it. The edges are quite rough in places. They're a later addition. Possibly quite some time later, looking at the weathering.'

'So what are the words?' Eddie asked. 'You said one of them was—'

'"Resurrection",' Cheng cut in. Nina and Eddie both looked at him in surprise. 'I, er . . . after I first saw Mr Krämer's pictures and thought the characters looked similar to the Atlantean alphabet, I worked on translating it.'

'What does that mean, then?' said Eddie. 'Stapper said a demon woke up and killed his friends, then it turns out he was holding something that literally says "resurrection" on it? What, did the key bring the thing back to life?'

'I don't know,' said Nina. 'But that's another reason why I *have* to help find it. There's . . . what we were talking about just now,' she nodded towards their room, not wanting to mention the Veteres in front of Cheng again, 'and the connection to Atlantis – what if it's another vault like the one from Turkey? We know that would be incredibly dangerous in the wrong hands. And there's the fact that anyone other than us won't have a clue what they're facing. We do – at least a little. But that might be the difference between coming out alive and ending up like Stapper's shipmates.'

'They could still be alive,' Cheng pointed out. 'If they are, then we have to rescue them.'

Eddie's expression made it clear he thought the odds of that were zero, but Nina nodded in agreement with her student. 'We do. And the sooner we start, the better the chances of finding them. And whatever they discovered in the ice.'

'I'll make preparations,' said Cheng, indicating his laptop, before hurriedly adding: 'If that's all right with you, Professor.'

'Go ahead,' she replied. 'Consider it another opportunity to impress me.'

He smiled.

The couple returned to their room. Eddie closed the door, then stood regarding his wife, arms crossed. 'So we're going, then.'

'Well, *I'm* going,' said Nina. 'You don't have to. I certainly know you don't *want* to – and it'd be better for Macy if you went back to New York.'

'I know,' he said, with a heartfelt nod, 'but if I *don't* go, and something happens to you that I could have stopped . . .' A long sigh. 'Not going to let that happen.'

'Thanks,' she said with a smile.

He didn't return it. 'Doesn't mean I'm happy about it. And I know Macy won't be. And nor will Holly or Olivia! So I'll let you break the news to them.'

It was her turn to sigh. 'I asked for that, didn't I?'

'Yeah. You did.'

'Okay. I'll call them. And,' she went on, 'I'd better do some shopping. We'll need to wrap up warm!'

6

The Southern Ocean

'Oiceberg, roight ahead!'

Nina smiled at her husband. 'I'm glad you've recovered your sense of humour.'

'Oh, I'm still pissed off, don't worry,' he replied. 'But how often would I get to make that *Titanic* joke for real?'

A week after the couple had left Rotterdam, iceberg D43 was now in sight. It had been a fraught seven days, the flight back to New York followed by a confrontation with an angry and upset Macy – understandably so, after being told her parents would be jetting off and leaving her behind again. At ten, Nina recalled with grim amusement, her daughter was old and savvy enough to protest that it was a form of child abuse, and she couldn't entirely disagree. It was certainly not an ideal situation; Holly couldn't take any more time off work, so childcare duties were being shared between her, Olivia and Lola Adams, a friend of Nina's from her days at the IHA.

But the sight of the iceberg reminded her there were other considerations. If the *Dionysius* remained intact inside, there was a chance, however slim, that its crew might still be alive. Imka was right: a rescue attempt had to be made.

And then there was the question of what *else* was inside. Nina still totally dismissed the idea that it might be demons or aliens, but there was *something* – something connected to the long-lost civilisation of the Veteres.

Which was why she *had* to be there, she told herself. As far as she knew, she and Eddie were the only people in the world with direct knowledge and experience of the ancient race. That edge could mean the difference between life and death.

She turned from the angular blue-white iceberg to the other people on the bridge. Three days earlier, the research vessel *Torrox*, sister ship to the *Dionysius*, had set sail from Sydney, Australia. Vorster had joined the mission, the bearded shipowner constantly lurking behind the *Torrox*'s captain as if itching to take command himself. Imka Joubert was also there, the stress and frustration of enforced inaction during the voyage clear on her face. Even if her fiancé was still alive, there was nothing the slender blonde could do to help him until they reached their destination.

But that time would soon come. Nina went to the last passenger on the bridge: Hui Cheng. The young Chinese was on his laptop, using a satellite link to download updated satellite imagery of D43. 'Anything new?' she asked.

'This is from yesterday,' Cheng said, showing her the picture. 'Some more pieces have broken off,' he indicated a cluster of white objects near the berg, ducklings trailing their mother, 'but none are very big.'

The captain, a languid Australian named Alan Tate, glanced at them. 'Doesn't mean it'll hold together. This latitude, the water's warm enough to work away at any cracks. The whole thing could split in half any time.'

'Let's hope it waits until we've finished,' said Nina as Cheng zoomed in. She was impressed by the speed of his satellite link; she had used similar technology in the past, but it always felt like going back to the days of dial-up modems compared to the unthinkingly accepted transparency of a Wi-Fi connection. This was practically broadband speed, though, even in the middle of the ocean. Technology kept advancing behind her back.

Imka regarded the icy peaks, then, frowning slightly, asked Cheng: 'Can you show me the picture Arnold sent when he first found D43?'

She had given him access to a cloud folder of files regarding the iceberg survey; it only took him seconds to bring up the picture. Nina also peered at the berg ahead before returning her gaze to the laptop. 'It's different.'

The South African nodded. 'The topography has completely changed. This formation here,' she pointed out a squared-off peak in the four-month-old photograph, 'has gone.'

'Wim said something . . .' Nina tried to remember the Dutchman's words. 'Something about everything turning over. That could be what he meant.'

'These things do roll,' said Tate. 'And you don't want to be anywhere near them when they do. You could be hundreds of metres clear and still have part of the berg come up under you like a bloody whale.' He stared at the distant iceberg. 'That looks like clean ice, no snow on it. It's been underwater. I'd say the whole thing flipped over.'

Imka looked stricken. 'If Arnold's ship was inside the iceberg when that happened . . .'

'There's still a chance,' Nina assured her, though she was far from confident herself.

The *Torrox* sailed on. Vorster surveyed the growing berg through binoculars. 'I can't see any caves big enough to take a ship.'

'Could be on the other side,' said Eddie. 'Anything on the radar?'

The iceberg's flank displayed as a crinkled, hazy line, smaller echoes dotted before it. 'The S-band radar should show a ship inside the ice, as long as it's not too deep,' said Tate. 'Or half a K underwater, which it might be after the thing rolled.'

The addendum was not something Imka wanted to hear. Nina gave the younger woman another look of reassurance.

Tate brought the *Torrox* into a clockwise orbit around the iceberg. Even though they were clear of the larger hunks that had calved from D43, growlers still occasionally clunked against the hull. Cheng flinched with every impact.

'You okay?' Nina asked.

'Yes, yes,' he said, looking anything but. 'I . . . don't like being on a ship.'

Eddie chuckled. 'You wait until *now* to tell us?'

'It makes me feel sick. I don't like high places either.'

'You'll be fine,' said Nina. 'You haven't thrown up so far, after all.' A mournful look from Cheng. 'Oh. You have?'

'In my cabin,' he admitted, a little shamefaced.

'Hope you mopped it up,' said Eddie with a smile hardly brimming in sympathy.

The ship continued on. After twenty minutes, Tate leaned closer to the radar screen. 'I think we've got something!'

The iceberg was now a ragged sweep across the screen's right, still fuzzy as the radar return bounced off different layers of ice, but a harder shape beyond its boundary had come into view. 'Is it the *Dionysius*?' asked Imka.

'Can't tell,' Tate replied. 'Might be two things close together; almost looks like they're overlapping.'

'Take us in closer,' ordered Vorster.

The captain turned the *Torrox* towards the iceberg. Everyone else went to the windows to gaze at the frozen cliffs. Even Cheng left his computer, transfixed. 'It is beautiful!'

Nina could only partially agree. In terms of colour alone, it was spectacular. The ice ran in stunningly vivid strata of white and turquoise and cyan, their steep angle confirming that D43 had indeed rolled over. It had shed some of its bulk, but was still over a mile and a half long. But the iceberg itself was only beautiful in the same manner as a painting by Francis Bacon or H. R. Giger, something dredged up from the darkest depths of the subconscious. Pillars of glossy ice resembling melting candles rose skyscraper-high above the water, leaning at impossible angles or merging together in unsettling primordial conjugations.

And according to Stapper, there was something even more bizarre inside. She turned her attention back to the radar. Tate was right: there did indeed seem to be two distinct objects within the frozen wall, but like the ice pillars, they were blended into each other, the radar struggling to differentiate them.

As for *what* they were, she couldn't tell. Neither looked like a ship – or a spaceship, for that matter . . .

Vorster still had the binoculars, staring intently at the base of the cliffs. 'I think . . . Yes! I can see an opening!'

'Big enough for a ship?' Imka asked hopefully.

'No, but . . . it goes into a cave. I can see waves inside.'

Nina and Eddie searched for what Vorster had seen. It was revealed as a low, dark mouth in the wall. 'Definitely too small for a ship,' said the Yorkshireman. 'If that's where the other one went in, it must be a lot bigger under the water. Good job it stayed at sea level when the iceberg rolled, or we'd never have seen it.'

'Yeah, lucky break,' said Nina, faintly puzzled. The topography visible in the picture sent to Imka was now part of the nine-tenths of the berg hidden beneath the ocean's surface, but if the odd radar return really was the *Dionysius*, then it was still roughly at sea level. The iceberg hadn't simply flipped over, but had rotated around an axis that somehow kept the cave containing the ship at the surface. She couldn't wrap her head around the complexities of motion that would have required.

Not that it mattered. The cave would be accessible by the *Torrox*'s boat, and according to the radar, whatever lurked inside was not too deeply buried.

'Okay, Al,' said Vorster, 'bring us in to five hundred metres, then heave to. We'll get the boat ready.'

Tate nodded. 'Who's going with you?'

'Imka, Professor Wilde and Mr Chase . . . and I think Mr Cheng is keen to set foot on something resembling dry land.'

'It's Mr *Hui*,' Cheng corrected.

Vorster spoke over him. 'Who's your best man with experience on ice?'

'Marc Naider,' said Tate. 'Good climber, knows his stuff.'

'Great. Hopefully we'll find the *Dionysius* – and everyone aboard it too,' he added to Imka. 'And Professor Wilde's archaeological discovery, whatever it might be.'

They all started to file from the bridge. 'Yeah, whatever it might be,' Eddie echoed in a whisper to Nina as she fastened her hair into a ponytail. 'You didn't mention the whole spaceship thing to them?'

'It won't be a spaceship,' was her taut reply. 'Besides, if I'd told them that was what we were looking for, they probably wouldn't have let me on the boat! As for what it actually is, well . . .' A glance at the opening in the ice. 'I guess we'll find out soon enough.'

The explorers donned cold-weather gear, loaded the *Torrox*'s boat, then set out towards their destination.

Imka sat at the bow, staring at the cave mouth with both hope and trepidation. Eddie and Nina were behind her. 'Christ, it's nippy,' the Yorkshireman complained, pulling his woolly hat lower.

'We're near the South Pole,' said Nina. 'What did you expect?'

'We're not even that near,' pointed out Vorster. 'We're only a few hundred kilometres closer to the pole than to the equator. Shows how bloody cold Antarctica is, hey?'

'Between the pole and the equator, I know where I'd rather

be,' Eddie told him. He checked on Cheng, who was beside Vorster, clutching his backpack and looking extremely unhappy. 'And I bet *you'd* rather be literally anywhere else right now.'

The RIB both pitched and rolled as it powered through the waves. 'I *really* don't like boats,' moaned the young Chinese.

Naider slowed to guide the craft around some bobbing chunks of ice, then brought it into the cave mouth. The growl of the outboard echoed back at the group as the walls closed in. The ceiling was about fifteen feet above; high enough to stave off claustrophobia, but far too low to accommodate the *Torrox*. If its sister ship was inside, it would have been unable to sail back out.

The light in the tunnel took on a sapphire hue as it cut through layers of dense ice. Ahead, the cave began to widen out. 'We're almost inside,' said Imka, turning her head to search for the *Dionysius*. 'Where is it? It was on the radar, we should be able to see it!'

Vorster used a walkie-talkie to call Tate aboard the *Torrox*. 'Al, how deep in were those radar signals?'

'Hard to say exactly,' came the crackling reply, 'but less than two hundred metres. The radar can't penetrate ice any deeper than that.'

'Then where *is* it?' Imka demanded in frustration.

Nina looked past her. The cavern became discernible as her eyes adjusted to the low light. The rear wall was well over a hundred metres away, but there was nothing there except ice. The wall to her left curved upwards out of the water until it became practically vertical, a sheer swathe riven by cracks and protrusions; at its far end was an ominous field of spikes. Icicles once hanging from the ceiling now stabbed upwards after the iceberg's roll. The right side of the cave narrowed to nothingness.

The water inside was calm – and empty. So where were the objects on the radar?

The answer came as they cleared the tunnel and entered the ice cavern proper.

The first thing Nina spotted made her blink in surprise at its incongruity: a ship's anchor, dangling from its chain about forty feet above. But surprise turned to shock as her gaze followed the chain upwards – and saw it was still attached to its vessel.

The *Dionysius* was embedded in the cave's ceiling almost a hundred feet over their heads.

The survey ship hung inverted, loose lines and chains hanging from it like vines. Metal and wood alike were coated in frost and ice. A ghost ship, suspended precariously from the roof of its frozen tomb.

Everyone stared in amazement at the gravity-defying sight.

'Oh my God,' Imka gasped. 'Look at that!'

'Definitely not something you see every day,' said Eddie. 'Even for us!'

Naider stopped the engine, the RIB coasting slowly into the cave. 'How did it get up there?'

'It must have gotten wedged in the ice,' Nina said. 'When the iceberg rolled over, it went with it . . . and then froze in place.'

'Not frozen enough,' Eddie observed. The glassy blue ceiling was split by numerous cracks around the *Dionysius*, icy fragments dropping in a faint but continual rain as the ship's weight pulled ceaselessly at its prison. With the outboard shut down, they could also hear noises from above. A low, creaking rumble formed a rolling bassline to intermittent cracks and bangs. 'It's going to break loose, and probably sooner rather than later. I don't want to be under it when it falls!'

Naider made a hurried course change to angle the boat out from beneath the suspended ship.

Imka cupped her hands to her mouth. 'Hello!' she cried. 'Can anyone hear me?' Her own echo was the only reply. 'Arnold! It's Imka! We're here, we've found you! Please, please answer me!'

Still no response. Eddie and Nina exchanged grim glances. After four months, the chances of the crew surviving were already slim, and now looked to be non-existent.

But they still had to be sure. The ship was here, but as yet there was no sign of people, alive or dead. Maybe they had found refuge deeper in the cave . . .

The drifting boat cleared the *Dionysius* to provide its passengers with an unobstructed view of what lay beyond. They all reacted with shock.

The research vessel was not the only thing trapped in the ice.

Startled gasps came from the explorers. 'Bloody hell,' said Eddie. 'You know what I think that is?'

'I do,' Nina replied. 'And the worst part is . . . I'm not sure you're wrong.'

If it wasn't a spaceship, she struggled to think of any alternative possibilities. The object was easily as big as the *Dionysius*, but it was hard to be certain of its exact dimensions; a large part of it was embedded in the cave wall, dimly visible through the stressed ice. The iceberg's roll had also left it lying at a steep angle. What she could see of it was a flattened cone in shape, jagged strakes and fins on its skin sweeping back into the cliff. Unlike its fellow prisoner, which was coated in frost, the metal hull was clearly visible. The *kind* of metal was a mystery, though. It had an oily sheen that her gaze almost slid off.

She shivered, not just from the cold. The object had an animalistic quality, reminding her of the head of a snake – or more fancifully, a dragon. Two elongated slits in its upper surface formed eyes, staring menacingly back at her. Windows? A pair of long, spear-shaped protrusions beneath its nose took on the role of fangs, increasing the resemblance.

She saw as they drew nearer that it was damaged. The hull was split and crumpled where it had succumbed to the pressure of the ice during its long entrapment.

But what was it? Had they *really* found a UFO?

'It *does* look like a UFO,' Cheng said, as if reading Nina's mind.

'Yeah,' agreed Vorster. 'And it's deep in the ice. How long has it been here?'

The astonishing sight had distracted even Imka. 'We . . . we estimated the deepest ice at over a million years old,' she said. 'This cave was at sea level when the *Dionysius* found it, and nine-tenths of an iceberg is underwater, so it's been buried for at least a hundred thousand years.'

'Same age as the UFO in *The Thing*,' Eddie noted with amusement.

Nina didn't smile. 'I was thinking more the same age as the Veteres,' she whispered to him.

'You're saying they built spaceships? Bit of a stretch.'

'This hasn't been into space. But we know the Veteres made it to Antarctica. It's got to be something they built. An outpost, or a ship.'

Vorster caught the end of the muted exchange. 'It's not a ship,' said the former naval warrant officer with professional certainty. 'Not one you could take across an ocean. It's got a flat bottom, no prow, no keel. You couldn't sail that across anything more choppy than a paddling pool.'

'Do you think we can reach it?' asked Imka. 'Arnold and the others . . . they might have taken shelter inside.'

Eddie surveyed the ice wall. The field of inverted icicles stood directly beneath the strange object, and the cliff leading up from them actually went beyond the vertical in places, overhanging the glinting needles. 'Wouldn't recommend going that way,' he said. 'I could do it, and Marc, you too?' Naider nodded. 'But probably not the best idea for the rest of you to climb a vertical line hanging over a load of six-foot spikes.'

Cheng regarded the icicles unhappily. 'I did tell you I'm not good with heights, didn't I?'

'So how do we get up?' Nina asked.

The Yorkshireman's gaze swept back across the cliff. 'There,' he said, indicating a jutting nose of ice rising from the water not far inside the cave entrance. 'We can get onto solid ground there, and I'll climb up to that ledge.' A ragged rift cut across the wall about sixty feet above until it met a thick, near-vertical pillar of ice standing out several feet from the face. 'There's a rope ladder in the gear. I'll haul it up, unroll it, then everyone else can climb up after me.'

'What about the rest of the way?' Imka said dubiously. 'The cliff's almost vertical, and there is that big column in the way – how will we get across to the spaceship?'

'It's not a spaceship,' Nina insisted.

Eddie smirked at her before answering the other woman's question. 'I'll set up pitons and ropes so everyone can get around that pillar. Once you get to the other crack,' he pointed out a weaving line beyond the obstacle that crossed the cliff almost the whole way to the mysterious object, 'it should be pretty straightforward to sidestep along it. I'll put in lines you can hold.'

'You make it sound so easy,' said Nina. She didn't doubt that the climb was well within his capabilities, but the constant creaking of stressed ice reminded her that they were in a cave that was slowly but inexorably melting. Surfaces that seemed solid could give way at any moment.

'Oh, you'll hear me complaining all the way up. But I think everyone'll manage it. Even you, Cheng.' The young man did not look reassured.

Naider brought the boat to the starting point. Eddie hopped out and the pair unloaded the climbing gear. The Yorkshireman donned a harness and equipped it with a light, an electric Fast Ice drill and several racks of six-inch ice screws, plus a set of foot-long ones. He then put spiked crampons over his boots, slung a coil of rope on one shoulder, and donned a climbing helmet as protection against falling debris. Finally he hefted a pair of folding ice axes. 'Anyone wants ice in their drink, just ask.'

'Mine's a double,' said Nina, amused. Then, more seriously: 'Be careful.'

'I somehow made it to fifty, so now I'm pretty determined to reach sixty!' He kissed her, then clomped to the cliff's foot. 'All right, let's go and meet the aliens!'

Nina's only reply as he started to climb was a long-suffering sigh.

7

Eddie's initial climb was straightforward. The ice was firm enough for his axes to bite deeply into, supporting his weight. A minor scare came when a tray-sized scab of ice sheared away as he dug in his crampon spikes, everyone below jumping back as it smashed at the bottom. But that aside, he reached the crevice with no difficulty.

He secured the rope ladder's top and let it drop down. It ended about six feet above the ground, but with Naider's help, even the non-climbers would be able to reach it. 'Everyone set?' he called to them.

All acknowledged in the affirmative, though Naider asked Cheng a question, pointing at his feet. 'I'm okay, I know what I'm doing,' the student replied impatiently, taking experimental steps on his spiked crampons.

'Shall we come up?' Nina asked.

Eddie pointed at the ice pillar. 'Give me a minute to get started on that, then yeah.'

He sidestepped to the column and crouched, using the powerful Fast Ice drill to screw one of the twelve-inch rods into the ice to act as a foothold. Once it was in place, he drilled in shorter screws higher up, then attached carabiners and fixed a rope to the first one before threading it through the rest. He then clipped the line to his harness and stepped on to the long peg, driving in more screws as he gradually worked his way around the obstacle.

A clatter and huff from the ledge announced Nina's arrival at the ladder's top. 'It's been a while since I've done anything like that,' she panted.

'Have you missed it?'

'I would say no, but . . .' She pointed. The object embedded in the ice was partially visible beyond the outcrop. 'There's *that*.'

'Still don't think it's a UFO?'

'I don't think we'll find little green men in it, no.'

He lowered his voice; Imka was starting her ascent. 'What about the ship's crew – Imka's fiancé?'

A grim shake of her head. 'I can't imagine they're still alive – not after whatever the hell happened here.' She looked up at the *Dionysius*. Dark portholes stared back like empty eye sockets. 'If anyone's here, alive or dead, they must be in . . . the other thing.'

'It's never a good sign when even you don't know what something is. Usually means we're going to find trouble inside,' he said, before quickly changing the subject as Imka neared them. 'Okay, I'll put ropes and pitons around the other side of this pillar, then go across the cliff. I'll shout as soon as I've got all the lines in place.'

'Don't go inside that thing without the rest of us,' Nina warned.

'Are you kidding? I've seen *way* too many movies about people who wander off on their own inside alien spaceships!'

'It's not— Oh just get going,' she said with amused exasperation.

Eddie laughed and continued around the outcrop.

At some point the bulging pillar of ice had been underwater, the sea washing it as smooth as glass. Fortunately, it was dense enough to take his weight, though the surface layers creaked and whitened with stress. He drilled in more ice screws and attached carabiners before securing the rope through them, soon stepping with relief onto the long ledge. It was narrow, ranging in width from roughly a foot to just a few inches, but would provide adequate footing for the group to traverse the cliff once he placed guidelines along its length.

He looked ahead. If the object trapped in the ice wasn't an alien spaceship, it was doing a damn good impression of one. He could see more detail on its glistening metal surface, including—

'It's got a door!' he shouted, seeing an oval void in its flank. 'It's open.'

'Can we reach it?' Nina called back.

'Should be able to, yeah.' The opening was higher up than the crack, but a few more screws would make it accessible. 'Okay, I'll climb over and set up the rope.'

He started across the ledge, drilling in more screws and attaching carabiners as he went. What had begun as a relatively straightforward journey became complicated by unexpected obstacles: debris from the *Dionysius* embedded in the icy wall. Barrels, tools, chains and pieces of broken crates were frozen into the cliff like flies in amber. Halfway along, a hunk of metal that he guessed was a ratchet from the ship's crane jutted out across his path like a claw. It was buried too deeply for him to dislodge, so he put an extra screw above it to serve as a handhold while he swung past the obstruction.

A glance at the source of the debris. The hanging anchor was now below him. From here, he saw that the *Dionysius* was pinned between two heavy sheets of ice, trapping it in its gravity-defying prison.

How long it would remain there was another matter. Icy flakes constantly fell from around it, the low moans of the overstressed ceiling louder and more alarming now he was closer.

The thought spurred Eddie to quicken his pace. He moved on, laying a trail for the others to follow, until he reached a jutting ledge just beneath the 'spaceship'. The inverted icicles stabbed up at him from below.

The view above was no less unsettling. He was almost underneath the looming metal shape, and something made a sixth sense clamour in warning. He couldn't escape the feeling that even after being buried for over a hundred thousand years, the object was not inert.

He put the disturbing thought aside and shouted back to the rest of the party. 'Okay, ropes are in place! Come across!'

Nina led the way, picking her way around the icy outcrop to the crack. With the line to support her, it did not take long to reach the frozen ratchet. 'Oh, this is conveniently placed!'

Eddie started drilling screws to act as steps up to the higher ledge leading to the opening. 'Hold the spike I put in as you go around, you'll be fine. Just make sure you're still clipped to the rope.'

'I wasn't planning to unfasten myself, don't worry.' She looked down. The drop to the frigid water below was an almost sheer sixty feet. 'Actually, I might put another clip on!'

Eddie smiled, then resumed his task.

She took hold of the protruding ice screw and leaned back as far as she could, pushing out her butt to clear the metal talon. 'This is dignified. I'm glad nobody's filming me!' The ice under her crampons crackled, but held. She brought herself around the ratchet and, relieved, continued onwards.

She soon reached the wider ledge. Her husband was above, finishing the steps to the object. This close, she finally got a full sense of its dimensions. Her first thought was that it was the size of a plane, a small commuter jet or large business aircraft, but that was doing it a disservice. An airplane's fuselage was a long, slim tube, but this was wide as well. Vorster was right that it couldn't be a ship; the underside was practically flat. A giant sled, able to be towed across the ice? It didn't seem likely.

So what the hell were they dealing with?

Eddie started to descend. 'Ay up. Here comes Cheng.' Cheng clumsily clambered around the outcrop. His movements were made more awkward by his backpack. 'What's he got in there? Bowling balls?'

'I think it's his laptop and satellite link,' said Nina.

He scoffed. 'What's he going to do, livestream everything?'

Cheng reached the ledge, relieved to have something other than steel spikes beneath his feet. He began the traverse, conspicuously not looking down. Imka appeared around the pillar behind him. Eddie watched with disapproval. 'Don't really want more than one person coming across at a time.'

'Won't the ropes take it?'

'I'd rather not find out. Imka!' he shouted. She paused. 'Wait until he's over here before getting on to the ledge.'

'I can't just hang on here!' she protested.

Eddie frowned. Amateurs becoming impatient was a recipe for trouble. 'At least let him get past that piece of metal.'

'Cheng, the ice is loose there,' Nina warned. 'Be very careful.'

He clutched the screw and swung around the ratchet. 'I'll be fine—'

The ice burst apart beneath his right boot.

He flailed his leg, trying to regain his foothold – and the crampon came off, flapping from his heel on its strap.

Cheng squawked in surprise and instinctively shifted his weight to regain his balance. His other foot slipped from the ledge. He fell—

The ropes caught him.

For a moment. Then one of the ice screws burst free.

Cheng screamed as he dropped again—

The other screws on each side held. He jerked to a halt three feet below the ledge. Gasping, he flailed at the wall, gloved hands struggling for purchase on the smooth surface.

Eddie was already moving back across the cliff. There wasn't time to clip his harness to the rope; instead he simply gripped it as he half walked, half leapt along the ledge. 'Cheng, I'm coming!'

The student was becoming panicked. 'Cheng!' Nina shouted. 'Use your foot, dig the crampon into the ice! No, not *that* foot,' she added almost with a disbelieving eye-roll as he kicked at the ice with his right foot, the loose crampon flapping beneath it. 'The one with the *spikes*!'

He made another attempt, this time with the fully attached crampon. Metal bit into the surface. That secured him just enough for him to raise himself. One hand found a hold on the ledge. He shouted in Mandarin, straining to bring himself up.

'I'll be there in a second!' Eddie yelled. 'Try and get hold with your other hand!'

The student did so, fingers clutching the edge. Eddie hopped sidelong to the nearest screw holding Cheng's weight. The ice around it had turned opaque under the strain, crackling and squealing. He wrapped his right arm around the rope leading back across the cliff, then took hold of the length supporting Cheng and pulled. 'Can you get your foot any higher?'

Cheng made a face of extreme effort. 'I . . . yes, yes, I can,' he said, inching upwards.

'Great. Hold on.' The Fast Ice and screw racks were still attached to Eddie's harness; he fumbled a foot-long rod into the chuck, then drilled it into the wall. Once it was in place, he gripped it with one hand and reached down as far as possible to take hold of Cheng's rope. 'Okay, I'm going to pull you up. Ready?'

Cheng nodded. Eddie braced himself, then hauled. Even with eight inches of steel embedded in the cliff, he still heard the ice around the screw moan, but it held. The youth rose higher, clawing at the ledge before finally bringing one elbow over it. 'Now lift your foot!' The Yorkshireman took Cheng's whole weight for a moment as he raised his leg and kicked his crampon spikes into the wall. 'That's it, keep going!'

Cheng brought himself high enough to hook his foot over the ledge. Eddie helped him fully onto it, then climbed up beside him. Crouching, he reattached the crampon to Cheng's footwear. 'For fuck's sake, son!' he snapped. 'It helps if you actually fit them to your fucking boots properly!' There was almost a centimetre of play around the toepiece. 'I thought you said you knew what you were doing?'

'I . . . I thought it was secure,' Cheng replied, unable to meet his eyes. 'I'm sorry, Mr Chase. I should have let Mr Naider check them . . . I just didn't want to seem useless.'

'There's useless, then there's *worse* than useless,' Eddie growled as he tightened the crampon. 'That's when you get other people hurt as well as yourself. At least if you're just useless, I can look after you.' He straightened, using the drill to attach a replacement screw and carabiner and clipping the line through it. 'All right. Wait for me to get across, then start after me. And don't fuck things up again.'

He made the crossing, shaking his head.

Nina awaited him. 'Kinda harsh, weren't you?'

'I should've been harsher. The kid could've killed himself.'

She shared her husband's view, but at the same time felt sympathy for Cheng. 'He's just young – and he's obviously a nerd. He probably felt threatened by you.'

'Well, he definitely does now.' Eddie stood with folded arms and watched as Cheng resumed his journey, considerably more carefully than before.

Eventually he reached the ledge. 'Are you okay?' Nina asked him.

It took him a moment to find his breath. 'Yes, thank you, Professor Wilde,' he said, still avoiding Eddie's hard gaze. 'I . . . I should have been more careful. I'm sorry.'

'You made it in one piece, that's the main thing. Let's try not to break rule number one again, huh?'

Imka resumed her crossing. Eddie watched her progress, but Nina turned her attention back to the strange object above them. Cheng stood beside her. 'It's so *big*,' he said, awed. 'I never thought . . .'

'Never thought what?' Nina prompted after a silence.

'That – that I would find something like this. An outpost of a lost civilisation, a lost race, hidden in the ice for all this time.'

'You think it's an outpost? Some kind of building rather than a ship?'

'I don't believe it's a UFO,' he said, directing a small smile at Eddie's back. 'And Mr Vorster is right. It's the wrong shape to travel on the sea. It must have been built in Antarctica.' He looked up at the dark, sinister shape. 'A fortress?'

'Protecting against what?' Nina asked, though she had her suspicions. The Veteres had travelled to the literal ends of the earth to escape their former slaves: humans.

Although that description wasn't strictly true, she reminded herself. The Veteres certainly considered humans as lesser beings, much as humans regarded apes and monkeys, but they had tried to teach and uplift them to something more. Their mistake was in not recognising until too late that distinctly human trait: applying any new knowledge first and foremost to the purposes of *violence*. They had given their primitive charges the most powerful weapon possible to use against them.

Imka arrived. Vorster began his traversal, Naider rounding the icy outcropping behind him. 'It's gonna get cramped on here,' Nina said to Eddie. 'Some of us should go up to make room.'

'"Some of us" meaning "the redhead New Yorker", right?' Eddie replied.

She grinned. 'Am I that transparent?'

'You're easier to see through than this ice. Go on up, then. We'll follow as soon as Marc gets across. Oh, and radio the *Torrox* – let them know we're okay and that we're checking the ship.'

Nina glanced between the inverted *Dionysius* and its shadowy companion. 'I guess we don't need to tell them *which* ship just yet, huh?' She took Eddie's radio, then moved to the ladder of ice screws. 'Cheng, with me.'

She started up the cliff face. Eddie had drilled in enough steel rods to make the ascent straightforward, but a glance at the icy stalagmites far below gave her added incentive not to get complacent. Before long she reached the upper ledge and clambered towards the unidentified object.

The tall oval opening loomed across a short expanse of exposed metal. She switched on a flashlight and shone it inside. A door made of the same faintly oily-looking material was revealed, a disc inset at its centre. Beyond was a passageway, tilted at the same steep angle as the rest of the object. Exploring the interior would be tricky; they might need ropes to stop themselves from sliding out of control.

She radioed Tate to update him on the situation. 'Roger that,' the Australian replied, crackling interference masking his voice. 'Any sign of the *Dionysius*'s crew?'

'Not yet,' she replied. 'We're going to start a search.'

'Understood. Keep us posted.'

Cheng had by now huffed and puffed his way up the ladder. As Nina stepped onto the hull to make room for him, the interference became audibly worse. 'Can you still hear me?' she asked.

'Just about,' Tate replied through the distortion. 'There's some really bad static. You standing next to a generator or something?'

'Something,' Nina echoed. 'Keep talking, I want to check this.'

'Keep talking? Sure, what about? I could tell you about the cricket, I supp—'

She stepped through the oval hatchway – and the moment she crossed the threshold, Tate was cut off. Back outside, and his voice returned. '—fifty runs!'

'Okay, thanks,' she said, before calling down to her husband. 'Eddie! This thing blocks the radio! Someone might need to stay outside so we can keep in contact with the *Torrox*.'

Eddie had just helped Vorster onto the ledge; he looked between him and Imka. 'Any volunteers?'

'I've got to find out what happened to Arnold and the others,' Imka insisted. The shipowner expressed a similar sentiment.

'Either me or Marc, then – and as much as I'd like to chill out, there's no way I'm letting you wander around an alien space-ship on your own,' the Englishman told Nina. A glance at the approaching crewman. 'I'll break the news to him.' He took back the radio and descended.

Nina peered into the opening again, Cheng using his own torch to illuminate the interior. He muttered something in Chinese. 'What?' she asked.

'It's the same metal. The hull and the door,' he clarified with unexpected emphasis, indicating the dark material. 'But it is different inside.'

'Orichalcum,' said Nina, aiming her beam at one wall. Panels of the red-tinted gold alloy shone back at her. Like the outer hull, there was a surprising lack of frost.

She leaned through the hatchway, after her experience with the radio now hesitant about setting foot inside. The light picked out something else protruding between the orichalcum panels. She thought at first it was ice, but then realised it was something altogether more unusual. 'It's *crystal*.'

Cheng looked for himself. 'Is it broken?'

'I . . . don't think so.'

She was distracted from his odd question by the arrival of the South Africans. Imka stared through the entrance with concern. 'Arnold!' she shouted. 'Arnold, it's Imka! Is anyone there?'

Only echoes reached them. 'I haven't seen anything yet,' said Nina. 'But this thing is big – someone might have gone deep inside to protect themselves from the cold.' It was a very long shot, and she was certain Imka knew it, but her companion was still clinging to any crumb of hope she could find.

Vorster's eyes went to the walls. 'That looks like gold!'

'It's orichalcum – an Atlantean gold alloy,' Nina told him.

His eyes narrowed calculatingly. 'You know . . . under the law of finds, this thing is ours! We're in international waters, so anything we discover here belongs to us.'

'We came here to rescue Arnold and the crew of the *Dionysius*,' said Imka with a hint of anger.

'Of course we did. But I'm just letting you know how the law stands.'

Eddie made his way back up. 'Well, Marc's thrilled about having to wait outside,' he said. 'What have we got?'

'Not much yet,' Nina told him. 'We were waiting for you before we went in.'

'Needed a canary, did you?' He peered through the entrance. 'Steep floors. We might need ropes.'

'Yeah, I thought that,' said Nina. 'How much do we have left?'

'Hundred and fifty feet, maybe. Don't know if it'll be enough. Looks like this thing's got two floors, maybe even three.'

'You're right.' Seeing the object almost in profile, it appeared they were about to enter it on the lowest level. The ceiling of the entrance passage was about twelve feet high, while the eye-like windows were at least fifteen feet above. There was also a bulbous section rising out of the top of the fortress that looked almost like a separate entity, nestled into the larger structure.

'We might need to go back to the ship for more,' said Vorster.

'We *need* to find Arnold and the others,' Imka insisted. 'Come on – we've got to go inside!'

'Okay, okay,' said Nina, gently but firmly moving to block her. 'But let me and Eddie go first? We've got experience of this kind of thing.'

Eddie sighed. 'Here we go again.'

Nina smiled at him, then raised her flashlight and stepped into the mysterious object.

8

Even though Nina had crossed the threshold once already, this time it felt different. More portentous . . . more *dangerous*. She was entering the unknown. The only people who had been in here before her were mad – or dead.

She examined the rib between the orichalcum panels. The material was definitely crystal, glinting under her light. 'Eddie,' she said quietly. 'Recognise this?'

He nodded warily. 'It's like the stuff inside the vault in Turkey. Think there's another bomb in here?'

Imka had pushed ahead of Cheng, anxious to be near the front of the search, and overheard. 'A bomb?'

'You remember three years back there was a massive explosion over the Persian Gulf?' said Eddie. 'It was an antimatter bomb – a thing called a spearhead.'

'An Atlantean relic,' Cheng clarified. 'Professor Wilde found it in Turkey.'

'There's another one here?' said Vorster in alarm.

'I don't know,' said Nina. 'The vault holding the spearhead was made of orichalcum and crystal, like this. But that doesn't mean this place has the same function. The vault was built by the Atlanteans, but this is much older. The same materials, but made by a different people.'

'What people?' Imka asked.

'That's a very good question!'

Nina cast her light over the walls as she moved down the short passage. It intersected with a curving corridor. From its arc, she guessed it ran around the whole interior of the ship/fortress/ whatever the hell it was. She settled on 'fortress' until seeing proof of anything else, still unwilling to give Eddie any points for his alien spaceship theory. The angle at which it was trapped meant the route to the right dropped steeply downwards, the floor more like a slide. It *might* be traversable without ropes, but she didn't fancy trying it.

She aimed her light upwards, to the left. The other direction curved inwards around the structure's centre, disappearing beyond a corner. Doorways lurked in the darkness. 'That way'll be easier,' she said. 'Looks like there are other rooms leading off it.'

'Space alien bedrooms, probably. But you're right,' Eddie went on before Nina could make another weary protest. 'One slip going the other way and we'll be whizzing down to the front of the ship on our arses.' He took off his helmet and crampons, the others following suit. 'If we jump across the corridor, we can use those ribs in the other wall like steps to go up.'

He readied himself, then made a running jump across to the inner wall. A tense moment as one foot slipped from the protruding crystal rib, but he caught himself and began to ascend. His progress became easier as he followed the corridor around, the wall's curve making the climb progressively less steep.

Nina vaulted after him and followed him to the first opening. 'What do you see?'

'There's a room here,' he said, aiming his light through the towering doorway. 'Full of benches – or could be beds, actually. If they are, whoever slept on 'em was tall.'

'Like the Veteres,' she said quietly. She aimed her light into the next room. The beam reflected back at her, and not off crystal. 'There's ice in there!' While the passages they had traversed so far had remained strangely free of frost, the room's rear wall had a thick translucent coating.

Eddie brought his light down to the floor of the chamber.

'Looks like it's been ripped open.' The metal was buckled, ragged tears disappearing into the icy wall. 'Or crushed. A hundred thousand years of ice must weigh a fair bit.'

'Yeah.' Noises from behind made her turn. 'Oh, you might want to help Cheng before he goes down the world's scariest Slip 'n' Slide.'

Imka had jumped after the couple, but Cheng was hesitating at the end of the entrance passage. 'I'm okay,' he protested. 'I can do it.'

'Well, let's make sure of that, shall we?' said Eddie, returning and extending his arms to catch him. 'Come on, kid.'

'I'm not a child!' Cheng leapt across, landing with a lurch as his backpack threatened to unbalance him. Eddie caught his harness before he could fall, giving him a patronising look. 'I'm not,' the younger man said with a huff.

Nina had already moved on. The next room was much like the first, a spartan dormitory, though the ice had encroached further into it. The rear of the fortress must have been badly damaged during its millennia of entombment. But why hadn't the ice kept advancing? There was no reason for it to stop . . .

The route ahead began to curve back downwards. They were at the fortress's rear; the passage looped around to head towards its front. In the higher wall was another door, with an ornate golden surround. She shone her light through the opening—

A tall figure faced her.

She gasped, flinching back before realising it was not alive. The menacing form was a suit of armour, embedded in more invading ice.

'Whoa!' Imka yelped. 'What is *that*?'

Nina edged up the slanted floor for a closer look. 'It's armour.'

'*Whose* armour? Whoever wore that must have been three metres tall!'

'It's the Predator!' Eddie joked as he, Cheng and Vorster hurried to see. '*Now* will you believe we've found a spaceship?'

Nina had to admit the armour was definitely made for someone – or some*thing* – far taller than even the lankiest human being. It was aggressively designed, a colourful mask resembling a devil's snarling face with protruding fangs fronting the horned helmet. She glanced at Cheng. 'It looks like a Chinese demon, don't you think?'

He nodded. 'It does. And there are more.' He pointed deeper inside the ice. Other figures were dimly discernible. 'But look at that! It must be a weapon.'

Nina spotted something within the frozen barrier. At first she thought it was a spear, as long as the armour was tall, then saw that instead of a blade, the head was an elongated metal bulb. More identical shapes were lined up beyond. 'Maybe it's an armoury.'

Eddie regarded the glowering metal figure with distaste. 'Whoever they were, I wouldn't want to fight 'em up close. It's got blades and spikes all over it.'

'Hopefully we won't run into the owner,' said Nina uncomfortably. The armour inescapably brought to mind Wim Stapper's demon. 'Let's keep going.' She set off again.

'What do you think of my theory now, Professor Wilde?' asked Cheng. 'A non-human precursor race – do you think that's what we've found?'

'I'll reserve judgement until I've seen more,' she replied. Something about his attitude felt . . . *off*. He seemed almost nonchalant about the discovery, regarding the giant armour with detached curiosity rather than astonishment. Her unease from her lecture returned; *did* he know more about the Veteres than he was letting on?

She put the thought aside – for now – as she continued around the curving corridor. There were more signs of damage, ice forming on the walls where the floor had buckled. She examined a rent between two frozen panels. One of the crystal ribs had been snapped by the ice's relentless pressure. The material wasn't indestructible, then. Had the intact crystals somehow held back the frost?

The passage ahead angled downwards towards the front of the fortress. 'It's getting steep again.'

'Think we'll need ropes?' Eddie asked. He shone his torch down the corridor. Metal and crystal glinted in the cold darkness – together with something else. Warning entered his voice. 'Everyone hold back.'

Standing out on the golden sheen of orichalcum was a darker splash, as if paint had been splattered over the walls and floor. At first glance it looked black, but as Nina's flashlight beam joined his, they saw with dawning horror that it was actually a deep red.

Blood.

'What is it?' Imka asked, trying to peer around the couple.

'Wait here,' Eddie said firmly. 'I'll have a look. Cheng, Janco, hold onto my rope.'

He handed the coil to the two men, who braced themselves behind him. Nina knew what her husband was doing – blocking Imka's view of what they both suspected he was about to find. He gripped the rope, then moved carefully down the steep slope.

Eddie soon reached the marks and played his torch over them. Bone fragments and shreds of flesh amongst the frozen blood confirmed his fears. Someone had been caught in an explosion, almost liquefied by the blast.

But what had caused it? To obliterate a human body so completely would need far more explosive than found in a hand grenade – which would also have ripped the passage apart. But there was no visible damage to the walls . . .

'What have you found?' Imka called.

'Someone was killed here,' he reported grimly. 'Looks like there was an explosion.' He aimed his light further downwards. 'Shit,' he whispered, seeing another dark burst twenty feet away. Gruesome confirmation that the remains were human came in the form of a booted foot wedged against a crystal rib, shards of bloodied bone jutting from it. 'There's another body – or what's left of one.'

'Oh . . . oh my God,' said Imka. 'Is it . . . is it Arnold?'

'I don't know.' She had shown them pictures of her fiancé during the voyage, but Eddie saw nothing here that could be used for purposes of identification short of a DNA test. He shone the beam past the grisly remains. Ice encroached into the corridor beyond a section of mangled wall. 'I don't think we can get down that way. We'll have to go back around past the entrance.'

'But we need to find out who they are!' the South African cried.

'We will,' Nina assured her. 'But we have to check the rest of the fortress first. There might still be survivors.' She didn't believe her own words, but Imka was desperate enough to cling to the tiny chance that she nodded.

The group helped Eddie back up, and they returned to the entrance. The demonic armour watched from its icy prison as they passed. 'Same drill,' said the Yorkshireman. 'Hold the rope, help me down, and I'll see what's there.'

'Be careful,' said Nina as he started his descent.

'Oh, I bloody will be, don't worry!

He held up his light as he moved down the slope, wishing he could exchange it for a gun. Stapper's story was looking less like the result of his madness and more like the cause. Something had killed two people in a truly horrific manner, enough to unsettle even a man who had seen every form of death imaginable.

And whatever had done it was still here, somewhere in the frozen darkness.

No sign of more bodies – or their splattered remnants – but before long his descent brought him to something else. 'There's some stairs here!' he shouted. They led to the higher deck. 'I'm going up.'

'What can you see?' Nina called after him as he ascended.

The low blue light of the ice cave surrounded him, coming through two elongated windows; the 'dragon eyes' they had seen from outside. One was broken, cold air wafting in. 'It's a big room,' he said. 'High ceiling, like a dome.'

He stopped at the top of the stairs, sweeping the light around. The room was oval, a large metal dais towards the rear. The underside of the egg-shaped object inset into the top of the ship rested upon it; it *was* a separate entity. Its nature and purpose remained a mystery, though.

Before it sat something he *could* identify – an ornate golden throne. Like the armour, it was on a considerably larger scale than human. 'It's a throne room!' he shouted. 'Nobody here, not that I can see. I'm going to look around.'

He moved cautiously into the steeply sloping chamber to continue his search for bodies, soles squeaking faintly on the floor. At its centre stood a large rectangular plinth. An altar? He headed towards it. His light picked out a recess set into its top.

He recognised the shape. The space was a perfect match for the key Krämer had stolen.

The realisation put him back on full alert. He turned to scan the whole room, shining the powerful beam into the shadows of the crystal pillars. Nothing there, no movement. Not reassured, he reached the altar. The upper surface was orichalcum and the same dark, oily metal as the hull, inset with numerous concentric circles of crystal and purple stone.

Noises drew his attention to the stairwell. 'Eddie?' Nina

asked, clambering into view. Vorster's voice echoed behind her as he shouted a situation update to Naider outside.

'Yeah, I'm here. Haven't seen any more bodies. Pretty impressive room, though.'

She brought up her own light. 'Oh wow! I see what you mean.' Her beam found the giant throne. 'And that's a hell of a big chair.'

He lowered his voice. 'So it's definitely the Veteres?'

'I can't think of anything else. The size matches, certainly. The bodies we found in Eden were at least seven feet tall.'

'That armour was getting on for ten feet, though.'

'Humans are different heights, so maybe the Veteres were too. Although yeah, three feet is kind of a big variance.'

'Maybe this lot played basketball.'

She smiled, then saw what he was examining. 'I recognise that shape.'

'Yeah,' he said as she came to stand beside him. 'The key's actually the ignition for the spaceship. Put it in, turn it on, and whoosh! Warp factor nine.'

A sardonic grin. 'It'd make getting back home to Macy a lot easier. But it's obviously where it's supposed to go. Stapper and his friend put it in there. Then . . .'

'Then all hell broke loose,' Eddie rumbled. 'Maybe literally.'

Nina surveyed the rest of the room. Another flight of stairs descended at the front of the oval chamber. Before she could investigate further, Cheng entered, Imka and Vorster behind him. 'Is there anyone else here?' Imka asked.

'Not that we've seen,' said Eddie, edging down the sloping floor towards the new set of stairs. 'Although we haven't checked the back of the room yet.'

Nina brought her light back to the huge throne, then the elongated golden sphere behind it. 'It looks a lot like the vault from Turkey,' she said, her flashlight beam sliding over a seemingly unbroken orichalcum surface. She started towards it. 'Maybe there's a door on the far side. Cheng, what do you make of it?'

She had assumed he was following her. But when she glanced around, he was standing at the altar with his back to her, his open backpack beside him. 'Cheng? What are you doing?'

'The key,' he replied. 'It fits here.'

'I know, it's—' His tone set off mental alarms at deafening volume. 'You've *put it in*? No, take it out!'

Cheng turned, revealing that he had indeed placed the golden artefact into the recess. 'I was just checking—'

'Take it *out*! Now!' She hurried back to him.

He didn't move, giving her a bewildered look. She reached past him and snatched up the relic – flinching at a sudden electric *snap* as she touched it. 'Ow! Dammit!'

'What?' Eddie asked urgently. 'You okay?'

'It gave me a frickin' shock!' She froze, listening intently . . . but the chamber remained silent.

'Nothing happened,' said Cheng, sounding almost disappointed.

She glared at him. 'Stapper said nothing happened until *after* they put the key in there!'

'What *could* happen?' said Vorster. 'You said this thing is over a hundred thousand years old. Even if they called it a key, it can't be like a car ignition key. They didn't have engines back then.'

'Not as we know them, no,' Nina said. 'But the Atlanteans used something called earth energy – or ley lines, feng shui, song lines, probably a dozen other names – as a power source, and crystals and a type of purple stone to channel it. And gee, look what we have here!' She pointed at the circles of said materials set into the altar.

'But this is older than Atlantis, isn't it?' asked Imka.

'Yeah, but it's the same kind of technology, if you can call it that. In the Turkish vault, the Atlanteans said it came from "those who came before"; I think this was built by the same people. They discovered the power, and the Atlanteans later used it as well. Which ultimately caused them to end up at the bottom of the ocean, because they couldn't stop fiddling with things they didn't fully understand.' She directed that last at Cheng, who averted his eyes.

'Nina,' said Eddie from the front of the chamber. 'There's something else down here.'

'What is it?'

'Buggered if I know. You're the archaeologist!'

'Put this away,' she ordered Cheng, thrusting the key at him before joining her husband. He was partway down the treacherously steep new stairs, shining his light downwards. 'It's another room,' he went on, 'but . . . well, see for yourself.'

Nina added her torch beam to his. What she saw below made her gasp.

The new room extended further forward into the fortress's nose, another oval chamber, forty feet on its long axis. Unlike the other rooms they had seen, this was built – grown? – entirely from crystal, the twin lights reflecting from facets beyond facets.

That was not what had stunned Nina, though. It was what was *inside* the room.

Coffins.

Towering cylinders of metal and crystal stood near-perpendicular to the floor, arranged in concentric rings. The one at the centre was the largest and most elaborate, all the others facing it. The sarcophagi were occupied, huge shadowy forms visible through the translucent covers.

The bodies had not been protected from the ravages of time, however. There were gaps in the rings, missing teeth leaving broken roots where they had stood. She redirected her flashlight. Several sarcophagi were piled amongst debris at the room's bottom end, cracked and broken. They had torn free and smashed into their companions when the iceberg rolled over.

But the majority of the ancient coffins were intact. The builders of the fortress were still here, preserved.

Eddie flicked his light at the nearest. 'This one's open.'

'More than that,' she said with sudden trepidation. The cylinder had split apart, hinging upwards to expose its interior. On its outer base was another recess matching the shape of the key – but she was more concerned with what was within.

Or rather, what was *not*. 'It's empty.' She gave Eddie an alarmed look. 'Whatever was inside . . . it got out!'

9

Captain Tate watched the ice cave's shadowy mouth with concern. Professor Wilde had forewarned him about the loss of radio contact, and Marc had checked in a few minutes earlier to let him know Janco had said everything was okay . . . but the inability to talk to the group directly was a growing worry.

He looked back at the radar. One of the signals within the iceberg, he now knew, was the *Dionysius*. Its being upside-down explained why he hadn't identified it at once. The second object, though, was still a mystery.

But now there was a *third*—

'What the *hell*?' Tate barked. A new shape had just appeared off to starboard. He darted to the windows. Another ship was rounding the towering wall of blue and white, about a kilometre away.

He grabbed binoculars and fixed them upon the newcomer. A freighter, one of the many independent tramp ships plying their trade between the widely scattered countries around the Southern Ocean. He focused on the name upon the bow: *Tahatu*.

Activity on the foredeck. Several men, a blond looking back through his own field glasses. One of his companions crouched, supporting a length of metal pipe on his shoulder and also staring at the *Torrox* through a telescope.

No, not a telescope. A *sight*.

Fear rushed through the Australian. The man wasn't holding a pipe. It was a *launcher*—

The blond shouted a command – and smoke and flame erupted from the tube.

The Javelin anti-tank missile took under two seconds to lance between the ships. Tate had just enough time to yell a terrified warning to his crew before over eight kilograms of high explosive blasted the *Torrox*'s bridge into flaming shrapnel.

'What do you mean, it got out?' said Eddie. 'They're coffins! Aliens I can believe in, but not bloody zombies.' He was about to say more when he heard a distant *boom*. 'What was that?'

'I don't know,' Nina replied, listening. The sound didn't reoccur. 'Ice cracking?'

'More than just a crack. That sounded big.' He returned to the stairs. 'Anyone else hear that?'

'Yeah,' said Vorster. 'Might have been part of the berg calving into the water. If it was too close, we'll need to leave.'

'Giving up your salvage?'

'Treasure's no use if you can't spend it,' was the pragmatic reply.

The Yorkshireman looked back into the crystal chamber as Nina examined first the open sarcophagus, then one of its intact neighbours. 'Are they the Veteres?' he asked.

She peered through the thick crystal at the figure within. Like the armour they had seen earlier, it was tall, and *big*, the shoulders broad and powerful compared to the elongated, almost willowy bodies of the extinct race. 'They must be, but . . . this one's much larger than the mummies we found in Eden.' She carefully crossed the inclined floor to another sarcophagus. All the coffins, she noticed, had the same recess for the mysterious key at their foot. 'So's this.'

Eddie shone his light at the debris below. 'You want a proper look at one, I think there's a body down there.' A long, pale arm protruded from beneath one fallen sarcophagus.

'Must have come from the open coffin.'

'A body?' cried Imka from the top of the stairs. 'Who is it?'

'It's not anyone from the *Dionysius*,' Nina hurriedly told her. 'This is . . . a mausoleum, I guess. The bodies of the people who built this thing are here.'

Cheng made his way down the steps, flashlight beam darting excitedly from one coffin to another. 'The shells aren't broken! They're intact!'

'Most of them,' said Nina. 'I think some came loose when the iceberg rolled over.'

Eddie made his way to the elaborate sarcophagus at the room's centre. 'Must be their king in here. Looks like he's wearing a crown.' Metal glinted around the head of the entombed figure as he swept his light over it, and he noticed secondary reflections from other items around its feet. 'They buried him with his stuff.'

Nina picked her way over to him. 'It's definitely an important figure. Although some of the others have things in their coffins as well. Maybe they were like the ancient Egyptians, and were buried with their greatest treasures?'

'That's not a treasure.' The sudden alertness in Eddie's voice made her look around. He was again aiming his torch at the bottom of the chamber. 'That's a *weapon*. It's a bloody trikan!'

'It *can't* be, they're Atlantean—' she began – but he was right. The beam was fixed upon a convex orichalcum disc resembling a yo-yo, three curved blue blades sweeping outwards from its rim. Macy's toy was based on a real example found in the sunken ruins of Atlantis . . . but now it seemed that that in turn had been modelled upon one even older.

And larger. The Atlantean weapon was sized to fit in a person's hand. This was more like a dinner plate, each sweeping blade almost a foot long. The weapons of the lost race were as super-sized as their armour – and themselves.

Cheng followed Nina's path down into the chamber. Imka hung back on the stairs, not wanting to enter, while Vorster took up station at the upper threshold. 'So if they're not from Atlantis, where *are* they from?' the shipowner asked.

'I don't know,' Nina replied absently. The leader's face was blurred and warped by the crystal, a yellow tint discolouring it, but she could see enough to tell that its head was not the same shape as a human's. It was larger, the rear of the skull extending backwards – like the image on the key.

Again, it wasn't the same as the remains of the Veteres. They too had elongated heads, facial features resembling the popular conception of a Grey alien – or perhaps that very image was some residual racial memory of *Homo sapiens*' former masters. But these seemed simultaneously somehow more and less like humans: the faces more so, the giant bodies definitely less.

Another species entirely? Could a *second* advanced race have existed at the same time as the Veteres? She doubted it. As history had proved several times, other intelligent hominids did not survive contact with a more advanced – or more violent – species.

Then there was the Veteres writing on the key. So were the bodies here some racial variant, or had the mummified remains in Eden been unusually small?

Answers would only come through detailed scientific analysis. Which meant the main issue now was how to deal with a find of this magnitude. 'Okay,' she said, addressing the others, 'we've made an amazing discovery. So we need to decide what to do next.'

'I told you, the law of finds applies here,' said Vorster without hesitation. 'The ship and everything in it are all ours – we just have to stake our claim, and we can do that by radio from the *Torrox*.'

'It's also an archaeological find, though,' Nina countered. 'And a burial site.' She indicated the sarcophagi. 'I should notify the International Heritage Agency. They're equipped to handle discoveries like this.'

'And then what happens to our claim?' Vorster demanded. 'We can't sit around waiting for lawyers to argue it out in some court. The iceberg's melting! It won't be long before it breaks apart – and then this whole thing will end up at the bottom of the ocean.'

'We still have to find out what happened to Arnold and the others,' Imka added quietly.

'But we must protect the find,' said Cheng. He gazed at the towering shape within the nearest sarcophagus, then regarded the recess near its foot. 'The key will fit in this . . .'

'Don't even think about it,' Nina cautioned. 'Nobody touches *anything* in here. This is a find on the level of the tomb of Tutankhamun. It needs to stay intact until it can be properly surveyed and—'

'By who?' cut in Vorster forcefully.

She ignored him. '—and catalogued. And we *still* don't know what happened to the crew of the *Dionysius* . . .'

Nina trailed off. Something had changed. The only illumination in the chamber had been the team's flashlights, but now she could pick out details in the shadows. 'What's wrong?' Eddie asked.

'I'm not sure.' She closed her eyes and clicked off her light. 'Everyone, turn your flashlights out.'

'Why should—' Vorster began.

'Just do it,' she snapped. The others switched off their torches. Nina waited a few seconds, then opened her eyes again.

The eerie sapphire light from above silhouetted Imka and Vorster on the stairs. But she could see her surroundings quite distinctly, lit by a low but clear white glow.

'That wasn't there before,' said Eddie. 'Where's it coming from?'

'I don't know.' The source was elusive yet ubiquitous, emanating from all around them. 'It's behind the walls . . .'

'It's not behind the walls,' said her husband with alarm. 'It *is* the bloody walls! The whole place is glowing!'

'What?' gasped Imka. 'How is that possible?'

'I don't know,' Eddie growled. 'But the last time we saw a crystal glowing like that, it blew up like a fucking H-bomb twenty-four hours later. Time to leave.'

'We don't know that it's anything like the Atlantean spearheads,' Nina protested.

'And we don't know that it isn't. We've seen weapons, we've seen armour – this place is a *military installation*. Come on!' He guided her upwards. 'For all we know, we've just set off a booby trap!'

'Captain, come in. Captain Tate? *Torrox*, can you hear me?'

Naider stood outside the fortress, the walkie-talkie raised to his ear to catch any reply through the radio interference. None came. His concern grew. Tate was a professional seaman and would never leave the bridge unmanned, especially with a shore party in a potentially risky situation.

Worried, he turned back to the hatch. He had to let the others know he'd lost contact—

A sound reached him over the ice's constant moans and creaks. An outboard motor, getting closer. Thank God! He went to the end of the ledge and looked towards the cave mouth. A boat came through it.

His relief only lasted moments, replaced by confusion. The *Torrox*'s only other craft was its lifeboat, bright orange with a fibreglass hull, but this was another rigid inflatable. And there was a second behind it. The new arrivals, four in each boat, weren't his shipmates. So who were they?

A man in the lead RIB pointed something up at him. He

stared at it, refusing to believe what his eyes were telling him. It *couldn't* be a gun—

It was.

A flash of fire – and Naider fell back against the icy wall as a bullet smashed through his right shoulder. He staggered . . . and slipped off the ledge.

He tumbled down the cliff, screaming – then his cry was abruptly silenced as he was impaled on the needle-sharp spikes of ice below.

The two boats pulled up beside the *Torrox*'s RIB. Their occupants jumped out and started to follow the explorers' path.

Eddie had just re-entered the throne room behind Nina when he heard the sharp crack. 'We didn't bring any guns, did we?' he asked Vorster.

'No,' said the shipowner, startled. 'But it might have been ice breaking.'

'That wasn't ice, that was a fucking rifle round. I think we're in trouble.' He hurried to the broken window and looked out at the ice cave. 'Oh, yeah. We're in trouble!'

'What is it?' asked Nina.

'Two boats full of guys, and they're all armed – and climbing up this way.'

'What about Marc?' said Imka. 'He was outside!'

Eddie couldn't see Naider, but a splash of bright red blood on the ice where they had entered the ship told its own story. 'They shot him. If he isn't dead, he soon will be.'

Cheng looked around in fear. 'What are we going to do? Hide?'

'If we hide, they'll find us,' Nina told him. 'They'll come *looking* for us – they must have known we were here.'

'How could they know?' protested Imka.

'Don't ask me, but they did. They want something – they

want *this*.' She held out her arms to encompass the structure around them.

'But they couldn't have known it was here,' Eddie said. '*We* didn't know it was here!'

'Maybe somebody else talked to Krämer, or Stapper. But it doesn't matter now.' She made her way to the altar. 'We can't fight them. But if we wait for them, we can find out what they want – and we might spot a chance to get away.'

Eddie was not happy, but he nodded. 'Okay. We'll let them make the first move. Just hope it doesn't involve pulling a trigger.'

Vorster looked towards the broken window. 'Are you crazy? We should get out while we can! We can jump from there.'

'Go for it,' the Englishman told him. 'It's only a sixty-foot drop into freezing water.' Vorster considered it, then let out an angry, frustrated breath.

Eddie joined Nina at the altar. Cheng followed, Imka holding back fearfully at the top of the mausoleum stairs. Vorster peered out cautiously from the window. 'They've reached the top ledge,' he reported. 'They'll be here any minute.'

'They didn't even give us time to work on our welcoming speech,' Eddie replied dourly. He squeezed Nina's hand, then noticed she appeared distracted. 'You with us, love?'

'It's getting brighter in here,' she replied. 'The crystals in the walls – they're glowing as well.' The crystalline ribs running up to the domed ceiling were indeed emitting a soft but gradually strengthening light. She examined the recess in the altar. 'I think my touching the key started it all off. Just like when I opened the vault in Turkey – it needed someone of Atlantean descent who could channel earth energy to provide the spark.'

'Great, so if we don't get shot, we'll blow up?'

'There's nothing like the spearhead here.' She glanced towards the lower chamber. 'I think these people were like the Atlanteans, and the Veteres. Some of them had the specific sequence in their

DNA that let them control earth energy, and they made use of it.'

'For lights?'

'And who knows what else? We've seen earth energy trap antimatter, levitate statues, make a sword chop through things like a *Star Wars* lightsaber. This place might use it for something just as incredible.'

'"Incredible" is the right word,' Imka said, disbelief plain. 'What you're saying sounds like magic.'

'It's not magic, it's science. Just . . . extremely *weird* science. And I don't pretend to understand it myself. All I can say is: it's real. I've seen it.'

'And you can control it,' Cheng observed.

'I wouldn't say *control*. Influence, maybe. There were people in Atlantis who thought they *could* control it, weaponise it – but they were wrong. They tried to use it to give Atlantis unlimited power, but it ended up destroying them.'

Vorster had made his way to the entrance. 'We've got more than mumbo-jumbo to worry about. I can hear them coming.'

'Get over here,' Nina told him. 'Don't give them any excuse to shoot.'

'They might not need one,' Eddie warned. 'They already killed Marc.' He moved around the altar. 'Get behind this thing. At least take some cover.'

She joined him and Cheng behind it as Vorster scrambled down to rejoin Imka. All eyes went to the entrance. Sounds echoed up from below, feet scuffing on metal and snatches of curt speech. Flashlights probed the stairs.

Nina tensed, holding Eddie. The muzzle of an assault rifle came into view, followed by a man wearing a black balaclava. He surveyed the room warily, eyes and gun locking onto the figures by the altar. 'They're in here!' he called. The accent was Nordic; Nina guessed Norwegian.

The intruder quickly and professionally checked for potential ambushers, then came fully into the room, the tactical light attached to his weapon fixed upon Nina, Eddie and Cheng. Another man in identical black cold-weather gear followed him in, his own gun aimed at Imka and Vorster. 'Are there any more people?' the leader demanded. 'If you lie, I shoot one of you.'

'We're the only ones here,' said Nina. 'Where's Marc, the man outside?'

'Dead.' The response was as icy as the surroundings. Imka gasped.

'What about my ship?' growled Vorster.

'Sunk.'

'Sunk?' The bearded man's eyes widened in fury. 'You bastards! Where are my crew?'

'They are dead too. We shot them.' Several more black-clad men had now entered; the leader pulled off his balaclava.

Nina recognised the hard face beneath. 'You!' It was the blond who had led the chase in Hamburg.

He had a red cut down one cheek where he had been hit by a stiletto boot. 'How are you *heel*ing?' Eddie asked mockingly.

The Norwegian gave him a hostile stare, then signalled for his men to spread out and cover the chamber as he made his way down the inclined floor to the altar. He regarded the recess at its centre, then looked back at Nina. 'Where is the key?' The gun came up at her for emphasis.

'I – I have it,' Cheng said fearfully.

'Give it to me.' He stared past the trio to Imka and Vorster. 'Where are the coffins?'

Both Nina and Cheng reacted with surprise. 'How did you know about them?' gasped the student.

The man did not answer. 'Maybe they talked to the guy in the asylum,' said Eddie.

'No, they couldn't have!' Cheng insisted. 'Professor Wilde was the only—'

'The key,' the man said with impatience. 'Now.' He swung his rifle towards the young man's chest. Cheng hurriedly delved into his backpack.

Eddie eyed the weapon. The SIG MCX, with its distinctive skeletal handguard around the barrel, was a relatively new weapon, and sales of the compact SB model the intruders were carrying was supposed to be restricted to police and military forces. Yet the accents he had heard as the group approached were varied enough to rule out their being from one specific country. Mercenaries, then – but who was paying them? 'What do you want?' he said. 'Apart from the key, obviously – you wanted that enough to chase us halfway around the world, but what else?'

Cheng had by now produced the artefact. Hands shaking, he held it out to the mercenary leader, who took it and called to one of his men. 'Roche! Carry this.' The other mercenary had also removed his mask to expose a craggy face with a bushy moustache. He slipped the key into a waterproof pouch on the harness across his chest. 'We want the key,' the blond man finally replied to Eddie, 'and the coffins.'

'Why?' Nina asked.

He turned to her. 'My employer needs them.'

'For what?'

'My employer needs something else as well,' he went on, ignoring her question. His eyes fixed chillingly upon hers. '*You*, Professor Wilde.'

10

Nina stared back, stunned. 'What?' That he knew her name was shocking enough, but she was his *target*? 'Why does your boss want me?'

'I don't know, and I don't care,' the man replied. 'But I'm being paid to bring them you, the key and the coffins – so that is what I will do.'

One of his companions checked what was down below. 'Harhund!' he called. 'The coffins, they're here.'

'Watch them,' Harhund ordered. Two more mercenaries kept their guns fixed upon Nina, Eddie and Cheng as he descended into the mausoleum.

'Why the hell do they want you?' Eddie whispered to Nina. 'How did they even know you were here?'

'I don't know,' she answered. 'Somebody on the *Torrox*'s crew told them, maybe?'

'If they did, they got killed for it.'

'There must be a spy,' said Cheng. 'Someone who knew about Krämer in Germany, and knew we were coming to this iceberg!'

'The only people who knew all of that are us three,' Eddie countered. 'Pretty sure me and Nina aren't spies – which just leaves you!'

'I'm not a spy!' Cheng protested, voice rising. 'Why would I—'

He broke off as Harhund returned. 'Most of the coffins are intact, but they are fixed to the floor,' he announced. 'We need to lift them out. Set up the winches.'

124

His team was apparently prepared for any eventuality, having brought coils of rope and a couple of ascender units: compact, self-contained powered winch systems able to haul several hundred pounds. They also had tools ranging from crowbars to drills – and, Nina saw with alarm, gas masks. Were they expecting a specific danger?

'They're going to drag those things out of here?' said Vorster in disbelief. 'They must weigh half a ton each!'

'Then you will help us move them,' Harhund said. 'You,' he pointed at Vorster, then at Eddie, 'you, and . . . no.' He drew back his finger from Cheng. 'A fat weakling is no use.'

Cheng's face flushed with outrage, but he said nothing.

'You got a problem with women?' Nina asked sarcastically.

'No. They make excellent hostages.' He turned away before she could come up with a suitably affronted response and started back into the mausoleum. 'Put on your masks. When we break the coffins free, gas will leak.' He and his men donned the masks, the black rubber and glass rendering them almost insectile.

'We'll just stand back and hold our breath, then!' Eddie shouted after them. He faced Nina. 'How would he know there's gas in those things?'

'He knows *way* more about this place than we do,' she replied. 'But how? If someone's spying on us, they'd have to be psychic, because *we* didn't know what was in here!'

She looked into the lower chamber. Harhund and his masked team were examining the central sarcophagus. Muffled discussion, then the leader retreated to give the others room to work. Clanks and scrapes echoed up into the throne room as they prised at its base, then—

'There!' one man cried as metal broke. 'Got it – oh shit!'

He and his companions hurriedly withdrew. 'Stay calm!' barked Harhund as a puff of yellowish smoke swirled around them. 'Don't let the coffin fall over.' They returned to support the metal and crystal container. 'Plug the pipe.'

'God, there really *is* gas!' Nina said in dismay. But they were already taking action to contain it, one man working at the base of the sarcophagus. The haze dispersed, slowly rolling down to the chamber's foot. 'Looks like they plugged it, though.'

Imka put her head in her hands. 'This is a nightmare. What is going on?'

'I don't know,' said Nina, 'but we'll get out of this.'

'How?'

'Let you know as soon as we've figured it out,' Eddie rumbled.

The men setting up the winch tossed a rope into the mausoleum, those below securing it around the sarcophagus. Harhund checked a reading on a device, then pulled off his mask. 'It is safe,' he announced. 'Bring the prisoners down here. Tell them to leave their gear.'

A guard gestured with his gun for Eddie and Vorster to descend. They reluctantly discarded their equipment by the altar and went down the stairs. The Yorkshireman sniffed the air. 'Someone have an egg sandwich for lunch?'

That produced chuckles from his captors. Harhund was not amused. 'Shut up. No talking, or I will make the women suffer.'

'Wouldn't recommend it,' Eddie told him with barely veiled threat.

Harhund merely sneered. 'Help the others lift it. But do not damage it. I will not need to shoot you if any gas escapes.'

Vorster and Eddie exchanged concerned looks, then joined the mercenaries to lift the sarcophagus. The Englishman noticed a lead pipe protruding from the floor, its end blocked by some kind of epoxy or superglue. As the men tilted the coffin, he saw a similarly plugged pipe in the bottom of the crystalline cylinder. The realisation that it still contained a deadly gas made him handle the heavy object with much more care.

They manoeuvred it between the other sarcophagi towards

the exit. Once it was clear of the obstacles, the powered ascender was switched on to help haul it up the steep stairs. Even with the machine's assistance, it was still a strain, but the glinting coffin and its bearers finally reached the throne room, Eddie giving Nina a look to assure her that he was still watching for any opportunity to escape. On the smooth floor, the sarcophagus's journey was much faster. It soon reached the entrance.

Harhund shut down the ascender and ordered two men to set up ropes in the curving corridor for the next leg of the ascent, then gave his prisoners a coldly thoughtful look. 'You, go back down,' he ordered Eddie.

'If you don't need me any more, I could just go home,' Eddie replied.

The Norwegian did not respond to the jibe. 'The rest of you, follow us. Braun, guard him,' he told the man watching Nina, Cheng and Imka.

'Where are you taking us?' demanded Nina. 'And why are you leaving Eddie here?'

'To make you do as you are told,' was the blunt answer. 'Now move.'

Nina reluctantly set off, the others following. She glanced at the altar – and stopped in her tracks.

Cheng almost bumped into her. 'What is it?'

'The crystals, look.' Like the walls of the sarcophagus chamber, those set into the altar's face had started to glow. These, however, were in different colours, reds and greens and yellows as well as blue-white.

The sight instantly brought to mind something more modern: a *control panel* . . .

'Keep moving,' Harhund ordered. She gave the altar a last uncertain look, then continued upwards.

Vorster and the mercenaries detached the sarcophagus from the ropes and carefully carried it down to the passage below.

Nina followed, looking back at Eddie, under guard on the mausoleum stairs. 'See you soon, love,' he called to her.

She wished she had his confidence. 'I hope so! I'll—'

She broke off and grabbed the wall for support as the fortress trembled. One of the men carrying the sarcophagus slipped and fell, the others barely catching it before it crushed his leg. 'What was that?' snapped Harhund.

'The iceberg's starting to melt!' said Vorster, recovering. 'It's full of fault lines – and they're breaking apart.'

'I guess you'd better work fast,' Nina told Harhund, but she wasn't sure Vorster was right. The shudder hadn't felt like a tremor shaking the fortress. It seemed more like a *vibration*, as if the structure itself were the cause.

The gold and crystal coffin was secured to the next set of ropes, then the ascender started to haul it up to the entrance. The crystal ribs were now aglow, giving the corridor the look of a neon-lit funhouse.

Harhund brought the prisoners past the sarcophagus and signalled for Vorster to join them. 'Wintz, go back to the boat,' he told one man. 'Bring it to the bottom of the cliff under the entrance. We will lower the coffin down to it.' Wintz scrambled ahead.

The fortress shuddered again, everyone stopping to brace themselves. Nina heard creaks and groans from all around, as if the structure itself was straining against its frozen prison. Were the glowing crystals melting the ice? She raised a hand to a rib. No heat, just light. That wasn't the cause – so what was?

Harhund spoke to Roche and another man, then faced his team. 'I will take Professor Wilde and the key straight to the ship,' he announced. 'Once the coffin is aboard the boat, bring these prisoners.'

'What about Eddie?' said Nina.

'If it is safe to take another coffin, he will come with it.' The blond man paused at another tremor. 'If it is not, we will all get out.'

'We're supposed to bring at least three coffins,' one of the mercenaries objected.

Harhund fixed him with a patronising stare. 'Do you want one of them to be yours?' He looked back at Nina. 'Now move. Quickly.'

They soon reached the entrance tunnel, blue light seeping through the open hatch. Under Harhund's watchful eye, Nina retrieved and donned her crampons before stepping onto the uppermost ice ledge.

Wintz had made quick progress across the cliff, clambering around the outcrop towards the rope ladder. But she was more concerned with her immediate surroundings. The ledge was littered with fallen chunks of ice. Looking up, she saw cracks weaving outwards from the embedded fortress.

Imka emerged behind her. 'Look!' she cried, alarmed.

Nina turned to see that the tremors had set the various chains and lines hanging from the *Dionysius* swinging. The heavy anchor rolled beneath the ship's bow like a pendulum. 'That won't hold for much longer,' she said as a man-sized hunk of ice broke from near the stern and tumbled into the water. 'Get Eddie out, now!'

'Quiet,' said Harhund. 'We may still have time to get another coffin.'

'Are you kidding me?' said Nina, but the Scandinavian pushed past her and re-entered the fortress to shout instructions. Roche gave the swinging chains a wary look, then took up position to guard the prisoners.

Wintz reached the ladder's foot and boarded one of his team's boats. He brought it deeper into the cave, giving the zone beneath the *Dionysius* a wide berth as more ice fell from above. He stopped at the bottom of the cliff near the forest of icicles. Naider was still impaled upon one, the blue ice beneath him stained red.

Harhund returned. The situation's urgency was instantly made clear; he was carrying ropes and ice screws himself rather than delegating the task. 'Martel, help me,' he told the second man with them. They started to drive screws into the frozen cliff face as Roche maintained his watch.

Another shudder rattled the cave. The ice around the trapped fortress crackled, a new stress line tearing across it. Nina gasped and shielded her head as debris clattered onto the ledge, a piece striking Martel's shoulder and making him swear.

The cold hail eased off. She peered up at the new crack, then turned to see if the fortress had suffered any damage.

It had. The already buckled section below the broken window had split wider. A light was visible within, brighter than anything she had seen inside. She worked out its position. Beneath the throne room, behind the mausoleum, under the snake skull's chin. What was it? Some kind of central focus for the fortress's power?

Grunts and huffs from the tunnel preceded the coffin's arrival, the other mercenaries bearing it into the open. Sapphire light glinted from it, unexpectedly highlighting the ancient figure within. Nina moved to let the men carry it past, gazing at its contents. A body so old she would have expected to be desiccated, naturally mummified, but this had held its form. Had the gas inside the sarcophagus preserved it?

The group attached the container to the ropes Harhund and Martel had secured and rigged the ascender, reversing its motor to lower it to the waiting RIB. It only took a couple of minutes to reach water level. The hard part was now getting it into the boat without swamping or capsizing it, but the heavy coffin eventually came to rest.

Wintz moved off. The RIB was clearly overladen, the mercenary pulsing the outboard with great care to back away from the cliff before slowly turning towards the cave mouth.

Harhund faced his companions. 'Now we go.'

Nina stood fast. 'What about the others? I'm not going anywhere until they're safe.'

The Scandinavian regarded her coldly, then called to a man near the hatch. 'August, tell Braun to kill Chase.' The man started back into the fortress. Imka made a sound of horror.

'No, wait, *wait*!' Nina cried. 'I'll come with you!'

August paused. Harhund kept his gaze fixed on the redhead for a long moment, then signalled for him to return. 'Do not push me, Professor Wilde,' he said. 'Now move.' He descended to the lower ledge and started across the cliff.

Martel set off after him, gesturing for Nina to follow. She hesitated – the ropes were already straining against the carabiners under their combined weight – but Roche pushed her. A furious glare at him, then she clipped herself to the line and stepped onto the crack.

The movements of the two men ahead made the rope judder in her grip. She sidestepped after them, keeping her body as close to the ice as she could. She would shed no tears if Harhund fell to his death, but she had no intention of joining him.

Roche obviously had similar thoughts, letting her open up a gap before following. Even so, the addition of a fourth person only added to the stress on the screws. Nina paused as she reached one, hearing faint crackles from the ice around it. Unnerved, she continued. Harhund passed the debris field where Cheng had almost fallen and headed for the outcropping, Martel not far behind.

The mercenary leader glanced back. 'Roche, keep up!' he shouted.

Roche made an annoyed sound, but increased his pace. The pouch on his chest meant he couldn't press himself against the wall, making his movements awkward. 'Go on, keep moving,' he told Nina as he closed the gap.

'We're too close together,' she shot back. 'If one of these screws breaks loose, we'll all—'

An impossibly deep *whump* of straining ice – and the whole wall shifted beneath her.

Nina gasped and flattened herself against the cliff. This was no mere tremor; her inner ear told her she was pitching forward. A hissing crash from below. The water churned and frothed, waves smashing against the foot of the glassy wall.

The whole *iceberg* was moving!

The two boats at the rope ladder lurched, breakers kicking them against the ice. Wintz desperately held on as his overladen craft rocked. He hurriedly increased power, putting speed over stability as he headed into the tunnel.

The falling sensation eased. Loud bangs came from behind Nina – not plummeting ice, but metal striking metal as the *Dionysius* shook. One of the hanging chains broke free and plunged into the water, kicking up an angry flume of spray. The anchor's swing became wider, wilder. 'Holy *shit*!' yelled Roche. 'Harhund, fuck getting more coffins – we've got to get out of here!'

Harhund watched the boat depart, then shouted a reply. 'Agreed! We have one coffin, the key and Professor Wilde – that is all we need. Tell the rest of the men to follow us.'

'What about the prisoners?'

The answer came without hesitation. 'Kill them.'

Roche turned to pass on the message—

Nina beat him to it. 'They're gonna kill you! *Run!*'

Her words echoed across the cavern. Imka and Cheng both stared at the American, disbelief and uncertainty momentarily paralysing them – but Vorster had spent enough years at sea to know that hesitation in the face of danger could be fatal. He charged at the nearest mercenary, knocking him over the edge to plunge to his death before shoving his companions through the open hatch. '*Go!* Get in—'

August overcame his surprise. His SIG whipped up – and a burst of fire erupted from its muzzle.

All three rounds hit Vorster in the back. He staggered, his last conscious act being to push Imka further inside before he toppled from the ledge, spinning into the deadly field of frozen spikes below.

Cheng and Imka had no time to look back. They ran into the crystal-lit tunnel as more bullets twanged from the walls behind them.

11

Eddie waited at the bottom of the mausoleum stairs, Braun standing guard at the top. The Yorkshireman's gaze never left him, waiting for some distraction that he could use to attempt an escape—

One came – but it caught both men by surprise.

The ship shook, knocking them both off balance. Eddie gripped the wall, about to charge up the stairs at his captor. But Braun also recovered and realised the Yorkshireman's intent. He spun to shoot his prisoner—

Eddie dived into the mausoleum.

He slammed against a sarcophagus, which lurched as its base cracked, then rolled over its side and dropped again to half run, half slide down the steep floor as bullets struck coffins behind him. The mercenary cursed and descended the stairs, searching for line of sight on his target.

Eddie wasn't going to give it to him. He landed at the room's foot, moving to put as many obstructions between himself and the gunman as possible. If the bastard wanted to shoot him, he would have to come and find him – and by then he would have armed himself . . .

One of the long spears lay near the dead giant, but he went for something smaller. Gold gleamed in the crystals' glow. The trikan.

He snatched up the ancient weapon. It was larger and heavier than the Atlantean version, but the basic design was the same – something to be hurled at enemies.

Which he did.

Braun climbed down through the outer ring of coffins, leaning around one to find his prey – and took the heavy, bladed discus hard in his face. Teeth broke, a thumb-sized chunk of flesh flayed from his upper lip and cheek. He screamed, stumbling and falling onto another sarcophagus—

The one Eddie had hit.

Its weakened base sheared apart. Man and coffin both bowled towards the bottom of the mausoleum. Eddie's eyes widened as the golden wrecking ball plunged at him. He flung himself clear, the falling container smashing down where he had been standing.

Braun tumbled off it into the broken debris. But even winded, blood streaming from his mauled face, he still twisted to aim his gun at Eddie—

Yellow gas gushed from a crack in the sarcophagus.

The toxic cloud caught the mercenary. He collapsed with a choked scream, flailing and twitching.

'Shit!' gasped Eddie, frantically clambering higher. Not only was the deadly gas welling below him, but there was another jet higher up where the sarcophagus had ripped away. He took in deep breaths, then held the air in his lungs as he angled as far away from the coffin as he could.

He passed the gap where the king's sarcophagus had stood and kept climbing. The gas was slightly heavier than air, slowly roiling downwards. Once he was above it, he should be safe. Just a couple more metres—

The room shook again.

He grabbed a sarcophagus as the ship – the whole iceberg – rolled. It went further than before, the chamber pitching several degrees towards the horizontal, then tipping sickeningly back. Cracks lanced through the glowing crystal walls with the noise of shotgun blasts. The whole place was tearing itself apart—

Another coffin broke loose above him.

He swung underneath the sarcophagus he was holding as the golden torpedo tumbled past. It hit another below, pounding it from its base. Both crashed onwards in a destructive chain reaction.

More gas escaped above. Eddie regained his hold, then scrabbled higher. Whichever way he went, he would have to pass through one of the streams to reach the stairs.

He readied himself – then closed his eyes and made a flying leap.

Even with his eyelids squeezed shut, the hissing gas still stung, but there was no time to think about it as he made a hard landing on the topmost coffin. He clawed at it, hauling himself upwards and groping blindly for the stairs. He couldn't risk opening his eyes until he was clear; some poisonous gases could destroy sight on contact.

His fingers found the lowest step. He pulled himself up, boots slithering on the smooth metal. The urge to breathe was rising fast, a balloon swelling painfully inside his chest. He kept climbing . . .

The ascent suddenly became easier as the ship tipped towards the horizontal once more. He increased his pace, opening his eyes. They stung, but he was clear of the gas. He took in more air and clambered into the throne room.

Gunshots rang through the ship. Not close – they were coming from the corridor with the armoury. What was happening – and where was Nina? He hurried to the broken window.

Pieces of ice fell past as he looked out, briefly disorientated; the whole cavern had changed, the once-sheer cliff now well off the vertical. This time, the berg had not rolled back to its original position. The water churned, the two moored boats tossed about like toys.

The *Dionysius*'s anchor swung towards the cliff – drawing

his gaze to Nina. She was about halfway along the narrow ledge. Harhund and another man were ahead of her, the mercenary carrying the key behind. All clung to the ropes as the wall shuddered, so nobody could threaten her . . . but nor could she escape.

That meant the gunfire in the ship was being aimed at Cheng, Imka and Janco – no, just Cheng and Imka, he realised as he saw Vorster's impaled body near Naider's. He hurried up through the throne room. As long as Nina could hold on, she was safe – and Harhund's employers wanted her alive.

Another burst made it clear that that didn't apply to the rest of them. He snatched up some of his abandoned gear from beside the altar, then ran down the stairs.

Nobody was in the passage below. He pounded up it, following the sound of the gunfire.

'Run, run!' gasped Cheng as he passed the armoury. The towering suit leered demonically at him and Imka.

'It's a dead end!' the South African protested.

'There might be another way out – Mr Chase didn't go all the way!' But the young Chinese lacked confidence in his own words. He had gone upwards at the end of the entrance tunnel purely on instinct, the primitive urge to find higher ground when threatened. But now there was no turning back – a mercenary was pursuing them.

The corridor ahead started to descend, not as steeply as before. The ancient vessel seemed to be pulling itself upright, somehow dragging the enormous mass of the iceberg with it—

Bullets ricocheted from the walls behind them. Imka shrieked. They raced down the slope. The glow of the crystals meant there was no need for flashlights. Cheng saw the damaged end of the passage ahead – and also the exploded remains of the *Dionysius*'s crew.

He averted his eyes as he ran past. They were almost at the crushed section of corridor.

But Mr Chase had been right. No way out—

Wait! An opening, half hidden by a buckled orichalcum panel. 'In here!' he cried, letting Imka slip through before squeezing into the narrow gap.

But his hope that it would lead to an escape route was instantly dashed. The small room had no other exits. Imka spun to face him, her expression almost accusing. They were trapped!

Nina gripped the rope as the cliff shuddered. Somehow, the fortress was trying to break free—

An explosive crack echoed around the cavern. She turned her head – and saw a truck-sized spearhead of ice plunge from beside the *Dionysius* to strike the water like a bomb. Smaller lumps skittered down the cliff from above, one forcing her to jerk aside to avoid it. Harhund and the other mercenaries faced the same danger, Martel taking a blow from a falling chunk and almost slipping from the ledge. 'Get to the boats!' Harhund roared.

He and Martel resumed as quickly as they dared. Roche started towards Nina – who remained defiantly still. 'What are you doing?' he yelled, stopping four feet away. 'Move, you stupid bitch!'

'Fuck you, asshole!' the New Yorker shouted back. 'Just climb past me! I'm going back to the fortress!'

'The hell you are!' He fumbled to unshoulder his MCX. Even in its short-barrelled model, the rifle was still awkward to manoeuvre at such close quarters. 'Move or I shoot you!'

'Whoever hired you needs me alive, moron! Think you'll get paid if you kill the only person who can make that thing work?' She jabbed a thumb towards the pouch containing the key.

Roche looked down as if he had forgotten it was there,

then his eyes flicked after Wintz's departed boat. 'They'll have the coffin, they'll have the key,' he said. 'Two out of three ain't bad.'

He aimed the SIG at her chest—

The cavern rocked again, a great swell of water smashing into the cliff's foot.

Both Nina and Roche were thrown against the wall. The iceberg continued its roll, metal groaning above as the hanging *Dionysius* was brought almost overhead. Nina gripped the ropes, flattening herself against the ice – which she realised with shock was now nearly thirty degrees from the vertical. The fortress would soon be on the level – would it stop when it got there?

The thought vaporised in the face of danger as Roche recovered. His expression was one of near-panic, self-preservation his only concern – and she was the biggest obstacle in his way. He brought the gun up again—

A *whoosh* from behind – and the *Dionysius*'s swinging anchor smashed into him with the force of an artillery shell.

August reached the corridor's end, spotting the opening and shining his light inside. Two figures were huddled together, nowhere to go. His finger went to the trigger—

Running footsteps, rapidly closing. He glanced back, expecting to see one of his comrades – but instead saw Eddie Chase charging at him with something in his outstretched hand.

He spun, raising the rifle—

Eddie reached him first, pulling a trigger of his own – on the Fast Ice drill.

A foot-long steel screw spinning at two thousand revolutions per minute punched into the mercenary's chest, its clawed tip cutting effortlessly through flesh and bone into the man's heart. August managed a gargling scream before crumpling.

'You know the drill,' Eddie told him. He detached the

bloodied rod from the chuck, then collected the dead man's gun. 'Cheng! Imka! It's me, Eddie – are you okay?'

'Yes, we're here!' was Cheng's fearful reply. 'What happened to that man?'

'He's screwed. Come on, the whole fucking place is coming apart!'

Imka emerged first, Cheng behind her.

'Where is Professor Wilde?' he asked, before gulping at the sight of August's chest wound.

'On the cliff – I hope.' He set off, hoping they would have the sense to follow.

They did – as far as the frozen remains. 'Oh no, *no*!' wailed Imka, staring in horror. 'It's Arnold!'

Eddie told Cheng to keep going before returning to her. 'You don't know that.'

'No, I do! This boot, it's a Scarpa, bright orange – I bought it for him! He . . . he was . . .' She struggled to breathe in her shock.

'I'm sorry,' said Eddie, grim-faced, 'but we have to go. Now!' As much as he wanted to offer sympathy, time was running out. He pulled her with him after Cheng.

'Jesus *Christ*!' Nina gasped. The swinging anchor had hit the base of Roche's spine, punching straight through his body to bury itself two feet deep into the icy cliff. The mercenary was still alive, twitching and shuddering – though he wouldn't be for long as his blood sluiced down the frozen slope. His gun fell from his spasming hand and slid towards the water, followed by one of his legs.

The most immediate threat had been removed, but she was far from out of danger. The anchor's impact had damaged the ledge, forcing her to dig her crampon spikes into the wall to keep from slipping – and the noise of half a ton of steel slamming into the cavern's side had drawn the attention of the two other mercenaries.

Harhund was partway around the outcrop, Martel just reaching the end of the crack. The leader shouted an order. Nina couldn't hear it over the crashing waves, but the gist was obvious: *get her!* Martel started back towards her.

The ledge broke away from beneath the anchor, taking a few feet either side with it. She yelped and shifted her footing as another lump beneath one boot disintegrated in sympathy. Her only chance of escape was to reach the fortress – but how?

Roche was by now mercifully dead. If she could jump across the gap and grab the anchor pinning him, she might be able to clamber around and reach the ledge on the other side.

Martel closed in. Nina unclipped her carabiner, then drew back, took a breath – and jumped.

She caught the anchor's long main shank with both hands, swinging for a moment before catching the end of its horizontal stock with one foot. Gasping, she pulled herself against it and looked along the ledge. The jump across the broken ice was about six feet, farther than the gap she had just crossed, but she was sure she could make it—

The cavern shuddered again – and the anchor burst free from the cliff.

Nina screamed as it carried her helplessly out over the freezing water.

12

Eddie entered the tunnel leading to the hatch, seeing a mercenary regaining his balance. He gunned him down without hesitation, then ran out onto the ledge – to see his wife sweeping across the cavern on the *Dionysius*'s anchor, what was left of another mercenary impaled upon it. 'Buggeration and fuckery!'

Martel was rapidly traversing the cliff towards him, Harhund on the outcrop beyond. The Yorkshireman whipped up his stolen SIG and locked on to the nearer man. One shot was all it took. A burst of blood from Martel's chest, then he spasmed and slipped from the ledge. The rope snapped tight, leaving him flopping like a fish on the sloping ice face.

Eddie didn't spare the dying man another thought, fixing his sights on Harhund. The Norwegian had already brought up his own rifle, but firing one-handed from his precarious perch, the best he could do was to unleash a frenzied hail of suppressing fire at the fortress.

It was enough, forcing Eddie to drop as rounds struck the hull behind him. He registered that the impacts sounded somehow *wrong*, but had no time to wonder why.

Harhund's magazine ran dry. Eddie rose and reacquired his target – only for the mercenary leader to scramble around the outcrop. He fired again, but the rounds only smacked against ice. 'Balls!'

Nina finally stopped screaming. He saw the anchor reach the far end of its arc, pausing for the briefest moment – before swinging back at the cliff.

★ ★ ★

Nina hadn't even heard the gunfire over her own terrified yell. She ran out of breath as the anchor came to the top of its sweep, gasping in more air – and felt the anchor chain shake as the *Dionysius* lurched.

She looked up with a new surge of fear. The ice trapping the ship was crumbling, the survey vessel slowly but relentlessly tearing free.

And now she was swinging back underneath it.

The chain jolted again, steel shrilling against steel as it snagged the edge of the ship's tilted deck. A sudden rush of wind hit her as the anchor's swing speeded up; with the pendulum effectively shortened, the laws of physics now forced it to move faster to conserve its momentum.

Sending her back at the ice cliff like a wrecking ball.

'Oh *shit!*' she shrieked as the frozen wall rushed closer—

She saw the ropes Eddie had placed across the cliff – *below* her.

Roche's remains were still mashed against the anchor's leading edge. Nina tore the waterproof pouch from his harness – and jumped.

She hit the cliff a few feet above the ropes as the anchor pounded into the ice overhead. The impact hurt, but before she could recover, she slithered downwards.

One spiked boot snagged the lines. They pulled taut, Martel acting as a counterweight to slow her—

An ice spike ripped from the cliff.

She dropped, hitting the ice face-first. Then the ropes jerked taut again, pitching her back.

She fell—

Her free hand caught the juddering lines. She slowed, Martel's body again acting as a shock absorber to ease the jolt. Gasping, grimacing, she wedged the pouch into her harness, then twisted to clutch the ropes with her other hand. 'Holy crap,' she wheezed.

'Nina!' She squinted to see Eddie outside the fortress. For a moment she thought the blow to her head had affected her vision, as colours seemed to be crawling over the ancient structure, but then she realised they actually *were*. Its metal skin was shimmering, a faint rainbow effect like oil on water roiling across its surface.

But she had more urgent concerns. 'Some of the ice screws are coming out!' Eddie warned. Martel's unsecured body was still swinging from the line, the steel shafts twitching and straining in the ice. 'I'll put some more in, then help you up.'

Nina dug her crampons into the cliff. 'No rush,' she said sarcastically. The iceberg's roll had brought the *Dionysius* directly overhead. Pieces of ice fell from around it, cracks widening. How much longer could it resist gravity?

He drove a new screw into the cliff face with the Fast Ice. 'I'll be quick. I don't want the ship to hit the *femme*.'

Despite the situation, she laughed. 'That was pretty good, for you.'

'Law of averages. If I do enough jokes, I'll manage a really clever one eventually.' The screw in place, he attached a carabiner and forced the tight rope through it before sidestepping along the ledge to fix another.

Cheng and Imka looked on from inside the hatch. 'Watch out!' Imka cried as a ten-foot spear of ice broke from beside the *Dionysius*.

Nina cringed and flattened herself against the wall. The icicle exploded into glittering rubble a few metres away, but she was still hit by flying fragments.

Eddie fixed another screw, then started towards her. The cliff's angle had changed so much he could walk across it, albeit hunched down to maintain his balance. A glance at the *Dionysius* looming overhead, and he quickened his pace. 'Try to climb up,' he called to Nina. 'I'll grab you and—'

A new noise over the crackle of ice. The mercenaries' boat roared into motion. Eddie hurriedly brought up his gun as he saw Harhund raise his own weapon, but the people on the cliff were not the Norwegian's target. Instead he strafed the explorers' RIB before bringing his outboard to full power and sweeping through the churning waves into the cave mouth.

Eddie sent a few angry shots after him, but hit nothing. 'Bastard!' he growled as he continued towards Nina. 'He popped our boat!'

'How the hell are we going to get out of here?' she asked, watching the Scandinavian disappear through the opening – which was getting taller but narrower as the iceberg rolled.

'Let's just get out from underneath this bloody ship first! Climb towards me!'

She used her spikes to drive herself upwards and sideways. Ever-larger pieces of ice fell and shattered around them. Eddie ducked as a wardrobe-sized hunk burst apart, a piece as big as himself barely missing him as it swept past.

Worse was about to come. A deep, sorrowful moan echoed from above, the *Dionysius*'s trapped hull straining to support the rest of the vessel's weight. Rivets burst from the plating like bullets. Either the ice was about to give way – or the ship.

And he and Nina were right in its drop zone.

'Nina!' he shouted. 'Let go – *jump*!'

'What? Are you crazy?'

'Slide down! It's the only way we'll get clear in time—'

The ceiling exploded as the *Dionysius* finally broke from its prison – and fell.

Eddie had already thrown himself down the slope, grabbing the redhead as he whisked past. He looked back – as the *Dionysius* smashed down like a hammer of the gods.

The blow shattered the frozen wall beneath it, a shock wave flinging Nina and Eddie into the air amongst a hailstorm of flying debris. They landed hard not far above the waterline where the slope shallowed, grinding to a standstill in the broken ice.

But they were still not safe. The *Dionysius* lay on its side . . . but then the crushed cliff beneath it began to slip away in a sparkling avalanche.

With an animalistic roar, the ship followed.

'*Run!*' Nina screamed. She yanked Eddie to his feet, then they charged across the bottom of the slope.

The *Dionysius* swept sidelong towards them, a hundred-and-twenty-foot plough scraping up everything in its path. Nina's crampons both helped and hindered, giving her grip, but also turning each step into a Frankensteinian stagger. Eddie was no better off, skidding on the loose, slippery surface.

The ice-encrusted juggernaut drew closer, snarling and screeching as it bore down upon them—

They dived over a ridge just as the ship's bow sliced past right behind, half burying them in a cascade of frozen rubble. The *Dionysius* hit the water, kicking up a massive wave. It rolled almost to the point of capsizing before swinging back upright. A crane on its aft deck collapsed and slumped over the gunwales like a broken-necked giraffe, the funnel toppling after it with a hollow crash.

Nina clawed her way out of the broken ice and stared in disbelief at the rocking ship. 'Oh my God! We made it!'

'We've still got to get out of here,' Eddie reminded her, a hand to his temple where he had been struck by debris. 'Christ, my head hurts. Got any ice?'

'Ho h— Oh *shit*.' She looked past the *Dionysius* to see the wave it had thrown up pound against the cavern's far wall . . . and rebound back at them.

This time it was Eddie's turn to pull her with him. They

scrambled away from the water's edge, but the smashed surface turned every step into a nightmare. The wave grew louder—

And hit them.

They were both swept up the slope by the freezing water – then dragged away by the backwash as it retreated. Nina gasped as the deathly chill penetrated her clothing. She fought desperately to keep her head above the surface, only to be slapped by choking breakers of salty froth. All she could do was try to stay upright until the wild ride eased.

She heard her name being shouted. 'Eddie!' she replied, spitting out seawater and searching for him. She belatedly realised she had lost the pouch containing the golden key, but that was now the least of her worries. 'Where are you?'

'Over here!' His voice came from the direction of the *Dionysius*. He was out of the water, on the mangled crane arm. 'Swim over here and climb up!'

Despite the draining cold and the still-turbulent water, she managed to make her way to the ship and hook an arm over the metal frame. 'Oh God! I'm freezing!' she gasped.

'Get out of the water, then we'll worry about warming up.' He helped her over the gunwale and they huddled together, shivering on the frost-covered deck. The ship's superstructure had been damaged by the fall, skewed sideways and every window smashed. 'What the hell just happened?'

'I don't know,' Nina replied as she fumbled to remove her crampons, 'but it's all to do with that.' She indicated the fortress – then spotted something bobbing amongst the broken ice below. 'And *that*.'

Eddie saw the floating yellow pouch. 'Suppose you'll want me to get that for you?' he grumbled.

'Normally I'd say yes, but it's not at the top of my priorities list. Where are Cheng and Imka?'

'In the UFO.' Two faces peered down fearfully from the

hatch. Eddie waved to them. 'We're okay!' he called. 'Use the ropes to climb down to us.'

'I need to get back into the fortress,' said Nina.

A moment of silence, then: 'You *what*?'

'I think I started all this when I touched the key after Cheng put it in the altar – so maybe I can stop it as well! Like in the vault in Turkey – I felt as if I could control the flow of earth energy. If I can do the same here—'

'This whole place'll come apart before you get the chance!' Eddie countered. Even though the fortress was approaching equilibrium, the iceberg around it was still racked with tremors, as if D43 was fighting back against whatever unnatural forces had rolled it around. Deep, dark cracks now sliced through the translucent sapphire ceiling, and the water's surface was alive with splashes as ice constantly fell from above. 'Wait here – I'll see if there's a lifeboat we can use to get out.'

He turned – and to his dismay saw a frost-shrouded orange fibreglass hull mangled beneath the fallen crane. 'Buggeration and fuckery! What are the bloody odds?'

Wait – the ship *itself* was still afloat . . .

A couple of life vests hung on hooks beside the crushed lifeboat. He looked up at the ledge. Imka had attached another length of rope to the carabiners and thrown it down the slope. 'Grab these and get onto the ship!' he shouted, before tossing both vests ashore.

'Shouldn't we swim out of the cave?' Imka yelled back.

'Only if you want to be stuck on a freezing iceberg with no food and no shelter! You know how ship engines work, don't you?'

'Yes, but—'

'If you can start this one, we've got a chance of staying alive!'

Imka seemed unconvinced, but nevertheless started down the slope.

Nina regarded him with equal disbelief. 'This ship's been frozen upside down for four months, and just got dropped from the ceiling! We're lucky it hasn't sunk already – I don't think we'll be able to just push the starter and chug out of here.'

'It's a big diesel engine – it takes a lot to fuck 'em up. And the fuel'll have loads of antifreeze in it. As long as it hasn't all leaked out, we might be able to get the ship running – *if* we can start it.'

'That's kind of a big if.'

'I'd rather try it than swim outside and climb the iceberg. Especially when Harhund's still out there.' That triggered a mental warning: where *was* the mercenary leader, and what was he doing? 'Keep moving, it'll help you warm up. I'll be right back.'

He hurried to the stern. The cave mouth was an irregular oval of glare. He squinted, trying to focus on what lay beyond.

No sign of the *Torrox* – but there was another ship, rust-streaked white above a grimy black hull. The sarcophagus was being brought aboard by a foredeck crane. He could just about read the ship's name: *Tahatu*? It sounded Indonesian, or Maori.

He frowned. Even if they started the *Dionysius*'s engine, they didn't dare leave the cave. There were at least two armed mercenaries on the other ship, maybe more—

A loud, crackling *boom* made him flinch. He spun, seeing broken ice fall from a huge new crack extending from the ancient ship to the hole in the ceiling where the *Dionysius* had been trapped.

Imka was almost at the bottom of the cliff, Cheng clumsily following her down. The student cried out as a chunk struck him, and lost his hold on the rope. He skidded down the slope, yelling all the way, and was about to slither straight into the water when Imka grabbed him and brought him to a halt just short of the sloshing edge.

Nina let out a relieved breath. 'God, I thought he was going in.'

'He'll have to go in anyway,' Eddie pointed out.

Imka helped Cheng up, then retrieved the life vests. She donned hers, and offered the other to him – only for him to hold up his hands in rejection, instead taking off his backpack. 'What's he doing?' Eddie asked in disbelief. He shouted across the water. 'Leave the bloody bag and put your vest on!'

Cheng shook his head, saying something to Imka that produced a nod of understanding. She gave him her own life vest before carefully tying his bulging backpack on top of the other. Eddie stared in angry bewilderment. 'No, just *leave* it! Don't— Oh for fuck's sake!' Imka jumped into the water, gasping with the shock of the cold before waving for Cheng to follow. He did so, letting out a stifled shriek as the freezing sea swilled over him. Imka started to pull him towards the *Dionysius*, Cheng towing his pack on top of the flotation device.

More icy fragments skittered down the cliff in their wake. Another echoing *crack* came from above as a new fault line zigzagged upwards from the fortress. A car-sized lump of ice plunged from it, slamming down on the shimmering metal hull – with a flare of light.

Nina's eyes snapped to it. It hadn't been caused by sparks; rather, the strange iridescent glow seemed to have reacted to the impact. To her surprise, the metal was undented despite being hit by a ton of frozen water.

The fortress had not escaped unscathed, though. The impact was transmitted through the rest of the structure – and part of the ice wall trapping it began to crumble.

With a tearing crunch, the fortress started to grind loose of its prison.

'Eddie, look!' she gasped, but her husband was focused on the two people struggling through the water. As they approached, he climbed down the crane to meet them.

'What the bloody hell are you doing?' he demanded as Imka

guided the young man and his bobbing cargo to the ship's side. 'Don't waste time faffing about with his luggage – this place might collapse any second!'

'His laptop is in it,' Imka said through chattering teeth.

'So? You planning to order some towels from Amazon so we can dry off?'

'It has a satellite link,' Cheng explained, with a hint of patronising exasperation even through his shivering discomfort. 'If we get out of the cave, we can use it to call for help!'

The Yorkshireman stared at him. 'Oh. Okay. Good idea,' he admitted after a moment.

Nina laughed. 'Mr Hui, you just earned yourself extra credit.'

Eddie helped Imka up, then snagged the backpack and passed it to her before bringing Cheng onto the crane. They clambered towards the deck. 'We can't send an SOS yet, though. Those arseholes have got a ship out there – if they know we're still alive, they'll come back and kill us.'

'Then we can't leave the cave even if you start the engine,' said Nina.

Eddie followed Imka and Cheng aboard. 'I know. I'm hoping they bugger off soon, otherwise—'

Deafening thunder from above – and a huge section of the icy ceiling plunged downwards.

It hit the fortress. Another strange flash from the rippling hull, but this time it could not deflect the damage. Thousands of tons of compacted ice sheared the exposed half of the ancient structure from the wall – and pounded it flat, the whole thing disintegrating in an explosion of mangled metal and shattered crystal.

The watchers on the ship dived to the deck as debris spun at them. The *Dionysius* shuddered as if struck by cannon fire. Nina clung to a stanchion as the ship reeled beneath her.

Not just the ship. The entire cavern – the entire *iceberg*.

The fortress was destroyed, and now whatever force had tipped the great mass of ice over was gone.

D43 was about to roll back upright – with them still inside it.

13

'If you can start the engine, now'd be a good time!' Eddie told Imka. He led her at a run into the ship.

Nina picked up Cheng's backpack and guided her student after them. 'Get inside,' she said. 'It might be a bit warmer – and there's less chance of getting beaned by falling ice!'

The redhead looked back at the remains of the fortress as they reached the hatch. A last residual glow from its heart flickered beneath the smashed ice and mangled metal . . . then faded to nothing.

'The key!' she suddenly cried, darting to the ship's side and looking down. The artefact was the cause of all this – and it was bobbing somewhere below. The surface was awash with floating ice. Where was the key? If there was any chance that the murderous Harhund might reclaim his prize, she had to stop it—

Yellow amongst the white and blue. The pouch was drifting towards the cavern's mouth, pushed by the rebounding waves.

Cheng still wore his life vest. 'Give me that!' she said, hurriedly pulling it from the surprised student. She put her arms through the straps – and leapt over the side.

She was already cold, but the freezing water was an even greater shock than before. The vest butting under her chin, she shook stinging brine from her eyes.

The pouch was nowhere in sight. She started to swim, hoping the exertion would counter the draining chill gnawing at her limbs. 'Cheng! Where's the key?'

Cheng gawped at her before looking hurriedly about, then

pointing past the ship's stern. 'There, over there!'

Nina still couldn't see the pouch, but she struck out regardless.

An almost impossibly deep rumble reached her, the vibration coming as much through the water as the air. The whole iceberg was straining as its weight began to roll it back over. A wave-smoothed outcrop of cyan ice near the entrance had been raised higher above the surface; now it sank again.

And the cave's mouth was shrinking too, slowly retreating into the water.

The realisation galvanised her to swim harder, determined to find the key – while she could still escape with it.

Imka took the lead from Eddie as they descended into the *Dionysius*'s dark bowels; the South African knew the ship's layout, and she still had a flashlight clipped to her harness. 'In here.'

She pushed open a hatch and stepped into the engine room. Eddie recoiled at the stench of oil, seeing the floor slick with dark, glutinous ooze. Even at freezing temperatures, some of the engine's lubricants had remained semi-liquid, leaking from the machinery while the ship hung inverted. 'Will it still run without all this?' he asked.

'I don't know if it will run at all!' Imka replied. The main diesel engine, a hulking dull-green block the size of a car, filled the room's centre. 'I'll use the compressed air system to move the pistons, but if there isn't enough air in the tanks, there's nothing I can do. There won't be any power to start the compressors.'

'You sure?'

'I smelled acid when we passed the battery room. It must have drained out when the ship turned upside down.'

'Glad we weren't barefoot, then. Where's this air system?'

'Over here.' She aimed her light at a panel beside a line of large grey cylinders, each the size of a bathtub. Steel hoses ran from valves to the engine. She tapped at a glass-fronted pressure gauge before turning a handle below it. Air thrummed through the pipes, the gauge's needle springing up.

'Will it work?' Eddie asked.

She pursed her lips. 'It might. But there isn't much air in the tanks. And the engine's cold; there's no way to pre-heat it. It might have seized up.'

'We've got to try,' he insisted. 'Otherwise we'll freeze – or get shot. Anything I can do to help?'

She pointed at a console. 'That's for engine control. The ship's pointing away from the cave entrance, so I need you to set it to reverse. Oh!' she added as he started towards it. 'And the turning gear interlock has to be disengaged. It's on the other side of the engine, a red valve.'

'Bit dark,' he said, rounding the block to see only shadows.

'Sorry.' She joined him and aimed the light at a protruding cylinder. 'There. Open it as far as you can.'

He started to turn the valve as she returned to the air tanks. 'You really know your way around a ship.'

'My dad was an engineer in the South African navy. I studied marine engineering at university. That was where I met Arnold, actually . . .' The moment of brightness at the thought of her fiancé quickly vanished.

'I'm sorry,' Eddie said quietly.

'Arnold . . . Arnold was inside the . . . the UFO when the ceiling fell in. There's nothing left, he's gone . . .' Her voice quavered.

He kept turning the valve. 'Imka. Imka! I know this is bad, but I need you. You're the only one who can start the engine. Keep your mind on that – tell me what to do.' The interlock reached its limit; he stopped, waiting for her response. When none came, he continued, more forcefully: 'Imka. The valve's open – now what?'

'The . . . the engine control,' she managed to say. 'There are two dials with speeds marked on them. The one on the left, set it to slow astern.'

He picked his way across the oil-smeared floor to the console, just able to read the controls in the wash of her light. He turned the left-hand dial one notch anticlockwise, bringing a marker needle to the first position in a red zone: the ship's reverse speeds. 'Done.'

'Okay. I'll set the valves to put air into the first cylinder. If there's fuel in the system, it'll ignite when the cylinder reaches maximum compression and start the cycle.'

'Will it work without the batteries?'

As with Cheng a few minutes earlier, there was a hint of condescension in her words. 'It's a diesel engine – it doesn't need spark plugs.'

He smiled in the darkness. 'You know this stuff better than me. Okay! Let's fire her up – and hope the propeller isn't still embedded in the cave's ceiling.'

Even with the life vest, Nina felt as if she was sinking. The cold water was rapidly draining her energy, and her fingertips and toes prickled with the onset of hypothermal numbness. If she stayed in the water for much longer, she might not get out of it . . .

'You're almost there!' Cheng had kept pace above, moving to the stern. 'To the left, you've almost reached it!'

She still saw nothing but icy slush rising and falling in the waves – then caught a flash of yellow. Twenty feet away, no more. The sight gave her new vigour. She ploughed towards it. The pouch bobbed into view again. Ten feet, five—

And there. She grabbed it with one cold-stung hand and forced it beneath her harness strap, then turned to swim back to the crane.

★ ★ ★

Imka made a final check of the gauges – and pulled a lever.

The steel hoses shook as a powerful *whump* of compressed air surged through them. Machinery groaned, forced into motion . . . then the engine abruptly clattered to life as the diesel fuel in the cylinder auto-ignited. The contained detonation drove the piston back, turning the great steel crankshaft. The other cylinders followed suit, the room filling with a ragged roar as the engine built up to speed.

Eddie gripped the console as the deck lurched. 'We're moving!' he cried. 'Let's get to the bridge – and hope we can steer this thing!'

A churning surge rushed up from beneath Nina. Froth rolled over her head. She surfaced, coughing and gasping—

And went under again.

Something was dragging her down. Even with the vest, she couldn't keep her head above the water. A pounding metallic rumble assaulted her ears. The ship's engine had started – and the propeller's vortex was sucking her in as the *Dionysius* reversed towards the cave mouth.

She kicked in a desperate attempt to make headway. But the force was unrelenting – and then the reversing juggernaut's stern rolled over her.

Nina clawed at the hull, fingers finding dents and barnacles, but nothing big enough to grip with her numbing hands. The propeller whirled below. The life vest strained uselessly to lift her, straps tugging painfully under her arms.

She slipped further down. The propeller was just feet away, slashing blades about to hack her apart—

Something writhed past her.

Rope, whipping like an angry snake as it was pulled towards the propeller. She grabbed it. For a moment both she and the line kept falling – then it yanked tight.

She clung to it. For agonising moments it remained still . . . before it inched back towards the surface.

Nina closed her eyes as she rose through the floating ice, then felt frigid air on her wet skin. The cold stung her throat as she took several deep breaths.

Even out of the water, though, she was far from out of danger. Cheng leaned over the railing above, face twisted with strain. 'Professor!' he gasped. 'I can't . . . lift you!'

'Get Eddie!' she cried. 'Call for help, get Eddie!'

He shouted her husband's name – but the rope was already slipping through his cold, wet fingers.

Eddie followed Imka back up through the ship. The engine was working, but it was far from healthy, bangs and rattles echoing through the vessel. If it kept going long enough to get them out of the cavern, though, that was all that mattered—

A shout from above. 'Mr Chase! *Help!*'

'Shit, it's Cheng!' he said, pushing past Imka and hurrying for the exit. What trouble had the kid got himself into now?

He ran into the open, the blue half-light dazzling after the darkness below – and realised to his horror that it wasn't Cheng who was in trouble. The student was on the verge of toppling over the railing as he held a taut rope. Eddie knew at once who was at the other end. 'Oh, for fuck's sake! *Now* what's she done?'

He ran to grab the rope and looked down. Nina was indeed clinging to the line. A glimpse of yellow under her harness straps told him exactly what she had been doing. He wasn't even surprised. Instead he helped Cheng lift her, then dragged her to the deck.

She flopped onto her back, water sluicing from her clothing as she looked up at him. 'Hi.'

'I'm not even going to ask,' he sighed, shaking his head. 'You okay?'

'Yeah. Although I'm frickin' freezing!'

'We got the engine started.'

'I noticed! What now?'

He looked out from the stern. Beyond the cavern, Harhund's ship had disappeared. A churned white wake and residual trail of diesel smoke told him it had left in a hurry, trying to get clear of the rolling iceberg.

The cave mouth had shrunk considerably since he went inside, its ceiling dropping inexorably towards the water. If the *Dionysius* didn't clear it in the next couple of minutes, they would be trapped.

'We've got to move.'

He, Nina and Cheng hurried into the reversing ship and made their way to the bridge. Imka was already at the wheel, facing the broken stern windows. 'What happened?' she asked.

'Archaeology,' was Eddie's sarcastic reply. He stared at the cavern mouth. 'Can we make it through?'

'I don't know. It's getting smaller.'

'Can you go faster?' Cheng asked.

'Perhaps, but a lot of oil leaked from the engine,' said Imka. 'If I push it too hard, it might seize up – or explode.'

'I'd kinda like to avoid the explosion option,' Nina said, huddling against Eddie for warmth. 'But I'd also like to get out of here before we become permanent residents!'

'You've got to risk it,' Eddie told the South African.

Imka chewed unhappily on her lower lip, but turned a dial to increase speed to half astern. The diesel's revival had also powered some of the electrical systems, a frost-covered light confirming that the command had been received by the machinery in the engine room. The raucous chug increased in tempo – and a grinding noise rose beneath it.

Eddie looked at the exit again, judging how long it would take the ship to reach it against the rate at which the ceiling was descending – and not liking the result. 'We won't make it,' he said. 'Imka, we've got to go faster!'

'If the engine breaks down, we'll be stuck in here!' Imka protested.

'We'll be stuck in here anyway!' She still hesitated – so he reached past her and turned the dial to full.

The engine's response was immediate, and alarming. A shrill screech came from the lower decks. Eddie forced himself to ignore it and looked ahead again as the *Dionysius* gained speed. Another rapid calculation. 'I think we're going to make it.' The ship drew closer to the icy tunnel. 'We're going to make it—'

A loud bang from below decks shook the bridge – and the survey vessel started to slow.

'Oh, you *had* to say it, didn't you?' cried Nina, clapping a hand to her forehead.

'We're still moving,' Eddie replied. 'If we can just keep going, we'll make it . . .'

'You did it *again*!' She made a plea to the heavens. 'Fate, if you can hear this: he's not with me!'

But the *Dionysius* somehow stayed in motion, trailing sooty smoke as it reached the icy passage. 'We can do it,' Eddie whispered, willing it onwards. 'Just got to get clear of this big lump overhead . . .'

Nina stared at the knobbly protrusion of glassy ice descending inexorably towards them. 'It's gonna be close,' she said. 'Very, *very* close.' It drew ever nearer. '*Too* close!'

Everyone grabbed the nearest solid object for support as the huge mass hit the ship.

With the funnel gone, the tallest part of the *Dionysius* was the radio mast atop the bridge, which toppled as it was ripped from its mount. Smaller masts for radars and weather sensors followed – then the bridge ceiling tore open, showering its occupants with freezing ice as the obstruction scraped over the superstructure—

Suddenly it was gone, the bridge moving clear, but the obstacle continued towards the foredeck, looking for all the world like a giant tooth about to gnaw on a snack. 'Hang on!' Nina cried.

It struck the deck just behind the bow. The whole ship lurched, the stern kicking out of the water – then smashing back down as thick metal plates tore and crumpled like paper. Its upper bow a mangled mess, the *Dionysius* veered towards the tunnel wall.

Eddie saw the new danger. 'Imka, we're going to crash!'

She hurriedly regained her hold on the wheel and spun it. The ship swung away from a solid collision, but not quickly enough to avoid a glancing one. It caught the ice in a series of stuttering blows, scattering the deck with frozen debris before finally pulling free.

But they were still inside the passage, open sea more than a ship-length away – and the ceiling kept dropping like a car crusher. The brightening daylight dimmed again, blotted out by a solid sapphire-blue firmament—

A thunderous roar came from behind, from above, even below – and the new sky split apart.

Icy meteorites bombarded the *Dionysius* as D43 tore asunder, cleaving along a line directly through the spot where the fortress had been trapped. The two halves peeled apart, the ship no longer in a tunnel but at the bottom of a widening chasm. Massive waves rushed down the channel, snatching up the battered ship and flinging it towards the open sea.

The diesel died as it was swamped by tons of water rushing down the stub of the funnel. More sluiced in through the broken windows, the bridge's occupants taking another soaking. But they were concerned only about holding on as the vessel pitched and rolled. Nina hooked one arm around a handrail, clinging to Eddie as they were flung back and forth over the wet deck . . .

Then the wild ride eased.

Nina shook wet hair off her face. 'Is everyone okay?' she gasped.

'Feel like the pea in a bloody whistle,' Eddie spluttered, 'but yeah.' He staggered upright. 'Imka! Cheng!'

Cheng had wedged himself between the bridge wall and a console, clutching his backpack. 'I'm . . . okay. I think.'

'So am I,' said Imka blearily as she slumped over the helm – only to gasp as she took in the view.

Nina had much the same reaction. Surrealistic spires and arches had risen from the sea, lancing almost horizontally from the iceberg's body. One half of D43 had rolled by nearly ninety degrees, submerged features brought spectacularly into the light. The other, larger part of the iceberg had not made such an extreme shift, but was still a good twenty degrees off its original alignment, newly exposed strata shimmering as water streamed down them.

The cavern was gone – as were the remains of the fortress. Everything they had discovered was now on its way to the bottom of the Southern Ocean. All that survived was the coffin the mercenaries had stolen, and the key inside the pouch on Nina's chest.

Eddie took in the incredible sight, but quickly moved past astonishment to concern. 'Where's the other ship?' His view was restricted by the walls of the newly formed fjord, and there was no sign of Harhund's vessel.

'Maybe it got squished when the berg rolled,' Nina suggested hopefully.

'I don't think the universe is *that* generous.' He turned to Imka. 'We need to make sure the ship isn't going to sink. Cheng, this'd be a good time to find out if your satellite link's working.'

'I'll check,' the student promised, shakily standing and bringing his pack to a plotting table.

'Great. Imka, let's go. If the ship's okay, we'll be back soon,' he told Nina as they headed for the exit. 'If it's not, we'll be back *really* soon!'

'"Okay" is kind of a relative term, isn't it?' she retorted, surveying the chaotic wreckage around them.

Eddie grinned, then followed Imka from the bridge.

Nina joined Cheng. He swept water from the table before sliding the laptop from its waterproof case. He then took out a black plastic tube containing the satellite link's folding antenna. 'It needs to point at the sky,' he announced.

She gestured at the gaping hole in the ceiling. 'That won't be a problem.'

Cheng managed a small smile, but it did not last. 'I . . . I can't believe we're still alive,' he said as he set up the antenna.

'Not all of us are,' Nina reminded him grimly. 'They killed Janco and Marc – and everyone on the *Torrox*.'

He sighed deeply, then regarded the yellow pouch, still wedged in her harness. 'If I'd known finding the key would bring so much danger . . .'

'You would have listened to my second rule? Kinda wishing I'd done that myself.'

He didn't reply, though his expression was troubled. Instead he turned back to his laptop, plugging in the antenna. 'Okay. I hope it's still working . . .'

He opened the computer. The screen remained dark for a moment – then to their relief it lit up, a login message appearing. Cheng tapped clumsily at the keyboard. 'Ow. It's hard to type when your fingers have no feeling.'

'They'll warm up,' Nina assured him. She watched as suspended programs came back to life, but all were in Chinese, indecipherable. 'You think you'll be able to call for help?'

'If I can get a satellite link.' No doubt behind his words.

Nina nodded and paced around the bridge to warm herself while he worked.

Eddie and Imka returned a few minutes later. 'Good news and bad news,' reported the Yorkshireman. 'Good news, the ship isn't going to sink. Bad news, the engine's wrecked. So unless we find some really big oars, we're not going anywhere.'

Imka went to Cheng. 'Is the satellite link working?'

The Chinese had been intermittently typing, waiting for responses over a messaging program. 'Yes. I managed to contact a friend in China. They reported our situation to the authorities, who will try to alert any other ships in the area.'

'They know the nearest ship's the one that stranded us out here in the first place, right?' said Eddie.

'Of course. I gave them our GPS coordinates, so they should—' A new bubble of text popped up. Cheng read it, then looked around with a smile. 'Yes! They've contacted another ship, which is diverting to find us.'

'How far away are they?' Nina asked.

'I don't know,' was the almost apologetic reply, before an idea came to him. 'But I can track them! Wait, please . . .' He turned back to the screen, bringing up an internet browser and performing a search. Most of the text on the page that came up was Mandarin, but a logo read *TrackShip*.

'The rescue ship is called *Destiny Sunset*,' said Cheng, typing it in. A pause, then a picture of a large bulk freighter appeared. He clicked a button beneath it. A world map loaded, zooming in on the southern hemisphere. 'It's here, heading for Melbourne, and we are . . .' He scrolled south-east to empty ocean, checking coordinates. 'Here.' He flicked between applications to make calculations. 'Oh. Over seven hours away,' was his unhappy announcement.

'We'll survive,' said Eddie. 'But we need to get out of this wind before we freeze. Pack up your computer, and— No, hold on!' He stopped Cheng from closing the screen. 'I saw Harhund's ship. *Tahatu*, I think it was called. Put the name in, see if you can find it.'

Cheng did so. The ship tracking website produced a new image, a much smaller black-hulled vessel. 'That's it,' said Eddie. 'What does it say about it?'

The Chinese read the text. 'Not much. It's privately owned, registered in New Zealand.'

'Can you track it?' asked Nina.

He clicked the appropriate button. The map reappeared, again showing an empty patch of the Southern Ocean. 'Not far from us.'

'On the other side of the iceberg, thank God,' said Imka.

'I can track its recent movements. Wait, please . . . Yes. It came from Auckland. It sailed four days ago.' The ship had come around the tip of New Zealand's North Island before angling south-west.

'That's before we left Australia,' said Nina, puzzled. 'They had to go farther, so they arrived after we did – but they knew where we were going!'

'How?' Eddie said in disbelief. 'We didn't tell anybody.'

'Nor did I,' Imka added.

Cheng looked up from the laptop. 'The only person I've spoken to is my mother, and I don't think she would send international mercenaries to kill me.'

'Depends; when did you last clean your room?' Nina said with a half-smile.

'Someone knows way too much,' Eddie rumbled. 'They knew how to find us, *and* what we were going to find inside the spaceship.'

'It *wasn't* a— Oh, you know what, forget it. But you're right, they knew a lot more than we did. Including,' she said, feeling a chill unrelated to the cold, 'that they'd need *me* to make the earth energy technology work.'

'What do they want it for? They stole a coffin – but what're they going to do with a prehistoric frozen corpse?'

'Nothing good,' Nina said. 'But we know where they're taking it.' She pointed at the map. 'If we contact the New Zealand coastguard or the authorities in Auckland, they should hold the ship and everyone aboard it until we get there. Then we can ask them ourselves.'

Eddie was not enthused. 'You want to go chasing after them?'

'Anything connected to earth energy always ends up with some lunatic trying to take over the world or start a war. Whoever's behind this and whatever they want it for, we can't let them go through with it.'

'She's right,' said Cheng. 'If there's a danger to world peace, you have to stop it. It's what you do. Both of you,' he added pointedly.

Eddie gave him an irritated glare, but said nothing.

Nina straightened. 'Once we're rescued, we'll go to New Zealand. I want to find out who's behind what just happened.' Her voice became as cold as her surroundings. 'And make them pay for it.'

14

Auckland, New Zealand

'There it is,' said Eddie, staring across the water. The *Tahatu* was moored on a long wharf west of Auckland's Viaduct Harbour. 'Let's find out what those arseholes have to say.'

'If they're still there,' Nina said. She, Eddie and Cheng had taken the first available flight from Melbourne, but the sea journey to Australia had taken four days, the Chinese bulk freighter that rescued them far from speedy. Even with considerably further to travel, the *Tahatu* reached its home port before them. She had already been informed that the Royal New Zealand Navy patrol vessel which intercepted the mercenaries' ship had let it sail on. There had been no evidence of their murderous activities, so no cause to detain them.

'*Somebody's* there, look.' There was a figure on the cluttered foredeck. 'Even if the mercs have buggered off, the crew must know something.'

They headed along the harbourfront, passing a ferry terminal and a sightseeing seaplane dock, an elderly de Havilland Beaver growling from its jetty. 'Shame the *Destiny Sunset* didn't have one of those aboard,' said Eddie. 'We'd have got to Melbourne a lot quicker.'

'Do you think Imka has found a flight to South Africa yet?' Cheng asked.

'I'm sure she has by now,' Nina replied. 'My God, though.

That poor woman. Not only is her fiancé dead, but she found his body. Nobody should have to go through that.'

'She found what was *left* of his body,' Eddie noted grimly. 'What the hell did that to him?'

'Maybe it was whatever the mercenaries were trying to find,' Cheng suggested.

Nina grimaced. 'That's a cheery thought.'

They reached the *Tahatu*. The tramp freighter was being unloaded, crates and pallets sitting on the quayside and more items stacked on its main deck. A large and muscular East Asian man carried another box down the gangway. He gave the new arrivals a look of deep suspicion.

'Hello!' Eddie called with affected cheer. 'You the captain?'

The man shook his head. 'On the bridge,' he replied. 'You cops?'

'No, we're looking to hire a ship,' said Nina. 'We were told the *Tahatu* might be available?'

He appeared conflicted, putting his cargo down and regarding the trio warily before finally nodding. 'Okay. I get Captain Nick.' He waved for them to follow him aboard.

'Huh,' said Nina quietly as they reached the deck. 'They were definitely geared up for anything they might find on the iceberg.' As well as numerous pallets of food and bottled water, enough to sustain an expedition for weeks, she saw cold-weather clothing and tents, climbing gear, scuba tanks and drysuits.

The crewman led them to the bridge. Its occupant turned to greet them. Nina had expected a grizzled old sea dog to match his vessel, but instead found a handsome and well-built Maori man in his forties, a small tā moko tattoo running down his chin like an ornate blue beard. It was partially obscured by several days' stubble, though, the captain looking sleep-deprived and harried. 'Yes?' he said. 'Can I help you?'

'Hi,' said Nina, extending her hand. 'Professor Macy Garde,

from Columbia University. In New York?'

He shook it, cocking his head quizzically. 'You're a long way from home.'

'I'm a climatologist, I travel a lot. Wherever you go, there's weather!' She laughed a little.

He managed a polite chuckle. 'Nikau Jones – but you can call me Nick. I'm the *Tahatu*'s captain. Thanks, Yuda.' He nodded at the crewman, who left the bridge. 'So what can I do for you?'

'We're looking to hire a ship to take us to . . . Campbell Island,' she said, drawing the name from some obscure corner of her memory. 'For climate research.'

'You'd be better off in Christchurch or Dunedin. You'd save a couple of days' sailing time, and there are people down there set up for going that far south.'

Eddie gestured at the equipment on the deck below. 'Looks like you've got the gear for it.'

A flash of anger in the captain's eyes. 'Previous clients. They left it behind; said they didn't need it any more.'

'That's some expensive equipment,' said Nina. 'You could probably get a lot of money for it.'

Jones shook his head. 'I just want it off my ship.'

'Not the best voyage?' said Eddie.

The Maori gave him a sharp look. 'I've had better. But the *Tahatu* isn't available for hire, for a very simple reason – most of my crew just quit. The only man who's stuck with me is Yuda, and the two of us can't run the ship on our own, so it's not going anywhere until I recruit some replacements. You'll have to find someone else. Sorry.' He nodded towards the exit.

Nina wasn't going anywhere. 'Why did they quit?' she asked. 'Problem with your clients?'

He scowled. 'You could say that. Now, if you'd—'

'These clients of yours,' Eddie cut in, 'you wouldn't know where we could find 'em, would you?'

The captain's eyes went wide. 'Aw, shit,' he muttered. 'Who are you really? Police?'

'No, but we can call 'em,' said the Yorkshireman. 'Unless you want to tell us who hired you to take them to the iceberg?'

The realisation that his guests knew about his last voyage knocked the wind from Jones. 'I . . . Okay, look, I don't know much about them. I didn't *want* to know.'

'Well, we *do* want to know,' said Nina. 'Because your clients sank our ship and tried to kill us!'

'I didn't know they were going to do that, I swear!' the New Zealander protested. 'When they started taking out guns and rocket launchers, I was whoa, what the hell? We tried to stop them, but they pulled guns on *us*! Har— The leader,' he quickly corrected himself, 'left three of his men aboard while the others went into the iceberg. We were all held at gunpoint until they came back!'

'We know his name's Harhund,' she said. 'And we also know most of his men *didn't* come back. I think he's got other things on his mind than threatening you.'

'Yeah, like explaining to his boss why he fucked up so badly and didn't even get everything he was sent for,' added Eddie.

'That coffin wasn't all he was after?' said Jones.

Nina shook her head. 'Not by a long shot.' She softened her tone, trying a different approach. 'Look, what did Harhund tell you? What exactly did he hire you for?'

Jones hesitated, then reluctantly answered. 'He hired us to catch up with a ship surveying an iceberg. The *Torrox*, right?' She nodded. 'They had all this gear,' he indicated the equipment below, 'so I figured they were planning to go onto the iceberg. I didn't know they wanted to go *into* it!'

'Or to attack the *Torrox*?' said Eddie.

'I told you, no! You think I would have taken them if I'd known? They paid a lot of money, but even if it had been ten times as much I wouldn't have let them use my ship for that.' He looked down at the deck, away from his interrogators. 'They killed all the sailors on the other ship, even . . . even the survivors in the water. They shot them. And there was nothing we could do about it.' His eyes flicked back to Nina, desperate. 'There was nothing I could do! You have to believe me – they would have shot us too!'

'There's *something* you can do,' she replied. 'Tell us how to find these bastards. We need to know who hired them.'

'We can protect you,' said Cheng, joining in with the exchange for the first time.

Nina gave him a look of mild surprise, but pressed on. 'Is there anything else you know? Any paperwork that might give us a trail to follow?'

Jones shook his head. 'Harhund took everything.'

'Did they leave any guns?' asked Eddie. 'I know people who can trace serial numbers.'

'No, they tossed them all overboard. The big stuff, anyway. They kept some pistols – must have been worried about us tossing *them* overboard after what they did.'

'What about the money they paid you?' Cheng said. 'That must have come from an account that can be traced.'

Another shake of the head. 'They paid in cash and bearer bonds.'

Eddie snorted. 'Bearer bonds? Were you hired by Hans Gruber?'

'Didn't that strike you as, y'know, incredibly dubious?' said Nina. 'Like a pretty obvious sign they were doing something criminal?'

'I didn't even know what a bearer bond was! I had to look it up. But I didn't think about it too much,' admitted Jones. 'I didn't *want* to think about it. It was a lot of money – more than enough to clear all my debts. And I just figured, maybe someone spotted a shipwreck on the iceberg and Harhund was in a rush to get there before the *Torrox* so he could claim salvage rights. It happens sometimes, there's a lot of money in it.'

Nina sighed in frustration. 'So you can't tell us *anything* about Harhund's employer? Didn't he report in after they found the coffin?'

'Yeah, but he made everyone leave the bridge while he used the satphone. I didn't hear what he— No, wait!' The Maori's expression intensified as he searched his memory. 'Before we left port, he talked to someone on his mobile. Must have been his boss, because he called him "sir". He said a name, but . . . It was an English name, something really ordinary . . . Miller!' he exclaimed. 'He called him Mr Miller.'

'Yeah, that *is* really ordinary,' Eddie noted sarcastically. 'Might as well be Smith for all the good it does us.'

'We can narrow it down when we start searching, though,' said Nina. 'Whoever it was is probably based in New Zealand, maybe even Auckland, because why send a ship from here when they could have beaten us to the iceberg if they'd gone from Australia?'

Her husband nodded. 'They'd need foreign connections to get hold of those weapons an' all. New Zealand cracked down on guns after that massacre in Christchurch.'

'Right. And someone with stacks of bearer bonds sitting around is probably very high up in the business world – they're mostly used by corporations.'

'The bonds Harhund gave me all have company names on them,' Jones said. 'They're like share certificates, right?'

'Sort of . . . Wait, what *kind* of corporations?' asked Nina.

'Mostly pharmaceutical companies. I checked that they were all still in business to make sure the bonds were worth what Harhund said.'

Eddie frowned in thought. 'So what does having a lot of bonds from pill companies mean?'

'It means,' said Cheng, 'that whoever provided them is probably a senior executive of a pharmaceutical corporation.'

'And he's called Miller, and he's based in New Zealand,' Nina added. 'Now *that* makes it a lot easier to narrow down the search!'

'I can narrow it down even more!' said Jones. 'You're not from here, so you wouldn't know him, but there's a guy called Donny Miller. He's rich, sort of a playboy, always in the news – *and* he's the boss of a pharma company.' He pointed towards the skyscrapers of central Auckland to the east. 'That tower there, with the blue logo? It's theirs.'

'Why would some yuppie hire mercenaries to steal a hundred-thousand-year-old coffin?' Eddie asked, glaring at the distant building.

'I don't know,' Nina replied. 'So let's ask him.'

15

'So is he the right guy?' Eddie asked.

Nina looked up from Cheng's laptop. 'Donny Miller is everything Jones said, according to the local news and gossip sites,' she said. 'Rich, powerful, connected – and the kind of asshole who'd be constantly getting the finger in New York because you *know* he'd always park his Ferrari in a disabled space.' She turned the screen to show him a picture of a man of around forty, whom she would have considered handsome if not for an expression of oily, self-satisfied smugness that she imagined was a permanent fixture. 'CEO of Miller & Family Inc., born in the States but emigrated to New Zealand about fifteen years ago, granted instant citizenship along with his mother on the grounds that they were rich and . . . well, that's pretty much all the Kiwi government cared about back then.'

'Let me guess – they came here because they think civilisation's about to collapse and they want to hide out in a bunker a long way from rampaging mobs of poor people?'

'Actually, he lives in a fancy penthouse right here in town.' Nina looked towards the window. They were in a room on the tenth floor of a hotel with a view across Auckland's central business district. The city's premier landmark, the Sky Tower – the southern hemisphere's tallest building, though rivals in Australia were under construction with the intention of stealing its crown – dominated the vista, a slender spire stabbing over three hundred metres towards the clouds. 'His mom fits the whole "ultra-rich survivalist" bill, though. She's got a big estate on South Island. She ran the company until a few years ago, when our smirking friend here took over.'

'The question is,' said Cheng, visibly fidgeting because someone else was using his computer, 'did he hire the mercenaries?'

'Like I said, let's ask him.' Nina, like her husband, had years before learned first-hand the benefits of a waterproof phone; hers had survived its immersions intact. A modicum of web searching provided contact numbers for various divisions of the Miller & Family headquarters. She decided to aim straight for the top and called the executive office, as expected reaching a secretary. 'Hi, this is Macy Garde, from the *Times* in New York,' she said. 'Is it possible to speak to Mr Miller?'

'I'm afraid he's very busy,' came the polite reply. 'You'd have to make an appointment. I'm sure something could be arranged for, let me see . . . the middle of next week?'

'That's a shame, I was kinda hoping to speak to him right now. Otherwise we'd have to run the story about Mr Miller's involvement in a criminal conspiracy without any comment from him, and I'm sure he'd like to put forward his side of the story before it goes to press. It might not even *need* to go to press if he can clear up a few questions.'

'I'll . . . I'll see if I can reach him. One moment, please.' Tinny hold music came down the line.

Eddie nodded approvingly. 'Nice.'

'You work at a university, you meet a lot of kids who fancy themselves as the next Woodward or Bernstein. I guess it rubs off.'

The secretary returned. 'Please hold for Mr Miller.'

'Thank you.' She switched her phone to speaker so Eddie and Cheng could hear.

A click of connection, then: 'Yes?'

'Mr Miller?' said Nina.

'Yeah. Who's this, and what's it about? Sounds like you were

175

making a threat, and let me tell you, people who threaten me regret it.' Despite having lived in New Zealand for many years, Donny Miller still had an American accent, though inflections on some of the vowels showed his adoptive country had taken a hold.

'My name's Macy Garde, from the *Times* in New York. I want to talk to you about iceberg D43, a man named Harhund, Professor Nina Wilde – and a golden coffin.'

There was a protracted silence. 'Mr Miller?' she asked.

'Yes, I'm here,' came the reply, the pushy arrogance gone – until it surged back at full force. 'I have no idea what you're talking about. I warn you, if you libel me I'll put you in debt for the rest of your life, and you'll never work—'

Nina looked to Eddie and rolled her eyes before speaking again. 'Mr Miller, there were survivors from the *Torrox*.' The revelation cut him off mid rant. 'They were picked up by a Chinese cargo ship and taken to Melbourne. I've spoken to them; they identified Harhund, and our investigations led to you.'

When Miller spoke again, his tone was guarded. 'What do you want?'

'I want to talk to you. In person. I want to hear your version of events. I'm sure a man in your position couldn't *possibly* have intended there to be any loss of life – you could set the record straight and make sure the right people are brought to justice.'

'I could . . . meet you today, yes,' Miller eventually said. 'Can you come to my office?'

Eddie put his hand over the phone. 'Not a fucking chance,' he whispered. 'Needs to be somewhere public.'

'I know,' Nina replied. 'But we don't know the city, so where . . .' She looked up – and saw the Sky Tower through the window. The hotel room had brochures for Auckland's tourist attractions; she signalled for Cheng to bring them. 'Does it have an observation deck?' she wondered, quickly flipping open the relevant pamphlet and finding that as well as various attractions involving dangling from its upper floors, it did indeed have a viewing deck, and places to eat and drink. 'Okay, that's about as public as you can get!' She gestured for Eddie to lift his hand. 'I'd prefer to meet at the Sky Tower.'

'The Sky Tower, okay,' said Miller. 'We'll meet in the Sugar Club at . . . noon. Okay?'

It was now just before ten thirty. 'Yes. I'll see you there.' She ended the call.

'We need to get over there right now,' said Eddie, eyeing the landmark. 'He's probably calling a goon squad to stake the place out already. If we get there first, we can watch for anyone turning up.'

Cheng stood, but Nina waved him down. 'No, no,' she told him. 'You stay here.'

'But you might need me,' he protested.

'I *do* need you – to look after the key.' She glanced at the golden relic, still in the waterproof pouch. 'As soon as Miller realises who I really am – and I doubt it'll take long – he'll want to know what happened to it. You have to keep it safe.'

'If anything goes wrong, you get it out of here,' Eddie told him. 'We'll use a warning code. If we phone you and say our names, like "It's Eddie," then you grab the key and go, quick as you can. If we say, "It's me," then it's safe.'

Cheng nodded. 'Okay. But I still think—'

'Stay here,' Nina insisted. 'You've been in enough danger already. Ah ah!' she added, raising a finger as he prepared to say more. 'You want to pass my class? Do what I tell you.'

'Yes, *Professor*,' Cheng replied with a huffy frown.

'We'll get a cab to the tower,' said Eddie.

Nina donned her boots. 'Think we'll make it before he can get anyone there?'

'Should do, unless he's got goons who literally live underneath it.'

'Dangerous place. You'd be constantly bombarded by jumpers.' She held up the brochure to show him one of the tower's main draws: the Sky Jump, where thrill-seekers could leap from on high.

Eddie grinned. 'I'll stick with the lift.'

'Okay, Cheng, wait here for us to call. Remember what Eddie said about the code?'

Cheng nodded. 'If you use your names, I take the key and go as fast as I can.'

'Good lad,' said Eddie. 'You all set, love?'

'Yeah,' she said. 'It's Miller time.'

From one hundred and ninety-two metres above the ground, the view across Auckland from the Sky Tower was spectacular. Both the east and west coasts of New Zealand were visible, the city built on one of the narrowest points of North Island. However, Nina and Eddie had other things on their minds than admiring the scenery. One was making sure Miller had not staked out the meeting; the other was right outside the window.

'You were right,' said Nina, watching as two attendants prepared a man in a bright blue-and-yellow coverall for the Sky Jump. The attraction's summit was directly beside the bar of the Sugar Club restaurant, occasional screams rising over the soft background music as leapers took the fast way down to street level. 'I think we'll stick with the elevator.'

Eddie chuckled. 'I've fallen off too many high things for free to want to pay to do it.'

She looked away from the platform outside into the main dining area, which curved around the circumference of the tower's fifty-third floor. 'What about in there? Anyone suspicious?'

He had recently returned from checking it out, pretending to admire the panoramic view while surreptitiously assessing the diners. 'There's only a few people. Two of 'em are an old couple, so I don't think they're hired goons, and the others were finishing their desserts. They'll be gone in ten minutes.'

Nina's watch told her they still had twenty before Miller was due to arrive. 'And anyone else who turns up, we'll see them.' The bar was at the restaurant's entrance; anybody arriving had to come past them. 'Okay, so I guess we wait. And listen to the screams.' The jumper finally plucked up the courage to step over the edge – and plunged towards the ground with a shriek, the cable attached to his harness rapidly winding out as he dropped in free fall before slowing.

'Nothing like that to help you relax,' said Eddie with a smile.

They had told a waiter they were expecting Miller, so were left alone while they waited. The dessert eaters departed. Another jumper was led to the platform, wobbling at the edge before disappearing with a Dopplering scream. It was clearly a popular draw, as the attendants bustled straight back inside to prepare the next customer for their vertical journey. Nina checked her watch again. 'Five minutes. Shame we're not planning to eat, I like the look of the menu!'

Eddie stood. 'I'll go and keep an eye on things.' He went through a door leading from the bar to the glass-walled corridor outside the Sky Jump waiting area, taking up position behind it to watch the restaurant through a porthole.

Nina waited, becoming increasingly tense even knowing Eddie was only yards away. From her brief talk with Miller, she had already pegged his type: an overprivileged, entitled product of money who became angry and aggressive if challenged, especially by a woman. She had run into a depressingly large number of them over the years, as they gravitated into business, law and politics as if considering such professions theirs by birthright.

But she was angry too. If Miller was behind what had happened in the iceberg, she would make him pay, even if that involved dangling him from the Sky Jump by his ankles . . .

The main doors opened. Nina turned – and instantly recognised Donny Miller. He was tall, well over six feet, and the smug expression from the photos was present in real life as if permanently etched around his mouth. There was, however, uncertainty behind it, which was a relief. If he had set up a trap, he would be a lot more confident.

The waiter, a cheery man with a nametag reading 'Simon', met him. 'Good afternoon, Mr Miller.' He glanced around, noting Eddie's absence with a small shrug, then led him to Nina. 'Your guest is already here.'

She stood, extending a hand. 'Mr Miller?'

He took it, giving her a perfunctory but still over-forceful power squeeze. 'You're Macy Garde?'

'I am, yes,' she replied – but he was already regarding her with suspicion, recognition starting to form. She distracted him by turning to the waiter. 'Can we go to our table, please?'

He led the way to the one she had requested, by the window just inside the dining section. She had chosen it because of its proximity to the entrance, allowing her to see anyone coming in – and also in case she and Eddie needed to leave in a hurry. She sat looking back towards the bar, Miller facing her. 'Two waters,' he told Simon brusquely. The waiter hurried away.

Miller checked no other diners were within earshot before he spoke. 'So. What do you want?'

'I want to know why you sent mercenaries to attack the expedition to iceberg D43,' she replied. 'Why you stole a coffin containing the body of someone who lived over a hundred thousand years ago – and why your men tried to kill me in Hamburg to get hold of the key that opens it.'

He blinked, taken aback by the barrage of accusations.

'Hamburg? You were— You're *not* a journalist, are you?'

'I'm not,' she answered stonily. Behind him, she saw Eddie re-enter the bar. 'I'm Nina Wilde.'

Miller stiffened, eyes widening before he covered his shock with clench-lipped indignation. 'So you brought me here under false pretences? I've got nothing to say to you.' He started to stand—

'Ay up,' said Eddie, putting a hand on his shoulder and pushing him firmly down. 'Not leaving already, are you? You only just arrived.'

'And that's my husband, Eddie Chase,' Nina told Miller. 'If you know anything about him, you won't try to stand up again until he lets you. He was in the SAS; he could kill you with his bare hands in a crowded room and make it look like a heart attack.'

Eddie gave Nina a crooked grin – the statement was a considerable exaggeration of his lethality – but Miller abandoned any further attempts to rise. 'All right,' said the Englishman, giving the younger man a patronising pat on the back before sitting between him and Nina, 'now we can have a nice little chat.'

Miller eyed him nervously. 'If I shout for help, the staff will have security in here in less than a minute.'

'If you shout for help, you'll have a fork in each fucking eyeball,' Eddie replied mildly, picking up two examples of said silverware and slowly flipping them over between his fingers. 'Just answer our questions, and you'll get to keep enjoying the view.'

'Start talking,' said Nina. 'Why did you steal the coffin?'

'The coffin,' Miller repeated, agitated. 'Look, what happened in Hamburg was a mistake, okay? I sent Harhund and his men, but that was, ah . . . premature. 'He looked down at the table, almost as if ashamed; his attitude was more that of a child being told off than the head of a multinational corporation. The arrogance quickly returned, though. 'But I didn't tell Harhund to kill anyone!'

'What about at the iceberg?' Nina snapped. 'He sank our ship with a rocket launcher! That's not exactly something you pack on the off chance it might come in useful.'

'That was out of my hands!' he objected. 'Yeah, I sent Harhund to Germany, but I already told you that was a mistake. I had nothing to do with anything that happened afterwards.'

'Then who did?' demanded Eddie. He looked around sharply at movement near the entrance, but it was merely the waiter returning from the bar with the water. The Yorkshireman pointedly held up a fork as the bottles were placed on the table, daring Miller to say anything. Miller remained silent.

'Would you like a drink, sir?' the waiter asked Eddie.

'No, I'm fine,' he replied. 'Can we have a few minutes before you bring the menus? We've got some business to discuss.' Simon glanced at Miller for confirmation, but he remained close-lipped, so nodded and departed towards the kitchen at the restaurant's far end.

'So who sent them to the iceberg?' Nina said. 'You expect us to believe you'd order Harhund to Hamburg to get the key, but then wash your hands of everything else?'

Miller gave her an unexpectedly calculating look. 'Do you have the key?'

'None of your fucking business!' Eddie growled. 'Answer her. Or you'll be taking the quick way down.' He gestured towards the long drop beyond the windows.

Miller swallowed, then lowered his voice. 'I had nothing to do with sinking your ship. It wasn't me. It wasn't!'

'Then who *was* it?' Nina demanded, anger returning at his prevarication. Was he trying to buy time? She glanced towards the entrance, but nobody was there.

Somebody was approaching from behind, though. Eddie

heard them too. 'Look, I said to give us a few min—'

'This cannot wait,' said a cold Scandinavian voice.

Nina and Eddie whirled – to see Harhund and one of his team from the iceberg. The mercenary leader had a hand in his jacket pocket, the unmistakable shape of a gun's muzzle pushing at the fabric.

'What the hell kept you?' said Miller with relief.

'I had to get my weapons past the metal detector.' The Sky Tower had the same security systems as an airport. 'And then I had to convince someone to let us come through the kitchen.'

The businessman nodded. 'You were right that they'd staked the place out.'

'It was predictable.' He regarded Eddie and Nina. 'Give me the key.'

She opened her hands wide. 'We don't have it.'

Harhund turned to his companion. 'Wintz, search them.'

The other man performed a rapid pat-down of Nina's clothing before moving on to Eddie. 'Ooh-hoo, that *tickles*!' the Yorkshireman cried in an exaggerated squeal. The other diners looked around, Simon giving them a curious glance as he headed for the bar.

Harhund was not amused. 'Shut up!'

'It's not here,' said Wintz, stepping back.

'We didn't bring it with us, dumbass,' said Nina. 'It's somewhere safe.'

'Then you will take us to it,' Harhund replied. 'I was hired to get the coffin, the key and you – and I always complete my contracts.'

Eddie made a sarcastic sound. 'Great. A killer with a work ethic.'

Harhund waved the gun again. 'Get up.'

Nina and Eddie reluctantly stood. Miller's habitual smugness returned, confidence rushing back now he had the upper hand.

'The Chinese kid must have the key,' he said as he rose. 'Where is he?'

Nina frowned. 'How did you know he was still alive? We didn't tell you.'

A flash of panic – which he tried to cover by counter-attacking. 'I *didn't* know, but you just confirmed it.'

Harhund's narrow-eyed disdain, however, told Nina that Miller had said too much. 'Let's go find him.'

'I'll have to phone him to get him to meet us,' she said.

Harhund shook his head. 'No phone calls, no warnings. Just take us to him.'

'I don't know where he is,' she shot back as they started out of the dining area, Eddie in the lead with Harhund flanking Nina behind him. 'We told him to walk around the city so that if anything went wrong you couldn't find him – or the key.'

'We *have* to get the key,' said Miller, perturbed. 'Let her call him.'

'No,' the mercenary replied, eyes fixed on Nina as Simon the waiter rounded the bar, carrying a bottle of wine and two glasses on a tray. 'She is lying, I am—'

Eddie passed Simon – and snatched up the bottle, smashing it against the counter's corner. Shards and liquid flew up into Harhund's face.

He shielded his eyes with his free hand, jumping back – as Eddie grabbed Miller and shoved the broken bottle's jagged end against his throat.

16

'Let her go!' Eddie barked as he backed towards the exit, pulling the taller man with him as a shield. 'Otherwise Donny Dipshit's next drink goes straight through his neck.'

Miller started to struggle, only to freeze as the razor-sharp glass sliced his skin. 'Jesus Christ, he's going to kill me!' he shrieked. 'Do it, let her go!'

Harhund instead grabbed the startled Nina, pushing his hidden gun against her back. 'He is bluffing. Let him go, Chase.'

Alarm from the diners as they saw the confrontation. The waiter hurriedly scrambled clear and took out a phone to call for help. 'I'm not fucking joking,' Eddie warned. Miller gasped as the jagged points drew blood, two hot red lines rolling down his neck to stain his pristine white shirt collar.

'Nor am I.' Harhund nodded to his companion. 'Get her to the car.' Wintz dragged Nina towards the restaurant's entrance. The mercenary leader then drew his gun and took aim – at Miller's torso.

Miller stared at the weapon. 'Uh, Astor, what the hell are you doing?'

Harhund kept his eyes locked on Eddie's. 'Do not worry. I will shoot him dead before he can cut an artery.'

'Yeah, but – but I'm in the way!'

'The bullet will go straight through you, but then tumble and tear organs when it enters his body. You will probably survive.'

'*Probably* doesn't cut it!'

'I'll cut *you* if you don't keep still,' Eddie growled – but the

185

situation was out of control. Despite Nina's best efforts to resist, the other mercenary had hauled her to the doors, and it was now absolutely clear that while Miller had once been Harhund's paymaster, he was no longer calling the shots.

Eddie backed towards the secondary exit. 'Nina,' he said, drawing his struggling wife's attention to him – and giving her a look that after seventeen years together he hoped she would understand. Her small nod told him she did: *distract him*.

'Watch her,' Harhund warned his comrade, detecting the unspoken message but not knowing what it meant. The mercenary held Nina more tightly as he forced the doors open. The Scandinavian advanced, eyes flicking towards movement on the Sky Jump platform before locking back onto the Englishman.

Eddie continued his retreat, giving Nina the look she had been waiting for—

She kicked out hard, catching one of the doors and driving herself back against her captor.

He staggered against the other door, which hit the wall with a bang. Harhund's head snapped around at the noise—

Eddie hurled the broken bottle at the mercenary leader's face.

Harhund lunged sideways to dodge the jagged glass missile – and Eddie propelled Miller at him with a forceful kick. The two men collided and fell.

'Nina, run!' yelled the Yorkshireman as he darted to the other exit. He looked back, hoping she had broken free – but the other man had kept his hold on her.

Harhund recovered, gun rising—

Eddie threw himself through the doorway as he fired. The bullet struck just behind him. He slammed the door shut, then ran down the curving corridor.

Glass walls revealed the Sky Jump to his left, Auckland sprawling beyond it. A woman was outside on the platform, attendants readying her for the drop. Eddie had reconnoitred when he and Nina first arrived; apart from toilets beyond the Sky Jump's entrance, the only accessible exit doubled back to the elevators in the central core. Harhund must have used a service door to enter the kitchens, but the Yorkshireman had no way to open it.

Not that he would even have time to reach it. The Norwegian charged into the corridor behind him.

Eddie barged through the door to the Sky Jump's reception area before Harhund could take another shot at his back. Outside the tower itself was another attraction, the vertiginous Sky Walk circling the entire floor. If he reached it, he might be able to loop round and find another way in, or at the very least evade his pursuer until the authorities arrived.

Another glass door separated reception from the chamber leading to the exterior platform. He hurried to it—

It didn't open.

The exit was locked. A warning sign explained why; it was effectively an airlock, preventing the high winds at almost two hundred metres up from gusting into the tower. Before one door could be opened, the other had to be shut – and the entrance door was still swinging closed behind him.

Harhund raced towards it. A nasty smile as he saw his quarry was trapped—

The inner door clunked shut – and Eddie threw open the exit.

Harhund shoved at the entrance, but it remained closed. A snarl as he realised what had happened, then he stepped back and aimed his gun at the glass wall.

Wind blasted Eddie as he entered the next room. A large piece of machinery occupied it: the descender rig and winch for the Sky Jump itself. Cables ran out above the open exit, in turn leading to pulleys over the end of the launch platform. The woman about to take the jump was still standing fearfully at the edge, two attendants trying to convince her to step off—

Harhund fired. Glass exploded, showering the room with glinting debris. He jumped through.

Eddie sprinted into the open, already knowing that his plan to escape on the Sky Walk was doomed. If he ran along it without a safety line, the constantly shifting wind would knock him to his death. But if he went any slower than a sprint, Harhund would shoot him.

There was only one other way: the Sky Jump itself.

He ran towards the jumper. If he held on to her, he could ride the descender rig to ground level—

An attendant saw him coming and shouted to her companion. He spun, seeing the man charging at him and flinching in surprise – catching the hesitant woman with his elbow.

She toppled over the edge with a scream. Eddie had nowhere to go—

Except after her.

He leapt over the platform's lip. Another bullet seared above his head as he plunged.

One death escaped, but now he faced another.

The wind tore at his face, forcing him to squint, but he couldn't close his eyes. He had only one chance of survival, and his timing had to be perfect. If he missed it, he would be dead in six seconds.

He saw a flailing blue-and-yellow shape sixty feet below. The woman, still in free fall . . .

She suddenly grew larger.

The descender was designed to bring a falling person to a gradual halt without the sudden jolt and rebound of a bungee jump. The cable was slowing her – and now Eddie was rapidly catching up.

He opened his arms wide—

The woman rushed at him – and he tackled her in mid-air.

Her scream became a wail of pure terror at the unexpected

impact. 'Sorry, but I need a ride!' he yelled, hooking his arms around her shoulders.

The buildings of Auckland's CBD rushed towards them. Half-way down and slowing, but not quickly enough. The descender had been set for her weight; Eddie had more than doubled it. Her harness cables lashed at him as emergency brakes kicked in.

The landing zone was on a platform at the tower's base, the tiny rectangle enlarging with frightening speed as they hurtled towards it. A red square appeared upon it, concentric white circles forming a target – a crash mat.

The name was appropriate. Even braking, they were going too fast. If he was still on the woman's back when they landed, he would crush her, breaking her legs, or worse.

A hundred feet up, fifty, thirty – and he let go.

The woman shot away as the descender caught her. Eddie fell the final yards, bracing himself—

He hit hard, rolling as if making a parachute landing to absorb the impact. The mat was padded, but it still felt like dropping onto concrete. Searing pain shot through his left ankle. He cried out, bowling to a stop on the platform's metal deck.

A shocked attendant rushed to catch the screaming woman. Another man ran to Eddie. 'What the hell happened? Are you all right?'

The Yorkshireman staggered up, ankle on fire. 'Yeah, I'm fine. Five-star experience, would recommend it to my friends. You'd better look after her, though.' He limped as quickly as he could down the spiral stairs to ground level, leaving the bewildered attendant to help the crying woman.

Some tourists gawped at him as he reached the street, but his plunge had barely been noticed. Aucklanders paid only passing attention to screams from the Sky Tower. Eddie turned back to the complex of buildings at the landmark's foot. Nina was still inside; he had to rescue her. He hobbled towards the entrance.

★ ★ ★

Wintz dragged Nina to the elevators, the panicked Miller following. 'Get your fucking hands off me!' she snarled, kicking and lashing at the mercenary. He grunted with the blows, but did not relinquish his hold.

Harhund ran out of the restaurant to join them, gun in hand.

'Did you get him?' Miller asked.

'He escaped,' was the frustrated reply.

'What do you mean, *escaped*? We're two hundred metres up!'

'Where is he?' Nina demanded.

'He took the Sky Jump.' Harhund jabbed at the already illuminated elevator call button. 'Mr Miller, you stay here and make up a story for the police. We'll get her to the car.'

'What – what story?' stammered Miller. 'What am I supposed to tell them?'

A shrug. 'You are a smart man, I'm sure you will think of something.'

'Like hell you're taking me with you!' said Nina. She tried to deliver a reverse headbutt to Wintz's face, but he jerked back just enough that she only caught his jaw a glancing blow. He still made a pained noise, which gave her some small satisfaction.

The elevator arrived. 'Get in,' Harhund told her.

'What, or you're gonna shoot me?'

'Yes.' He drew a second gun with his free hand – a Taser.

'Oh, *crap*,' said Nina – as Wintz let go and twin electrified barbs stabbed into her chest.

The Sky Tower's security personnel had responded to the chaos within, uniformed guards preventing people from entering the building complex and hurriedly ushering others already inside through the exits. Eddie cursed as he watched from behind a concrete pillar. There was a good chance the waiter had already given his description to the authorities, and the Sky Jump employees would also have reported him by now. He wouldn't be able to get back in without risking being caught – which meant he would have to wait for his enemies to bring Nina *out*.

At least he knew where they would emerge. Donny Miller didn't strike him as the kind of man who used cabs; he would almost certainly have a chauffeur, and he had noticed a VIP drop-off and pick-up point at the tower's foot. They would have to come this way – he hoped.

A squeal of tyres. He turned to see a black Porsche Cayenne SUV rounding the tower. The rear windows were heavily tinted, but the driver was visible: a man in a dark suit and peaked cap. The vehicle screeched to a halt outside the entrance. The driver jumped out to open the rear door.

Eddie looked towards the building. The passengers must be on their way . . .

Harhund hurried out, flanked by Wintz – with Nina between them. She appeared only semi-conscious, both men supporting her.

Eddie rushed from behind the pillar. Pain flared in his ankle, but he refused to surrender to it. The mercenaries bundled Nina into the SUV, the chauffeur watching in confusion before hurrying back to the driver's seat in response to Harhund's shouted order.

The mercenary leader saw the Englishman running towards him—

Eddie tensed, ready to dodge gunfire – but instead Harhund dived into the Cayenne. 'Go!' he bellowed. Wintz scrambled in after him as the vehicle powered away.

The Yorkshireman swerved to intercept, but his aching ankle slowed him. '*Shit!*' he roared as the escaping Porsche bounded onto the street, making a skidding left turn. He ran after it, reaching the pavement just in time to see it run a red light at a crossroads and swing out of sight to head south.

Despite having no chance of catching up, he didn't slow. He now needed to get clear of the Sky Tower before the cops arrived – which they soon would, sirens rising. He angled across the road, then around a corner. The street ahead sloped down towards Viaduct Harbour to the north.

Walking as quickly as he could, he called Cheng. 'It's me,' he said. 'Listen, they've got Nina.'

'What?' said Cheng. 'Oh no! What are we—'

'Just take the key and get out of the hotel. Meet me at, er . . .' He didn't know the city, and the only landmark he could think of was the Sky Tower itself. 'Meet me at the dock where we went onto the ship. There was a ferry terminal, I'll see you outside it.'

'Are you okay? What about Professor Wilde?'

'I'm fine. Just get there.' He disconnected and continued down the street as more sirens sounded behind him.

An hour later, Eddie saw Cheng nervously approach along the waterfront. As well as his backpack, the young Chinese was carrying the few items Nina and Eddie had left in the hotel room. 'What took you so long?' the Englishman demanded.

'I wanted to make sure nobody was following me,' Cheng replied. 'Do you know what's happened to Professor Wilde?'

'No, and that's worrying, 'cause I would have expected them to call me by now – to exchange her for the key. You got it?'

He nodded. 'Are you going to give it to them?'

'To get Nina back? Course I fucking am.'

Cheng was surprised, even alarmed. 'But . . . but Professor Wilde almost died to keep it from them.'

'Professor Wilde's almost died for a lot of stupid archaeological crap. I've been telling her ever since we met that she's more important, but she never listens.' Eddie saw the younger man trying to hold back a smile. 'What?'

'It's funny, but . . . in her lecture, she said her number one rule is that no archaeological find is worth risking your life for. I suppose she doesn't even listen to herself.'

'Sounds like Nina,' said Eddie, with a half-smile of his own. It quickly faded. 'I don't trust 'em to make a swap without trying something on, though. They need her as well as the key and the coffin. They won't let her go until they've made her do what they want.'

'So how are you going to get her back?'

'That's a bloody good question. I wish I had a bloody good answer!'

'I'm sure you'll rescue her,' Cheng told him. 'You've done it before, after all.'

'Too many times. This needs to be the last.' He frowned in frustration. 'But I can't do anything until I know where she is.'

'Have you tried calling her? She may still have her phone.'

'No, but they just kidnapped her – they're not going to let her put that up as a Facebook update.'

'You said you were waiting for them to call you. Perhaps you should take the first step.'

'Huh. Perhaps I should.' He called Nina's number.

To his surprise, it was answered. It was not his wife's voice, though. 'Chase?' said Miller cautiously.

'Yeah. Where's Nina?'

'She's here, with me.' There was an echoing background noise; the sound of an aircraft in flight.

'Let me talk to her.'

'Ah . . . okay, but before you do, let me tell you what's going to happen—'

'What's going to happen is that I will hunt you down and pull your tongue out via your arsehole if you hurt her,' Eddie growled. 'I've killed richer people than you, so don't think I'm bluffing. Where is she?'

'She's, she's right here. Hold on.' The echo changed as the phone was put into speaker mode.

'Nina, you there?' Eddie asked.

'Eddie! Yeah, I'm here,' she replied.

'You okay?'

'That son of a bitch Harhund zapped me with a Taser, but I'm fine now. They took me to the Miller building and we got a helicopter to the airport. We're in his private jet. Pretty small one, I expected it to be bigger.'

Miller's annoyance at having his planehood disparaged was practically audible. Eddie grinned. 'Where are you going?'

'We're going to Queenstown,' said Miller, reasserting himself. 'And that's where you'll be coming too. Now, wait.'

A pause, then Eddie heard him muttering in the background. 'What's going on?'

'He's called someone else,' Nina told him. 'I'd imagine it's whoever's *really* behind whatever's going on – the person who paid Harhund to raid the iceberg after Donny botched things in Germany.'

'Great, another arse to kick.'

'All right, be quiet,' said Miller irritably. The other conversation had not left him in a good mood. 'Now here's the deal. Chase: you bring us the key. Professor Wilde: you use the key. If it works, we let you both go.'

'What do you want it for?' Eddie demanded.

'To coin a phrase, none of your fucking business.' Miller sounded far too pleased at turning the Englishman's words back upon him. 'Once you—' He broke off in response to something Eddie couldn't hear, muttering again.

'You know,' said Nina with clear amusement, 'I think he's being told off for swearing.'

Eddie laughed. 'Who's he talking to, his mum?'

'That's not important,' snapped Miller, aggrieved. 'Chase,

you get on the midday flight to Queenstown tomorrow. We'll meet—' Another interruption from his other phone. This time, he was sufficiently wound up that his side of the discussion was audible. 'Are you *sure*? You really can't wait one more day— Okay, all right, okay.' A huff of surrender, then he returned. 'We'll arrange a business jet to bring you to Queenstown today. Go to the NjetZ offices at the international terminal; they'll be ready for you. You'd better be on the plane, though.'

'Oh, I will be. Can't wait to see you fist to face,' Eddie said.

'Remember, you bring us the key first. *Then* we let her go.'

'Yeah, I remember. Nina, I'll see you soon.'

'Stay safe,' Nina managed to reply before the call was cut off.

'What happened?' Cheng asked, having only heard one side. 'Is she all right?'

'For now, yeah. But they want the key before they'll let her go. I'm going to fly to Queenstown and make the exchange.' He had already dismissed involving the New Zealand authorities; he couldn't risk being arrested for the trouble at the Sky Tower, and Miller was powerful and well connected, which would make the police hesitant about storming in to carry out a hostage rescue.

Cheng nodded. 'I'll come with you.'

'No you won't.'

'But I—'

'No.' Eddie put a firm hand on his shoulder. 'Thanks for everything, but this is as far as you go. I'm sure Nina'll give you an A – if she gets back to the university.'

'But I can help you!' Cheng protested. 'I'll find out where Miller will be taking her in Queenstown, and—'

'I'll just have to play it by ear. Usually works out – I'm not dead yet. Give me the key.'

Cheng reluctantly produced the pouch. 'I really can help, you know.'

'I'm sure you could.' Eddie checked the ancient artefact was

195

inside it, then shoved it into his jacket. 'But I don't think you'll be able to give me the kind of help I'll need. Now if you could bring me a gun, *that* might be handy . . .'

'I can't do that right now, I'm afraid.' The student sounded genuinely apologetic.

'You get back to New York – and hopefully Nina'll be back in class soon. I need to get to the airport too, so we'll share a cab.' He held out his hand. 'You've done a good job, mate. Thanks.'

Cheng gave him a surprised look, then shook it. 'Thank you, Mr Chase.'

'Call me Eddie. All right, let's get going. Those arses won't kick themselves.'

17

Queenstown, New Zealand

Nina normally had no concerns about flying, but the trip from Auckland to Queenstown left her clutching her seat's plush armrests. The business jet was much smaller than a regular airliner, far more affected by turbulence – and the winds on the approach to her destination, flying through a valley with snow-capped mountain peaks rising high on both sides, were far from gentle.

'Nothing to worry about,' Miller said through his teeth as an especially harsh jolt shook the cabin. 'I've made this flight hundreds of times.'

'Yeah?' Nina said. 'And how many barf bags did you get through?'

He gave her an irate look, then concentrated on holding himself in his chair as the plane touched down with a bone-jarring thud. His sigh of relief was audible even over the roar of the thrust reversers.

A helicopter awaited them when the jet pulled up. Nina shivered as she stepped out; even at ground level, the wind was fierce and bitterly cold. The two mercenaries flanked her as the chopper's pilot came to meet Miller. A short exchange with his boss, then he led the way to his aircraft. Some of the airport's ground crew were not far away, and Nina considered raising the alarm – but Harhund was right beside her, one hand in a pocket. She didn't know if he was holding the gun or the Taser, but nor did she want to find out.

The chopper took off, its flight quickly bringing it past the heart of Queenstown. Nina looked down. The lakeside town sat at the foot of a mountain, a cable car line rising to its cloud-shrouded summit. Even though the weather was far from idyllic, people were still enjoying the water; as well as wind- and kite-surfers, she saw numerous boats blasting across the whitecaps at high speed. New Zealand had a reputation for extreme sports, and its people seemed keen to live up to it.

The helicopter continued along the lake for several miles, then descended towards the western bank as it curved to the north. Mountains rose ahead, but there was a shallower sweep of green land above the waterfront – and on it she saw a lone building. A *big* building, she realised as they approached. A mansion overlooked both arms of the lake. The imposing structure was traditional in style, with high, steep rooftops and exposed wooden beams, but clearly modern in construction; one wing was still being built, steel and concrete behind the facade.

Nina regarded it quizzically as they approached a helipad. It was a large house, sure, but there was far more construction equipment than she would have expected. Several concrete silos, a veritable squadron of earth-movers, portable cabins and pallet after pallet of materials . . .

The helicopter touched down, a large man in a dark suit coming to the aircraft to open the door for Miller. He bent low and scurried from the pad. The two mercenaries followed, pulling Nina between them. They made a beeline for a veranda and went inside.

A tall and severe besuited man in his sixties greeted them,

head tipped slightly back as if snootily regarding the new arrivals – even Miller – down his nose. 'Good afternoon, Master Donny.' His accent was refined English. 'A pleasant flight, I hope?'

'Not really, Broates,' Miller replied, looking faintly seasick. 'Where is she?'

'Waiting for you in her study. She is eager to meet Professor Wilde.' The way he said *eager* made Nina suspect he actually meant *impatient*.

Miller nodded. 'Good, good. Okay, let's go.'

Harhund and his comrade fell in behind Nina as Miller and Broates proceeded into the mansion. Its owner clearly had old-fashioned tastes; the walls were panelled in dark wood and the furniture was all either replica Victorian or actual examples from the era. They also liked it warm, Nina already finding the air uncomfortably stuffy.

The study was a large room overlooking the lake. Broates led the group inside. 'Your son, and Professor Wilde,' he said respectfully.

Within was a wizened old lady in a wheelchair. She sat hunched in the seat, right hand clawed around a control lever. Blue-rinsed hair rose in an elaborate beehive. Her face was pinched, wrinkled not only by age but by attitude. 'About time,' she snapped.

Miller stepped forward, hands raised in apology. 'I came as quickly as I could, Mother.'

'Not quickly enough. And you didn't even get the key!'

'It's on the way. Chase will be here with it soon.'

'As long as you haven't screwed it up like everything else you touch.' She pushed the lever, guiding the chair across the room to stop before Nina. 'So you're Professor Wilde.'

'Yeah,' said Nina, folding her arms. 'And you are?'

The old woman gave her son a withering look. 'You haven't even *told* her?'

Miller couldn't meet her iron gaze. 'I figured the less she knew, the better—'

'Well, you're the expert on knowing less.' Like Miller, her accent was American – Nina placed it as from one of the south-eastern states – but unlike his, there was no influence from her adoptive country. 'Since my son doesn't have the manners to make proper introductions, Professor Wilde, I'll take the burden. As usual.' She glared at Miller before turning back to her guest. 'I'm Eleanor Miller, the founder of Miller & Family. And still having to keep a very hands-on role even though I've officially retired. It's a pleasure to meet you.'

'The pleasure's all yours,' Nina replied, scathing. 'You'll forgive me if I'm not exactly thrilled to meet someone who's kidnapped me.'

Eleanor smiled, a tight-lipped contortion of her lower face that didn't reach her eyes. 'You've got spunk. I like that in a woman.'

'My British husband would be smirking like a teenager right now. So why did you bring me here?'

'Straight to the point, too. Good. Saves time, and at my age I hate to waste it. I'll do you the same courtesy.' She reversed, gesturing at an armchair near the windows. 'Take a seat.'

'That's okay,' Nina replied, not moving. 'I like to stand.'

Malice flared in the wheelchair-bound woman's eyes. 'You watch that tongue of yours, missy. If it gets too sharp, I may just have to blunt it.' She gestured, and Harhund shoved Nina forward.

'Hey!' the redhead said. 'Watch it, asshole.'

Eleanor frowned. 'If there's one thing I can't abide, it's potty-mouth.'

'You'll probably die of apoplexy when you meet my husband, then.'

She shook her head. 'It's a sign of no class. I expected more from a professor. Even one from New York. But anyway.' A dismissive wave, then she continued: 'You want to know why you're here – and why I need the key and the sarcophagus as well.'

'The sarcophagus is here?' Nina asked.

'I'll show it to you soon. Now, what do you know about Miller & Family?'

'The company, or the jerks?'

'Watch your damn mouth,' said Miller angrily.

Eleanor, however, was almost amused. 'You *are* defiant, aren't you? It really must be the red hair.' She said the latter almost in confirmation rather than comment, but Nina had no time to dwell upon it. 'I founded the company almost fifty years ago. I don't expect you to know this, but I have a doctorate, just like you. Although mine is in chemistry rather than,' a twinge of disdain, 'the soft sciences. I prefer learning to have some practical value.'

'If my doctorate didn't have any practical value, we wouldn't be having this conversation right now,' said Nina snippily.

'True, true. But you'd have to admit that the creation of new pharmaceuticals has been of greater benefit to the world than digging up its lost past, wouldn't you?'

She folded her arms again. 'I doubt the victims of thalidomide or Vioxx would agree.'

The sour scowl returned to Eleanor's face. 'Not a single one of Miller & Family's products has ever been recalled, I'm proud to say. Everything I've worked for has been to improve the health of humanity, to increase our lifespan. With great success, I might add. People are living longer than ever before. And that,' she said with a sudden flourish, 'is the problem.'

Nina cocked her head. 'How is that a *problem*?'

'Because, Professor Wilde, it's going to bring about the collapse of civilisation. There are now nearly eight billion people on the planet. Eight *billion*. Twenty-five years from now, by 2050, it will be *ten* billion. They'll all need food. They'll all need water. And houses, and medicine, and fuel, and a hundred and one other things. Competition for resources will change to *fighting* for them – first on a local scale, then nationally, then internationally. I guarantee you that within ten years, we'll see a full-scale war over control of water supplies. Probably between Egypt and Sudan or Ethiopia for the Nile, but it could be anywhere. Wars mean refugees, who add pressure in other countries, and the whole thing spins out of control.'

'You've been reading your Thomas Malthus,' said Nina. 'I know the theory: population growth leads to catastrophic collapse as demand for food outstrips supply. But it didn't happen in the nineteenth century, or the twentieth, because we came up with more efficient ways of producing food. Why would it be different now?'

Eleanor was clearly not used to being challenged on her assertions, nor did she welcome it. 'I know what I'm talking about! I've spent the last twenty years of my life researching it. It *will* happen! Why do you think I moved to New Zealand?'

'For the bungee jumping?'

An angry laugh. 'I'm not the only wealthy person – or *smart* person – to move here. Civilisation as we know it is unsustainable. The crash is coming, believe me. The rest of the world will tear itself apart as everybody fights over the remaining resources, and billions of people will die.'

'But not you? You've built yourself this nice little bolthole and are going to hide out while the world burns?'

'I have a more worthy goal, but yes. This is the ideal place. Isolated, but with resources – water, geothermal power, farmable land. I'll be able to wait out the crash in safety.'

Nina couldn't help noticing that she was speaking in the singular – and her son was aware of it too. However, there was another point she had to make. 'Forgive me for pointing out the obvious, but I don't think you'll be around long enough to do that, however many Miller & Family vitamin pills you take. You're in your eighties, I'd guess? And you don't look in good shape. Another five years will be pushing it, never mind ten or twenty.'

'Hey!' cried Miller, outraged. 'You shut up.'

'She's right,' Eleanor told him. 'Left to my body's own devices, I'd be lucky to last another ten years, even being optimistic. But that's where you come in.'

'Me?' said Nina. 'What, you think I know a way to extend your life?' She tried to cover her unease. In her adventures, she had indeed discovered not one but two separate means of prolonging the human lifespan: one was a rare yeast found in the Pyramid of Osiris deep beneath the Egyptian desert, and the other the Fountain of Youth, hidden behind a trail of clues left by Alexander the Great.

Eleanor, however, had something else in mind. 'No, no,' she said. 'But I believe you can help me *suspend* it.'

'What do you mean?'

The old woman turned the wheelchair to gaze through the windows. 'I realised that prolonging life is worthless if you're going to end up living through hell. So I began an alternate line of research: suspended animation.'

'Like cryogenics?' Nina asked, surprised. 'Freezing people?'

'That was one avenue, yes. There have been numerous recorded cases where people were revived from a state of effective death at low temperatures. But the problem is that no *repeatable* techniques have been found. The risk of cell damage during freezing is too high. I also tried chemical stasis using anaerobic gases, but again, the process is unreliable – at least in any form we've yet developed. It *is* basically filling every cell in the body with poison, after all.'

Nina's unease returned as she remembered the toxic yellow gas that had escaped from the sarcophagus in the frozen fortress. Was that what Eleanor was after? 'But you think you've found a new approach, right?'

'I have.' The wheelchair turned to face her again. 'Several years ago, I was approached by a Chinaman who knew about my interests in suspended animation. He offered me a deal: if I helped him get out of China with a new identity – and a large sum of money, naturally – he would provide me with technical details of China's research in that area.'

'And he gave them to you?'

'He did.'

'But I'm guessing the information wasn't any use, since you still need me.'

'On the contrary, it was *very* useful. So useful that I haven't gotten him out of China yet.' A mean little smile. 'He's far too valuable where he is.'

'I'm sure he's delighted.'

'There's nothing he can do about it. If he raises a stink, he'll be arrested – and boy, is China hard on traitors! But I keep my promises. I'll get him out . . . once I've got everything I need from him.'

'So if he's supplying you with the technology to put yourself in suspended animation,' said Nina, 'why do you need me?'

'Because the Chinese are in the same boat: they can't make it work.' Eleanor's expression became almost conspiratorial. 'They didn't build the technology. They *found* it. Those coffins you discovered in the iceberg? The Chinese found some too. They've had them for nearly fifty years.'

Nina was stunned enough by the revelation to be lost for words. Miller excitedly filled the silence. 'I've seen pictures of the bodies. They look like aliens, but the Chinese did DNA tests – they're related to humans.'

'Very closely related,' added Eleanor. 'But at the same time, different. Meaning there's something about their DNA that lets them use their technology, while we can't.' Her gaze focused laser-like upon Nina. 'At least . . . *most* of us can't.'

Nina realised where she was leading. 'And you think I can?'

'I *know* you can. You brought the ship trapped in the iceberg to life when you touched the key. You're one of the few people in the world with the right DNA profile to manipulate earth energy – or as the Chinese call it, qi.' She pronounced it *tchee*. 'In Chinese mythology, it's a life force that runs through the whole planet. Seems there's more than a little truth to the legend. But you'd know all about that, wouldn't you?'

'Would I?' Nina shot back, challenging – and wanting to find out how much the Millers knew.

'Yes, you would. You found King Arthur's sword, Excalibur – a conductor for earth energy that could cut through almost anything. Then there were the levitating statues that led you to the lost cities of Paititi and El Dorado in South America, the Atlantean spearhead that almost blew up a big chunk of the Middle East, and I suspect some other things you didn't mention to the International Heritage Agency.' Eleanor smiled again, but the only humour behind it was gloating. 'Oh yes, missy. You know.'

'And how do *you* know?' Nina demanded. 'A lot of what I discovered with the IHA is still classified.'

'And which country is one of the IHA's biggest funders through the United Nations?'

She let out a soft moan at missing the obvious answer. '*China*. Of course.'

'They know everything the IHA knows – and thanks to my man on the inside, I know everything *they* know. When it comes to earth energy, at least. But the Chinese know a lot more than the IHA. They know that to activate the technology they found, they need a key. They found one – but then they couldn't find anyone who could use it. Which brings us to you.'

'You want me to use the key to open the coffin,' said Nina. 'But why? What use is a hundred-millennia-old dead body?'

Eleanor laughed again. 'You haven't realised yet? It's not a coffin. The body inside it isn't dead – it's in suspended animation!'

18

Nina stared at the old woman, thinking she had misheard. 'You're kidding.'

'Do you think I'd go to all this trouble for a joke?' Eleanor replied. 'During their nuclear testing, the Chinese discovered a fortress hidden in the Gobi Desert. It was smashed, all the sarcophagi damaged and the people inside them dead, but they also found and translated the records buried with them. They were very clear.'

Despite herself, Nina couldn't help but be intrigued. 'What did they say?'

'The sarcophagi are filled with a gas that suspends cellular functions – and they also use qi, earth energy, to somehow put the whole body into a state of indefinite stasis. My man in China sent me as many technical details as he could, including the gas's chemical formula; I've already had large quantities manufactured. But recreating the sarcophagus has been harder. It requires some kind of crystals that even the Chinese haven't been able to find or duplicate. All the ones they have are broken, useless.'

'So you thought it'd be easier to steal a sarcophagus instead.'

'I wanted more than one.' She gave Harhund a critical stare.

'We were only able to get one before the iceberg broke up,' the mercenary told her, unfazed.

Eleanor huffed. 'Excuses, excuses. I've had enough of them.' Her glower turned upon her son. 'Especially from you, Donny. But I suppose I should be glad I have even one sarcophagus, after you almost wrecked the entire plan before it started.'

'I did what I thought you wanted, Mother!' Miller protested. 'If you'd told me more—'

'I told you as much as you needed to know!' she snapped, making him flinch. 'If I'd wanted you to send people to get the key in Germany, I would have *told* you to.'

'You didn't know what he was doing?' asked Nina.

Eleanor shook her head, still glaring at her contrite son. 'I *wanted* you to get the key, Professor Wilde, so you would follow the trail to the Dutchman in the madhouse, then hopefully get enough out of him to find the iceberg. That way, I would have the key, the sarcophagi *and* you, all in one go. But my idiot boy almost ruined everything by trying to steal it in Hamburg!'

The redhead let out a dismayed sigh. 'So the whole thing was a set-up? Oh, man! Eddie keeps warning me, and I keep stepping right into them!'

'Like I always say, there's book smarts, and there's common sense,' said Eleanor with mocking amusement. 'Just because you have one doesn't mean you have the other. Donny's living proof of that.' To Miller's relief, her gaze finally went back to Nina. 'But I got all three eventually.'

'You haven't got the key yet,' she reminded her.

'I will soon.' She turned the wheelchair and headed for the door. 'I want to be ready when your husband arrives. Broates, show her down to the bunker.'

Broates gestured for Nina to follow. 'This way, please, Professor Wilde.'

'Thanks, Alfred,' Nina replied sarcastically. 'You know you're complicit in a kidnapping, don't you?'

'I have faith in Mrs Miller and her lawyers to successfully navigate the legal system on my behalf,' he replied, with a mocking smile.

Miller, Harhund and Wintz at her back, Nina followed Eleanor and Broates to an elevator. The only buttons inside were for the ground and upper floors – but then the old woman flipped the whole panel open to reveal another behind it. She put her hand on a palm-print scanner, then pressed the lowest button. The doors closed, and the car began to descend.

The ride continued downwards for longer than Nina expected. 'Where are we going, Mordor?'

'I don't merely want to live through the fall of civilisation,' said Eleanor. 'I want to rebuild it afterwards. This bunker isn't just for me – it's for the survival of the whole human race.' The elevator eventually slowed. 'We're now two hundred feet underground. This place can survive a direct nuclear strike. Not that it should need to; I came here precisely because it won't be on anyone's list of targets.'

The doors opened. Broates held the others back so Eleanor could exit first. 'Welcome to my redoubt, Professor Wilde,' she said proudly.

Nina was impressed only by the engineering needed to carve such a place from the mountain's root. Compared to the old-world luxury of the mansion above, this was stark, almost brutal in its use of bare grey concrete. 'Going for Soviet chic, I see.'

'Decoration is not my top priority,' Eleanor said as she led the way down a long, curving passage. Other corridors headed off it; Nina saw an evacuation plan at a junction that revealed the underground complex as a veritable maze. Their location by the elevator was marked by an arrow, but a tunnel at the bunker's opposite end appeared to lead to stairs to the surface. 'All the essentials are in place, though. It's completely self-sufficient for power and water – it has a geothermal generator, and two separate wellheads. Then there's storage for vacuum-preserved food, seed banks, tools, machinery, weapons; everything people will need to rebuild.'

'Weapons, huh? So you're not planning to make a new start preaching peace and love.'

'You can't remove violence from man. If you have something others want, they *will* take it by force – unless you can defend yourself.'

'And conveniently, if someone else has something *you* want and you've got lots of guns . . .'

Eleanor gave Nina a cutting look. 'And then there's the archive. A print and digital library of the sciences, medicine, engineering, our history, our religion – everything worth preserving.'

'*Our* history? Whose exactly?'

There was a patronising tone to her reply. 'The ascent of civilisation in Greece and Rome, the rise of Christianity, the Old World discovering the New, and then through to the present day. Enough for people to see where mistakes were made, and correct them next time.'

'Damn, I'm glad you weren't my history teacher,' said Nina in disdain. 'What about, well, the rest of the *entire world*? The Egyptians? The Chinese? The Aztecs and Mayans and the other pre-Columbian civilisations? What about the rise of Islam? That's had kind of an influence on events for the past fourteen hundred years.'

Eleanor scowled. 'None of that is important.'

'Who are you to decide what's important?'

'The person who built the library! I'm the one preserving knowledge for the future.'

'No, you're *censoring* it. The things you decide are worthless could be of huge value to someone else. If you were really concerned about preserving knowledge, you'd put everything you could in there. Not just dry technical stuff; where's the art, or literature? Music, movies, everyday culture?'

The old woman stopped the wheelchair. 'Are you suggesting I should preserve every trashy paperback novel? Every obscenity-filled rap song? Every self-aggrandising selfie and internet comment?'

'If you can, why not?'

The proposal genuinely angered Eleanor. 'That would be a signal-to-noise ratio so poor, the garbage would drown out everything of value!'

'That "garbage" might tell someone in the future more about our society than any list of kings and queens.'

'Liberal nonsense,' she spat, setting off again. 'Exactly the kind of weak, woolly thinking that's accelerating the collapse, giving equal weight to all sides. It's probably for the best that the end comes quickly, so people have to focus on what's important!' She reached a set of doors, impatiently waving for Broates to open them. 'Now, in here.'

Nina followed her in. The room appeared to be a workshop or laboratory. Doors led off to each side, but Eleanor headed to one opposite: a gleaming metal vault. 'This, Professor Wilde,' she said, anger replaced by triumph, 'is where I will sit out the fall of civilisation.'

There was another palm-print reader on a console before the oversized entrance. She placed her hand upon it. The door slowly slid open with a low growl of motors. Beyond, another large room was revealed, the concrete walls reinforced by steel beams. 'Here he is,' she proclaimed, going to the object at the vault's centre: the stolen sarcophagus. 'The last of the Nephilim.'

Nina stopped in shock. 'The . . . the *Nephilim*?'

'You know what they are?'

'Of course I do! "There were giants in the world in those days" – from the Book of Genesis.'

'Chapter six, verse four,' Eleanor said with a nod. '"When the sons of God came in unto the daughters of men, and they bore children to them."'

'The offspring of angels and human women. They were supposedly cast out by God and imprisoned beneath the earth for all eternity. But why do you think *this*,' Nina pointed at the towering figure inside the coffin, 'is one of them?'

'Because that's what they called *themselves*, according to the Chinese.'

'But the entire myth of the Nephilim originated from the Middle East, not China.'

'You found them in an iceberg that came from *Antarctica*,' the older woman pointed out. 'It seems they got around. According to my contact, the Chinese took the name directly from the records they translated. And I don't mean a transliteration from an ancient text. They had some kind of audio recording.'

'I've seen them before,' Nina said, remembering a Veteres artefact. 'Clay cylinders inscribed by a needle as they rotate, like a kind of primitive gramophone.' She approached the sarcophagus. It stood at a steep angle so its occupant was resting almost vertically. 'They actually used the name Nephilim?'

'Everything else my man has given me panned out. I have no reason to believe he's lying about this.'

She stared up at the indistinct form behind the crystalline cover. 'And you think – *they* think – this guy is still alive?'

'They do, yes. They've spent decades, and a lot of money, trying to rebuild what they found. Not just these coffins either; they found other artefacts as well. But none of them work; they were all broken. Even if they'd been intact, though, the Chinese wouldn't have gotten anywhere. They need a key – which they don't have – and a priestess. Which ditto.'

Nina raised an eyebrow. 'They need a priestess to make their technology work? Just so you know, I haven't been ordained.'

Eleanor smiled thinly. 'I doubt it's the title that matters. It's the DNA. It seems Nephilim men could use some of the items the Chinese found, but all the important matters were jobs for the ladies.'

'*Plus ça change* . . .' Nina walked around the sarcophagus. The section of broken pipe under its base had been connected to a hose running to a long rack of large metal cylinders. The skull-and-crossbones symbol signifying poison gas was prominently displayed upon them. 'When you had the gas manufactured, you brought it *here*?'

'Ready for use. I was hoping to recover at least a dozen stasis chambers; that's why the room's so big. But if one is all I could get, then one will have to do.'

Nina gave Miller a look of sardonic pity. 'I guess you get to experience the apocalypse first-hand while Momma sleeps through it.' His flash of tight-lipped bitterness told her it was not the first time he had thought about it.

A soft buzz sounded. 'Excuse me, please,' said Broates, answering a cell phone. 'Yes? I see, excellent. I'll tell her at once.'

'What is it?' Eleanor demanded.

'Mr Chase is on the way,' the butler replied. 'His plane will arrive at Queenstown in just over an hour.'

'What about the key?' asked Miller anxiously. 'Has he got it?'

'I've been informed he does, yes.'

The younger man was relieved.

Eleanor nodded in approval. 'Good. Donny, you go meet him.'

'You want *me* to go?' Miller said, suddenly concerned again. He fingered the cuts on his neck.

'Take Harhund and his man as well, and some of the security staff. And *don't* let him escape this time.'

'He jumped off the Sky Tower!' was her son's exasperated cry. 'What was I supposed to do, jump after him?'

'If you screw up again, Donny, you might wish you had. Now get moving.'

Miller bit back a rejoinder and instead turned to Harhund. 'Well, come on, then! Let's go.' He strode out, fists clenched. The two mercenaries exchanged dismissive glances, then followed.

Eleanor turned back to Nina. 'I wouldn't consider doing anything foolish now we're alone, by the way. Broates is armed, and very capable.'

The Englishman moved to stand impassive guard beside her.

'Just what you want from a butler,' Nina said acidly. 'A propensity for violence.'

'You never know when it might come in useful. And knowing what I do about your husband, I want as many armed men on my side as possible.'

'It won't be enough.'

'We'll see.' She looked back at the frozen figure. 'And when he arrives with the key, we'll find out all the secrets of the Nephilim.'

'If I agree to help you,' said Nina.

The old woman smiled, painted lips drawing tight like a razor slash across her wizened face. 'Oh you will, missy. You will.'

19

Under other circumstances, Eddie would have enjoyed being the only passenger on a private jet. The NjetZ crew had no inkling of the reason he was flying to Queenstown and did their professional best to keep him happy on the two-hour journey, to the point where just before touchdown he apologised for his curt and unfriendly attitude. They were only doing their jobs.

On landing, he saw others who were also doing their jobs – but these would receive no apologies for the damage he hoped to inflict on them. He had a reception committee: Donny Miller, Harhund, Wintz, and three other men in dark suits with the chunky build and scowling demeanour of private security guards.

The latter, he guessed, worked at the Miller estate. Cheng had used his laptop to show him aerial photos on the cab ride to Auckland airport; Eddie was sure that was his destination, and wanted to carry out a virtual recce. The house was isolated, the landscape bleak and exposed with no trees for cover and the only road through the mountains long and circuitous, but at least he now knew what to expect.

He approached the waiting men. 'Ay up. Been waiting long? Hope you haven't caught pneumonia.'

'Shut up,' snapped Miller. The businessman wore an expensive padded coat, but still looked cold and miserable. 'Where's the key?'

Eddie reached into his leather jacket. Harhund immediately brought up his right hand inside his own coat pocket. The Yorkshireman saw the shape of his gun clearly, even through the fabric, but also something else; every other man bar Miller reacted similarly. They were all armed. 'Here,' he said, slowly taking out the waterproof pouch.

'Open it.'

He did so. Orichalcum gleamed within. 'Happy?'

'Give it to me,' Miller snapped, clicking his fingers.

Eddie slapped it down hard on his open palm, making him flinch. 'Where's Nina?'

'We're taking you to her. Don't worry, she's safe. We need her. You? Not so much, but while I'd like to kick you out of the chopper mid-flight, you've still got some uses. Like making sure your wife does what she's told.'

'Good luck with that. I've been trying for seventeen years!'

One of the guards chuckled.

Harhund was not amused. 'Move.'

A helicopter waited nearby. The men put Eddie in the centre-rear seat before surrounding him. Harhund sat to his right, pressing his gun against the Englishman's side. 'Try anything and I will shoot you,' he said.

'I preferred the service on the plane,' Eddie sighed.

The helicopter took the group past Queenstown and along the lake. Their destination was indeed the Miller estate. On landing, they were greeted by another thick-necked security guard and escorted into the mansion. Miller led the way to a lift, pushing the call button. The doors opened. 'After you,' he said with mocking politeness.

Harhund ushered Eddie inside, a jab from his gun telling the Yorkshireman to stop in the centre. 'Face the door,' he said as first the guards, then Miller filed in. Eddie reluctantly turned. Both mercenaries took up position behind him, guns fixed upon his back. Two of the guards stood side-on to keep their own watch on the prisoner, the remaining pair flanking their boss.

Miller opened a panel and put his hand on a scanner, then

pushed a button. The lift began its descent – a long one, Eddie soon realised. They were going deep underground. How far? He listened to the keening song of the elevator cables, and watched Miller. He would know how long it took to reach the bottom . . .

Which would be Eddie's only chance to act.

The lift continued downwards, the steel lines whining faintly outside – then their pitch shifted as the machinery began to slow. At the same moment, Miller straightened, readying himself to exit. The four guards took their cue from him, relaxing slightly in anticipation of the end of their claustrophobic journey.

Eddie turned his head slightly, glancing back and down at Harhund's gun arm. The pistol had drifted fractionally from its original position; it was still pointed at his back, but now more to the side than directly at his spine—

He threw himself backwards, twisting and sweeping his right arm to drive the gun away from him as he collided with the Norwegian. Harhund pulled the trigger as he hit the cabin wall. The gun fired – the sound deafening in the confined space, as powerful and disorienting as a stun grenade.

Eddie staggered, but was first to recover. For once, his partial hearing loss – the result of far too many close encounters with gunfire and explosions – worked in his favour. The other men took a second longer to regain their senses—

That was enough.

He whirled and smashed his left elbow into Wintz's cheekbone, knocking the mercenary down into the corner, then spun back to drive his other elbow into Harhund's stomach. The Scandinavian let out a breathless gasp as he doubled over. Eddie tore the gun from his hand. He belatedly realised that one of the guards had fallen, hit by the bullet. Another round took a second man down in a grisly explosion of blood across the metal wall. Miller screamed at the noise of the shot mere inches from his head.

The doors opened. His own ears still ringing, Eddie snatched the pouch from the reeling businessman's hands, then threw him against the remaining guards and stabbed at the control panel as he barged out. The doors rumbled shut behind him. A mechanical whine came from beyond them as the elevator started to ascend, taking his captors with it.

Panting from the sudden burst of violence, he turned – to see Nina.

Any relief vanished when he realised she was not alone. An old woman in a wheelchair was beside her – and behind his wife stood a tall, supercilious-looking man. 'Mr Chase,' said the woman. 'Good afternoon. Now, drop your gun. My butler has one of his own pressed into your wife's back.'

Eddie didn't move, assessing his chances of taking down Nina's captor. Slim; the butler was using her as a shield. 'Who are you?' he said instead, stalling for time.

'Eleanor Miller,' came the reply, faintly affronted that he didn't know.

'Oh, Donny Dipshit's mum.'

A purse-lipped smile. 'He's been called many things, sometimes by me, but that's a new one.' Her eyes went to the pouch. 'Mr Chase, there's no need for violence – well, further violence. I only want the key. Perhaps Professor Wilde could explain?' She turned to Nina.

'Perhaps I could say hi to my husband first?' Nina fired back. 'Eddie, are you okay?'

'Yeah,' he replied, not taking his eyes off the butler, who watched the Yorkshireman with equal intensity, waiting for the first micro-flash of movement that would signal an impending attack. 'The lift was a bit crowded, though. What about you?'

'Oh, super-fine. Eleanor here's been telling me about her plans to set herself up as the next Queen of Thunderdome after civilisation ends by putting herself into suspended animation.'

'She looks more like Davros to me,' he said, indicating the wheelchair, before fully registering what she had said. 'Wait, suspended animation?'

'The creature inside the sarcophagus from the iceberg isn't dead,' said Eleanor impatiently. 'It's in a state of stasis. The key can be used to open the sarcophagus and resurrect it – or close it and restart the suspension process.'

'That's what she thinks, anyway,' said Nina. 'What she's pinning her chances of survival upon.'

'There's one way to find out, isn't there?' Eleanor told her. 'You have to use the key.'

'Nina's the only person who *can* use it, right?' said Eddie, glancing at the old woman.

'That's right.'

'Then . . . you can't risk anything happening to her, can you?' He looked back at the butler, readying himself—

'Before you do anything foolish,' Eleanor said, her voice taking on a commanding tone, 'bear in mind that I'm still alive despite being confined to a wheelchair for almost twenty years. Broates's gun is pressed against the base of your wife's spine. She probably won't die if he shoots her there – but do you want her to live the rest of her life like me? Knowing it was your choice that crippled her?'

Eddie hesitated – and Eleanor smiled. 'You have two choices: cooperate, and you'll both get to see your little girl again. Or . . . well. I always get what I want. One way or another.'

The Englishman looked at Nina. They both knew there was no way out of the stand-off without one or both of them being shot. 'Buggeration and fuckery,' he muttered.

Eleanor glowered. 'Gutter language. Now, are you going to put your gun down?'

Eddie tossed it aside angrily. 'I suppose you want this thing too.' He threw the pouch to the floor in front of Eleanor's wheelchair. 'There. Get it yourself.'

'I don't like your sense of humour, Mr Chase. Professor Wilde, pick up the key.'

Nina did not respond immediately, prompting Broates to jab her with his gun. 'Do as Mrs Miller says.'

She reluctantly picked up the pouch and opened it. The key rested inside, precious metal reflecting the harsh overhead lights.

Eleanor eagerly craned her neck to see. 'Good,' she said. 'Good!' She turned, gesturing down the passageway. 'Well, what are you waiting for? Let's wake our guest.'

20

By the time Nina, Eddie, Eleanor and Broates reached the chamber housing the sarcophagus, Miller, Harhund and the other men had come back down in the elevator and caught up, guns drawn. Miller glared at Eddie. 'Why is he still alive?'

'Because I need him,' said Eleanor. 'Which is something I often wonder about with you.' She waved for the newcomers to lower their weapons, then moved to the great crystalline coffin at the room's centre. 'Although I have a better use for him than a mere hostage.'

'Just don't ask me to do any sex stuff,' Eddie told her. 'You're not my type.'

Her face crinkled in disgust. 'Has anyone ever told you that you have the attitude of an especially unpleasant teenage boy?'

Eddie grinned. 'Been hearing it from Nina ever since I met her. She still married me, though. Dunno what that says about her tastes in men.'

Nina sighed. 'I'm still questioning them.'

'Broates, bring me the key,' said Eleanor. The butler took it from Nina and handed it to the old woman. 'Thank you. Now that I *finally*,' a pointed glance at Harhund, 'have the key, the sarcophagus and Professor Wilde, we can find out if the Chinese theories were correct.'

'If they're not, a lot of people have died for nothing,' Nina told her.

She didn't reply, instead dismissively turning to face the sarcophagus, arms outstretched to bring the key to the matching recess in its base. Broates moved to assist her, but she waved him back. 'I want to do this myself,' she said, straining to slot it into place. 'There!'

The frisson of anticipation amongst the observers quickly turned to disappointment when nothing happened. 'It's not working,' said Miller.

'Of course it isn't,' snapped his mother. 'Do you ever listen to a word I say? It needs somebody with the proper DNA profile to activate it – someone of Atlantean ancestry.' She gave Nina a probing look. 'Or Nephilim ancestry, perhaps.'

'You think the Atlanteans are descended from the Nephilim?' Nina replied dubiously.

'The Chinese think it's highly likely, based on their genetic testing.'

'Seems like pointing out the obvious, but Nina's not ten feet tall,' said Eddie.

'Probably a result of cross-breeding over hundreds of generations,' Eleanor said, gazing up at the figure inside the coffin. 'The human genes controlling the physical form became dominant. But there are more important questions to answer right now. The first is: can a human be put into stasis in this sarcophagus?'

'I guess you'll find out for yourself in a hundred years,' said Nina.

A thin smile – with a hint of cruelty behind it. 'Do you really think I'm going to climb into an ancient contraption filled with poison gas without knowing if it works? Somebody else will test it first.' She pointed a bony finger at Eddie. 'Him!'

Miller's expression brightened. 'And if it kills him, nothing lost!'

'If it kills him, we'll have to seriously rethink the plan,' Eleanor chided. 'But everything provided by my Chinese source suggests it should work. So Professor Wilde will get that,' a flick of her hand at the frozen figure, 'out of there, then we'll prepare Mr Chase for the experiment.'

'Like fuck you will,' Eddie growled.

Harhund stood before him and brought up his gun again, while Wintz and one of the security guards moved to flank the Englishman.

'You should be honoured,' said Eleanor. 'You'll effectively become humanity's first time traveller, skipping over the period in stasis. Assuming you survive, that is.'

'I don't even know how to make that thing work!' Nina protested.

Another nasty smile slit the old woman's face. 'Having your husband inside should give you an incentive to learn quickly.'

Eddie shook his head. 'Typical. After fighting loads of evil billionaires, we finally met one who was half decent, then the next one's right back to being evil!'

'I resent that,' Eleanor sniffed. 'Wanting to ensure that humanity doesn't disappear from the world like the Nephilim is anything but evil.'

'The ends justify the means, huh?' said Nina.

If she had hoped to land a stinging rebuke, she failed.

'Always,' the older woman replied. 'History has proven that over and over. You of all people should know, Professor. Decorum and timidity achieve nothing – only strong, decisive action gets results.'

'And if anyone's killed in the process, it's just their tough luck?'

'There are people who shape history, and people forgotten by it. I intend to be one of the former. Now, use the key to open the sarcophagus.'

'Wait!' Harhund said urgently, glancing towards her. 'The gas will leak—'

Eddie saw the mercenary's momentary distraction – and leapt at him.

He collided with Harhund, both men reeling as he tried to grab his weapon. The gun went off—

The round lanced past the Englishman – and hit one of the gas tanks.

The bulbous cylinders were thick steel, strong enough to resist a bullet impact, but the shot struck the valve assembly on its end. It fractured a hose connector – and a shrieking jet of highly pressurised gas burst free.

Wintz threw himself clear, but the yellow rush caught the unprepared guard. He staggered, choking on the toxic miasma.

An alarm blared, amber warning lights flashing. Harhund retreated fearfully from the expanding cloud, Eddie moving with him – then letting go to deliver a punishing kidney punch. The Scandinavian fell. 'Nina!' the Yorkshireman cried, running for the exit.

She sprinted after him, weaving past Miller and the remaining guard, but their adversaries quickly overcame their shock. Guns came up—

Eddie shoved Nina sidelong as they cleared the chamber's entrance. Shots tore through the opening behind them, hitting the console beyond the doorway. 'Through here!' he cried, heading for one of the lab's side exits.

'We've got to get to the lift,' he said as he hurried through the next room.

'They'll shoot us before we reach it,' Nina replied. 'But I saw a plan of the bunker when I arrived – there's another way out!' They ran on through the underground maze.

'Shut the door!' Eleanor cried as Broates pushed her out of the chamber at a run. 'Switch on the extractors, vent the gas!'

The butler hurried to the control panel – only to look up in alarm. 'It's not working!'

She saw the bullet holes in the console. 'You *idiots*!' she shouted at her men, before glaring at the side exit. 'They must be trying to reach the emergency stairwell. Get after them! *Now!*'

Wintz and the last guard raced in pursuit. Harhund and Miller, though, headed for the main corridor. 'Where are you going?' she demanded.

'Are you *kidding*, Mother?' Miller said, jabbing a finger back at the roiling poison. 'I'm getting away from *that*!'

'I suggest you do too,' Harhund added as they exited.

Broates hurried to Eleanor. 'Mrs Miller, I can't stop the gas from spreading. You *must* get out of here. Quickly!' He pushed her after the two men.

Miller and Harhund charged through the bunker to the elevator. Behind them, more alarms sounded: the toxin was spreading through the ventilation system to other rooms. 'Come on, come on,' Miller gasped as he stabbed at the call button. 'Come *on*! We were the last people to use it, why the fuck isn't it—' The doors slid open. He rushed inside, Harhund joining him.

'Donny! Wait!' They looked back to see Eleanor, Broates propelling her at a straining run. 'Hold the door!'

Miller reached out to stop it from closing – then caught Harhund's eye. A pause, mixed emotions crossing his face . . . and he stepped back.

Eleanor's own expression was one of disbelief. 'What are you doing? Donny! Hold the door!'

He said nothing, remaining motionless – until the doors started to close again. He held up his hands in a shrug as if there was nothing he could do as metal slammed shut between them.

She stared at the elevator, speechless, before exploding in anger. 'You little *shit*!'

Broates quickly turned her around. 'I'll get you to the emergency stairs.' He pushed the furious old woman back down the corridor.

★ ★ ★

'This map you saw,' Eddie said to Nina as they ran pell-mell through the concrete warren. 'Don't suppose you remember any details from it? 'Cause I think we're lost!'

'The other exit was at the opposite end to the elevator,' she told him. 'If we keep going this way, we should reach it. Eventually.'

'Be just our luck if it's at the end of a five-mile tunnel!' They reached a T-junction. 'Okay, which way?'

Nina looked in both directions, seeing numerous doors, but neither option appeared preferable. 'Uh . . . left?'

Over the spreading cacophony of alarms, Eddie heard a shout behind them. 'We'll try it.' They set off. 'So this whole place was built for Eleanor to sit out the apocalypse? Why's it so huge?'

'She was planning to preserve all human knowledge down here – at least, the parts she thought were worth keeping. So it's got archives, tools, weapons—'

'Weapons? Why didn't you bloody say so? These are all storerooms!' The doors they passed bore signs, but in her hurry, Nina hadn't read them. Eddie glanced at the next as he ran past. 'Seeds – not much use!'

'Maybe these?' she suggested. There were three more doors ahead before the passage made a right turn.

But the labels told them the rooms' contents were no more use than the seed bank. They rounded the corner – only to stop in dismay. 'Shit!' said Eddie. It was a dead end, a last door in the far wall thirty feet away. 'We'll never get back to that junction before they catch up.'

'Eddie, wait!' Nina cried, hurrying onwards. 'You want weapons? Here you are!'

The door's sign read *Arsenal*. 'Hope it's not just because Ellie supports the Gunners,' he said, joining her. He tried the door, and was surprised when it opened. 'What, they don't even lock their fucking gun room?'

'Eleanor meant for everyone down here to be asleep,' Nina pointed out as they entered. 'But they only recovered one sarcophagus. And maybe she planned to lock up properly before entering stasis.'

'Still slack. Works for us, though!' The walls were lined with hundreds of metal drawers. Eddie pulled one open at random. 'All right!' he said, taking out an M16, the US Army's standard infantry weapon. 'Now just need some ammo . . .'

He opened more drawers nearby, but found only guns, all lacking magazines and ammunition. 'This is no bloody good!'

Nina joined in. 'Guns, guns, guns – but no frickin' bullets!' She reached for another handle, then paused: bullets would be stored in large quantities, a heavy load, so most likely were in the larger drawers at floor level. She tried one, and was relieved to find it full of neatly packed cardboard boxes. 'Got them!'

Eddie shook his head. 'They're nine mil – I need five-point-five-six. And a mag.' He opened more drawers himself. 'Nine mil, nine mil, fifty cal . . .'

A noise over the alarms: running footsteps. Getting louder.

'Someone's coming!' Nina cried, trying more drawers.

More nine-millimetre ammunition, shotgun cartridges—

'Yes!' Military-issue cases stencilled *5.56 mm*. She pulled one open and withdrew a card sleeve holding thirty gleaming rounds. 'Got the bullets!'

'Magazine?'

'Oh, God *damn* it!' She hurriedly gave him the bullets before yanking open more drawers. 'I can't find any!'

They were out of time. Their pursuer rounded the corner, pounding towards the arsenal—

Eddie tore a bullet from the sleeve and pulled back the charging handle to open the rifle's chamber. He pushed the round inside and tipped the weapon slightly upwards to minimise the chance of a slamfire – an accidental weapons discharge – then thumbed the bolt release.

Clack! The handle sprang back into place. No slamfire. The M16 was ready for action.

But he only had one shot.

And the guard had heard the unmistakable sound of the bolt closing. He ran into the room, gun raised—

Eddie whipped up the rifle – and fired.

The bullet hit the guard's chest just as he pulled his own trigger. The impact threw off his aim, the pistol round clanking into a drawer beside the Yorkshireman. The man spun, blood spouting from both the pencil-width entry wound and the much larger exit wound in his back, and fell nerveless to the floor.

Ears ringing, Eddie exhaled. 'Shit! That was close.' He picked up the fallen man's SIG Sauer P320. 'Get another bullet,' he told the wincing Nina.

'What for?'

'For you. I've got this,' he waved the pistol, 'so you can have this.' He held up the rifle.

She collected another round, then joined him. 'There's no magazine – it'll still only have one shot.'

'One shot's better than none.' He quickly reloaded the M16. She reluctantly took it. 'Okay, we took a wrong turn somewhere. Hopefully the other way isn't a dead end too!'

They ran back towards the junction as more alarms sounded.

Broates had taken a different route from Nina and Eddie, pushing Eleanor into a machine room. 'If I remember correctly, this service passage cuts behind the archive wing and leads almost directly to the emergency stairs,' he said as he let go of the wheelchair and went to a door. 'We can get ahead of Professor Wilde and Mr Chase. I'll deal with them.'

'Good,' Eleanor replied. 'But keep her alive if you can. I still need—'

He opened the door – and reeled as dirty yellow gas rushed through it.

Eleanor pulled back on her chair's control stick in fright as the butler collapsed. 'Broates!' she cried, but the cloud had already rolled over the convulsing man. A new alarm sounded as sensors in the machine room detected the contaminant; the service passage, intended only as a conduit for water pipes and electricity cables, had not been similarly equipped.

Panic rising, she spun and retreated at top speed, the chair's motors whining. With the shortcut blocked, she now had to navigate the whole underground maze to reach the other exit.

An exit with no elevator, only stairs.

To Nina and Eddie's relief, the other route beyond the junction led deeper into the complex. They entered a wider corridor that curved away into the distance. 'It's got to be this way,' said Nina, panting. The wail of alarms faded behind them. 'And we're clear of the gas; now we've just got to—'

An echoing gunshot – and a red-hot spike tore through her left arm.

Eddie whirled to see Wintz in a doorway a hundred feet away. He snapped off a shot, forcing the mercenary back into cover.

But they were completely exposed in the stark concrete passage. 'In here!' he shouted, pushing Nina to a nearby door. Another bullet impact blasted stinging cement fragments at his head as they rushed through.

The new room was a large archive, tall shelving racks filled with countless white-spined hardback volumes. Nina crashed against the long shelves, clutching her wounded arm. 'I'm fine,' she gasped.

'Let me see.' She winced as she lifted her hand. There was

some blood, but the bullet had only clipped her. 'It'll need treating, but you'll be okay. See if there's another way out, I'll hold him off.'

'Eddie—'

'Just go!' He returned to the doorway, watching for Wintz—

The mercenary was already running towards him.

'Shit!' Eddie threw himself back as more bullets slammed into the door frame. He loosed a couple of suppressing rounds to force the other man to swerve, then scrambled away from the entrance. 'He's coming! Is there another exit?'

Nina ran down the aisle, reference volumes flicking past on both sides. She reached its end – and found the wall ahead was an unbroken barricade of books. 'Oh, crap!'

'I'll take that as a no!' He heard motion outside and sent another shot through the doorway. A thump and a grunt as the other man flattened himself against the wall.

That gave him a few extra seconds. But he had nowhere to go, trapped in the archive. And the rising cry of alarms warned that the gas was still spreading. If Wintz pinned them down until it reached the door, they were dead . . .

He had to take the mercenary down, fast – which meant drawing him into the archive. He shouted at the top of his voice: 'Nina! Get out of that back door, now! I'll be right behind you!'

Praying she wouldn't instantly blow his ruse by yelling '*What* back door?' he ran a short way, then used the shelves as a ladder to climb onto the top of the stack. The ceiling was mere claustrophobic inches above him. He slid over so Wintz wouldn't see him when he entered, then waited. Faint steps outside – then the mercenary darted through the door.

Eddie glimpsed the top of his head as he swept his gun from side to side, seeing no sign of his prey. Wintz hesitated, then headed deeper into the archive.

The Yorkshireman slid quietly to the edge. A shot to the back was hardly sporting, but survival trumped honour – and Wintz wouldn't hesitate to do the same to him.

The mercenary passed him. Eddie swung his legs over the edge, finding a narrow foothold on a shelf and easing himself out—

His boot slipped.

He clawed at the shelving's metal top, but found no purchase – and fell.

He made a hard and painful landing, toppling backwards. Wintz spun at the unexpected noise, his weapon aimed at chest height before he realised his target was sprawled on the floor.

The gun came down at Eddie's head.

21

Triumph filled Wintz's face as his finger tightened on the trigger—

A shot – but much louder than a handgun.

A bloody fist-sized hole exploded in Wintz's torso, white books nearby suddenly splattered with red. Mouth gaping, he fell against the racks. Nina stood behind him, smoke curling from the M16's barrel.

A moment of horror at what she had just done, then she dropped the empty rifle and hurried to her husband. 'Are you okay?'

'Yeah,' he said as he got up. 'He didn't shoot me – I just fell on my arse. Fuck's sake. Can't believe I ballsed up the landing!'

'You're fifty, not twenty,' she reminded him, before adding with a faint smile: 'You're lucky you didn't break your hip!'

'Ha fucking ha. Let's find that bloody lift.'

They hurried into the main corridor. The sound of alarms followed as they ran. 'How much gas does she *have*?' Eddie asked in disbelief.

'Enough to preserve herself and anyone else with her for as long as it took,' Nina replied. The corridor's end came into view, a large red-painted door in its wall. 'Think that's the way out?'

'Either that or the world's most inconveniently placed toilet.'

'You know, Eleanor was right. You really *are* a teenage boy at heart—'

She broke off at an echoing shout from behind. It was Eleanor herself, but her cry was not one of anger or threat – it was a desperate plea for help. The matriarch rolled at full speed after them, wheelchair twitching and juddering as she fought to keep it under control.

'What the hell's *she* still doing here?' said Eddie.

'I think Donny's speeding up his inheritance,' Nina realised. 'He must have taken the elevator up without her.'

'Stop, stop!' Eleanor wailed, frantically waving at them. 'Please help me! I—'

Her other hand twitched on the joystick as her weight shifted – and the wheelchair veered sharply. The turn threw her against the armrest. The chair tipped, rocking on two wheels . . . then overturned, pitching the old woman onto the concrete. She shrieked in pain—

Then in terror. Gas roiled from a vent not far behind her. 'Help! Help me! *Please!*'

Eddie looked at Nina. 'Should we?' She didn't need to speak for him to know her answer. 'Oh, sometimes I fucking *hate* being the good guy! Get the door open!' He ran back down the passage as Nina rushed to the exit.

The cloud's hazy edge rolled ever closer to Eleanor. She tried to drag herself away, but lacked the strength to do more than slither clear of the wheelchair.

Eddie reached her, holding his breath – and hoping the poison was not absorbed through the skin. He scooped her up as yellow tendrils reached her feet. She was shockingly light, useless legs withered to sinew and bone. He raced back towards the corridor's end.

Nina reached the door. It had a handprint scanner like the elevator. 'Eddie, it's locked!'

'Aren't you glad you saved me now?' Eleanor rasped. 'Hurry up and get me to the door!'

'I'm not your bloody butler,' he replied. A glance back. The grimy yellow cloud swallowed the wheelchair. 'You just get your bony hand ready!'

'Come on, come on!' Nina shouted. 'Quick!'

'Oh great, now I've got it in stereo!' Eddie complained as he arrived. There was no time for gentleness or even courtesy; he flipped Eleanor's legs downwards, one arm around her lower chest to support her as he brought her to the scanner. She gasped, but pressed her hand against it.

An agonising pause – then a hefty bolt retracted. Nina hauled the thick barrier open. A bare concrete shaft lay beyond, stairs sloping upwards at a steep angle. The top was an alarming distance away. 'We've got a hell of a climb!' she said.

Eddie threw Eleanor over his shoulder in a fireman's lift, ignoring her angry protestations as he started up the stairs. 'And I thought living eight floors up was bad enough when the lifts are out.'

'It's good for your butt, though,' said Nina behind him, regarding said body part.

The old woman made a disgusted sound. 'Please, spare me.'

'We already did,' Eddie reminded her. 'You want me to leave you here?'

'You'd regret it. You'll need my handprint to open the top door as well.'

'Does the rest of you need to be attached to it?' Eleanor fell silent.

The forced pace of the ascent was exhausting. Nina looked back. Amber warning lights flashed at the bottom of the shaft; the gas had reached the emergency exit. But the climb's end was in sight. Leg muscles burning, they finally arrived at a landing. Another door awaited them, this time a large steel one set in reinforced concrete. Eleanor's bunker had been built to withstand even the most determined intruders.

'Okay,' Eddie wheezed. 'Get this . . . bloody thing open.' He slid Eleanor down.

Even though she had not been running, the jolting journey had left her breathless. 'Just a moment,' she said between inhalations. 'I need some air.'

'You can get it outside,' Nina said impatiently. 'It won't be fresh in here for much longer!'

Eleanor clenched her jaw in annoyance, but slapped her hand on the scanner. The great door began to slide aside.

'Where does it come out?' Eddie asked, regaining his breath.

'At the foot of the mountain,' she replied. 'The estate was a sheep ranch. The old farmhouse is still there. It's ruined – but there's a hatch inside it.'

'What're we going to do when we get out?' Nina asked Eddie.

'I'm thinking it'd be best for everyone if we got the hell out of here and went home to New York with as little trouble as possible,' he replied, giving the woman he was holding a look of meaningful menace.

Eleanor scowled, but nodded reluctantly. 'Agreed.'

Nina glanced back. 'The key's still down there, though.'

'Well, let it bloody stay there!' her husband exclaimed. 'Besides, you'd need a full hazmat suit to get it out now.'

'And how long will it take for someone to rustle one up? They could get the key *and* the sarcophagus – then this whole thing would start all over again.'

The door opened far enough for them to slip through. Eddie checked the room beyond, a small bare space with a ladder running up one wall, then carried Eleanor in. 'Maybe we should get the IHA involved.' He looked up the ladder. 'There a lock on this hatch?'

'Just a bolt on the inside,' Eleanor told him.

'Okay. Nina, you go up first and open it, then I'll bring her out.'

Nina ascended the ladder. The bolt was set into the hatch's underside, and moved easily. The same could not be said of the hatch itself, a solid piece of cast metal. She climbed higher and pressed her shoulder against it, using both legs for maximum leverage to lift it.

A cold wind blew in. Dusk had fallen, just enough light in the leaden sky for her to pick out the ruined building around her. She forced the hatch up and climbed out, shivering as chill gusts caught her.

Eddie, bearing Eleanor over his shoulder, climbed up behind her. 'There any more cars at the house? I don't want to walk all the way back to Queenstown.'

'Yes, two,' the old lady told him. 'And there's also the helicopter.'

'Donny's probably taken it already,' said Nina. 'I can't imagine he'll want to stick around.'

'Donny!' Eleanor snapped. 'That ungrateful little—' She scowled. 'He left me to *die*!'

'You can give him a nice surprise by turning up while he's delivering your eulogy,' Eddie said, picking his way over rubble to a collapsed section of wall. The lake was a pale swathe of reflected sky against the dark mountains, the mansion's lights lower down the hillside. 'Through here. We can get back to the house.'

He clambered over the tumbledown wall, Nina behind him. 'I don't know how we're going to—'

'Don't move.'

The words were snarled, venom behind them. Eddie and Nina froze at the cold click of a gun's hammer. Harhund rounded a pile of rubble, Miller lurking behind him. 'I *told* you we needed to check the emergency exit,' said the latter, voice tinged with both triumph and nervousness. 'Where's Broates?'

'Dead, thanks to you,' Eleanor shot back.

'Oh? Well, good,' her son said with unconvincing bravado. 'I never liked him. Patronising bastard.'

'Enough,' said Harhund. 'We found them, so now we kill them.'

Nina faced Miller. 'I don't think you'll get to claim your inheritance if your mother has a bullet in her head.'

'That . . . that's a good point,' Miller replied. 'Okay, new plan. Go back into the bunker. Harhund, once they're inside, you pile rubble on the hatch so they can't open it again. If the gas doesn't get them, they'll starve.'

Eleanor glared at him. 'You don't even have the guts to lay a single stone on my grave yourself? Donny, you're a disgrace. I've never been more disgusted with you in my entire life.'

'Yeah, well,' he stammered back, 'it doesn't matter now, does it? I'm finally free of you. The company's mine, and—' his voice rose an octave, 'and I won't have you telling me what to do any more!'

She shook her head. 'Pathetic. You're still a child, Donny. A weak, cowardly child. Enjoy running the company while you can – with you in full charge, I doubt it'll last a month before being torn apart by predators.'

'We'll see. We'll see.' Miller gestured angrily at the trio. 'Go on, then! Get into the bunker.'

'Like hell we will,' said Nina.

Harhund flicked his gun towards the hatch. 'Go back inside or I will shoot you right here. I will count to three.' He aimed the gun at Eddie's heart. 'One, two—'

His head exploded.

A spouting fountain of gore sprayed across the broken stones as a high-powered rifle round punched through the back of Harhund's skull, a blizzard of lead and bone fragments erupting from his face and dragging pulped brain matter in their wake.

Eddie was the first to recover, pulling Nina down with him.

The shot's angle told him it had come from lower on the hillside, and the sound of its firing belatedly reached him; not the sharp crack of gunfire, but muffled, like a sheet being torn. The weapon was suppressed, hiding the sniper's position.

Miller stayed standing, staring in horrified shock at the headless corpse. 'What – . . . holy shit!' he cried. 'What the *fuck*? What, what—'

'Get down, you idiot!' said Eleanor. 'Do I have to tell you how to do *everything*?'

He scrambled behind a collapsed wall, panting in fear.

Nina was almost as terrified. 'Who the hell did that?'

'Dunno, but they did us a favour.' Eddie slid Eleanor to the ground and crawled to a small gap in his cover. He was all too aware he was risking his life – even in the low light, the sniper might spot the movement, and if they were using a night-vision or thermal scope he would stand out as brightly as a flare – but he had to know who they were facing.

Not the local police, that was for sure. Several shadowy figures were making their way up the hill. All wore black clothing, faces masked. They also carried weapons, the sky's grey sheen reflecting faintly from gunmetal.

He drew back. 'Whoever they are, they'll be here in a minute,' he said. 'At least six armed men.'

'Can we get away?' Nina asked.

'With that sniper down there, they'd pick us off before we got fifty yards.' He went to Harhund's body and took the gun from his still-twitching hand.

'You're gonna shoot it out with them?' asked Miller in disbelief.

'No, but I want to stop them from walking right up and killing us without a fight.' He checked the remaining rounds, then moved to a new vantage point. 'Get back behind the biggest wall, see if you can—'

'Professor Wilde! Mr Chase!' A woman's voice, accent revealing she was not a native English speaker. 'We are here to help you. Please show yourselves.'

Nina blinked in surprise. 'They knew we were here?'

'Better that than they're just randomly walking around New Zealand looking for heads to blow off,' said Eddie. He raised his voice. 'Who're you?'

'We are here to help,' the woman repeated.

Eddie took another peek through the wall, seeing the black-clad figures spreading out to flank the ruined cottage.

'You and Professor Wilde will not be hurt.'

'And what about the Millers?' Nina asked.

There was a conspicuous silence.

'Oh shit,' gasped Miller. He scrambled to Nina and put a beseeching hand on her shoulder. 'You've got to help me!'

Nina looked back at him, eyes hard. 'Why?'

The younger man had no answer to that.

'I would have to agree with her,' Eleanor said icily.

The new arrivals reached the ruins. Eddie gave Nina a look of concern, then slowly stood. Harhund's pistol was in his hand, but he kept it at his side. Sub-machine guns snapped up at him – but the closest figure, the woman, gestured and they were lowered again. 'You do not need the gun,' she said.

'Need and want are two different things, as I've told my daughter about twenty million times,' he replied. 'I'll keep it until I know what's going on. Unless that's going to be a problem?' He put an edge of threat into his voice.

The masked woman's eyes narrowed, but she shook her head. 'No. I understand that you do not trust us.'

Nina joined her husband. 'So who the hell *are* you guys?'

Two more figures had caught up with the others during the conversation. One was the sniper, carrying a long-barrelled rifle with a telescopic sight. The other, trailing behind him, was unarmed, and noticeably fatter than his companions. The woman stood back to let the second man approach. 'He will tell you.'

The newcomer took a moment to recover his breath before pulling off his mask. Eddie and Nina both reacted in shock.

It was Cheng.

'Sorry it took so long,' he said with a smile. 'But I told you I could help.'

22

China

Nina stared frostily at Cheng across a table in the business jet's cabin. 'So everything you've told me, everything you've done, was all part of a plan to get hold of *this*?' She held up the resurrection key.

Cheng met her gaze, albeit decidedly shamefaced. 'I'm afraid so, yes.'

The group that had saved Nina and Eddie was a Chinese special forces team, which after securing Eleanor and Miller sent members in full hazmat gear into the bunker to plug the gas leak and recover the key and the sarcophagus. Once brought back to the surface, the artefacts were taken to a waiting boat, then the entire group travelled back to Queenstown. The jet, a spacious Cessna Citation Longitude with a Chinese registration, awaited them at the airport; somehow, passengers and cargo all boarded without a single official check. Nina had no idea how that had been arranged, but she doubted the entire customs staff could have been bribed, so it seemed more likely that they had orders from above to let them pass. Diplomatic dealings, faked instructions or high-level corruption? She didn't know, and her rescuers remained tight-lipped.

The flight, Cheng told her, would take over twelve hours. She had plenty of questions, not least why they were being taken to China at all – while they were not technically being *forced* to make the journey, unlike Eleanor and Miller, their new travelling companions had made it clear they would not accept a refusal – but she was also exhausted from the frenzy of the previous day. Reluctantly, she and Eddie used one of the cabin's private berths to find restless sleep.

Now it was morning, and they were cruising high over the endless rocky deserts of western China. Cheng shifted awkwardly before continuing. 'I didn't find the key on the dark web myself. Chinese intelligence spotted it, and bought it from Krämer – but without someone of the correct bloodline, it was useless.'

'So you thought, "Hmm, who do we know who's got Atlantean DNA? Oh, right, the woman who discovered Atlantis! Let's trick her into helping us!"' Eddie said sarcastically.

The young Chinese's discomfort increased. 'Ah . . . yes. We paid Krämer to cooperate and gave the key back to him, then I did everything I could to convince you to meet him in Hamburg. We were sure that if you got the key, you'd be intrigued enough to talk to Stapper in Holland, and then, if he gave you any useful information, follow it to the iceberg.'

'You knew about the iceberg?' Nina asked. 'Why didn't you just find the fortress yourselves?'

'Krämer didn't know which iceberg it was. We sent someone to talk to Stapper,' he glanced down the cabin at the rescue team's female leader, now named as Major Wu Shun, 'but all he did was babble about demons. We already knew what they really were, of course.'

'The Nephilim.'

'Good band,' said Eddie. 'Preferred the Sisters of Mercy, though.'

Cheng gave him a puzzled look, then nodded to Nina. 'The sleeping giants. We found one of their buried fortresses during our nuclear tests.'

'Yeah, Eleanor told us.' It was Nina's turn to glance down the cabin. She and Eddie had stayed in luxury up front; the Millers were in considerably less comfortable compartments at the rear. While the jet was supposedly a commercial charter aircraft, it seemed its only client was the Chinese government – whose operatives might occasionally require an onboard cell.

Wu Shun had apparently been eavesdropping; now she joined them. She had changed from her black special-ops gear into civilian clothing, but even that seemed stiff and formal on her. 'We are very interested to learn how Eleanor Miller knew about it,' she said. 'The discovery of the Nephilim is one of China's most closely guarded secrets.'

'She said somebody who knew she was researching suspended animation sold her the information,' said Nina. Too late, she registered Eddie's subtle warning look: *don't tell them anything*. She cursed inwardly. While the couple were not literal captives like the Millers, right now they might as well be.

Luckily, she had not revealed anything the Chinese did not already know. 'Yes. We are investigating,' Wu told her. 'She did not tell you a name?'

'No, sorry.'

Wu regarded her impassively. Nina looked back, sizing her up. To have become the leader of a special forces unit at a relatively young age – she doubted Wu had yet reached thirty – meant she was dedicated both to her career and to the Chinese state. She couldn't tell if the major's cold, hard exterior was a necessary defence in a male-dominated environment, or her natural personality all the way through.

'We will find out soon,' Wu eventually said. She returned to her seat without a further word.

'She's got a lovely smile,' Eddie said quietly. Nina gave him a quizzical glance; Wu's mouth had been resolutely downturned. 'Problem is, she keeps it in a jar under her desk.'

Cheng chuckled – then froze as if worried Wu had overheard. But the Chinese officer showed no reaction.

Nina's own smile quickly vanished. 'So you did all this in the hope that I'd find the fortress and activate the key for you,' she said to Cheng. 'How long have you been planning it?'

'Ever since we got the key,' he replied.

'Stapper was rescued, what, four months ago?' He nodded. 'Wait, the semester started less than two months ago! Were you already enrolled, or did someone throw a lot of money around to get you a place?'

'I'm afraid it was the money thing.'

Nina did not hide her disapproval. 'So somebody who actually wanted to be an archaeologist lost their place so you could play international spy?'

'I really *do* want to be an archaeologist!' he insisted. 'I was going to study in Beijing. But when we found the key, you were the only person we knew who could activate it, based on your experiences with Excalibur and the vault in Turkey – so we came up with a plan to get you to do that.'

'Good plan,' Eddie scoffed. 'It almost got us killed – it almost got *you* killed.'

'And other people *did* die because of it,' Nina added angrily. 'Their deaths were your fault!'

Cheng was abashed. 'I'm . . . I'm sorry. But it did work. So . . .'

'So here we are. You got this,' she tapped the key, 'you got an intact sarcophagus complete with occupant – and you got me. Now what are you intending to do with your new collection?'

He had still not recovered from her verbal lashing, keeping his eyes lowered. 'We want you to open the sarcophagus so we can learn how it works. We found several like it in the Gobi, but they were broken, like all the other Nephilim technology. The theory is that the crystals were damaged by neutron radiation, but nobody knows for certain. But now we have an intact sarcophagus, we can find out.'

'What do you want it for?' Eddie asked.

Cheng looked up at him. 'If we can put people into suspended animation, we can send them into space, to other planets! And there are many medical uses too. A critically wounded person can be put into stasis until they reach hospital, or someone suffering from a disease could be frozen until it can be cured.'

'All very noble,' said Nina scathingly. 'And what about the *other* technology you found? If it's like what was in the iceberg, some of them are weapons. Do you want to use the key to make them work too?'

Before she could press him further, the plane's engine note changed. Wu approached them. 'We are coming in to land,' she announced, collecting the key. 'Take your places.' Cheng's laptop was on a table across the aisle; he switched seats with a hint of relief. Wu returned to her own position.

Annoyed, Nina peered through the window at the vast expanse of the Gobi. Other than a single road angling across the pale brown landscape, there was no sign of human activity. 'That's a whole lot of nothing out there,' she said. 'Where are we?'

'That is classified,' Wu intoned from down the cabin.

'I'm not asking for GPS coordinates, just a general idea.'

'Professor Wilde has agreed to help us,' said Cheng. 'There's no reason why we can't be polite hosts.'

Wu frowned at him, then spoke in Mandarin. After a brief exchange with the student she withdrew, irate. Cheng smiled.

'Do you outrank her or something?' Eddie asked.

'No, no. I'm not in the military. But the research into the Nephilim is a scientifically led project, and I'm a member of the archaeological team.' His smile became almost bashful. 'And it helps that my mother is in charge of it.'

'Your mother?' said Nina, a thought coming to her. 'Wait – your family name is Hui, so . . . is your mom Dr Hui Ling?'

He nodded with enthusiasm. 'She is. You've heard of her?'

'Yeah, but not for a while. She wrote several papers about comparative mythology that I used as reference for my graduate thesis, which was – God, nearly twenty-five years ago. I haven't seen any new work from her for a long time, though.'

'She's been very busy here. She started work on the project seventeen years ago, and became its director ten years ago.'

'So you grew up where we're going?' said Eddie.

'Mostly. My father stayed in Xi'an, so I travelled between them. But then he, um . . .' His lips pursed. 'He left, so I stayed with her. I grew up at the base.' An overly casual shrug. 'It's probably why I wanted to become an archaeologist, huh?'

'I know all about sharing your parents' obsessions,' Nina said quietly.

An uncomfortable silence followed, which Cheng broke. 'Anyway! Look over here – that's the city nearest to us.'

Nina and Eddie leaned across the aisle to see. Visible in the distance was a grey sprawl against the sandy brown, endless ranks of tower blocks surrounding a core of mirror-walled skyscrapers. 'Big place,' said the Englishman. 'What's it called?'

'Xinengyuan.' He pronounced it *khu-seen-ang*. 'The name means "New Energy City" – it'll be a showcase for renewable energy and solar power when it's finished.'

'It's not finished? But it's massive!'

'It's still being built. In five years, there'll be eight million people living there.'

'How many are there now?' Nina asked.

'About . . . ten thousand.' He seemed almost embarrassed by the admission.

'A ghost city?' She had seen photographic examples in the past of the peculiarly Chinese phenomenon of newly built megacities with barely any inhabitants, but thought changes in government policy had ended the *Field of Dreams* approach to urban development: *if you build it, they will come.*

'It will be ready for them,' Cheng insisted. 'I've been there, it's very cool. It has the world's second-largest indoor ski run!'

'Only the second-largest?' said Eddie with wry amusement. 'I thought China wanted to be number one at everything.'

'The Arabs built a bigger one right after it was finished.' The fact seemed almost a personal insult to the young Chinese man. 'We're going to Cangliang air force base, about forty kilometres away.'

The plane banked, slowing further as it continued its descent. The pilot's voice came over the cabin speakers; Cheng translated. 'We're about to land. You need to put on your seat belts.'

Nina and Eddie did so.

There was little to be seen of the airbase itself as they approached. Two tall rings of wire-mesh fences with guard towers dotted along their length enclosed thousands of acres of barren sand. Occasional masts and towers of indeterminate function were the only other structures visible until after the jet touched down and began to taxi. The heart of the base finally swung into view. A tall control tower, hardened hangars, fuel dumps and warehouses, banks of grim barracks; military functionalism was much the same anywhere in the world.

The plane took them to an area somewhat detached from the central complex. Apart from a water tower and a large bank of electrical transformers, the only structure was a squat concrete bunker. 'We're here,' said Cheng, standing as the plane halted. 'Come on.' He gathered his belongings and headed for the exit.

Eddie and Nina followed. They descended the steps to see Cheng embracing a woman; several other people, a mix of civilians and military personnel, waited behind her. 'Professor

Wilde,' said Cheng, 'I'd like you to meet my mother – Dr Hui Ling.'

Hui extended her hand. 'Professor Wilde. It is a very great honour to meet you.'

'You too, Dr Hui,' Nina replied, shaking it. The Chinese woman was around fifty-five, small in stature with her greying hair cut in a bob, her eyes alert and intelligent. 'Your papers were an inspiration for my own early work.'

'Really?' Hui smiled, pleased. 'We must find time to discuss archaeology in general later. But we have a more specific subject for now.' She looked down the plane's length, where a forklift was unloading a large crate containing the sarcophagus.

'The Nephilim.'

'Yes. Cheng has told you, then. Good; that will save time.' She turned to the Chinese officer beside her, a stocky, stern-faced man of about Eddie's age. 'This is Colonel Commandant Wu Jun, the military commander of this base.' The slight emphasis on the word *military* was clearly intended to differentiate her side of the work from his.

'Colonel Wu,' said Nina, receiving a stiff, formal handshake. His features were oddly familiar – then the reason came to her. 'You're Major Wu's father?' She glanced back at the special forces leader.

'Yes,' Colonel Wu replied gruffly. 'I very proud of my daughter.' He struggled with even those few English words.

Hui continued to make introductions, ending with a moon-faced middle-aged man. 'And our translator, Zan Zhi.'

'Good to meet you, Professor Wilde,' said Zan.

'And you.' Nina shook his hand before turning back to Hui. 'But it doesn't seem like you need a translator – you all speak English.'

Hui laughed. 'Zhi does not translate English. He translates *his* language.' She gestured at the crate as it was carried towards the bunker. 'The language of the Nephilim!'

Nina remembered what Eleanor had told her. 'How much have you translated?'

'I will show you. Please, come.'

Nina was about to follow her when a commotion at the plane caught her attention. Donny Miller, hands cuffed behind his back, struggled with three of the Chinese commando team. 'Fuck you! Let me go, you slant-eyed bastards! I'm still a US citizen, and a rich one too – you have no idea of the amount of shit that's going to come down on you!'

Two other men carried Eleanor out behind him. She was not cuffed, though they held the frail old woman in such a way that there was little she could do to resist. 'Donny!' she snapped. 'At least show some dignity. You're a Miller; behave like one.'

'Fuck you, Mom!' he shouted back.

It was plain from her affronted expression that her son had never spoken to her like that before – at least not within earshot.

'I bet that's been about thirty years coming,' said Eddie.

Colonel Wu gestured impatiently to the Millers' escort. The pair were frogmarched towards the bunker.

'What are you going to do with them?' asked Nina. She had no love for either, but the People's Republic of China was not a nation with a kid-glove reputation for the treatment of prisoners.

'We find out who give them classified information,' he replied. 'We interrogate them.'

'Interrogate?' Miller yelled. 'Bullshit – they're going to torture us!' He shouted pleadingly to Nina. 'You can't let this happen!'

To their mutual surprise, Eleanor let out a small laugh. 'You're going to torture my son? Well, that saves me the trouble.'

'*Mother!*' Miller cried, appalled.

The commandos hauled the pair through the entrance.

Hui spoke quickly to Nina. 'I'm sorry. We should have waited until you were inside before taking them from the plane.' The comment was addressed as much to the facility's commander as the redhead.

'*Are* you going to torture them?' Nina demanded.

The colonel eyed her coldly, but his daughter was the one who replied. 'They are responsible for espionage against the People's Republic. The United States has in the past abducted Chinese nationals, even senior government officials, accused of similar crimes against America. We are following your example.'

'You didn't answer my question.'

'We will get truth,' said Colonel Wu, his curt tone making it clear further discussion of the matter was over. He turned and headed inside.

'Nice to meet you too,' Eddie called out to his retreating back.

His daughter shot him a disapproving glare.

'My apologies, Mr Chase,' said Hui. 'We did not mean to ignore you.' She shook his hand. 'Now, please come inside. We have a lot to talk about.'

A bank of elevators was set back inside the bunker's entrance. The sarcophagus and the prisoners had already descended; Hui called another lift. 'I will give you the background on our discoveries,' she said. 'If I tell you something Cheng has already mentioned, please stop me.'

Nina nodded. 'Go ahead. I'm very interested to hear the full story.'

'China began nuclear tests in this region in 1964. It was while examining the crater left by a test in 1976 that something incredible was discovered.'

'The buried fortress?'

'Yes. A structure twenty metres beneath the sand, constructed from materials unknown at the time. It contained several sarco-phagi made of the gold alloy now called orichalcum, thanks to your discovery of Atlantis; a harder metal we call adamantium – my son chose the name—'

'From Wolverine's claws,' said Cheng, with a slightly embarrassed smile.

'—and a crystalline substance,' Hui continued. The elevator arrived, and everyone filed in. 'The occupants of the sarcophagi were all dead, but as the records we recovered were translated, it became clear they expected to be revived.'

'Has everything been translated?'

Hui nodded towards Zan. 'We are as fluent as we can be in their written and spoken languages. Zhi is an expert. I am . . . fair. Cheng is better.' Her son grinned. 'But we also have a computer program that can translate.'

'You've heard them talk?' asked Eddie.

'As well as inscriptions, there were audio recordings of the Nephilim voices.'

'Clay cylinders that use a needle and a metal cone for recording and playback, right?' said Nina.

'Yes. Did Cheng tell you about them?'

'No, I've seen them before.'

Hui was surprised. 'You have already found a Nephilim site?'

'Not Nephilim,' Nina told her. 'I knew them as the Veteres. They weren't the same species as the occupants of the sarcophagus, though. They were smaller, more slender.'

'And they looked like space aliens,' Eddie added.

Nina fought the urge to sigh.

However, Hui nodded. 'We have theorised that the modern image of a spaceman is an ancient racial memory of the Nephilim. We do not know for sure – but it is more likely than aliens coming to earth in flying saucers.'

The Yorkshireman was disappointed.

His wife couldn't resist smiling at him. 'Told ya.'

The elevator stopped. 'We have also analysed the technology found in the structure,' Hui went on as the doors opened. 'It was all damaged beyond repair, but we still learned much from it. We could not replicate any of its functions, though – until recently.'

She led the group into a lobby area painted in an institutional pale green. A security barrier stood a short way beyond the elevator bank, armed guards watching their approach. Hui merely waved at them, and the barrier opened. Corridors led off in different directions, but she headed for a set of large doors straight ahead.

'How were you able to get it to work?' said Nina. 'And if you did, why do you still need the key, and me?'

'We still could not make it function. But we repaired some items. We think the key now *will* make them work – if you are willing to help us.'

'Well, we'll see,' said Nina. 'You'll need to convince me to trust you. I don't like being deceived.' A pointed look at Cheng, who wilted a little.

'I apologise,' his mother told her. 'But we did what needed to be done. As we did with what you are about to see.' They reached the doors, Hui entering a code on a keypad before opening them. She led them into a large, brightly lit chamber.

'Why, what am I—' Nina began – before halting in shock.

She had seen the object it contained before.

23

The room was occupied by a slightly flattened sphere, over twenty feet across. Its skin of red-tinted gold gleamed under the banks of overhead lights. A door was open in its side, revealing tantalising hints of what lay within.

It was the vault she had discovered in Turkey, a repository for one of the Atlantean spearheads, the crystalline bombs trapping particles of antimatter within. It had been buried beneath a hilltop overlooking the ancient city of Gobekli Tepe; the Atlanteans had hidden a doomsday weapon on the doorstep of the rival civilisation that could be activated by an emissary of Atlantis should its adversary pose a threat – and only be *de*activated upon total surrender, the alternative being complete destruction.

How it had been removed from the hillside was a worrying mystery in its own right. The Turkish government had grudgingly allowed the International Heritage Agency to oversee the site's excavation – but the night before the IHA was due to begin work in earnest, the entire hilltop was dug out and the vault removed. Since it weighed in excess of twenty tons, the effort needed to carry out the raid would have been phenomenal.

There were few groups in the world with the necessary resources . . . but the Chinese government was one of them.

'You!' Nina cried accusingly. '*You* stole the vault from Turkey!'

'We did,' Hui admitted. 'After the IHA became involved, China, as the agency's biggest source of funding after the US, was informed of what you had found. We immediately realised the crystals inside it were the same kind used by the Nephilim – but these were intact. We *had* to have them. So an operation was carried out to bring the vault here.'

'Hell of an operation,' said Eddie. 'How would you even move that thing?'

'Three heavy-lift helicopters were flown to Turkey by air freighters,' said Wu. From her matter-of-fact attitude, she had been involved in the operation, perhaps even planned it. 'Excavators broke into the outer vault, then the helicopters lifted it out. We had to rent a Russian freighter to fly it here; it was too big to fit into any of our own aircraft.'

'And you did it all in one night. I'd be impressed, if I wasn't appalled.' Nina folded her arms. 'This thing is dangerous!'

'We have taken all possible precautions,' insisted Hui. 'And with the spearhead gone, it poses no threat. Let me show you.'

She went to the vault's door. Nina followed her inside. One difference from her previous visit was instantly obvious: the crystals, then alive and glowing with earth energy, were now inert, dull and clouded.

Another was more alarming. Sections were missing, parts of the crystalline pillars running from floor to ceiling cut away to expose the metal behind. 'What did you do?' she demanded.

'We used them to repair the damaged Nephilim artefacts,' Hui replied. 'Successfully, we believe, but we have been unable to test them.'

'Why not?' asked Eddie, entering behind them.

'Because they haven't got anyone with Atlantean DNA to activate them,' said Nina in realisation.

'What, out of every single person in China? I know it's rare, but it's still something like one person in every hundred, isn't it? And China's got, what, a sixth of the entire world's population?'

'The DNA profile is extremely rare amongst Han Chinese,' explained Hui. 'We are quite ethnically homogeneous. It is a strength that gives us unity – but in this case it hinders us. Other races in China may possess it in greater numbers, but this is a top-secret project. Even if we found someone with the DNA profile to channel qi, the only way to test it would be to have them try to activate a piece of Nephilim technology. That would require bringing dozens, even hundreds of civilians here. It is too great a security risk.'

'So you decided to get *me*, huh? Great.' Nina turned to exit.

'That makes *us* security risks too,' Eddie muttered as they left the vault.

'I know.'

Cheng had not heard the exchange inside, and greeted the redhead with puppyish enthusiasm. 'It's amazing, isn't it, Professor? And we know how the Atlanteans got it to Turkey. The vault can levitate!'

'And I can float on a cloud of my own farts,' Eddie said sarcastically.

'It's true!' Cheng protested. 'The Nephilim records describe what they call vimanas. It's an ancient Sanskrit word, it means—'

'Flying machine,' Nina cut in. 'We know, we found one in the Vault of Shiva in the Himalayas. It was just a glider, though.'

He shook his head, eager to correct her. 'No, no. The Hindus took the word from the Nephilim! It can also mean "flying palace" or "flying castle" – and the Turkish vault was one of them. The Atlanteans somehow flew it to Gobekli Tepe. The fortress we found in the iceberg might have got there the same way.'

'So it really *was* a UFO?' Eddie said dubiously. 'As in, literally an unidentified flying object?'

Nina looked back at the vault, seeing it in a new light. 'We *have* seen things levitated by earth energy,' she said. 'Big things, like the Sky Stone. That was the size of a house.'

'The Sky Stone?' Hui asked.

'A meteorite found by the Atlanteans. Earth energy let it levitate against the planet's magnetic field. Certain people, Atlantean priestesses, could also use it to channel and direct huge bolts of earth energy. They intended to use it as a weapon, but it went catastrophically wrong.'

'How so?' said Cheng.

'Remember how Atlantis dropped into the sea?' Eddie told him. 'There you go.'

'That's what you get when you try to turn things you don't understand into superweapons,' said Nina. 'Hard to think of a bigger example of hubris. Although people keep trying to beat it.' She gave her hosts a pointed look.

Wu merely frowned in return. Hui, on the other hand, became defensive. 'This technology has far more uses than weapons! It is a non-polluting source of power. No more coal, no more oil, no more nuclear. That is why we are so determined to unlock the past – to build a new future.'

'With China controlling the technology, of course.'

'If America had it, they would do nothing different. Nor would Britain,' Hui added to Eddie.

The Yorkshireman snorted. 'If we had it, I guarantee we'd hand most of it straight over to the Yanks in exchange for a better trade deal on haggis and strong cheese, then privatise the rest and flog it off for a tenth of what it was worth.'

'This technology can change the world,' Hui insisted. 'If we can make it work. Professor Wilde, *please* hear us out. I am sure we will be able to convince you to help us. Not only for China, but for the rest of the planet.'

Nina did not answer, instead turning at someone's approach: Colonel Wu, accompanied by two soldiers. He spoke to Hui and his daughter in Mandarin, then issued a command.

'Come this way, please,' said Hui, starting for an exit.

'Where are we going?' Nina asked.

'To see the sarcophagus. To meet our . . . guest.'

'That doesn't sound ominous or anything,' rumbled Eddie as they followed.

Colonel Wu led the way through a minor maze of corridors. He strode past a door, but Hui stopped at it, calling out to him. He gave her an impatient reply, but halted. 'I wanted to show you this,' Hui told Nina, entering a code to open the door. 'It is our main archive.'

'It's very cool,' Cheng added with enthusiasm.

Nina and the others followed them in. He was right; it *was* impressive. The archive contained bank upon bank of relics, presumably recovered from the buried Nephilim fortress. She recognised some immediately: fired clay cylinders inscribed with fine lines, the same kind of primitive audio media used by the Veteres.

Also on display were hundreds of clay tablets. Many were damaged, but still intact enough for her to make out what was written upon them. It was a mixture of languages; some were in the elaborate Veteres alphabet, while others used the more angular proto-Atlantean script cut into one side of the resurrection key. The switch between the two seemed to have taken place over a long period – some of the ancient records revealed intermediate states. The Nephilim had developed their own system of writing over time.

Eddie took an interest in something more sinister. 'Ay up. They've got some of those spears over here.'

Nina came to look. The weapons were like those she had seen frozen inside the fortress's armoury, long golden rods with seed-shaped metal pods on one end, carrying chains running half their length. One of the pods had been dismantled, the components laid out inside a glass case. 'What are they?'

'We call them qiguns,' said Hui. 'Somehow they release raw earth energy.'

Nina looked more closely at the pieces. Inside the golden cover was a fragment of crystal and a sliver of purple stone, contained inside a spiralling cage of dark metal. Ordinarily she would have been dismissive of Hui's words, but she had just minutes earlier mentioned the Atlanteans' attempts to do the same thing. 'Are you sure?'

'That's what their own records say,' Cheng told her, gesturing towards the tablets. 'We don't know how they work, though. We've never been able to activate them.'

'But you've tried, eh?' Eddie noted acerbically, moving on to examine a clutch of trikans. The golden discs had their long blades retracted, the oversized weapons stowed in their metal handgrips. 'I bet Macy'd love to play with one of these.'

'I'm glad she can't,' Nina replied. 'She'd probably take somebody's arm off!'

Colonel Wu gave a brusque command. Hui reluctantly ushered everyone back to the door. 'The colonel wishes us to move on.'

They resumed their trek through the underground complex, reaching another room. One half was a laboratory, computers ready for a new round of scientific analysis, and a large high-definition screen on one wall; the other was a glass-fronted isolation compartment containing the canted sarcophagus. Numerous cameras and sensors overlooked the crystal coffin from a lighting rig resembling that of an operating theatre.

The colonel spoke to Zan, the translator nodding obsequiously. He collected a laptop, which he plugged in on a bench at the armoured glass wall. 'He is going to test our translation program,' Hui told Nina.

'I thought you said it worked?'

'It does – based on the records we found. But we need to know if it will work with a real Nephilim subject.'

Nina stared at the shadowy giant behind the crystalline cover.

'You want to wake him up? Rather – you want *me* to wake him up?'

'You can do it, Professor,' said Cheng. 'You powered up the fortress in the iceberg, so you must be able to do this as well.'

'It's not whether I *can* do it that matters, it's whether I *want* to do it!' she objected. 'For one thing, this guy's been frozen for over a hundred thousand years – his body might be preserved, but for all we know, his brain's turned to mush. For another thing, I really don't like being used. Sorry to be blunt, but for all your talk about changing the world for the good of humanity, I still don't trust you.'

Her hosts' expressions darkened, none more so than Colonel Wu's; his understanding of English was apparently better than his ability to speak it. The only exceptions were Cheng, who seemed mortified at the criticism, and his mother, now pensive. The colonel was the first to respond. 'Professor Wilde,' he said, voice stern and utterly cold. 'You will use key to wake the creature.'

'I will not,' she replied firmly.

The commander scowled, unused to direct disobedience. His daughter spoke for him. 'If you do not do it voluntarily, we will make you.'

'What're you going to do, drag me in there and force my hand onto the key?' said Nina. 'That might start the process, but it won't finish it. If it's anything like the vault from Turkey, getting it to do anything more than power up takes an active effort of *will* – I have to control it, guide it with my mind. And y'know, I need to be in a good mood to do that.'

'Like emptying the dishwasher,' Eddie noted from beside her. '*So* not helping.'

Wu was unimpressed. 'Then we will force you to cooperate.'

Eddie sighed. 'Let me guess. Torture? Been, seen, done.

Won't be the first time – and I've got the drill scars to prove it.'

'We do not need to torture you. We have something more effective.'

She spoke to one of the soldiers, who went to a door across the lab. He entered, speaking briefly to another man, then they both came back out – with someone else between them.

Macy.

The breath froze in Nina's throat at the sight of her daughter. 'Oh shit. *No*,' she gasped, gripped with terror.

Eddie's response was more vocal, murderous rage in his eyes as he spun to face the Wus. 'If you hurt her—'

'That is up to you!' the younger officer barked. 'Do as we say and nothing will happen to her.'

Macy's expression as she emerged had been one of relief at seeing her parents, but it now turned to confusion and alarm. Her toy trikan was in one hand; she clutched it more tightly. 'Mom? Dad? What's going on?'

'What are you *doing* here, Macy?' Nina cried. 'Why aren't you with Olivia and Holly? Are they okay?'

'Yeah – of course they're okay,' was the bewildered reply. 'What do you mean, what am I doing here? You told me to come!'

Nina ran to Macy and hugged her. 'Oh my God, my God! I didn't tell you to come here! I wanted you to stay in New York, where it was safe!'

Eddie joined them, fists clenched and giving Macy's two escorts a glare that promised instant and painful retribution if either interfered. Both men retreated, slightly. 'What did you do to her?' he snarled at Wu.

'Nothing,' the Chinese woman replied. 'She came with the permission of her guardians. Lam Chi,' she glanced at the man in civilian clothes who had been with Macy, 'met her at the airport and travelled with her.'

Eddie's gaze snapped to him. 'Did he hurt you?' he asked Macy, straining to control his fury.

She shook her head. 'No, he looked after me on the plane. Dad, what's going on? Why were you so surprised to see me?'

Nina gave Wu a hostile look of her own. 'I think we're owed an explanation.'

Wu seemed about to refuse, but her father said something to her with a small shrug. 'Very well,' the major said instead. 'I will show you.'

She logged into a computer. 'Here,' she said, gesturing at the large wall screen. 'Watch.'

The screen lit up. Nina saw . . . herself.

The frozen image appeared to be from a computer's webcam, her other self looking directly into the lens. Inset into one corner was a smaller picture of Macy; it was a recording of a video call. Nina didn't recognise the background. It looked like a hotel room, but not one she had stayed in recently. Confused, she watched as Wu started playback.

'Hi, honey, it's me,' said the Nina on the screen. 'Are you okay?'

The inset Macy replied with a smile. 'Yeah, Mom, I'm fine. What about you? Are you in New Zealand now?'

A pause, longer than Nina would have expected to allow for transmission delay, then her doppelgänger spoke again. 'No, we had a change of plan. We discovered something amazing – in China.'

'China? What did you find?'

Again there was a slightly over-long pause before the reply. 'I can't tell you over an unsecure line. But it's amazing. Daddy and I want you to fly here and join us. We're going to get a friend of ours, Lam Chi, to meet you—'

Wu paused playback. 'We convinced your grandmother to let Macy go with Lam.'

Nina was still staring at the frozen image. 'That's not me. It's not me! I never said any of that.'

'But it *was* you, Mom,' said Macy with rising concern. 'I talked to you, I could *see* you! I even spoke to Dad, too!'

'It wasn't us, love!' Eddie told her, before turning back to Wu. 'What the bloody hell is this?'

'CGI,' Wu replied. 'Computer graphics, the latest deepfake technology. Professor Wilde is famous enough for there to be large amounts of reference material that an artificial intelligence program used to replace another person's face with hers. Her voice was also simulated on the supercomputer at this base, all in real time.'

'*I'm* not famous, though. You couldn't have done that for me.'

'We only needed to fake your voice, and we had enough recordings of you to do so.'

'What recordings?' Eddie demanded, only to notice Cheng looking ashamed. 'You were taping me on your bloody laptop, weren't you!'

'I didn't know it would be used for this,' the young man replied quietly. 'I'm sorry.'

Nina turned away from the screen. 'Okay, so . . . you've got us,' she said, defeated. 'Now what?'

Colonel Wu pointed at the shape inside the sarcophagus. 'Now? You wake it up.'

24

Nina heard her own breath hiss inside the tight-fitting rubber face mask, sounds from outside muffled by a thick neoprene hood. Her captors knew the sarcophagus contained a lethal gas, and since they needed her alive – for now – they had taken steps to ensure she stayed that way.

They had not given her a fully sealed hazmat suit, though. She needed to touch the resurrection key with her bare hand. As Eddie had angrily pointed out, if the poison was absorbed through the skin, she was screwed – along with the entire Chinese plan. But the protest had been to no avail.

The key itself was heavy in her hand. She regarded the inset stone and crystal, then looked back through the glass wall. Eddie and Macy stood beyond the barrier, watching with deep worry. They were under guard, a loose semicircle of armed men around them. Also observing were the two other family pairings in the lab: father and daughter, mother and son. The Wus looked on with stony dispassion, while the Huis at least appeared concerned.

Major Wu Shun spoke into a headset, her words inaudible through the thick glass but instead crackling in Nina's left ear through a small receiver. 'The door is secure. Take the key to the sarcophagus.'

Nina knew that only her eyes were visible behind the mask. Nevertheless, she tried to give Macy as reassuring a look as possible before turning away.

The sarcophagus stood before her, fourteen feet of precious

metals and strange crystal. Even with the amount of light upon it, the figure inside was still indistinct, somehow menacing despite its stillness. 'Put the key in the recess,' Wu ordered.

'I'll do it when I'm goddamn good and ready, okay?' Nina shot back through her throat mic. 'I need to make sure there aren't any nasty surprises.'

'We examined the broken coffins. There are no traps.'

'The key word there is "broken", and I know from experience that the traps on these things aren't mechanical. I'm the archaeologist, not you, so let me do my job, okay?' She glanced at the window. Eddie's smirk told her that her side of the conversation was on speaker.

'Just do it,' the Chinese woman snapped.

Nina ignored her, crouching to examine the sarcophagus for breaks in the metal or hidden panels. There were none. She checked the underside. The broken pipe had been replugged.

No evidence of any physical booby traps. Nor, for that matter, any way of opening the coffin without using the key – or brute force. 'Okay,' she said reluctantly. 'I'm putting the key in.'

She hesitated, then inserted it into the recess. It was a perfect fit, nestling into place with a surprisingly satisfying *click*.

Nothing happened – yet. She had deliberately kept her hand off the central insets, knowing the purple stone was a conductor for earth energy. Wu impatiently demanded a progress report, but again Nina ignored her, unwilling to take the next step until she was ready.

As far as she could tell, there was no danger – other than the unknown. 'Right,' she finally said, 'here we go.'

She placed her palm flat on the key.

Even expecting the shock of contact, it still made her flinch. The sarcophagus was indeed alive with earth energy, the mysterious lines of force weaving over the entire planet. She could *feel* them, some inexplicable sixth sense revealing them to her not just within the coffin, but in the chamber outside, the base – and beyond.

She knew from her experiences with the vault in Turkey that she could do more than feel the energy flow. She could *shape* it, her willpower alone enough to influence its course. She focused her attention on the sarcophagus. Somehow she could make it open, wake the sleeper inside—

Someone else was in there with her.

Nina broke contact, jerking back as if from an electric shock. 'Nina!' Eddie shouted in her earpiece, his cry loud enough to be picked up by Wu's headset. 'Are you okay?'

'I – I'm fine,' she stammered.

'What happened?' demanded Wu.

'I'm still trying to figure that out!' She took a moment to compose her thoughts. 'Okay. When I touched the key, I felt the flow of earth energy – qi, you called it. I was trying to direct it so I could open the sarcophagus when . . . when I felt the person inside it. He's still alive. He's *conscious*.'

Shock from the observers. Dr Hui wore a headset of her own, her voice coming through the earpiece. 'That is not possible. How can he still be conscious?'

'I don't mean he's fully awake and aware of what's going on,' said Nina. 'But there's . . . a *spark*, some part of him that's still active.' The implications hit her. 'My God. He's been in there for over a hundred thousand years – and at some level, he's been conscious all that time. What the hell will that have done to his mind?'

'We will find out soon,' said Wu without sympathy. 'Go back to the key. You have wasted enough time – open the sarcophagus.'

'All right, but you can pay for the guy's shrink.'

Now prepared, she placed her hand back on the key. Her external perception fell away as an inner eye reopened. The energy flow surrounded her again. She concentrated upon the coffin. Again she made contact with the spark of life inside. But this time she forced herself past it, searching for some other mental handhold. The Turkish vault had had a way to stabilise the spearhead once it was triggered; there had to be something similar here . . .

There was. The lines of power flowed together, concentrating in one particular place. She fixed her mind upon it. She didn't know *how* to manipulate it, only that she *could*—

That was enough.

Her will shaped the phantom world – and something changed, the lines reconfiguring. The jolt of transition was enough to make her release the key in surprise. Reality snapped back around her, leaving her momentarily confused – then she hurriedly retreated as a low thud came from within the sarcophagus.

The crystal lid began to open.

Yellow gas swirled through the slowly widening crack – and alarms sounded, the isolation chamber's sensors detecting the poison. The dirty mustard-coloured miasma rolled across the room after Nina. 'Okay, you can let me out now,' she said, reaching the door. 'Seriously, I'm done here!'

The exit remained closed. 'The ventilation filters will quickly clear the air,' Wu told her as powerful fans started to thrum.

'That's great – unless this stuff kills me on contact!' She flattened herself into the furthest corner, watching with growing fear as the expanding cloud came closer . . . then began to rise, swirling into a vortex as the extractors drew it upwards. In seconds, the escaping gas became a yellow tornado as it was sucked from the still-opening sarcophagus.

Clean air pumped into the room to replace it, rustling Nina's clothing. Soon the cloud became translucent, the discoloration thinning, then vanishing.

'The air is clean,' Wu reported. 'You can take off the mask.'

'Y'know, I'll give it another minute, just in case,' Nina replied.

Cautiously returning to the now-open coffin, she looked beneath the cover – and gasped.

The giant figure within, naked except for a broad golden circlet around its head, was entwined in what at first glance looked like silver threads until she realised they were tendrils of crystal, extruded from the inner bed on which it lay. The occupant's genitals were concealed beneath the covering, but she knew at once from the hard, angular features of his face that he was male.

That face was . . . unsettling. The mummified Veteres bodies in the Garden of Eden had been of a related but separate species to *Homo sapiens*, as Hui had suggested, resembling popular culture's idea of a Grey alien. The man before her was somewhere between the two. Even had he not been ten feet tall, one look would have been enough to know he was not quite human. The face was longer, eyes larger and more canted, the proportions of the features *off*. He had an almost predatory feel, giving Nina a brief, involuntary shiver. *The offspring of angels and humans . . .*

'Our instruments do not show any change in his condition,' said Hui. 'Is he waking?'

'I don't know,' she replied. The figure hadn't moved at all; if not for the small but powerful sense of life she had felt, she would have assumed him to be dead.

'Use the key again,' ordered Wu. 'Wake him.'

'Don't I get a coffee break first?' Her joke was met with stony silence. 'Okay, okay. Let's see what I can do . . .'

She placed her hand back upon the key. This time, she brought her attention to the point of life within the patterns of force. Somehow she had to free it, wake it up. But how?

The question, the mere desire to do so, was already guiding her invisible hands. The flow of energy shifted. The sense of contact with the sleeper's consciousness returned—

Cold shock, almost fear, nearly jerked her hand from the key, but she forced herself to maintain her hold.

He was awakening. And he knew she was there.

But somehow, she knew there was more she needed to do. Something scraped at her subconscious, a discordance telling her that whatever process was bringing the man from his stasis was not going smoothly. Again, she didn't know exactly how to fix it, but the application of her willpower reshaped the earth's invisible forces. The discomfort began to ease.

She became dimly aware of a voice saying her name. Not the sleeper: Hui, penetrating her fugue state. '. . . you all right? Can you hear me?'

'I'm fine.' Her own voice sounded distorted, slowed, as if what she perceived internally was happening much faster than the outside world. 'He's coming around. I think.' But she was now sure; the discordance faded, the rasping on her soul gone. From here, it was all up to the sleeper himself.

Nina let go of the key. The snap back to reality this time left her dazed, her mind reluctant to leave the unseen world. There she had power, could shape and control what happened; here, she belatedly remembered as she turned, she was a prisoner. The Chinese scientists and soldiers were still watching her intently. Eddie and Macy's concern became relief as they saw she was unharmed.

'I'm okay,' she said. 'That was, uh . . . a hell of a thing.'

'What happened?' asked Hui. 'Did you manage to alter the qi forces?'

'I think so, yeah. He should start to . . .' She trailed off as she saw the crystalline tendrils slowly shrink, retracting and being absorbed into the translucent slab on which the Nephilim lay. The crystal itself changed colour, taking on an eerie turquoise hue.

More of the giant's body was gradually revealed. The aeons motionless inside the coffin had not diminished him; his muscles were still sharply defined, a lean but powerful frame. She watched as the thin creepers withered to nothingness. 'Okay, I've never seen anything like that before – and I've seen a lot of weird things.'

'Is he awake?' demanded Wu.

Hui checked readings on a laptop. 'I do not know if he is awake – but he is definitely *alive*. Look!' She turned the machine.

It displayed a thermographic feed of the isolation room, heat sources in lurid false colour against a dark background. Nina herself was an inverse silhouette of hot orange and yellow and white – but behind her, a new form took shape, shimmering blobs of purple and blue spreading to create a supine humanoid shape. The colours shifted, greens and reds appearing as the body grew warmer.

One of the scientists called out in excitement. 'He has a heartbeat,' Hui reported breathlessly. 'Slow – but it is getting faster!'

Nina again regarded the figure inside the sarcophagus. He had still not moved, but his pale grey skin had taken on a warmer tone at his extremities. 'Is the air definitely safe?' she asked. Wu confirmed it was. 'Okay, I'm taking off the mask.'

'No, wait,' said Hui. 'It will affect our readings of—'

'Sorry, but I've had enough of being the gimp.' She unzipped and tugged away the covering hood before fumbling with the gas mask's buckles. The inner seal came free from her face with a wet pop. Her skin suddenly felt cool where she had been sweating beneath the enclosing rubber. She took in a long, unfiltered breath. Relief; she didn't drop dead on the spot.

Another look at the Nephilim. His face was now changing colour as long-static blood warmed and pulsed through his arteries. His natural skin tone was unlike any of humanity's many variations, though, with a distinct blue cast resembling pale marble. 'What's his heart rate now?'

'Rising, but below normal,' Hui replied. 'Though we do not know what *is* normal for him.'

'Just the fact that it's beating at all after longer than the whole of recorded human history is amazing in its own right,' Nina noted. 'How about his body temperature?'

'Close to human normal,' the scientist replied.

The being's chest remained motionless. 'Is he breathing?'

'There is no way to tell.' Hui's tone was a little accusatory. 'Your breath is affecting the carbon dioxide readings.'

'Have to check the old-fashioned way, then.' She retrieved the mask and held the glass eyepieces below the Nephilim's nose. No sign of misting. 'Nothing. He'll have to start soon, though.' She leaned closer, seeing a faint pulse beneath one eye. 'Blood flow without fresh oxygen is going to cause him some major problems in—'

The eye snapped open.

Nina stared at it, frozen in surprise – and before she could react the towering man grabbed her by the throat.

25

Macy's scream was audible even through the isolation chamber's thick glass. Nina tried to pull back, but the huge hand clamped crushingly tight around her neck.

The Nephilim drew in a deep, gasping lungful of air, then exhaled, his first breath in untold millennia. Another gasp, then he swung his legs from the sarcophagus and stood – hauling Nina off her feet. She fought to break his grip, but his tendons were like steel.

Frenzied activity outside the transparent wall, Colonel Wu shouting orders and the soldiers scrambling to respond as the scientists backed away in shock. Only Eddie held his position, pushing Macy behind him and yelling his wife's name as he pounded helplessly on the armoured barrier.

She couldn't hear his voice – but instead heard another, in a tongue not spoken since the dawn of humanity. The Nephilim shouted something at those on the other side of the glass. Both confusion and anger were clear in the unknown words. His voice was powerful, deep, with a strange echo from the depths of his broad chest.

The chamber's door opened. Several soldiers burst in. Major Wu followed, barking orders. The Nephilim whirled to face them.

Nina was still trapped in his grip. She clawed at her captor's unyielding fingers – then changed targets, kicking at his exposed genitals.

The Nephilim was surprised by the attack, but twisted just

quickly enough to take the blow on his upper thigh. He grunted, then glared at her, teeth bared. His grip tightened still further. Nina let out a silent cry as darkness swallowed her vision—

The pressure suddenly eased. She drew in a painful breath. The Nephilim's eyes went back to the soldiers – who had moved closer, raising their guns. He looked from one man to another, gaze flicking over their weapons . . . then his hand opened.

Nina fell to the floor, weak and breathless. An order from Wu, and two men dragged her through the door.

Eddie was already there. 'Get off her!' he growled, shoving a soldier aside to pick her up. 'I've got you.' He carried her clear.

'Mom!' Macy wailed, running to them. 'Mom, are you okay?'

'Jury's . . . out,' Nina gasped. 'Jesus! I thought . . . he was gonna . . . kill me!'

'He did too – until he saw the guns,' said Eddie, looking back through the window. The giant and the soldiers remained in a stand-off. 'How the hell would someone from a hundred thousand years ago recognise an assault rifle?'

Nina had no time to ponder the question. Hui issued rapid commands. Zan Zhi hurriedly worked his laptop, donning a headset. A window opened on the screen; he checked it, then spoke. The language was not Mandarin, the words glottal and strange.

The Nephilim looked in surprise at the voice coming from loudspeakers in the ceiling. Zan spoke again, a longer sentence. The giant gave the soldiers a wary glance, then advanced to address the Chinese man through the glass. Nina saw words flash up on the screen, one set in the Nephilim alphabet, the other in simplified Chinese. The computer was translating the ancient being's speech.

Zan didn't need the machine to understand, replying before the full translation had appeared. The Nephilim regarded him with evident suspicion, but his anger lessened.

'What's he saying?' Eddie demanded as Hui joined Zan.

'He wants to know where he is, and where the rest of his people are,' Zan replied. His English was as fluent as Cheng's.

'Probably best not to tell him they're at the bottom of the Antarctic Ocean.'

'I told him that he's safe, and in China. Near the Nephilim site we found, I mean – I wanted to see if he recognised the name from the records. He wouldn't know what China is.'

'Did he recognise it?' Nina asked, recovering her breath. Her throat felt bruised, aching from her attacker's grip.

'I think so, but—' Zan broke off as the Nephilim spoke again. The tone was commanding, but less hostile. The translator replied, nodding, then hurried across the lab to a water cooler.

'What are you doing?' Hui demanded.

'He asked for water.' He filled a cup, then a second. 'He'll be very thirsty after all this time!'

'You're going in there?' asked Eddie in disbelief. 'He just tried to kill Nina!'

'No, this is good,' said Hui. 'It will establish trust. Take it to him, Zhi.'

Colonel Wu appeared unconvinced, but nevertheless waved Zan into the isolation chamber. The soldiers parted to let him through. He cautiously approached the watching giant, speaking to him in his own language. The Nephilim's expression was equally wary, but he took the proffered water, sniffing it before gulping it down.

That seemed to be the ice-breaker. The tall man returned to the sarcophagus and sat upon its end, holding out a hand in a clear gesture: *more*. Zan bowed his head and hurried back out to bring him two more cups. A short exchange followed, the Nephilim giving the observers a look of assessment before concluding.

Zan emerged, face filled with nervous enthusiasm. 'I've spoken to him!' he announced proudly.

Wu was unimpressed. 'Yes, we saw.'

'What did he say?' asked Hui.

'His name is Gadreel. He is the leader of the Nephilim!'

'Gadreel?' said Nina, just as Hui echoed the name with equal surprise. 'That's a biblical name!'

'Well, you said the Nephilim are from the Bible,' Eddie pointed out.

'From Enoch,' said Hui. 'One of the non-canonical books. It describes the fall of the angels who copulated with humans to create the Nephilim, the giants.'

'You've done your research,' said Nina.

'As soon as it became clear that this race called itself the Nephilim, we collected as much information and folklore about them as we could. Most of it came from the Old Testament of the Jews, even those parts that became apocryphal.' Hui gave the being beyond the glass a quizzical look. 'But the biblical Gadreel was not one of the Nephilim – they were the offspring. He was an angel, one of those responsible for their creation.'

'The story might have become garbled over time,' suggested Nina. 'In this case, a very, *very* long time. I've seen it before – with Atlantis, for one. The myths that led me to it were distorted versions of the true history.'

'I'd say it was like a game of Chinese whispers, but I don't want you to think I'm racist,' Eddie said with a grin.

Hui gave him a puzzled look. Cheng explained in Mandarin. 'Ah, yes; we call it geese to geese,' she told the Englishman.

'It's telephone in America,' said Nina, 'but whatever it's called, it would explain it.'

She was about to describe how Abrahamic religious lore had been based upon the history of the Veteres when Colonel Wu interrupted. 'He must be questioned.'

The translator nodded in response to the officer's further instructions, then went back to his laptop and began a new exchange with Gadreel. This was less straightforward than before, Zan occasionally appearing confused and rephrasing his words. 'What's wrong?' Nina asked, seeing flashing question marks in the computer's translations.

'We translated all the records we found,' explained Hui, 'but he is using words we do not know.'

'He looks worried,' said Macy. 'Maybe he's asking for help?'

'He's ten feet tall and can pick someone up with one hand,' said Eddie. 'I don't think much'll worry him.'

'Macy's right, though,' Nina realised. The man before them was not human, but the subtleties of his expression were still recognisable. For all Gadreel's imperiousness, there was a concern, even anxiety behind it that was nothing to do with the guns still trained upon him. 'Something's bothering him. Mr Zan?' Zan glanced back at her. 'He wanted to know where his people are. I think we should tell him.'

Hui was dubious. 'Is that wise?'

Colonel Wu was less circumspect. 'Do not tell him anything! If he knows they are dead, he will not tell us location of fortress!'

Nina looked sharply at him. '*What* fortress?'

'Nephilim records say a big fortress hidden somewhere. He,' he pointed at Gadreel, 'knows where. He tell us where to find it.'

'Colonel!' said Hui. It was obvious that he had said something she did not want revealed. The soldier responded in Mandarin, equally pointed and with clear impatience.

'Oh, you haven't told us everything? Golly gosh, I'm shocked,' said Eddie, deadpan.

'That is not how I wanted you to find out,' Hui told Nina. 'Yes, according to the records, there is another Nephilim outpost buried somewhere in this region, but finding it was *not* my first priority! I was—'

'It is the first priority of the People's Liberation Army, Doctor,' cut in the younger Wu. 'It must be located.'

'What's in this fortress?' Eddie asked. 'More Nephilim?'

'That . . . is possible,' said Hui. 'According to the records, it was built as a last defence for them – a hiding place. If the fortress still exists, they could still be there, in stasis.'

'In which case,' said Nina, 'telling you how to find it is the only way he'll see them again.' She faced Colonel Wu. 'We have to tell him. It might be your only chance to get what you want.'

He scowled, but after a moment spoke curtly to Hui. She bowed her head to him, then faced Nina. 'The colonel has decided that as the scientific leader of the project, I should make that decision,' she said, with just a hint of snideness.

'Passing the renminbi, huh?' said Eddie, grinning. 'Senior officers, same in any country.'

Neither Wu appreciated his joke, but they let it pass. Instead the colonel issued more commands. The soldiers in the isolation chamber backed out, keeping their weapons fixed on Gadreel until the door was closed in their wake. 'Now,' said the commander, 'tell him. And hope you are right.'

Hui stepped up to Zan, about to speak – then gestured for Nina to join her. 'You should tell him, Professor Wilde. You saw the fortress in the ice, what happened to the rest of his people. I did not.'

'He strangles me for waking him, then I get to be the bearer of bad news? I'm glad there's a thick piece of glass between us!' Nina reluctantly stepped forward. 'All right. What the hell do I say?'

'Tell him the truth,' Macy suggested.

She smiled at her daughter. 'Honey, I love you. You're right; I should. Okay.' She took a breath, then stood at Zan's shoulder. 'Let's do it.'

She looked up at the Nephilim, who had realised she was now the focus of attention in the lab and was watching her intently. 'Gadreel? My name is Nina Wilde.' Zan began a simultaneous translation, speaking in the giant's language into his headset. 'I'm an archaeologist.'

No sooner had Zan tried to relay that than the computer brought up a warning. Flashing question marks appeared in the Nephilim text, though not the Mandarin; the machine was transcribing as well as translating both sides of the conversation. 'I don't know how to say that,' he warned.

'Okay, how to phrase it? I'm a . . . chronicler of the past?' she offered. Zan made a hesitant attempt to translate. Both he and Nina were a little surprised when it seemed to succeed, Gadreel cocking his head, intrigued. He spoke in reply.

Zan translated. 'Are you a priestess?'

'Ah . . . no,' she replied. 'A . . . discoverer of how things used to be?' The explanation sounded lame, childish, but it was the best she could improvise.

Again, though, Gadreel appeared to understand. 'You have the red hair,' Zan said for him as the giant indicated Nina's locks. 'Like a priestess. But you are like me. You seek understanding.'

'That's a good way to put it, yes.'

Gadreel's eyes narrowed. 'You were with me when I woke. My priestess is not here. Do you have the gift? Did you wake me?'

'Yes.'

The answer surprised him. He looked at the key in its recess, then put a hand to his chin in a very human expression of thoughtfulness. A long pause, then he spoke again. 'Where are my people?'

Nina did not answer at once, trying to think of a way to break the terrible truth gently – but that in itself was enough to make Gadreel's face fall. 'I'm sorry,' she said. 'You're the only one we were able to get out.'

'What happened to them?'

'We found your fortress in the ice.' The computer baulked at translating the last word, and Zan gave her a helpless shrug; it had clearly not appeared in the records found by the Chinese. 'The, ah . . .' Nina recalled a similar term used by the Veteres. 'The cold sand?'

Understanding came to the giant's face. 'Cold sand?' asked Hui.

'The Veteres came from a hot climate; they'd never encountered snow until they fled to Antarctica,' Nina replied. '"Cold sand" was their very literal way of describing it. And it looks like they share a lot of their language with the Nephilim.' She turned back to Gadreel. 'Your fortress was trapped in the ice.' Zan adapted his translation to include the new term, though the computer was still puzzled. 'We found you and your people inside. But something went wrong,' she decided not to complicate matters by giving him the whole violent story, 'and the fortress fell into the sea.'

'They are all . . . gone?'

'I'm afraid so. I'm sorry.'

Gadreel's expression of loss was entirely clear. He stared down at the floor, whispering something.

'What did he say?' asked Hui.

Zan shook his head apologetically. 'I couldn't hear it well,' he said, checking the laptop's screen. 'I think . . . "We failed"? Or "We lost"? And . . . I don't know. "Escape", perhaps. It was too quiet for the computer to hear.'

Colonel Wu was devoid of sympathy. 'Where is fortress buried? He must tell us, now!'

'Colonel!' Hui rounded sternly upon the officer. 'This man is not our enemy, or our prisoner. He has just learned he has lost everything – his people, perhaps his family. Have some decency. Give him time.'

The commander regarded her, tight-faced, but eventually

nodded. 'I give him time. But not a lot. Now, I deal with people who *are* our enemies, and our prisoners. We question him when I come back.' He spoke to his daughter, then marched from the room.

Nina looked back at Gadreel. He had not moved, eyes downcast. His face was not grieving or disconsolate, though; more contemplative, lost in thought. 'I think we should leave him alone for a while.'

Hui nodded in agreement. 'Come, in here.'

She led the way to a side door. The others filed after her. Nina glanced back at Gadreel. He had registered the exodus, but did not react to it, still thinking.

She and her family followed the Chinese into a conference room. Hui picked up a remote and activated a wall screen, bringing up a video feed from inside the isolation chamber. 'We will see if he needs us,' she told Nina. 'Now, what are we to do?'

Major Wu remained standing as everyone else sat. 'Finding the buried fortress is our top priority.'

'We will find it,' Hui replied dismissively, 'but we have much to discuss first.' She opened a laptop and started a search of the project's records. 'The name, Gadreel,' she said to Nina, indicating the results, 'in biblical apocrypha is indeed one of the angels who fathered the Nephilim. He was known for two things – the first is that he was the tempter of Eve, an aspect of the serpent responsible for the expulsion from Paradise.'

'Great,' said Eddie. 'So we've woken up a literal devil.'

'History is always written by the victors,' Nina pointed out. 'In this case, the Veteres.'

'The Shangdi, as we call them,' said Cheng.

His mother nodded. 'Shangdi in ancient Chinese theology is the primal deity, the creator of all things. We named the progenitor race mentioned in the Nephilim records after him.'

Macy gave her a curious look. 'What did the Nephilim call them?'

'They didn't give them a name,' Cheng explained. 'At least, not in the records we found. They only ever referred to them as "the pursuers" and "the persecutors".'

'Not best mates, then,' Eddie noted.

'That's interesting, though,' said Nina. 'The Nephilim obviously saw themselves as victims, the oppressed – but the Veteres had a completely different view. Their side of the story is the one passed down to us through the Book of Genesis and the other early books of the Old Testament – including ones that didn't make the final cut, like Enoch. The Nephilim were bad guys, abominations, who were eventually cast out and imprisoned for all eternity.' She regarded the figure on the screen. 'Two very different stories. But now we get to hear *his* side of it – firsthand.'

'Why were they cast out?' asked Macy, intrigued.

Hui brought up more records, switching the wall screen to display them. All were written in Mandarin, but they included photographs of the artefacts discovered by Chinese archaeologists. 'The Nephilim say the Shangdi accused them of great crimes – the crime of being children of the Shangdi who were born to humans.'

'Hybrids,' said Nina in understanding. 'The Nephilim are a product of both races. In the Bible, they were the offspring of *angels* and humans – ancient humans saw the Veteres, the Shangdi, as angels. Or at least that's how the Veteres *wanted* to be seen.'

'So some of the Veteres couldn't keep it in their pants around human women – and then the rest took it out on the kids when they were born?' Eddie said.

His wife nodded. 'The mindset of the slave-owner throughout history. The Veteres may have claimed to have lofty ideals about uplifting and educating humans, but they still used them as slaves. In a society like that, punishing the individual slave-owner for those kinds of transgressions is a bit close to the bone; it's almost a criticism of the society itself for allowing it to happen. So the victims take the brunt of it instead.'

'Scumbags,' he growled, disgusted.

'I guess it at least proves hypocrisy isn't a human invention.' Nina turned back to Hui. 'So the Veteres were hunting down their own forbidden offspring?'

'They chased them across the world,' the scientist replied. She brought up a map. Dots connected by arrows formed a ragged path from the heart of Africa through the Middle East and into Central Asia. 'Each point is a reference to a place from the Nephilim records. Most have not been specifically located, only the general region, but a few we have narrowed down to smaller areas.'

'Like the one near here?'

'Yes. We believe the fortress is within sixty kilometres. But our aerial surveys have not found any trace.'

'Which is why we must question him,' Wu commented pointedly.

'As you can see,' Hui continued, 'the Nephilim travelled a long way to escape their pursuers.'

'A very long way,' Nina agreed. 'But they *were* still being pursued?'

The Chinese woman nodded. 'The longest they stayed in one location before Shangdi scouts found them was twenty years. Whenever this happened, they moved on before a larger force could capture them.'

'Capture them?' Eddie asked. 'Not kill them?'

'The Veteres considered themselves *civilised*,' said Nina, giving the word a caustic edge. 'Abominations or not, the Nephilim were still their offspring. Imprisoning instead of executing would let them feel they had the moral high ground.' Something she had said earlier came back to her. 'Wait . . . in the Bible, the Nephilim were supposedly imprisoned for eternity. And they have a way to *sleep* for eternity – are the two things connected?'

'We think so,' Hui told her. 'What the Nephilim used by choice, the Shangdi imposed on them by force. The Nephilim feared being taken to Tartarus, where they would be trapped in torment beneath the earth, alive but unable to move.'

Nina nodded thoughtfully. 'A place from Greek and Roman mythology,' she added for Eddie's benefit – from Macy's look of recognition, her daughter had encountered the name in her explorations of ancient legends. 'A prison at the end of the world for those who challenged the gods, and for the worst sinners. The version in the Book of Enoch is where fallen angels are imprisoned.'

Eddie glanced back towards the laboratory. 'So that sarcophagus was originally built as a sort of eternal torture chamber? And the Nephilim used them *voluntarily*?'

'They might not have had a choice,' she mused. 'If it came down to freezing to death in the Antarctic or putting yourself into stasis, even knowing what that meant, in the hope of being rescued later, what would you do?'

'Put it that way . . . yeah, I'd probably chance the freezer,' he admitted.

Macy had another question. 'What was the *second* thing Gadreel was known for?'

Before Hui could answer, there was a knock at the door. A guard entered and spoke briefly to Wu. 'He wants us,' she announced.

Hui quickly switched the screen back to the isolation chamber. Gadreel had stood, donning a robe taken from a previously unnoticed compartment inside the sarcophagus. She rose and signalled for everyone to follow her into the laboratory.

Zan scurried back to the translation laptop. Gadreel waited until he was ready, then spoke. 'What is he saying?' asked Hui.

'He wants to talk,' Zan replied.

'Good,' said Wu. 'Ask him about the fortress.'

'No, no – he wants to talk to *her*.' He gestured at Nina. 'Alone.'

The Chinese officer turned on the American with deep suspicion. 'Why you?'

'Yeah, why me?' Nina asked, equally mystified.

Zan asked a question in the Nephilim language, getting an answer. 'He says you were there when the fortress was destroyed. He wants you to tell him exactly what happened to his people.'

'There's not really much more to tell,' she replied. Gadreel watched her from behind the glass. His unblinking gaze was distinctly unnerving.

'No, it could be a good idea,' said Hui. 'Not only were you there, but you are the only archaeologist with personal know-ledge of the Shangdi – the Veteres. You know things about them we do not. You may be able to use that to gain his trust.'

Nina was not convinced, but she nodded. 'Okay. I'll give it a try.'

'No,' said Wu. 'A foreigner, talking to him alone?'

'I won't be alone,' Nina pointed out. 'I can't speak Gadreel's language, so I'll need Mr Zan.'

'And the whole talk will be monitored and recorded,' Hui added. 'We can watch from the conference room. There will be no secrets.'

Outmanoeuvred, Wu gave way, but with poor grace. 'Do it, then. But do not try to hide anything from us,' she warned Nina.

'Like what, the recipe for the Nephilim's special sauce?' She joined Zan at the window. 'All right, let's see what he has to say.'

Cheng brought Nina a chair, then the guards retreated to a far corner, while the others returned to the conference room.

'Mom, will you be okay?' Macy asked as she went with Eddie.

'I'll be fine,' Nina assured her. 'Don't worry.'

'I can't help it.' Her daughter's eyes flicked towards the giant. 'He's . . . scary. I don't like him.'

'I'm going to find out if we can trust him,' Nina said. 'I hope we can. And I hope he can trust us,' she added, giving Wu a meaningful look.

'Good luck,' said Eddie as he and Macy reached the door. 'And if he starts talking about fava beans and a nice Chianti, *run*.'

Nina stifled a laugh, but as she turned back to Gadreel, it struck her that her situation did indeed resemble a famous scene from the movie *The Silence of the Lambs*. She was about to question a man through a glass wall – and for all she knew, the Nephilim was every bit as intelligent and cunning as Hannibal Lecter. As dangerous, too; the sight of his eyes fixed upon her triggered an almost physical reminder of his unbreakable grip on her throat.

She covered her concern and went to the chair. Gadreel tipped his head to indicate that she should sit. Faintly annoyed that by doing so he had, consciously or otherwise, assumed the dominant position in the impending discussion, she sat and leaned back, adopting the same *okay, now impress me* pose as she did when dealing with students one-on-one in her office. 'You want to talk? Let's talk.'

26

Zan relayed Nina's words through his headset, then Gadreel's back to her when he replied. 'Yes. I first want to, uh . . .' He checked the computer, but it was unable to help. 'I don't have a direct translation,' he admitted, 'but I think he's apologising for hurting you.'

Nina's attention had not left the Nephilim while he spoke, and there was little in his expression to suggest contrition. 'Tell him thank you,' she replied, giving him the benefit of the doubt. 'He'd only just woken up, and was in a strange situation, confused – I'm sure it was just a misunderstanding.'

The Chinese made the translation. Again Nina watched Gadreel closely. A moment of satisfaction, she thought – but was it because his apology had been accepted, or because it had been *believed*?

He spoke again. Zan translated. 'You said those who travelled with me are all dead. Where are the rest of my people?'

'I don't know,' Nina replied.

The simple answer unsettled him. 'You have not found them?'

'No. These people,' she indicated Zan, 'found one of your fortresses. But everyone was dead.'

'What about . . .' Zan stopped, frowning. 'I know the words, but I don't understand what they mean. He said "the People of the Tree".'

'The Veteres,' Nina said, for the benefit of those listening in the conference room as well as Zan. 'The Shangdi – that's what they called themselves. It represents knowledge – it's where the myth of the tree of knowledge originated in the Book of Genesis.' She looked back at the Chinese man. 'What else did he say?'

'He asked, what about the People of the Tree?'

'They're . . . gone. They don't exist any more.'

The revelation shocked Gadreel. 'How can they be gone? What happened to them?'

'They were driven out of Eden by . . . by us. By humans.' The computer flashed up an error when Zan attempted to translate the word, and he looked at her for an alternative. The term the Veteres used to describe their slaves came to her. 'By the beasts.'

Another flash of shock on Gadreel's face. 'You killed the Shangdi?'

'Yes. Not us, now – it happened a long time ago.'

He considered the revelation for a long moment. 'The beasts were always violent,' he eventually said. 'But not like animals, killing for food. They *needed* violence. It . . .' Zan paused to find the best word. 'It *excited* them. Of all their tools, it was the most powerful.' The Nephilim leader looked back at Nina. 'How long ago?'

The Veteres had used the same odd, non-linear numerical system as the Atlanteans; even though Nina's innate skill at mental arithmetic meant it only took a few moments to convert one hundred and thirty thousand years into an Atlantean figure, she then had to get Zan to translate it correctly. She could tell they were finally successful when Gadreel froze, drawing in a long breath before sitting, shaken, on the foot of the sarcophagus. Zan strained to hear his disbelieving whisper. 'So long . . . so much time . . .'

'I'm sorry,' she said quietly.

The tall man was silent for the better part of a minute, Nina not wanting to disturb him as he came to terms with the new reality. At last he spoke again. 'You are a discoverer of how things used to be,' he said. 'Does anything remain of the People of the Tree?'

'Only legends, stories,' she replied. 'I followed their trail across the world, from where they began to where they ended. Everything was destroyed.'

'Eden was where they began.' Nina found it faintly unsettling that the name was the same in both the Nephilim language and English. 'Where did they end?'

'They had a city in Antarctica – the land of cold sand. We found your fortress trapped in ice that had broken away from it. Were you looking for them there?'

'Yes,' he replied. 'To find and free my people.'

'Were your people in Antarctica?'

'I do not know where they were taken. To Tartarus, a place of great power, but that is all we knew. We made ourselves stronger in our exile. We had new weapons, new armour, powerful fortresses.' Zan hesitated over that last, checking the computer, but it had apparently decided upon the same word. Nina understood his confusion: surely a better descriptor for a fortress would be *strong*? But there was no time to dwell upon it, as Gadreel was still talking. 'They had hunted us for . . . centuries.' Another pause as the Chinese worked out an appropriate equivalent. 'But then we became the hunters. I led the search for our people.'

Nina felt there was something personal about the Nephilim's description of events. 'How long were you hunted? You yourself, not your people as a whole?'

'This is getting hard for me to translate,' Zan complained. But he did well enough, Gadreel replying: 'I do not know exactly. We travelled so far and for so long we lost count of the seasons. But I led my people for more than—' Zan looked at Nina, startled. 'Three hundred years.'

'You're over *three hundred* years old?' she gasped.

'I am older than that,' Gadreel responded. 'That is how long we were hunted. I was more than two hundred years old when we began.'

Nina stared at the Nephilim with renewed astonishment. He was over five hundred years old – and had stepped out of the past after more than one hundred *thousand* years as if not a day had passed. The technology, if something that used crystals and stones rather than gears and circuitry could be so described, of the Veteres and their Nephilim cousins was far beyond anything previously known. 'So you chased the Veteres to Antarctica?'

Gadreel's face darkened. 'Yes. We knew they would hide where the lines of qi were strongest.' Zan put the translation into terms with which he was familiar. 'My priestesses followed the lines. But we went into a night that did not end, with a terrible storm. We could not go on.'

An Antarctic winter, Nina realised; for all their advances, the ancient race would probably have been unaware that the continent was plunged into darkness for part of the year. 'So you put yourselves into the sarcophagi?'

'Yes. Our supplies ran low. Only a priestess can put us to sleep, or wake us. One chose to remain, to wake us when the storm passed and the sun returned.' A flicker of sadness. 'She must not have lived.'

'I'm sorry,' Nina said. 'Was she one of your family?'

'My people are all my family – I don't think he means in a literal way,' Zan interjected, before continuing to translate. 'But my wife and son were safe; they were sleeping in another place. Before I left, I hid the rest of my people to wait for our return.'

'But you never did return. So – they might still be there, still sleeping.'

'Yes . . .' He straightened, suddenly hopeful. 'If I help you find them . . . will you help me wake them?'

'I'll do what I can, yes. Are they in another fortress?'

'Yes. It is bigger than the one in which you found me.'

Nina glanced up at the cameras. Gadreel had just confirmed he knew where the main fortress was buried – but that triggered a different thought. She turned back to Zan. 'The word we're using, *fortress* – that's definitely the correct translation?'

He prickled as if she were accusing him of making a mistake. 'Yes, of course!'

'It's okay, I'm not saying you're wrong. But a fortress is a fixed defensive structure – yet the Nephilim travelled across Antarctica, and an ocean before that, until theirs got trapped in the ice . . .' She faced Gadreel through the glass. 'Your fortress – how did you get it to Antarctica?'

Gadreel looked back – then, just for an instant, his gaze flicked away before he spoke. 'How would you cross a sea?'

'By boat?' Nina replied, suddenly suspicious. Was he dissembling, hiding something?

'Yes, by boat,' came the reply. 'That is how we travelled there.'

'That's not what I asked.' But before she could press him further, the laboratory's main door opened, and Colonel Wu and his escort entered.

Anger flashed across the commander's face at the sight of the American talking to the Nephilim. He shouted a command to the guards, who rushed to take up positions at the window, and gestured firmly for Nina and Zan to follow him to the conference room.

His daughter and Hui had seen his arrival on the monitor, meeting him at the door. A heated exchange followed, the younger Wu taking almost as much flak as the scientist. The exasperated Hui switched to English so Nina could understand the argument – and participate. 'We were learning what happened to the Nephilim,' she insisted. 'He asked to speak to Professor Wilde, alone.'

'Why her?' snapped Colonel Wu.

'She woke him – she is the only person here who *could*.'

'And I'm the only person who's found archaeological sites belonging to the Veteres – the Shangdi,' Nina added. 'They were enemies of the Nephilim. Gadreel was telling me how they were hunted by them.'

'It is true,' said Wu, sounding almost unwilling to agree with Nina in front of her father. 'He gave us information. He mentioned their weapons,' she added, with more enthusiasm.

That caught the colonel's attention. He looked across at Gadreel, who was observing with interest. 'What about fortress?'

'He must know where it is, because he said he'd help us find it – if we agree to wake his people,' Nina told him.

'There are more? How many?'

'I don't know. But his wife and son are with them.'

'That is good,' said the major. 'It gives us leverage. He will have to cooperate if he wants to see them again.'

'He is not our prisoner!' Hui insisted.

By now, Eddie and Cheng had joined the little group. 'What about your *actual* prisoners?' said the Yorkshireman. 'Got anything from Eleanor and Donny yet?'

'Not yet,' said Colonel Wu. 'But soon.'

'You got them to talk?'

Wu asked much the same question in Mandarin, the reply drawing a small smile of satisfaction. 'The man did not know anything about the spy,' she said, 'and the old woman would not talk, even when we put pressure on her son.'

'You tortured him, you mean,' Nina said in disgust.

'But he knew other things that were useful,' Wu went on, without acknowledging her. 'Passwords to the Miller & Family bank accounts and financial systems.'

Eddie's eyebrows rose. 'Torturing Donny didn't help you – so you're going to hit Eleanor where it *really* hurts.'

'We take her money,' Colonel Wu said smugly. 'One million American dollars at a time. If she does not name spy, she soon have nothing. She *will* talk.' He looked back at Gadreel. 'But fortress more important. Professor Wilde, you say he tell us where it is?'

She nodded. 'If we agree to help wake his people.'

'Of course we agree.' He addressed Zan. 'Tell him.' The translator hurried back to his station.

'But does that mean you'll actually *do* it?' Nina demanded.

Wu turned away without answering. 'Finding the fortress is a matter of the highest national security,' his daughter replied instead. 'You will get him to tell us where it is.'

'And then Eddie, Macy and I can leave, right?' Now it was the younger Wu's turn not to answer. 'Y'know, I'm not exactly overflowing with trust for you guys right now.'

Macy emerged from the conference room. 'Mom, what's going on?'

'We're just . . . debating what to do next, honey,' said Nina, putting a protective arm around her shoulders.

'I would let you go home,' Hui assured her. 'But getting Gadreel to tell us the location of the fortress will be the best way to persuade the colonel, I am afraid.'

Nina reluctantly made a decision. 'Colonel Wu!' The commander turned. 'I'll do it. I'll ask Gadreel where to find the fortress.'

For the first time since their meeting, he smiled, though the expression did not suit him. 'Good. Do it.' He gestured towards her seat at the window.

'He'll be more cooperative if it's just me and him again,' she said.

'Professor Wilde,' said Hui, collecting a headset like Zan's. 'If you wear this, we will be able to hear you more clearly – and we will also be able to speak to you.'

Nina donned it. 'Just don't have everyone gabbling in my ear at once, okay?'

Hui smiled, then told the others to return to the conference room. 'Come on, love,' Eddie said to Macy. 'We need to let your mum work.'

'Mom,' mother and daughter corrected as one.

He grinned. 'We're in China, talking to a five-hundred-year-old man who looks like a space alien . . . and my family still find time to take the piss out of me.'

'You'd miss it if we didn't,' Nina replied.

'Yeah. I would.' A moment of utter seriousness behind his grey eyes. 'Let's make sure we can keep doing it, eh?'

'Yeah,' she replied in kind, before turning to Macy. 'Go with your dad, okay?'

Macy gave her an unexpected but welcome hug. 'I'll watch you on the big screen.'

'Thanks, honey. Hope I give a good performance.' She went to Zan's station, finding him already speaking quietly to Gadreel. 'What's he saying?'

'He was . . . asking if we had agreed to help him,' came the hesitant reply.

'What did you tell him?'

'Nothing! I thought I'd leave that to you.'

Nina got the feeling that the conversation had been more involved, but Hui's voice in her ear pushed further questions aside. 'Professor Wilde? We are ready.'

'Okay,' she replied, taking her seat. Gadreel still rested on the sarcophagus; he had leaned forward while talking to Zan, but now sat up straight and imperious. 'Gadreel, I've spoken to the other people here, and they've agreed to help you revive your people – if you tell us how to find them.'

'You are not a leader?' Zan's voice was flat as he delivered the translation, but the Nephilim had asked the question with surprise.

'No. I'm from a different country, a different . . . tribe. They don't have anyone who can use the key.'

Gadreel said a word Zan couldn't translate, the Chinese shaking his head apologetically. But the Nephilim's expression was one Nina knew from university, both as a student and a teacher: she could only think that he had said *interesting*, waiting for the other to elaborate on their theory – or dig themselves deeper into a hole. A pause, then he spoke again. This time Zan knew the words. 'Do you know how to follow the lines of qi?'

'I don't, no,' Nina admitted. 'The knowledge was lost.'

'Then I do not know how to show you where it is.'

'Oh . . . okay. That kinda puts the kibosh on the plan, then,' she said to the cameras.

Hui's voice came through the headset. 'Colonel Wu suggests we show him a map of the region.'

'The landscape's probably changed a lot over a hundred and thirty thousand years,' she replied. 'It'd be like burying a pirate's treasure chest in the woods on Manhattan Island in the seventeenth century, then asking them to take you to it today.'

'Then what can we—' Hui broke off as Colonel Wu spoke in Mandarin. Whatever was being said, it became more heated, the commander's voice rising. The scientist eventually addressed Nina again, sounding both angry and defeated. 'The colonel has a new *suggestion*. Please tell Gadreel to wait.'

'Tell him . . . okay, tell him somebody's had an idea, and he'll have to wait to find out what it is,' Nina instructed Zan. 'I'll be interested myself, actually!'

Leaving the translator to relay her words, she returned to the conference room. 'What's going on?'

'There is a device,' said Hui, with a brief glance at Eddie and Macy that immediately made Nina concerned for their well-being – not from anything the scientist might do, but because she was warning the redhead that she and her family were about to hear something the Chinese military kept at the highest levels of secrecy. 'We call it a qi tracker – it shows the flows of earth energy on a global scale. It was built using Nephilim technology.'

'I thought you couldn't make it work,' said Eddie.

'The rest of it, no. But this . . . It is hard to explain in English,' she said, frowning.

'I'll do it, Mom,' said Cheng. 'We used a crystal from the vault. Even though it wasn't active enough to power any Nephilim tech, we could still test it to see how it *reacted* to different qi flows, first around the country and then around the world. The changes were at a very low level, but we could still detect them. It let us build up a map that showed us how qi flows around the planet – and now we've packed enough computer power into it to see changes in real time.'

'Oh, you have, huh?' said Nina, taken aback. 'So, what – you're going to wheel this thing in and get Gadreel to point at the fortress on its map?'

That was exactly what Colonel Wu had in mind.

The qi tracker was not what Nina had expected. The name suggested a device resembling a radar dish, but what two men actually brought in on a small pallet was a skeletal torus made of orichalcum and the dark metal she had seen in the ice fortress, crystals and purple stone arranged within amongst a complex web of wiring and microcircuitry. A laptop with the hefty ruggedised casing of military hardware was mounted above it, linked by cables. The whole apparatus stood about two feet tall.

The archaeologist part of her was already seething at the thought of the artefacts that must have been torn apart and melted down to make the machine. Macy's thoughts were more prosaic. 'Does it work?' she asked, regarding the tracker with curiosity.

Hui smiled at her. 'It does. It is still being developed, but it is much more accurate than when first tested. We can track lines of qi energy across the world to within one hundred metres.'

'Why?' Nina asked. 'I mean, why build it in the first place if you can't actually *use* earth energy?'

'Knowing where the lines of qi flow will let us perform experiments. Once we know the power is there, we may be able to harness it – without needing a person to channel it. We could have limitless electricity without burning coal or flooding farmlands.'

'So why's the military in charge of it and not the Ministry of Energy?' said Eddie sceptically.

Major Wu overheard the discussion, and moved to end it before further awkward questions could be asked. 'Professor Wilde, once the tracker is running, you will ask Gadreel for the location of the buried fortress.'

'What if he can't find it?' said Nina.

'That is not an option. He *must* find it.'

'Good to know you're flexible.' She examined the machine as it was placed alongside Zan's station. One of its bearers opened the laptop, pecking out commands on its keyboard. LEDs inside the torus lit up to indicate that it was now active. Nina glanced at Gadreel, who watched with fascination. Amazement that the savage beasts who had been humanity at the time he entered stasis had now created their own technology, perhaps? Or was he containing his contempt that for all their advances, they still couldn't replicate that of the Veteres and the Nephilim?

The man working the laptop called out to Colonel Wu, who nodded. 'It is ready,' his daughter announced. 'Display the map. Professor Wilde, ask him to show us the fortress.'

Nina took her seat beside the softly humming tracker. Its operator gave the trackpad a final tap before retreating.

Two maps appeared on the laptop's screen. One was a Mercator projection of the world, the other a computer-generated globe. Red lines began to appear on both, a twisting web spreading over the earth's surface. 'Are those the lines of earth energy?' Nina asked, watching as the network grew ever more dense.

'Yes,' Wu replied. 'The tracker will take few minutes to show them all, but now it is calibrated it can identify them even on the other side of the planet.'

Gadreel moved closer to the glass, crouching for a better look. The laptop was on a swivel mount; Nina turned it towards him. 'Well, he's got to see the thing to find the fortress,' she pointed out as the Chinese officers expressed silent disapproval.

Gadreel's expression became one of amazement as he stared at the screen. For all the ancient race's achievements, television had not been one of them, a moving picture as remarkable to him as an artefact levitated by earth energy was to a modern human. Nina spoke to him. 'This is a map of the world. The red lines are where earth energy is flowing.'

'I understand,' came the translated reply. Gadreel stared intently at the image. Ever-finer lines were being drawn, curling and weaving across continents between much heavier currents of natural power. 'I recognise some places.' He pointed, Nina leaning to see where he was indicating. It seemed to be the region of the Persian Gulf. 'That sea. We explored it.'

'I don't know exactly where he's pointing,' Nina told the observers. 'Is there a way to zoom in?'

'It is a touchscreen,' Hui replied. 'You can use it like the map on a phone.'

Nina hesitantly put her thumb and forefinger over the Gulf on the Mercator projection and slid them apart. The map expanded. The CGI globe followed suit, the world turning to bring the Middle East to the sphere's centre. Even through the glass, she heard Gadreel make an exclamation. A moving picture was impressive enough, but an *interactive* one was on another level entirely. She pointed out the enclosed waters. 'Is this the sea?'

'Yes,' came the reply. 'From it, we travelled east.'

Nina zoomed back out. Gadreel gazed intently at the map, taking in the shapes of the coastlines and the paths of energy crossing them. She had an idea and scrolled to Asia, then downwards to reveal Antarctica. 'This is where the Veteres hid their city,' she told him. 'Where your fortress was trapped in the storm.' There were several places on the frozen continent where major lines crossed each other: confluence points. From past experience, she imagined that if she moved the map to Europe, she would see another over Glastonbury in southern England.

'Go up,' the giant ordered. She dragged the map back towards the equator. 'Stop.'

Australia, the vast island chain of Indonesia and the Philippines, and the Malaysian peninsula were now on view, more confluences dotted amongst them. 'Do you recognise it?' she asked.

Another long pause, Gadreel absorbing the image before replying. 'We passed many islands when we travelled to Antarctica. But I do not know these places for certain.'

'Show him where we are now,' said Major Wu. 'See if he recognises it.'

Eddie, standing with Macy and Cheng at the lab's rear, offered another suggestion. 'Better idea – show him where you lot found the fort at the nuke test site. If that was like an outer defence for his main fortress, he'd know how far apart they were, and in what direction.'

'Good idea,' said Nina, before turning to the Chinese. 'Where *was* it found?'

Zan reached over to scroll the map. China came into view, along with parts of the surrounding nations. He pointed out a particular spot in the country's west, then returned to his computer, speaking in the Nephilim's own language.

Gadreel examined the map thoughtfully. It was some time

before he replied, and he did so carefully, mind still hard at work. 'The fortress' – Nina noticed that he now used a word she recognised, vimana – 'is to the east. It is . . .' the translator used a calculator app to make a unit conversion, 'ninety-five kilometres from it, at the foot of a mountain. It was placed . . .' Zan hesitated again, this time frowning as if unsure he had chosen the correct word, 'at the meeting of several lines of qi.'

'He must show us,' Colonel Wu demanded.

'It'll probably be easier if you just do what Gadreel tells you,' Nina told Zan. The translator nodded and began an exchange with the Nephilim, adjusting the map with each response. Sensing the task might take some time, Nina rejoined her family.

'You okay?' Eddie asked.

'Yeah, I'm fine. Why?'

He glanced at Colonel Wu and his daughter, both watching Gadreel with hawkish intensity. 'Don't like those two,' he said quietly. 'I reckon they're up to something.'

'Haven't doubted that since we arrived here. I'm amazed they left me alone with that machine.'

'You weren't alone,' Macy pointed out. 'Mr Zan was with you.'

A small laugh from Nina. 'You know, you're right. You kind of forget he's there. But it definitely feels like there's more to the tracker than just, y'know, tracking. It can trace flows of earth energy, sure – but why's that so important to the Chinese military?'

Eddie lowered his voice still further. 'Some sort of weapon? Jack Mitchell and DARPA tried to use earth energy to blow stuff up.'

Nina frowned at the thought of the operative from the Defense Advanced Research Projects Agency, America's secret weapons think tank. He had worked with her to locate King Arthur's sword Excalibur, itself a conduit for earth energy, before a Russian oligarch could put it to destructive use – only to reveal his true colours and force her to become a living component of his own deadly weapon system. 'Maybe. But it won't be any use without someone who can activate it.'

'Someone like you.'

'If they try, I'll make them regret it,' she promised. 'I can channel earth energy – and now I know I can *control* earth energy. It won't go where they point it, believe me.'

'Let's hope it doesn't come to that, eh?'

'Yeah. Oh, what's happening?' Zan was calling to Colonel Wu. The commander and his daughter strode to him. Dr Hui followed as the translator pointed out something on the screen.

'Better go and find out before they decide we're done here,' said Eddie.

Nina took his point and quickly joined the little group. 'Has he found it?'

'I think so, yes,' said Hui excitedly. 'About fifty-five kilometres from here. Somewhere north of Xinengyuan.'

'The new city? At least it wasn't right in the middle of it.'

'There were several qi confluence points in the region,' said Zan, indicating the intersections of red lines on the map, now rendered with extra detail to show topography, 'but Gadreel remembered the mountains nearby. We used them to find the correct location.'

'He sure?' asked Colonel Wu. The translator nodded. 'Good. We begin now.' He summoned the two men who had brought the tracker, then gave them orders. Hui reacted in alarm.

'What's going on?' Nina asked.

'I don't know,' she replied. 'Colonel Wu!'

He ignored her until he had finished, his subordinates saluting and going to the tracker. They closed the laptop and carried the machine away. Major Wu went with them, taking out a phone to issue orders of her own. The colonel summoned Hui to follow as he moved out of Zan's earshot. 'Professor Wilde. You too.'

Nina and Hui exchanged worried looks, then went to him.

'What are you doing?' the scientist demanded.

'We have location of fortress,' he said. 'We now find it.'

'It is an archaeological site,' Hui protested. 'I am in charge of—'

'*I* am in charge!' Wu interrupted.

Hui tried to stifle her shock at the abrupt usurpation of her position. 'I was appointed by the Central Committee,' she said stiffly. 'You have no right to overrule me on any matters concerning the Nephilim.'

'I have orders,' growled the colonel. 'You obey, or I remove you.' As Hui stared at him, speechless, he turned to Nina. 'Now we know where to look, this project no longer scientific. It now military. No more delays. We fly there in helicopters and search.'

The way he was regarding the two women gave Nina the feeling she was about to receive some very unwelcome news. 'You mean "we" as in "me and my team of soldiers and nobody else, especially not any Americans"?' she asked hopefully.

'You both come. And him.' He pointed at Zan, who was back at his computer and speaking into his headset. 'And . . . that.' A final stab of his blunt finger at Gadreel.

'Why do you need *me*?' Nina protested.

Colonel Wu indicated Gadreel again. 'He say only women can open fortress.' He added some Mandarin.

Hui translated for Nina. 'Priestess,' she said. 'Gadreel told Zan that only a priestess can open the fortress.'

'Like I told Gadreel, I'm not a priestess!'

'You come with us,' said the colonel. It was a direct order, anger rising behind it.

'What's going on?' Eddie demanded, coming closer with fists balled. A sharp look from Wu prompted guards to block his approach.

'They're taking me with them to find the fortress,' said Nina. 'And I'm *sure* they'll honour their deal with Gadreel and wake up his family once we get inside, right?'

'This is not my doing,' Hui protested. 'Colonel, I am still in charge of this operation! I will take this to the highest authority if I have to.'

'Do that,' Wu snapped. 'But later. Now, you have orders.' He called out to Zan, who reacted in dismay as he was given his new assignment. Then the commander turned on his heel and marched away, two guards falling in behind.

'This – this was not supposed to happen!' Hui told Nina. 'I am sorry, I thought . . .'

'You thought the military would just stand back and let you run things?' Eddie offered as a worried Macy joined him. 'Sorry, but that's never happened in the entire history of the world. Would have thought an archaeologist would know that.'

Hui spoke to Zan. 'Have you told Gadreel what just happened?'

'No,' he replied, flustered. 'I was . . . asking him if he knew any more about the fortress.'

'Do not tell him the situation. We do not want him to think that we have lost control to the military.'

'Y'know, he's probably figured that out already,' said Nina. The Nephilim now stood with arms folded and feet apart in an unmistakably dominant pose, looking down on the aggravated humans beyond the glass as if observing the reaction inside an ant farm after he had shaken it. 'He might be five hundred years old, but he's not senile.'

'I still have to tell him the colonel commandant wants him to go with us,' said Zan.

'Do that. But . . . be subtle. Make it seem we still have authority.'

'Good luck with that,' said Eddie.

301

Zan turned pensively back to Gadreel. Nina's expression as she faced Eddie and Macy was equally concerned. 'Somehow I doubt the colonel's going to let you come with me.'

'So do I,' the Englishman replied. 'Still, at least we're not prisoners. We might be inside a secret lab in an underground bunker guarded by hundreds of soldiers on a military base in the middle of a desert in China, but they haven't actually locked us up. Yet.'

Nina smiled, then crouched to hug Macy. 'Afraid I'll be taking another trip without you. Will you be okay?'

'Daddy'll be with me, so . . . I guess.' Not even her father's presence was enough to overcome her misgivings. 'Why do they need you to go? Daddy said it was because you're the only person who can control earth energy.'

'That they know of,' Nina clarified – uncomfortably aware that there was a good chance Macy shared the same genetic key, and that if the Chinese had not yet come to the same realisation, they might do at any time. 'They need me to open the fortress. If it's still there – it could have been destroyed thousands of years ago.'

'Let's hope,' said Eddie. 'I get the feeling nothing good'll come of it if you find the thing.'

'Same here.' She looked around as a phone rang.

Dr Hui answered, face falling in resignation as the caller spoke. 'That was Major Wu,' she said. 'Professor, we are to meet the colonel and his team in fifteen minutes.'

'I'll get my gear,' said Cheng.

His mother shook her head. 'No. I'm sorry, but . . . the major's orders were that only myself, Professor Wilde and Zhi are to come. And Gadreel.'

The young man was outraged. 'But this is an archaeological mission! If soldiers start crashing around inside the fortress, they could wreck everything!'

Eddie grinned. 'You really are Nina's student, aren't you?'

'I'm being serious!' Cheng looked back at Hui. 'This is *your* project – you're in charge. You don't take orders from them!'

'I'm afraid I do.' She sighed. 'Everyone does, if they know what is good for them.' A moment of maudlin defeat, then she raised her head. 'Professor Wilde, Zhi? We must go.'

Zan hastily concluded his exchange with the Nephilim. 'I'm ready! But I need to get some things.'

'You have fourteen minutes,' Hui told him. The translator hurried away, Gadreel watching him go. She turned back to her still fuming son. 'Just because the military want to secure the site does not mean there will be nothing left to discover.'

'I hope so,' Cheng replied, unconvinced.

'We will set up a live video feed to the control centre. I want you to monitor it. And take Mr Chase and his daughter. If anyone questions their presence, tell them you are all there on my authority.'

'What if they call Colonel Wu and he orders us out?'

'I think the colonel will have more important matters on his mind.' She kissed Cheng on the cheek. 'But you should get there quickly. If you are already inside when the military observers arrive, they will be less likely to make you leave.'

He gave her a reluctant nod. '*Zàijiàn,*' he said, before facing Eddie and Macy. 'She's right. We should go to the control centre.'

'Okay,' said the Yorkshireman. 'Nina, you take care.'

'Don't I always?'

'I wouldn't need to remind you if you did!' They shared a smile. 'Come on, Macy. Let's see if there's anything expensive you can break.'

'Daddy!' Macy objected as they followed Cheng from the lab. 'You're the one who always breaks things.'

'Are you ready?' Hui asked Nina.

The redhead sighed. 'No, but that's never stopped me before.'

★ ★ ★

Ten minutes later, the two women headed for the elevators. Hui had detoured to collect a hastily assembled pack of archaeological tools and an expensive camera. Nina almost started to gather equipment of her own, but suppressed her professional urges; the operation was still in the hands of the Chinese military, and she was being forced to help them. Her cooperation would be the bare minimum she could get away with.

'I do not know how long this will take,' Hui said as they entered the corridor leading to the Atlantean vault's hangar. 'Gadreel may recognise the landscape when we arrive, but—' To her surprise, Zan emerged from the archive ahead of them. 'What are you doing?'

'I – I was checking the original inscriptions,' he replied. 'I wasn't sure I'd translated some of Gadreel's words properly. I wanted to look at the source.'

'Yeah, I thought some things didn't seem right,' said Nina. 'Like when you said the fortress was "placed" on an earth energy confluence; I could tell you thought that wasn't the right word.'

'Come on,' said Hui, looking at her watch. 'We have to go.'

They set off again. Zan, suddenly sweating, put one hand in his pocket, something small clutched tightly in his palm.

27

Two military helicopters waited outside the bunker's entrance, transport aircraft that nevertheless had guns mounted on each side. A troop of soldiers stood before one, a smaller group with a large case that Nina guessed contained the qi tracker at the other. All were armed.

'Going in heavy for an archaeological expedition, aren't you?' she said, ostensibly to Hui but deliberately loudly enough for both Colonel and Major Wu to hear.

'This is a matter of national security,' the younger Wu snapped. 'The area will be sealed off and any civilians removed. For their own safety,' she added, almost as an afterthought.

'Uh huh.' Nina, Hui and Zan stopped at the helicopter. 'So where's Gadreel?'

Colonel Wu looked back. Nina turned to see three more soldiers escorting the Nephilim into daylight. Gadreel was now shrouded in a camo-patterned tarpaulin hastily repurposed into a cloak, sandals on his feet. 'Nice camouflage. I almost didn't see the ten-foot-tall man.'

'It will be windy in the mountains,' Hui told her. 'We did not want him to die of exposure – and,' a small smile, 'we did not have any coats in his size.' Nina half smiled too. 'There was something else inside the sarcophagus as well as his clothing,' the scientist went on, serious again. 'A trikan. Like the Atlantean weapons, but larger.'

'Yeah, we found one in the ice fortress.' Nina watched the approaching Nephilim survey his surroundings. Some of the soldiers, having not seen the giant before, looked on with wonderment, uncertainty and even fear. 'He took the clothes, but left his weapon?'

'He knows we outgun him,' said Major Wu.

Hui had her own view. 'Perhaps he trusts us and does not think he needs it?'

'Or he's got something better,' said Nina, more cynical.

'He has been searched,' Wu informed her. 'He is not a threat.'

The American reserved her judgement on that. Now that he was out of confinement, Gadreel's confidence had grown to match his stature, looking down on everyone else literally and figuratively. He spoke to Zan, who replied in the Nephilim language before translating for the other Chinese.

'He told him that we are taking him in a flying machine to find the fortress,' Hui said for Nina's benefit.

'He doesn't seem impressed,' the redhead replied.

Gadreel, whose head reached almost to the helicopter's stationary rotor blades, seemed distinctly underwhelmed by the aircraft. There was a roar, and he looked around. Across the sprawling airbase, an angular Chinese stealth fighter hurtled along the runway with afterburners blazing before rocketing skyward. Again, while he now appeared more intrigued, there was none of the shock Nina would have expected from a man from the past seeing twenty-first-century technology for the first time.

Colonel Wu waited for the thunder to subside, then gave orders. The larger group of soldiers boarded their helicopter, one of the men with the qi tracker opening the other's cabin door to let the commander enter. Major Wu stood back, directing the scientists inside.

Nina clambered in. The cabin was outfitted with metal and canvas seats designed for lightness rather than comfort, and while the space was about thirteen feet long, it was not high; even at only five foot five, she had to hunch down to move around. 'Damn. Gadreel'll have to fold himself in half.'

Colonel Wu took the seat closest to the cockpit. He gestured towards the cabin's empty rear, where blankets and bed rolls had been laid out. 'He sit on those.'

'If that's your idea of first-class flying, I'd hate to see your economy section.' Nina sat as far from the colonel as she could, Hui taking the seat beside her and Zan settling himself opposite. The soldiers then guided Gadreel into the aircraft.

The Nephilim was far from pleased by the interior, glaring at his fellow passengers as he lowered himself onto the bedding.

'Tell him that at least he won't have to eat an in-flight meal,' Nina said to Zan. Hui chuckled, but the translator did not pass on the joke.

The tracker's case was secured, then finally Major Wu boarded. The helicopter's engines started, the rotors slowly beginning to turn. Gadreel reacted in alarm to the initial rumble of machinery, but quickly calmed on seeing that the others were not concerned.

Before long, they were airborne. The helicopter wheeled into a wide banking turn, heading east. Even wearing headphones, Nina found the noise almost intolerable. She didn't want to imagine what Gadreel, whose head was too large for the ear protectors, thought of his first flight. 'How long before we get there?' she asked Hui.

The reply came through the internal intercom system. 'About thirty minutes.'

Wu heard the question through her own headphones. 'When we arrive, we still have to search for the location.'

'I hope Gadreel's got a good memory for topography,' Nina noted. 'The landscape will be totally different. The desert's expanded, rivers have changed course, forests are gone . . .'

'The *mountains* have not changed,' Wu replied, with a snide edge. 'He will recognise them.'

Annoyed, Nina looked back at the Nephilim as he asked Zan a question, the translator having to yell a reply before giving his companions a nervous look. 'What did he say?'

'He does not like this,' Zan told her, one hand in a pocket. 'Nor do I.'

'Afraid of flying?'

Neither he nor the Nephilim answered. Nina sighed, then sat back to endure the rest of the journey.

After twenty-plus minutes, Colonel Wu peered through a starboard-side porthole in response to a gesture by his daughter. Nina followed his gaze. Xinengyuan was visible, concrete and brick dotted with countless tower cranes spreading across the desert. The helicopter's course would take it north of the city. She peered through the cockpit entrance, seeing mountains ahead. Not far to go.

Another few minutes, then the aircraft began to descend. Beyond the city was a barren, dusty wilderness. Whatever had prompted the Chinese government to build an enormous new settlement here, it wasn't the fertile farmland – more likely the combination of a need for jobs and housing for an ever-swelling population, the hope of bringing investment to an isolated region, and somebody aiming to get rich from property sales.

Colonel Wu gave an order to the pilots, then called to Zan, who translated for Gadreel. The Nephilim's shouted reply was relayed back to the commander. 'The helicopter is going to circle so he can view the mountains,' Hui told Nina. 'When he recognises the landscape, he will tell us where to land.'

'*If* he recognises it,' said Nina. Part of her hoped the fortress would remain lost, her doubts about the Chinese military's ultimate motives still strong. That led to other worries: if Colonel Wu couldn't claim his prize, what would happen to her and her family? They had already seen far too much of the secret operation – she couldn't imagine they would simply be allowed to return home with that knowledge . . .

The helicopter banked into a lazy, sweeping circle. Gadreel looked out at the mountain peaks rising above the distant horizon. If he did recognise anything, he showed no sign. Minutes passed—

The Nephilim suddenly shouted. Zan hastily relayed his words, Colonel Wu barking a command to the pilot.

The helicopter slowed. Gadreel watched the ground slide by. Nina saw nothing but rock and sand and occasional scrubby vegetation, but he was clearly searching for something specific. He looked up at the mountains as if getting his bearings, then back down—

Another urgent call. Colonel Wu issued a new order. The helicopter pitched back into a hover. It hung in the air while the Chinese urgently consulted amongst themselves, then descended. A thump as it touched down, dust swirling outside. The engines powered down.

A thudding roar told Nina the second chopper was landing nearby. She looked out to see what had caught Gadreel's attention, but found nothing. They were near a low and barren dome-shaped hill, the mountains to the north rising beyond it.

The chopper's occupants disembarked. Everyone moved clear of the aircraft, regrouping nearby. 'Okay,' said Nina, surveying their surroundings, 'what have we found?' They were in the mountains' foothills, a cold wind blowing down the rocky slopes. The sprawl of Xinengyuan began several miles to the south, past nothing but desolation. There was no need to worry about keeping civilians away; there was nobody else remotely nearby.

'He says the vimana, the fortress, is here,' Zan announced, also looking around. 'But I don't know where.'

'He does,' said Wu Shun, the young woman striding to Gadreel. He was almost twice her height, but she put her hands on her hips like a teacher sternly addressing a pupil as she spoke to him. Zan translated. The Nephilim gave Wu a disdainful look, then turned to the nearby hill, speaking again.

'He says it's here, under the hill,' Zan announced.

Nina regarded the rise. It was roughly eighty feet at its highest, a near-symmetrical mound of sand and broken rock perhaps a hundred yards across. The fortress from the iceberg could have fitted into it several times over. 'Hope you brought shovels, because you'll need to do a lot of digging to find it.'

Even though Gadreel could not have known exactly what she said, he still picked up the gist from her tone. The towering figure smiled, the expression disturbingly out of place on his not-quite-human features, then said something to her.

She looked back at Zan. 'What did he say?'

'He said,' the translator replied, 'it will not be hard to find. It is not buried underneath the hill.' His eyes widened in surprise. 'It *is* the hill!'

Gadreel directed the group to one side of the mound, climbing roughly halfway up it. The soldiers from the second helicopter had indeed brought digging equipment; Colonel Wu waited for Zan to relay the Nephilim's instructions, then ordered his men to start excavating.

The hill's upper layers were little more than sand and scree, the soldiers making rapid progress, but before long the ground became more densely packed. Even so, with so many people working hard, a large hole was soon opened up. Four feet deep, five, six, the crater widening.

Nina stood near the edge to watch. Assuming Gadreel was right and the fortress was indeed here, how deep down would it be? The passage of over a hundred millennia could have deposited an awful lot of debris upon it . . .

Major Wu took a phone call, then spoke to her father. The

colonel's response was simultaneously satisfied yet impatient.

'What was that about?' Nina asked Hui.

'They think Eleanor Miller will soon tell them the name of the spy,' she replied, before shaking her head. 'What sort of woman would let her son suffer to protect a secret, but break because her money is being taken away?'

'A very rich and unpleasant one,' said Nina. 'Mind you, her son *did* leave her to die from poison gas, so even if they get out of here, I'd imagine the family Christmas dinner would be kinda awkward.' She gave the other archaeologist a penetrating look. '*Are* they going to get out of here?'

Hui wore a headset to communicate with the base; suddenly uncomfortable, she muted the microphone. 'That is . . . unlikely,' she whispered.

'And what about me and *my* family?'

The Chinese avoided Nina's gaze. 'I will do everything I can to help you. But . . .'

'But Colonel Wu's in charge, right?'

A shamefaced nod. 'Yeah.'

A shout from the pit drew their attention. A soldier jabbed into the soil with his shovel, each strike producing a metallic *thunk*. An order from the colonel, and the other men converged, working at a more hurried pace. 'They've found it!' said Nina as a dark grey plate was revealed beneath the dust of ages.

Gadreel, makeshift cape flapping in the gritty wind, stood with the Wus and Zan observing the excavation. He spoke, the translator passing on his words. 'He said the fortress was buried to hide it from the Shangdi, but there is a way inside. We will have to dig to find it,' Hui told Nina.

'That's one good thing about involving the military, I guess,' the redhead replied as the soldiers tore into the surface. 'When they're told to dig, they dig – no standing about drinking coffee or posing for selfies.'

The other woman smiled. 'I can tell you have worked with students.'

The hole grew steadily larger. Gadreel spoke again once enough metal had been exposed for him to assess where it sat on the fortress's exterior. Nina noticed he was no longer addressing Zan directly; rather, he made proclamations and expected the Chinese man at his side to pass them on to everyone within earshot as if he were a medieval herald. Colonel Wu glared at the pair, then gave stern instructions of his own. The men concentrated their digging in a new spot. 'I don't think the colonel likes anyone challenging his authority,' Nina whispered to Hui, faintly amused.

Something else was soon found. As more of the metal surface was uncovered, it was revealed to be curved, matching the domed shape of the hill – but the soldiers now reached a flat-floored recess cutting into it. They quickly cleared it of dirt, exposing what lay at its end.

A door.

It was oval, much taller than it was wide, like the entrance to the icebound fortress. This one, however, was closed tight to protect whatever awaited inside. The only feature on the otherwise smooth surface was a disc inset into its centre.

Nina knew what it was. 'It's like the lock on the vault from Turkey,' she said. 'It channels earth energy.' She addressed Gadreel. 'Am I the only person who can open it?'

The Nephilim's amused condescension was clear even before Zan translated. 'Some tools of the Nephilim can only be used by priestesses, but a fortress that even the ruler could not enter would be useless.'

'Then tell him to open it,' said Colonel Wu firmly as Nina frowned. 'Now.'

Zan passed on the command. The giant glowered at the officer, but climbed down into the trench. The soldiers backed away – though at another order, they brought up their weapons to cover him.

Gadreel eyed them, then spoke, Zan acting as relay. 'He said, "Do you not trust me?"' Hui told Nina. '"It is just a door."'

'A door that only he knows what's behind,' she pointed out.

'Do *you* not trust him?' asked Hui.

Her reply was sardonic. 'My trust supply's pretty depleted right now.' She lowered her voice. 'He lied.'

'What do you mean?'

'At the base, he said that only a priestess could open it. He wanted me here for something.'

The older woman shifted uncomfortably. 'Colonel Wu would have made you come here no matter what.'

'Why? What's *he* got in mind for me?'

Hui was reluctant to answer. She looked around in relief as father and daughter concluded a muted discussion of their own. The major told the soldiers to lower their weapons. Gadreel waited for them to retreat, then placed his palm against the disc.

Nothing happened. Colonel Wu's face darkened, and even Gadreel appeared concerned – then the metal underfoot shuddered with a deep, heavy thump. Another sound, the grind of a mechanism moving for the first time in untold centuries, and the door began to open.

A gust of escaping air kicked up a whirl of sand around Gadreel's feet. The fortress had been tightly sealed. He stepped back as the oval hatch swung inwards.

Colonel Wu entered the trench, standing beside – and just ahead of – Gadreel as the interior was revealed. A passageway disappeared into darkness. Hui began excited commentary into her headset for the benefit of those at the base.

Nina moved for a better look. Major Wu was about to wave her back when her father interceded. 'Come, look,' he said, gesturing at the opening. 'You went in other fortress. You know what inside.' A meaningful look at the Nephilim. 'You tell us if he try tricks.'

She watched as the door jolted to a stop, fully open. 'So . . . who's going in first?'

'You,' said the major. 'As long as your husband and daughter are our *guests*,' a thin smile, 'we trust you.'

Colonel Wu called out to his men, several hurrying back to the helicopters. They soon returned bearing assorted equipment, including hand-held and clip-on flashlights – and the qi tracker's crate. 'Why are you bringing that?' Nina demanded.

The colonel ignored her, staring into the shadows beyond the hatch. 'Professor Wilde,' he said. 'Lead the way.'

Nina sighed, then took a flashlight from Hui. 'At least the floor's level this time.'

She stepped across the threshold – becoming the first living thing to enter the buried fortress for one hundred and thirty thousand years.

28

The passageway beyond the entrance was much like the one in the iceberg, but almost twice as long. Nina made her way to a T-junction at its end. Others followed; first Hui, relaying what she saw to base, then Colonel and Major Wu. Behind came the first of the soldiers guarding Gadreel, then the Nephilim himself, Zan at his side. The other two guards were behind their charge, and finally came the men carrying the qi tracker.

'Which way?' Nina called back. 'In the other fortress, we went right to get to the throne room.'

Gadreel waited for Zan to translate, then replied. 'Go left,' Zan reported.

She raised an eyebrow – the layout so far seemed to match the other fortress, just on a larger scale – but took the left path as suggested. Orichalcum and adamantium and crystal gleamed in her torchlight, the new passage curving out of sight. Nina followed it, the rest of the team behind her.

'*Mā?*' said Cheng into his headset, frowning first in confusion, then rising concern. 'Mom, can you hear me?'

A camera on one of the helicopters had relayed the exploratory team's arrival at the hill to the control centre, but once they started digging, they passed out of sight over its crest. Eddie had spent the time since being as unobtrusive as possible, watching Macy show off what he had to admit were impressive yo-yo moves with her toy trikan while listening to Cheng's progress reports. The worry in the young man's voice made him hurry to his workstation. 'What's going on?'

'I don't know,' said Cheng. 'Mom was describing what she saw as they went inside, then she just . . . stopped.'

'It's like the one in the ice,' the Yorkshireman realised. 'We lost radio contact with the ship, remember?'

Cheng called to one of the other staff, who spoke to someone via his own headset. 'We can still talk to the chopper pilots and the soldiers guarding the site,' he said after receiving a reply. 'But they can't reach the people inside either.'

'We should get out there. If anything goes wrong, they'll need help.'

'I don't think they'll let us borrow a helicopter,' Cheng told him unhappily, casting a glance at the hard-faced captain overseeing operations.

Macy came to her father. 'Is Mom going to be okay?'

Eddie gave his daughter a reassuring smile. 'She'll be fine. Just a radio glitch, that's all.' He looked at the screen. The image had not changed, a handful of men visible around the hill. 'She'll be fine,' he repeated, concealing his own disquiet.

Nina led the way around the curving passageway. The fortress's interior was indeed a scaled-up replica of the one in the iceberg. Doorways opened into the same barracks-like rooms she had seen there, except these were larger, with more beds. If the similarities continued, she would soon reach the armoury. Was Gadreel deliberately taking them that way so he could grab a weapon?

But she was certain Colonel Wu was planning something too. The qi tracker's presence proved that. What was he so keen to find that it couldn't wait until the archaeological team had checked the entire fortress?

She put that question to the back of her mind as she reached a new opening. The armoury, as expected, her flashlight beam dancing across unsettling forms within. Towering suits of armour loomed over her, the black voids inside the helmets somehow more unnerving than faces.

Colonel Wu let out an exclamation, pushing past Hui to see for himself. Each suit was different, custom-made for an individual warrior. Some were dark metal, raw and unadorned; others were brightly painted with elaborate patterns worked into the plating. Helmets bore spikes, wings, horns, even the faces of grotesque beasts sneering down at the new arrivals.

Hui gasped in pure exhilaration. 'These look like the "shining armour" of the Song dynasty!' she cried. 'The plate design, the decorations – they are very similar. Bigger, of course.'

'The Chinese armour might have been a throwback to an earlier civilisation,' Nina mused. 'I've seen it before – like the carved ceiling in the Alhambra in Spain. The artwork was Islamic, but the actual design was taken from an Atlantean piece.'

Gadreel gazed at the armoury's contents. Zan now needed no prompting to translate as he spoke. 'They have not been used. My people have been safe for all this time, waiting for my return.'

Colonel Wu took an interest in something beyond the hollow platoon. '*Wǔqì!*'

Nina and Hui added their lights to his. A rack held dozens of the spear-like weapons Hui had called qiguns. '*Baraka,*' said Gadreel.

Zan was apologetic. 'It . . . it's a word I don't know.'

'I do,' Nina said, to the surprise of the others. 'It's a lot like the ancient Hebrew word for lightning.'

'Hebrew?' said Major Wu dubiously. 'You mean the Jews?'

'Nephilim is a Jewish word itself,' the redhead pointed out. 'Or more likely, it was a word the ancient Hebrews adopted to describe . . . giants.' She indicated Gadreel. 'Their name lived on even after they disappeared.'

'They disappeared, but now we have found them again,' said

Hui. She spoke into her headset – but received no reply. 'The radio is not working!'

The announcement raised alarm. The major took out her phone and saw it had no signal, then took a walkie-talkie from a soldier. Nothing came from it but static. 'The same thing happened in the ice,' said Nina. 'As soon as we went inside, we got cut off from our ship.'

Wu rounded angrily on her. 'And you did not warn us?'

'It wasn't exactly the foremost thing on my mind!'

The colonel also gave Nina a nasty look, but pointed impatiently along the passage. 'We move on. Go.'

Nina again took the lead, following the corridor around. To her relief, no exploded human remains awaited. A flight of steps led up to somewhere behind the armoury, but Gadreel signalled for her to continue past. Side rooms turned out to be other barracks and storage areas, whatever they contained long decayed to dust, but at the end of the passage more stairs led upwards. She warily ascended.

Her footsteps started to echo as she neared the top. She shone the flashlight around. A throne room, on an even grander scale than the one she had seen previously. The domed ceiling was adorned with elaborate reliefs in precious metals, another egg-like chamber set behind three gold and orichalcum thrones. Several altars were arranged in a semicircle in front of the seats, facing the elongated crystalline windows. Only dirt and stones were visible beyond.

She advanced into the chamber, the others entering behind her. On the room's opposite side she saw another set of stairs leading downwards – in the same relative position as in the smaller fortress. They would have reached the throne room much sooner had they turned right at the first junction. Her suspicion of Gadreel's motives deepened. He would have known that – so why had he taken them the long way round? To make sure the armoury and its contents were still intact?

Before she could voice her thoughts, a harsh command from Colonel Wu made her turn. Gadreel had started towards the front of the throne room, heading for stairs that Nina assumed led to another mausoleum, only to halt when his escort raised their guns. The Nephilim regarded the commander with hostility as he spoke. 'I want to see my people,' Zan translated.

Colonel Wu's reply was both negative and devoid of sympathy. He waited for the soldiers to place bright LED lanterns around the room, then signalled to the men carrying the qi tracker. They brought it to the central altar.

Major Wu took Nina by the arm, directing her towards it. She angrily tugged free. 'What are you doing?'

'You will use the resurrection key to activate the fortress,' Wu replied, holding up a satchel containing the ancient artefact.

'Like hell I will.'

'If you do not, your daughter and husband will suffer.'

'You fucking bitch,' Nina snarled. She glared at the Chinese officer's companions. Her father was stony-faced, having approved of the plan, or even conceived it. Hui, on the other hand, displayed shock at the turn of events. 'What for? Why do you want to power it up?'

The colonel spoke. 'To give China most powerful weapon in world.'

Nina blinked. 'Okay, not the answer I was expecting.'

'You have seen something like it before,' Major Wu replied. 'The American earth energy weapon.'

She remembered the container ship DARPA had secretly converted into a mobile weapons platform, able to direct a blast of the planet's raw power at a target thousands of miles away. 'You know about that?'

'Our spies are effective. But it was a crude toy compared to this.' She gestured at the dark and silent fortress around them.

'These crystals allow qi to be directed with great accuracy – and power. The potential of a large, flawless crystal to do this is almost limitless.'

'And Nephilim records,' said Colonel Wu, 'say this fortress built around such crystal.'

Nina stared at him, dismayed, then turned to Hui. 'So all the talk about changing the world was bullshit? You just want to use this thing as a big *gun*?'

'It *will* change the world,' Wu Shun said smugly before Hui could reply. 'China will take its rightful place as the greatest superpower. No one will be able to challenge us.'

'They bow to us,' her father added, 'or be destroyed.'

'You're crazy,' Nina exclaimed. 'You think America will bend over just because you've got a new weapon, however powerful?'

'You will have no choice,' said the colonel ominously.

'We can destroy your entire nuclear arsenal in minutes,' his daughter elaborated. 'And you will not even know who did it, or how.'

'That's why you want it, isn't it?' the redhead realised. 'It's a *stealth* weapon. No warning, no defence – and no way to know where the attack came from.'

The major nodded. 'America planned to do the same thing. So do not lecture us. It only exposes your own hypocrisy.'

'Not *my* hypocrisy. I blew the damn thing up! And I'll do the same to yours if I get the chance.'

'Our weapon is not as vulnerable as DARPA's. There are no masts or antennas—'

'*Antennae*,' Nina corrected.

The Chinese woman gave her a cold glare for her sarcastic pedantry, then continued. 'The earth *itself* is the antenna. The qi tracker is more than a detection device. When connected to the large crystal, it will not only show us the flows of qi; it can *redirect* them, force them together at a target until the energy that builds up is released – as an explosion. The Nephilim spear weapons do the same, but only on a limited scale.' She gestured at Gadreel. 'Your daughter asked: what was the *second* thing he was known for? He was the creator of weapons of war! He designed them, he built them. But we *improved* upon them.'

'We can destroy a building,' added Colonel Wu, 'or a city.'

'And you need me to start the whole thing up, huh?' said Nina, disgusted. 'Well, screw you. I'm not helping you do a damn—'

Major Wu abruptly punched her hard in the stomach. Nina folded in breathless pain. Hui gasped. 'You will do as we say,' the major hissed. Two of Gadreel's guards hurried over and grabbed Nina's arms, then Wu held the key up before the American. 'You will power up the fortress.'

'Fuck you,' Nina wheezed.

Wu drew back her arm as if about to hit her again, then scowled and gave another order. The soldiers hauled Nina to the central altar. Like the one in the first fortress, it had a recess in the ornate surface. Wu Shun placed the metal disc into it. She did not even offer her prisoner an ultimatum, instead forcing her hand towards it. Nina struggled, but the soldiers were too strong. She clenched her fist to stop her palm from being placed against the key—

It made no difference. Her knuckles were pressed against it – and she felt the almost electric shock of contact as earth energy was channelled through her. She jerked back. The men pushed her hand down again, but Wu Shun spoke, and they released her.

She had served her purpose, providing the spark that would re-energise the ancient structure, bringing its deadly secrets back to life. Fear rose inside her. If the Chinese decided she was no longer necessary, they wouldn't need to keep Eddie or Macy alive either . . .

Wu Shun's cold eyes were fixed upon her. Nina retreated from the altar, expecting a fatal order to be snapped out—

It didn't come. The major gave her a last dismissive sneer, then turned to the qi tracker. Its operators began to set it up.

With nowhere else to go, Nina rejoined Hui.

'I – I am so sorry,' the scientist said, appalled. 'I did not know any of this would happen!'

'Cram it,' Nina growled. 'What did you *think* was going to happen? The Chinese army was going to use all this to spread love and harmony around the world?'

Hui seemed about to protest, then sagged in defeat. 'I . . . Yes, you are right. I should have known. I . . . *did* know. But I denied it to myself.' She straightened, drawing in a determined breath. 'I will try to make it right. Colonel Wu!' She turned to the commander and spoke in firm Mandarin.

Nina noticed Zan talking quietly to Gadreel, but her attention was dominated by Colonel Wu's fiery response to Hui. The officer did not like what she said, nor was he shy about letting her know. She tried a couple of times to reply, but his verbal steamrollering could not be stopped. Only when he paused for breath did Hui manage to interject, the word 'Beijing' the only one Nina understood – she guessed the scientist was threatening to take the matter to his superiors.

If Hui had hoped he would back down, she was completely mistaken. A cold, frightening anger entered the colonel's voice, the tone of someone used to wielding power – and who would not hesitate to use it. The archaeologist shrank back as he jabbed his finger at her, voice rising with each stab. A final outburst, almost roared into her face, then he shouted an order to his daughter. She hurried over, the soldiers who had forced Nina to the altar going with her, and they took up menacing positions around Hui.

'What are you doing?' Nina demanded. Hui might have been naïve – or wilfully blind – but she had still tried to stand up for her.

'Colonel Commandant Wu has removed Dr Hui as director of the archaeological project,' Major Wu told her stonily.

'You can't do that!' She looked back at Hui. 'You're in charge! He doesn't have the authority!'

But Hui, utterly crushed, had nothing to say. 'Take her away,' said the colonel – in English, to make it absolutely clear to Nina who was in control. Major Wu and a soldier led the scientist from the throne room.

Colonel Wu watched them leave, and was about to turn back to Nina when something caught his eye. He looked around the chamber. Nina did the same, seeing faint swathes of light in the shadows; the crystals in the walls had started to glow. Only faintly – but they were growing steadily brighter. 'It's happening more quickly than in the ice fortress . . .'

'This place at meeting of many lines of qi,' the colonel replied. 'More energy here, it charge faster.' He went to the tracker. The device was now fully set up, several cables running to the key upon the altar. A custom-made clip secured them to the artefact.

Gadreel spoke with barely restrained anger. Colonel Wu gave a dismissive reply, which Zan passed on with obvious nervousness. 'He demands to see his people,' the translator then told Nina. 'The colonel said . . . he does not take orders from monsters.'

'Yeah, I can tell that went down well.' The Nephilim had the same look of cold fury Wu himself had displayed just minutes earlier – but rather than unleash his anger, he contained it, fuel for his next action.

And Nina knew he was *planning* that action, waiting for the right moment. But to do what?

One of the technicians ran a program on the tracker's laptop. Status reports flashed up. She couldn't read the text, but the numbers were clear – as were their colours. The majority of the results were in either orange or red, falling short of some desired level. The technicians exchanged worried looks, then reported their findings to the colonel.

He was not pleased, marching to the machine as if his glare could force all the numbers into the green.

'Got a problem?' Nina asked.

Colonel Wu ignored her, making demands of the technicians as he looked over their shoulders. She turned to Zan. 'They ran a test program,' he said. 'It . . . didn't work.'

'Really? Oh gee, I guess we'd all better go home and forget this happened.'

Wu did not appreciate her insolent tone. 'It should work. But it did not. Something missing.' He advanced on her, signalling for the remaining guards to block her retreat. 'You! Americans needed you to make their weapon work. So you make *our* weapon work.'

'The hell I will,' Nina replied. 'I didn't let DARPA use me to start a war, and I won't let you do it either.'

'Then your family pay.' The colonel's eyes turned more pitiless than ever. 'Choose your husband, or your daughter. One will live – and other will die!'

29

'They're coming out,' said Eddie. Figures crested the hilltop on the control centre's screen.

'There's Mom,' said Cheng with relief. 'Major Wu's with her.'

'Where's *my* mom?' Macy asked.

'I don't see her,' Eddie replied. The little group moved clear of the buried entrance. Nobody else followed.

'I'll call her,' said Cheng. He spoke into his mic. On the screen, his mother reacted by raising her head, then starting to talk – but Major Wu yanked off her headset.

Eddie watched with growing concern as the officer donned it herself. 'What's going on?'

Cheng listened in as Wu spoke to the captain in charge of the control centre – then drew a shocked breath. 'They – Mom's been removed from her post!' he whispered.

'What? Why?'

'I don't know. The major says—'

Everyone looked around in surprise as a young officer ran into the room, urgently shouting in Mandarin. The captain quickly patched him through to Wu. Cheng let out a startled exclamation.

'What the hell's happening?' Eddie demanded.

'Mrs Miller just gave up the name of her spy,' Cheng told him. 'It's Zan Zhi!'

'The translator?' Eddie looked back at the screen in alarm. 'But he's still in there with Nina!'

Major Wu had realised the same thing, starting back towards the entrance – but she only managed a few steps before stumbling. The image shook, dust kicking up from the hill. Macy gasped. 'It's an earthquake!'

'It's not an earthquake,' Eddie growled. 'It's the same thing that happened in the iceberg – Nina's powered up the bloody spaceship!' The picture jolted again. 'It's trying to pull itself out!'

'Choose now,' said Colonel Wu, watching the horrified Nina with unblinking basilisk eyes. 'Eddie, or Macy? Who lives, and who—'

The crystal columns in the walls suddenly pulsed, light rippling through them – and the throne room lurched.

Nina reeled against a guard, knocking him to the floor. She managed to regain her balance, but the Chinese soldiers were all thrown off their feet.

Zan also staggered – but Gadreel grabbed him, the Nephilim prepared for the sudden shift. He muttered something. Zan hurriedly tugged a cloth-wrapped object from his pocket and gave it to him.

The truth came to Nina: *Zan* was Eleanor's spy, selling his intimate knowledge of the Nephilim and their technology in the hope of finding wealth and freedom outside China. The Millers would eventually expose him as a traitor under interrogation – so he had turned to the only person who could now help him escape.

Zan must have taken the object from the archive. What it was, and what Gadreel meant to do with it, she had no idea. But it was also *her* only way out: the only way she could protect her family from Colonel Wu.

A rumbling sound echoed through the chamber. Nina looked towards the windows – and saw the packed earth outside shifting, slowly sliding over the crystal.

The fortress was *moving*, the entire structure burrowing up through the thousands of tons of dirt and debris that had buried it for millennia.

Hui had only just recovered from the shock of the quake when the ground trembled again, less violently – but more insistently, the tremors like the thrum of some giant machine.

Which, she realised, might just be the cause. 'It's the fortress!' she shouted. 'We need to move!'

She ran for the helicopters. Both aircraft were parked well clear of the domed hill, but still shook, rotor blades flapping and bouncing. Wu recovered and chased after her, the soldiers following as the earth began to slide away underfoot.

A hole opened up before Wu. She almost fell into it, but leapt the widening gap just in time. Behind her, a great ragged cleft tore the hillside apart.

Hui finally reached the bottom of the slope and risked a look back. To her shock, she saw that the hill had *grown*, its summit rising. She ran faster, hearing panicked cries from the soldiers behind—

One shout became a scream as a man was swallowed by an opening crevice – only to be silenced as tons of dirt rolled over him.

Wu Shun cleared the mound and raced after Hui, enmity forgotten in her fear. 'What's happening?' she cried.

'The fortress,' Hui panted in reply. 'It's coming out of the ground!'

'*How?* How is that possible?'

The scientist's reply was cut off by a roar of falling rubble as *something* pushed up through the hill – and continued skywards, the dark shape masked by a cascade of sand and stones. A soldier who had just reached level ground was crushed by a churning wave of falling debris. Another man further back was caught in the landslide and plunged with it over the rising edge, screaming all the way down before vanishing into the chaos.

Dust gushed around the two women, who shielded their faces. The landslip's fearsome noise reached a crescendo . . . then faded.

Hui squinted through the swirling cloud. To her shock, the hill was gone.

An empty crater was surrounded by a ragged ring of piled debris, the earth and stone that had fallen from the fortress as it rose – but where was the fortress itself?

She looked up . . . and got her answer.

Panic and confusion ran through the control centre as churning earth and billowing dust clouds filled the screen. 'Mom!' cried Cheng as he spotted a figure running towards the camera.

'She's okay – but where's Nina?' said Eddie. Others were behind Hui, but his wife was not one of them—

The image cleared enough for him to see what lay behind the running figures. It took him a moment to process. 'Okay,' he said in disbelief. 'Tell me that's *not* a bloody UFO!'

Something hovered over the crater where the hill had been, dust streaming from its dark metal hull. It looked like the fortress Eddie had seen trapped in the iceberg – but much larger, more menacing.

Hui and Wu Shun stood in the image's foreground, staring up at the impossibly floating juggernaut. Cheng was similarly awestruck. '*Fuzanglong* . . .' he whispered.

'What does that mean?' Macy asked, wide-eyed.

'It means a dragon – a treasure dragon,' he replied. 'It's a Chinese legend – it lives underground, but can come out and fly.' He pointed at a detail on the screen. 'And it has a pearl under its chin, a symbol of qi.'

Eddie saw what he meant. The fortress did indeed bear a

distinct resemblance to the head of a Chinese dragon, the windows on its upper section forming sinister eyes – and on its underside, below the elongated snout from which fangs protruded, was a brightly glowing sphere, mostly hidden behind curved plates of armour.

There was more to the fortress than the head section. It had a snake-like rear body, tapering back to a point, though the camera's angle meant he couldn't judge its size. All he knew for sure was that it was *big*.

And Nina was still inside it.

'We've got to get out there,' he told Cheng. 'I'm not sitting around while my wife's trapped in that thing!'

'I don't know how!' the young man replied. 'If my mother's no longer in charge, the scientific team won't have any authority—'

He broke off at the sight of Wu hurrying towards the helicopter, Hui and the surviving soldiers behind her. Cheng covered his microphone as he overheard an exchange between the major and the captain in the control centre. 'She's calling for backup,' he whispered. 'Colonel Wu is still inside – and so are Professor Wilde and Gadreel. And Zan,' he added.

'I'm assuming the sentence for treason in China isn't two weeks' community service,' said Eddie. 'He'll do whatever it takes to escape.'

On the screen, Wu Shun issued orders to the soldiers. Cheng looked at Eddie with sudden hope. 'She didn't say anything else about my mom – and she told the captain to call the airbase and get more men out there. He's the only officer here who knows my mom's not in charge any more—'

'And he's got more important things to worry about,' Eddie finished as the captain made a frantic phone call. 'You think we can hitch a ride?'

Cheng nodded. 'If I tell the pilot my mother authorised us to go, they should believe me. I hope.'

'Only one way to find out.' Eddie spoke quietly to Macy. 'Normally I'd want you to stay here where it's safe. But right now, I don't want to let you out of my sight! So do you fancy a helicopter ride?'

'Not really,' she admitted. 'But I want to help Mom.'

'Me too. Let's see what we can do.'

Cheng surreptitiously checked that the military personnel were not paying him any attention, then they followed him to the exit.

Nina blinked as daylight flooded into the throne room. The dirt covering the windows slid away – to reveal that the fortress was now above the ground.

High above the ground. 'Oh my God!' she said, running to the nearest window. 'We've taken off!'

The fortress hovered some sixty feet up. Colonel Wu gestured for the guards to watch Gadreel, then hurried to see for himself, uttering a shocked exclamation.

Gadreel spoke. Nina and the colonel turned as Zan translated. 'You have seen what our fortress can do. This is the power of qi – the power of the Nephilim. Now you will honour our agreement, and help me wake my people.'

Colonel Wu's initial response was a mocking chuckle. He then gave his reply, which Zan dutifully relayed to Gadreel.

Nina sighed. 'I don't even speak Mandarin, and I know that was not a big helpful yes.'

'Did you think I give this . . . *caveman* anything?' sneered Wu.

'Oddly enough, no. And I don't think he did either.' Gadreel's expression was not outrage at the betrayal; rather, it was almost . . . *expectant*.

Wu didn't notice. 'It does not matter. Fortress is ours. It can fly? Good! He fly it to Cangliang. If he not do as I say, I have his people destroyed, one by one.'

330

Zan passed on his words. Gadreel's face tightened. 'I knew you would say that,' the Chinese translated. 'So I . . . prepared—'

Before Zan could finish, the giant brought his hands together – and snatched the wrapping from the hidden object.

The colonel saw the movement and shouted a furious command to the guards. Their guns came up—

Gadreel curled the first two fingers of his left hand around a piece of crystal inside an adamantium spiral. He aimed it at the soldiers – and pressed his thumb against an exposed facet.

The crystal glowed. A crackling ball of what looked to Nina like heat haze erupted from the strange object's end—

Both soldiers *exploded*.

One instant they were there – the next they burst apart in a red mist. Only extremities remained intact – a forearm, a lower leg, the top of one man's skull. Their rifles spun from the eruption of gore, the stock of one split and mangled as if a small bomb had detonated inside it.

Gadreel still held his weapon, but part of his hand was gone, his first two fingers and a chunk of the palm blown away. But even with his face twisted in agony, he rushed towards the grisly remains of the dead soldiers.

Nina stared in horror at the carnage – then fear and adrenalin took control, sending her diving behind the nearest altar. Her action snapped Colonel Wu out of his shock. He snatched for his holstered pistol—

The Nephilim scooped up the undamaged rifle with his right hand. It looked almost toy-like in his grip – but was still deadly. Gadreel jammed his forefinger's tip into the trigger guard as he whipped around, a blaze of fire cutting down the two military technicians.

The colonel's gun was only halfway clear. He threw himself behind another altar as Gadreel rounded on him. Bullets shrilled off metal in his wake. Then the gun ran dry, bolt clacking on an empty chamber. The Nephilim looked at the empty weapon in confusion.

Colonel Wu jumped up, automatic in hand—

Another shot struck his cover, forcing him back down.

Zan had recovered the damaged rifle, gingerly holding the blood-splattered weapon as if it were dripping in acid. The spy sent two more rounds at Wu's cover.

The Nephilim dropped his useless rifle and shouted to Zan. The translator looked at him – and the colonel used his distraction to race for the nearest stairwell. Zan spun back, but hesitated, unable to fire on a live target.

Gadreel had no such qualms. He ran to the translator and snatched the rifle from him – but Wu had reached the stairs. He dived down them as bullets tore past.

The giant shouted in anger, then returned the gun to Zan, giving an order that Nina guessed was an instruction to guard the chamber. He came to her, putting down the damaged Nephilim artefact. A strained breath at the pain from his ruined hand, then he spoke. 'You will help me if you want to stay alive,' Zan translated.

She eyed Gadreel's left hand. Blood dripped from the wound, as red as any human's. 'You'll need help yourself if you don't want to bleed to death.'

'I will live. I will endure any pain for my people's freedom.' He looked towards the mausoleum's entrance. 'Bring the resurrection key. It is time to wake them!'

Cheng emerged nervously from the bunker, Eddie and Macy following. A Z-20 transport helicopter, an updated copy of the American Black Hawk, was taking aboard a hurriedly assembled squad of troops. A second aircraft was on its way from the main airbase to collect another group. The captain from the control centre climbed into the waiting chopper. The Z-20's engines screamed to full power, and it hauled itself skywards, turning east.

Eddie watched it go, then regarded its approaching twin. 'He didn't see us. Think you can bullshit your way aboard this one?'

'I'll try my best,' Cheng replied.

'Daddy!' exclaimed Macy. 'You swore!'

Her father grinned. 'Afraid you might hear a lot more rude words from me, love. I can only watch one thing at once, and if anything kicks off, it won't be my mouth.'

The second helicopter landed. The assembled soldiers shielded their faces from the gritty wind, then hurried to it. 'Come on,' said Cheng, running after them.

Eddie and Macy followed. A junior officer counted the team into the cabin; he looked in surprise at the civilians, deep suspicion rising when he realised two were not Chinese. Cheng shouted an explanation over the idling engines. Eddie tensed. If the soldier knew that Dr Hui had been removed from her post, the only place they would be taken was a cell . . .

The man seemed unsure what to do – but the situation's urgency, and the presence of the project director's son, overcame his concerns. He pointed into the cabin. Cheng thanked him, then squeezed inside. Eddie and Macy went in after him, the lieutenant boarding and slamming the door.

With two gunners, ten soldiers and their gear already within, the cabin was a tight squeeze. Cheng took the last empty seat, holding his backpack on his thighs. The Englishman pushed his way up the central aisle and crammed himself into a corner behind the cockpit seats. There were no spare seat belts; the best he could do was wedge his feet against the seat frames and grasp a cargo strap. He used his free arm to hold Macy on his lap. 'You okay?' he asked her.

'I don't think this'll be as nice as the flight to China,' she replied, worried.

'So long as we get there in one piece, that's the main thing.' The engines rose in volume. 'And then we'll see what trouble your mum's caused this time!'

The Z-20 lumbered into the air, following the first aircraft towards the distant mountains.

Gadreel disconnected the cables and lifted the key from the altar, then led Nina to the mausoleum. Zan took up position at the top of the stairs to watch the throne room's other entrances. 'He wants you to open his wife's sarcophagus,' the translator told her. 'There's a hole, like the one in the altar – put in the resurrection key, then place your hand on it.'

'Yeah, I know what to do,' Nina replied. 'I woke *him*, remember?'

'Of course. Sorry.' Zan nodded apologetically, then resumed his sentry duty. 'I'll translate if you need me.'

'You might have to shout.' Like everything about the new fortress, the crystalline chamber below was larger than its frozen counterpart. The glow from the translucent walls revealed at least fifty sarcophagi, four rings of ancient coffins standing like golden tombstones around a trio of more ornate examples at the room's centre.

The most elaborate was empty. Gadreel went to one of its neighbours, gazing at the shadowy figure inside before moving on to the third. He indicated the recess at its foot, speaking loudly so Zan could hear. 'My wife,' the translator called back to Nina. 'Wake her first.'

'What about the poison gas?' she asked. 'I don't see any gas masks in here!'

Zan passed on her concerns. 'He says the gas will be . . . taken away when the sarcophagus opens. I didn't understand all the words, but he's not worried.'

'I wish I had his confidence in something that hasn't been

used in a hundred and thirty thousand years.' A sigh, then she held out a hand. 'Okay. Let's get this party started.'

Gadreel didn't need to understand English to recognise her mockery. He scowled, slapping the key down with more force than necessary. She set it in the recess, readied herself – then placed her palm upon it.

Even prepared for contact with the planet's hidden energies, the sensation still came as a shock. A moment to recover and gather her thoughts, then she focused her temporary sixth sense upon what she felt around her.

Both Gadreel and Colonel Wu were right: the fortress was at a confluence point for earth energy. An almost overwhelming power flowed through it, irresistible as a tsunami. She fought to ride the current to the far smaller conjunction controlling the sarcophagus. *There*; her mind felt the flow of force around it, sensed the hint of consciousness within. There were many more nearby, waiting – pleading – to be awoken, but she kept her attention on the closest. Guide the lines, shape them the way she needed—

Done. She withdrew her hand, blinking in momentary confusion as reality inverted. Gadreel spoke as she retreated from the sarcophagus. 'Did you wake her?' Zan asked from the stairs.

'Yeah, I did – and this thing's about to open, so I'm standing well clear!'

The Nephilim, though, did not move. The crystal lid began to rise. Wisps of gas rolled out – but then a hollow moan came from beneath the coffin. The few vaporous coils that had escaped rolled slowly down to floor level, but the yellow miasma still inside the sarcophagus was drawn into its base. The tubes the mercenaries had broken in the iceberg were not to keep it filled with the gas, Nina realised; rather, to extract it safely before the sleeper awoke.

The crystal took on a turquoise tint. The lid rose higher, revealing the figure within. Another giant, though not so tall as

Gadreel. A woman. The fine crystalline tendrils wrapping her body began to retreat, exposing bare pale skin. Nina felt a frisson of primal fear at the sight of her face. Though she had the same non-human features as her husband, she was beautiful – in the dangerous, predatory manner of a lioness or a bird of prey. Nina's unease was compounded by the Nephilim's hair. It was red, like hers – but of a shade no human had ever naturally worn, almost the colour of blood.

Gadreel made a deep, breathless sound, his expression beatific. 'Sidona,' he said, putting a hand on the motionless body.

'Sidona – my wife,' echoed Zan.

'Yeah, I figured that part out for myself,' Nina snarked.

'The high priestess of the Nephilim,' he continued. 'She is safe, and now she will awaken the rest of my people.'

'Okay, great,' she said with forced cheer. 'Well, if he doesn't need me any more, I'll be on my way!'

Gadreel looked at her with annoyance, pointing at the key. 'You will wake my son, Turel, then my warriors. She will take . . . I think he means a few minutes,' Zan said, 'to recover.'

Nina reluctantly returned to the coffin, but other than an unpleasant bleach-like odour, the air was clear of residual gas. She took the key and went to the third central sarcophagus. The shadowy form inside was almost as tall as Gadreel, but even through the distorting crystal it was noticeably more slender, wiry rather than muscular. Under Gadreel's watchful stare, she activated the key.

Again a new eye opened inside her mind, drawing her into the strange parallel realm of energy. This time, the process of awakening the sleeper was almost routine. She took a moment to widen the scope of her perception, trying to feel the fortress itself. The result was unnerving. The forces lifting its mass clear of the ground in defiance of gravity were vastly more powerful than she had imagined.

Could she affect them? Not from here, she realised. The key was merely a conduit, while the central altar in the throne room was indeed a kind of a control panel, intimately linked to the fortress's levitation.

Shifts in the energy flow brought her mind back to more immediate matters. She released the key, drawing back from the opening sarcophagus. Gadreel leaned over Sidona's coffin. The glassy strands enveloping the Nephilim woman had now fully withdrawn, patches of warmer colour appearing on her pallid skin.

He glanced impatiently at Nina. 'Now wake my warriors,' Zan intoned from the stairs.

The revival process became practically rote, setting several more Nephilim on the road to recovery. She released the key – to find another person in the chamber. Sidona was now standing, her back to Nina as she donned a long purple robe.

The priestess turned and regarded her with barely veiled contempt. She spoke, her voice having the same strange reverberation as her husband's. Zan's translation was tinged with nervousness; Nina guessed she had treated him with the same disdain. 'She wants you to give her the key.'

'She's welcome to the damn thing,' she replied, holding out the artefact to the giantess – who looked down at the floor as if expecting Nina to kneel at her feet before handing it over. 'Not gonna happen,' she muttered. Sidona's almond-shaped eyes narrowed, but she snatched the key away, then turned and spoke to Gadreel.

He gestured at the figure in the third central coffin. For the first time, the leader's face revealed genuine pleasure. His wife's resurrection had been a relief; his child's was a source of delight. The youth stirred, slowly opening his eyes. He blinked, bringing his parents into focus. All smiled as the family was reunited after one hundred and thirty millennia. Gadreel spoke, but Zan opted to let them share the moment in private.

Turel was helped out of his sarcophagus. If he were human, Nina would have guessed him to be in his mid teens, but considering the race's extended lifespan, for all she knew he was in his fifties. He started to dress, donning a blue robe and a belt on which was hung a trikan, its blades retracted. Nina backed quietly towards the stairs, but the Nephilim leader gave a sharp command. She halted. 'He wants you to go to the throne room,' Zan told her.

'That was kinda my plan,' she said. 'Although I meant to keep on going to the exit!' That made her think of Colonel Wu; he had not reappeared, but with the fortress floating high above the ground, there was no way he could escape it. Where was he, and what was he doing?

She climbed the stairs. Gadreel and his son followed as Sidona checked the other sarcophagi Nina had activated. The crystal pillars in the throne room's walls were now brightly aglow. More daylight shone in through the long windows. She glimpsed parts of the outer hull, seeing the same iridescent shimmer that had appeared on the fortress in the ice. Some other earth energy effect, but what?

Gadreel went to a window with Turel, the two men gazing across the landscape, then spoke again. 'What's he saying?' Nina asked Zan.

'I have returned to you in victory,' the translator replied. 'Our persecutors are no more, we have . . . outlasted? Outlived them. Now we must claim our inheritance. We will awaken our people here, then find Tartarus.'

The truth dawned as Nina heard the name. 'The Nephilim captured by the Veteres were put in stasis in Tartarus just like Gadreel's people here,' she realised, 'except the Veteres had no intention of ever reviving them. They could still all be there – and Gadreel wants to wake them!'

'But where *is* Tartarus?' said Zan.

'I don't know . . . but he's got a good idea.'

The Nephilim leader kept glancing at the qi tracker while talking to his son – at the Chinese base, he had seen the map of earth energy flowing around the entire globe.

Sidona, carrying the key, emerged from the mausoleum and called out to her husband. His interest in the tracker was confirmed when he pointed at it. She gave the Chinese technology a quizzical look, then went to it. The two Nephilim men started towards her, Gadreel issuing instructions. 'What does he want her to do?' Nina whispered to Zan as she set the key in the altar.

'He says it will lead them to Tartarus – and we will show them how it works.'

'Oh, *we* will, huh? This might be a good time for you to tell him that not only am I not a weapons designer, I can't even read Mandarin—'

Movement behind Gadreel and Turel, a shadow shifting in the stairwell – and Colonel Wu appeared, pistol raised.

Nina instinctively dropped behind the nearest altar. Zan stared at the officer, frozen in surprise, but he was not Wu's target. The gun found Gadreel—

His son reacted to Nina's movement, realising there was a threat. He spun and shoved his father aside – as Wu fired.

The first bullet slashed Gadreel's forearm. The next two slammed into the younger Nephilim's chest. Turel fell, knocking down his father and crashing limply to the floor.

Zan snapped out of his shock and sent a burst of fire at Wu. The colonel fled back down the stairs.

Sidona screamed and rushed to her family. Gadreel gasped as he flexed his wounded arm, but forgot the pain as he saw his son slumped beside him. 'Turel!' he cried. The youth did not respond, eyes wide and unmoving. Sidona crouched beside him, breathlessly repeating his name.

There was no reply.

She sagged, starting to sob. Gadreel's face, however, filled with pure fury. He glared at Nina and Zan with such intense hatred the archaeologist feared he would kill them on the spot – then snatched the trikan from Turel's belt. He clenched his fingers around the handgrip and raced after Wu.

Nina looked back at Sidona as she wept over her son, feeling a gut-wrenching pang of parental sympathy. But then survival instinct took over. This might be her only chance to escape . . .

Gadreel charged down the stairs. Zan started after him – then fell with a cry as Nina body-slammed him to the deck. The rifle spun away across the smooth metal.

She snatched the key from the altar and sprinted for the stairwell where she'd first entered. Zan scrabbled to retrieve his weapon. She reached the stairs—

Sidona shouted behind her, voice filled with rage and grief – but she was still in control, issuing an order. Nina glanced back. To her horror, she saw two of the Nephilim warriors she had revived emerge from the mausoleum. They didn't need to understand what was going on, what had happened to the world during their long hibernation; all that mattered was that their high priestess had commanded them to kill her.

She jumped down the stairs and sprinted along the metal and crystal corridor.

The giants pursued her.

30

Colonel Wu ran for the exit tunnel, cursing. His ambush had failed; the presence of more of the monsters had caught him off guard, making him hesitate before firing. A second, less, but it had saved Gadreel's life.

And now the giant was pounding after him. There was no way he could outrun him, and even if he got outside, the fall to the ground would be fatal. He had to stand and fight . . .

He darted into cover behind one of the glowing crystal ribs. However big Gadreel was, three shots to the centre of his mass would drop him like any man. The thudding footsteps grew louder. Wu readied his gun as he came into sight down the curving corridor—

Gadreel's right hand lashed out as if cracking a whip. A blur of golden metal flashed from it. A trikan, Wu realised – but the yo-yo-like weapon was heading well wide.

He locked his gun on the giant's chest—

The trikan swerved at him.

Its whirling blades snapped out and hacked chunks of flesh from his raised arm. Wu fell back with a scream, a reflexive shot clanking uselessly from the ceiling. The trikan whisked back towards Gadreel on its wire. The Nephilim held up his hand – and the weapon returned to its resting place in the handguard with a clack, the blades retracting.

Pain almost overcame Wu, but he forced himself upright. Ragged strips of bloodied muscle cut to the bone hung from his arm, tendons severed. The gun fell from his paralysed fingers.

He crouched to find it with his other hand, but froze as Gadreel advanced. His expression filled the colonel with a new fear. The Nephilim's rage would only be satisfied by his death. He turned and ran.

Gadreel raised the trikan – and flung it again.

Wu heard the shrill of the wire and the blades slicing through the air. He lunged behind another crystalline column—

The trikan made another impossible change of direction in mid-air.

It struck just below his right shoulder. The blades carved straight through skin and bone like an axe. The colonel screamed. Gadreel yanked his hand back, the trikan whirling home – and Wu's arm fell to the floor amidst a fountain of blood.

Somehow, he overcame the agony and shock, stumbling along the wall into the passage leading to the hatch. Dust gusted past him in a stinging vortex. He tripped, thudding face-first to the dirty floor when he tried to catch himself on an arm that was no longer there. Whimpering, he shuffled forward on his knees.

Gadreel rounded the corner behind him. He saw the wounded man and stopped. The trikan, blood dripping from the softly glowing blades, remained in its grip. Wu glanced back, hoping to see some glimpse of mercy in his pursuer's eyes – but instead he knew he was about to die.

The knowledge galvanised him. He staggered to his feet and faced the towering Nephilim. 'Well? What are you waiting for, you shit? We should have burned you and your bastard breed the moment we found you!'

Gadreel's lips curled in disgust – then he burst into a run with the force of an Olympic sprinter, scooping up the colonel like a child in his free arm.

He didn't stop, charging through the hatch and across the fortress's upper hull. The surrounding landscape opened out before him. He barrelled onwards as if to hurl himself over the edge with his prisoner – then halted abruptly just short of the sixty-foot drop.

A rasping cry escaped from the injured man. Gadreel grabbed his chest, buttons popping and seams tearing as he clutched his uniform like a claw. Wu gasped again – then cried out in fear as the Nephilim held him over the edge.

'Major!' said a soldier, pointing. 'Up there, look!'

Wu Shun broke off from her call over the helicopter's radio. She saw two figures on top of the hovering fortress. One was Gadreel, the Nephilim leader holding a man over empty air.

Her father.

She dropped the handset and ran towards the crater. 'Father!' she shouted. '*Dad!*'

Colonel Wu dimly heard his daughter's cry. He forced open his agony-clenched eyes to see her running towards him.

Knowing she was there ignited a last spark of defiance. He would not die without a fight – especially with his only child watching. He kicked, trying to overbalance the giant and send them both over the edge—

Gadreel suddenly stepped back – and let go. Wu landed heavily at the hull's lip. He groped at the shimmering surface, feeling an odd vibration even before he touched it, but then his hand found the strange metal.

He looked up. The Nephilim towered over him, staring down dismissively as if he were nothing more than a bug . . . then turned and walked away.

Despite his pain, fury rose within the colonel. This *thing* had attacked him, maimed him – and was now *insulting* him, not even bothering to finish him off. He managed to stand, swaying in the wind. 'Hey,' he snarled. 'Hey! Look at me, you coward! You piece of pigshit! *Face me!*'

Gadreel kept walking . . . but then the trikan slid from its guard.

And Wu realised with horror that the Nephilim had not finished with him. He had merely paused, to give him a moment of false hope before delivering the final strike.

The weapon started to spin, blades charging up with rippling light – and Gadreel snapped around to face the Chinese. The trikan became a blur—

Then it sliced at Wu in a sweeping arc.

The colonel brought up his remaining arm in a futile attempt to shield himself. The trikan slashed through bone as if it were paper, then continued into his torso, blood splattering from a diagonal slash that cut from his shoulder down to the opposite hip – and out, arcing back to clank into its guard.

Wu coughed, crimson gushing from his mouth . . . then fell backwards. His legs and lower torso slumped onto the hull, spilling organs across the shimmering metal.

The rest of him plunged towards the ground sixty feet below.

Colonel Wu had just enough air in his lungs for a final scream—

It ended with a sharp crack as he hit the broken rocks at the crater's edge.

Major Wu saw the burst of red erupt ahead of her. '*No!*' she wailed, scrambling up the slope – to see her father splayed across the bloodied stones.

She knew there was no way he could still be alive, but ran to him anyway. 'Dad!' she gasped, clutching his hand. Every finger was broken, bone grinding in her grip. He did not react, his pain over.

Her own welled within her. She dropped to her knees,

holding his hand against her forehead. Tears rolled down her cheeks – then she looked up at the dark shape hanging above. 'You bastard,' she gasped with sudden venom, standing. 'I'll kill you. You *bastard*!'

The last word was shrieked at the sky. Not caring if it had been heard, she ran back to the helicopters. 'Take off!' she shouted. 'Shoot that fucking thing down!'

Gadreel hurried back into the throne room. Sidona was still slumped over Turel's body, sobbing. He glared at Zan, waiting nervously near the altars. 'Where is the woman?'

Sidona raised her head. 'She took the key.'

His gaze snapped to the empty recess in the central altar. 'We can't wake the rest of our people without it!' He rounded on Zan. 'Why didn't you stop her?'

The translator cringed at the giant's fury. 'Sh-she took me by surprise,' he stammered.

'Stupid *beast*,' Gadreel growled. These *animals* had wiped out the People of the Tree? He could hardly believe it possible.

'Two warriors chased her,' said Sidona, looking up as another newly awoken man emerged from the mausoleum. 'Where is the one who killed Turel?'

'Dead,' Gadreel replied with no small satisfaction – though not enough to dampen his rage. He ordered the newly arrived warrior to join the hunt for the woman, then looked out at the distant city. It was huge, larger than any he had ever seen before. The humans had done much in his long absence . . .

But it was time to remind them they were not the *true* inheritors of this world.

He marched back to the central altar and held his hands over the crystals and stones set into it. Only a priestess could control earth energy for complex and subtle purposes – but all Nephilim, men and women alike, could use it in more simple ways. And *simple* did not necessarily mean *weak*. 'Help me fly the fortress,' he said.

Sidona came to him. 'What are you going to do?'

Another resurrected warrior entered, unsure what was happening. 'Go below and charge the lightning spears!' Gadreel told the man, who hurried from the chamber. The Nephilim leader put his uninjured hand flat on the console. He felt the tingle of force run through it – a force he could guide. 'We shall show these beasts the true power of the Nephilim!'

An effort of will – and the energy he felt through his hand changed, its flow altering as if rounding a stone dropped in a stream.

The entire fortress responded.

Sidona braced herself as the floor tilted. The city slid across the windows until it was directly ahead. Gadreel moved his hand again – and the fortress slowly picked up speed, gliding away from its burial pit.

A voice echoed from the altar, one of the glowing crystals pulsing. Sympathetic energy vibrations linked it with another in a room below, allowing the man he had dispatched to communicate with him. 'The lightning spears are ready, my lord.'

Yet another warrior emerged blinking from the mausoleum, realising from his leader's look that he was needed for immediate action. 'Go to them,' Gadreel ordered. 'Raze that city to the ground!'

Both helicopters' engines were running, but their rotors were not yet at take-off speed. Wu Shun used her angry impatience to dam her tears. The monster who had killed her father would pay, no matter the consequences—

Shouts and gasps from the soldiers nearby. She turned – to see the fortress *moving*, blotting out the sun as it passed overhead. The very air trembled with some invisible force, dust swirling across the ground. From below, it resembled a dragon more than ever, an elongated body behind the head bearing elaborate fins and spines. The iridescent glow rippling across the hull grew brighter.

Her rage surged: they were escaping! She snatched a rifle from the closest man and opened fire on the behemoth. The other soldiers followed her lead, sending a storm of bullets up at the dragon's belly.

At a range of twenty metres the clamour of rounds hitting metal should have been as loud as a hailstorm on a tin roof – but instead she heard a strange echoing hiss. Little flares of light erupted across the fortress's underside. Not sparks on the hull, but just *below* it, as if the bullets were being stopped before they hit—

'It's got a *shield*!' she cried, simultaneously aware of how ridiculous it sounded – and that it was the truth. The qi energy levitating the leviathan also protected it, deflecting their attacks. Hammering the point home, one of the soldiers yelped as something hit him: a still-searing bullet, flattened by its impact against the shimmering forcefield wrapped around the fortress.

Those men familiar with the concept from superhero and fantasy movies ceased fire. It took the others a few seconds longer before they too realised that their guns were causing no damage. 'Major! What do we do?' one demanded.

Wu Shun watched the fortress gain height and speed as it headed for Xinengyuan's distant sprawl. 'We've got to bring it down before it reaches the city!' The helicopters neared take-off revolutions; she moved clear of the blasting downwash.

Another soldier indicated the Z-20s' twin miniguns. 'Our rifles didn't hurt it – what if those don't?'

'Then we need something bigger,' she said firmly. 'Get me the airbase!'

★ ★ ★

347

Nina's rush through the lower level was disrupted first by the lurch when the fortress began its flight, then by the echoing cacophony that followed. Hundreds of oddly distorted hammer blows rang up through the floor. It took her a moment to realise that the troops on the ground were shooting at the vimana. Despite the fury of the assault, though, the bullets didn't seem to be penetrating.

Thankful that she wasn't about to be shot in the butt, she continued her run. Ahead was the armoury. The giant suits watched her approach through empty black eyes.

Knowing the room had no other exits, she almost ran past to head for the exterior hatch – then swerved inside as she saw the racks of spear-like Nephilim weapons. The qiguns, or baraka, as Gadreel had called them. He had used the crudely repaired core of one to kill his guards, his touch enough to trigger it. Presumably the full weapons worked in a similar, though less self-destructive, way.

If he could fire one, maybe she could too . . .

She ducked around the towering armour and pulled down one of the heavy, ungainly spears. How did it work? What she assumed was the business end was enclosed by an ovoid orichalcum cover, seams suggesting that it opened up. But how? Was there a trigger? She shoved the key into her clothing, then examined the spear as she hurried back to the entrance. The only visible feature on the shaft was an indentation about two inches across, a sliver of crystal set into polished stone within it—

An inhuman shout from the passage. Two Nephilim ran towards her. Both carried trikans. The leader whipped out his arm, the disc spinning from the handguard. Its blades sprang out, shimmering with strange energy – just like Excalibur—

She threw herself into cover behind the doorway as the trikan flashed past, then reached the end of its wire and whipped backwards. She saw it coming just in time to drop. The weapon clipped the door frame, chopping a thumb-sized chunk from the metal before returning to its owner.

Nina recovered from her shock and sprang up, leaning out to point the spear down the passage. The leading Nephilim was less than thirty feet away, trikan spinning again—

She jammed her thumb into the recess and *willed* her weapon to fire.

It did.

The cover at the spear's end snapped open, revealing a spiral of metal and crystal identical to Gadreel's makeshift weapon – and the air before it split apart.

A crackling, shimmering bolt of heat haze lanced from the qigun. The Nephilim tried to dodge, but wasn't quite fast enough. The disruption caught his arm – which exploded like an egg in a microwave. His trikan fared no better, its disc-shaped body bursting apart.

'Holy *shit*!' Nina gasped, horrified by her weapon's destructive power – and relieved that she was wielding rather than facing it.

The wounded Nephilim crashed against the wall, screaming and clutching at the blood-spouting remains of his arm. The second giant hastily flattened himself behind a crystalline rib, then glanced out to locate Nina.

She thrust the spear at him and thumbed the trigger again—

Nothing happened.

The warrior flinched, then stepped out further, throwing his trikan.

It rushed at her, blades singing. She shrieked, instinctively ducking as it shot past – a move that saved her life. The disc reversed and spun back along its line, rolling ninety degrees in response to a flick of the Nephilim's hand and slicing just above her head.

Panting in fright, she peeked around the doorway. The first Nephilim was still slumped against the wall, moaning as blood gushed over his body. The second advanced again – and a third warrior hurried into view further down the corridor. She looked at her weapon. The cover had clapped shut. Either it could only fire a single shot, or it took time to recharge.

Hoping it was the latter, and that the recharge time was seconds rather than minutes, she jabbed the spear back out and pressed the trigger again—

Another crackling burst of energy erupted from the qigun. The nearer Nephilim dived, but the man behind him was caught by surprise. Only luck saved him as the rippling burst of earth energy missed by inches and struck the wall. A dazzling flash came from the adamantium panels, sparks flying and the metal glowing red hot. He darted into a storeroom.

Nina pulled back. The gap between her shots had been about ten seconds. It possibly took less time than that to recharge, but she couldn't risk being caught in the open with a useless weapon.

She listened. Footsteps thudded softly against the metal floor: the new arrival joining his comrade. If they advanced on each side of the corridor, she could only target one – and the other would reach the armoury before her weapon recharged.

She didn't entertain even for a moment the fantasy that she might be able to beat them in close-quarters combat. Instead she continued her mental countdown. Six seconds, muttered discussion audible over the injured man's fading groans. Three, two—

Movement. Nina couldn't wait any longer – they were coming. She lunged back out. Both Nephilim ran at her, trikans whirling, widely spaced to make targeting both impossible—

She found a *different* target.

The wounded Nephilim was at death's door. Nina ended his agony, blasting him into a gory haze – which hit the charging warriors with explosive force. They both reeled back, blinded by the stinging red spray.

Nina hauled the clumsy baraka with her as she rushed into the corridor. The exit to the fortress's exterior was ahead. What she would do when she reached it she had no idea, but anything was better than waiting to be carved to pieces.

Behind her, the two warriors recovered, wiping blood from their eyes before pursuing. Their intent had already been murderous; now it was personal.

31

The first Z-20 took off from the crater, followed by its twin. Both helicopters climbed to follow the fortress towards the city.

Wu Shun watched them go, then resumed her radio exchange. 'No, Colonel Commandant Wu is dead! I've assumed battle-field command. Yes, *battlefield* – this is a combat situation! There is a UFO heading for Xinengyuan; it's hostile, and must be destroyed before it reaches the city.' She paused, listening to the inevitable disbelief and resistance from the airbase's watch officer. 'Yes, I know it sounds crazy, but it's true! It killed Colonel Wu! I need gunships and fighter jets, now! This thing has to be taken down before there are civilian casualties!'

'Uh, yes, ma'am,' the officer replied. 'There are two armed transports on their way to you already. Gunships will take fifteen minutes to arm up and get airborne.'

'Too long! What about jets?'

'We weren't expecting combat, so twenty minutes to fuel and load ordnance – but they'll reach you much faster than the gunships.'

'Just get them here,' she snapped. 'And institute a total communications blackout on Xinengyuan and the surrounding region – my authority. Phones, internet, radio, everything. If a single picture of this thing appears on social media, somebody will be executed for it!'

She angrily switched channels to talk to the helicopter pilots.

The Z-20s closed on the fortress, moths against the dragon. 'This is Major Wu! Get in close, find a weak spot – and fire!'

A compartment in the throne room's rear wall had once contained medicines and bindings for wounds, but everything within had long since turned to dust. Sidona ended up tearing off part of her gown to bandage her husband's mutilated hand. He grimaced at the pain, but said nothing, concentrating on flying the vimana. The strange city grew steadily larger ahead. So many tall towers! They couldn't all be temples, surely?

The highest were at its centre. They would be the first targets for his vengeance, an example of the Nephilim's power. After they fell, he would obliterate all the others, one by one—

'Gadreel!' Sidona shouted, running to a window. 'There's something out there!'

Zan hesitantly followed. 'It is one of our flying machines.'

Gadreel remembered that the aircraft carried objects resembling the noisy human weapons. 'Does it have a *gun*?' he said, using Zan's own odd-sounding word.

'Yes, a . . . turning cannon?' The human was far from confident he had translated correctly, but the concern in his voice told Gadreel it was something powerful.

But he had something powerful of his own. 'Use the lightning spears!' he shouted into the speaking crystal. 'Destroy those machines!'

'In range!' said the lead helicopter's gunner, bringing his minigun – a near-clone of the American M134 six-barrelled Gatling gun – to bear on the fortress. Major Wu had said the dragon's eyes were the windows of a control room. He squinted down the gunsight, finding the elongated porthole – and pulled the trigger.

Fire blazed from the whirling sextet of muzzles. Tracer

rounds lanced across the gap between the helicopter and its target like laser beams, hitting home—

The UFO's port side was engulfed in a dazzling fireworks display, a hundred rounds per second producing a storm of sparks as they slammed into the iridescent energy field. The second Z-20 opened up from starboard.

The dragon banked as if trying to escape – but the barrage seemed to be cutting through its shield. He saw metal spall below the window as fire hosed over the area. A weak spot! He fixed his aim upon it. More shards ripped away under the onslaught.

'I'm getting through the shield!' he cried. 'Keep firing, it—'

Movement in his peripheral vision. Finger still tight on the trigger, he glanced at the fortress's nose – to see one of the long fangs pivot towards him.

Nina ran around the looping passage, seeing the way to the outside ahead. But the Nephilim were catching up fast.

A trikan whirled—

A hideous noise – and the fortress banked, pitching her towards the wall. She caught herself, then staggered onwards. One of her pursuers fell, barking a Nephilim curse as his trikan clanged to the deck. The other grabbed a pillar for support.

The thud of rotor blades and the chainsaw rasp of a minigun told her Major Wu had ordered an air assault. The bizarre ringing of bullet impacts was almost deafening, but the noise changed under the relentless barrage, becoming flatter, weaker. The guns were getting through—

Another lurch – and she heard metal scream and tear somewhere above. The fortress was not invulnerable.

She reached the tunnel to the hatch. A trail of blood gave a clue to Colonel Wu's fate. She rounded the corner, then looked back. Both Nephilim were recovering.

Ten seconds was up—

She fired the baraka again – just as the fortress jolted, making her stagger. The energy burst exploded beside her target, throwing sparks into his face. He yelled, shielding his eyes.

Nina ran down the dusty passage. One of the Chinese helicopters was visible through the hatch, fire blazing from its minigun. She stopped. If she went outside, she would be exposed, a target—

A fierce crackle of thunder – and the helicopter exploded.

'Evade, evade!' shouted the lead gunner as the fang-like weapon locked on. 'They're going to shoot—'

The other Z-20 suddenly blew up, burning wreckage spinning from the fireball. The first aircraft's pilot made a rapid descent, but too late. The air rippled and tore – and the chopper and its occupants were blasted apart in a fiery explosion.

Nina threw herself clear as a chunk of flame-wreathed metal shot through the opening with cannonball force. 'Jesus!' More debris rained down outside. She waited for the barrage to end, then looked out.

A greasy black cloud was the largest remnant of the helicopter. Burning scrap littered the adamantium expanse. The other helicopter must also have been destroyed, the only noise now the rush of wind.

Clutching her oversized weapon, she hurried outside. The slipstream almost knocked her over. She used the spear for support and squinted ahead. The fortress was already approaching Xinengyuan's outskirts, tower blocks rising like dominoes. But its course would take it to larger structures: the skyscrapers at the city's centre.

A chill beyond the tearing wind. Gadreel wasn't heading there to meet the civic leaders. He was out for revenge for his son's death – and she had just witnessed the fortress's firepower, the spear in her hands scaled up many times to deliver enormous destructive force.

And there was nothing she could do to stop it.

But she *could* stop the Nephilim from waking any more of their forces. She still had the resurrection key. Without it, they couldn't release anyone else from the sarcophagi – and if the fortress lost power, they wouldn't be able to restore it.

Simply throwing the key over the side would be the easiest way to keep it from them, but it might be recovered. For all she knew, Sidona could use the earth energy fields to sense its location. She either had to destroy it, or leave it somewhere it could never be retrieved.

The sight of numerous tower cranes amongst the city's sprawl gave her an idea. Construction sites were full of deep pits – and newly poured concrete. If she could reach one, she could render the key inaccessible, if not permanently then at least long enough for the Chinese military to blast the vimana from the sky.

Only one catch: she was two hundred feet above the ground . . .

Noises behind her. The Nephilim were coming. She dropped low against the wind and ran clear of the hatch.

It felt as if something was pushing back against her feet, the oily shimmer of colours roiling over the metal reacting to each step with a pulse that spread outwards like pond ripples. The entire hull was charged with some kind of earth energy field. An experimental stamp with one boot; the flash and the feeling of resistance both intensified. A shield, a counter-force to impacts? All she knew for sure was that it made traversing the exterior more difficult.

Aft of the exit, large strakes swept backwards to the hull's edge. She had no idea of their purpose, but they stood tall enough to provide some cover. She clambered over the nearest, ducking and scurrying along for several metres before clearing the second. She readied the spear and peered back over the metal ridge.

Both pursuing Nephilim were outside, robes flapping violently. The wind affected the giants more strongly than Nina, forcing them to hunch down. That would even the odds somewhat – as long as she stayed clear of their trikans.

The fortress banked, sweeping around an unfinished apartment block. A second turn to avoid another tower, and it resumed its original course. Either it couldn't fly any higher, or Gadreel had some reason for holding this altitude. Neither option helped her, though; she was still high enough for any fall to be fatal—

If she landed on the *ground*. But on a building . . .

Staying low, she scurried to the hull's edge. More of the city came into view. There were plenty of smaller buildings between the large towers, some at least ten storeys high. If the fortress passed close enough above one, she might be able to jump down without breaking both legs—

A shout as the first Nephilim saw her.

'Shit!' she gasped, bringing the baraka to bear and firing. The warrior threw himself sidelong. The energy blast passed through the shield as if it didn't exist, one form of earth energy unaffected by the other. It hit the hull just beyond him, spraying sparks.

The second Nephilim ducked low and scurried towards her, trikan ready. The first jumped back up and hurdled several strakes before closing in. They were trying to catch her in a pincer – and she could only attack one threat at once.

No way to retreat. Buildings and roads rolled past below; the latter were practically empty, only a handful of vehicles in sight. The newly built city still awaited the majority of its inhabitants. She looked ahead, seeing an expansive multi-level freeway intersection. Even the highest overpass was over a hundred feet below – but beyond the knotted roads she saw a cluster of luxury apartment blocks around a large park. If Gadreel held his course, the floating behemoth would pass over one of them, perhaps thirty feet above the roof.

A potentially fatal drop. But she might have no other choice. The Nephilim were getting closer.

Ten seconds. The baraka should have recharged by now—

Nina looked for the nearest threat. The warrior to her right, partially exposed. She aimed the weapon at him—

A glint at the edge of her vision. She instinctively jerked back as the other Nephilim's trikan sawed through the air. It missed her – but hit the spear hard enough to knock it from her grasp. It spun over the edge into open air.

The nearer warrior straightened, setting his trikan spinning. Nina ducked back behind the metal wall, only to see the other man vault into her channel.

Nowhere to hide – and nowhere to go.

A desperate glance over the side. The building was coming up, still thirty feet below – but light shimmered off something on its roof . . .

The Nephilim raised their trikans—

Nina leapt backwards over the edge.

Both men reacted in surprise, one sending his trikan whizzing after her – but she had already landed with a splash in a rooftop swimming pool. The weapon smacked against the churning water. The warrior angrily recalled it as the gasping Nina resurfaced.

Eyes stinging from the over-chlorinated water, she swam to the poolside. The vimana swept past above.

She still had the key – and Gadreel didn't know she had escaped. By the time the warriors returned to the throne room to warn him and the fortress turned back, she could be clear. If she lost her pursuers, she could ensure they never recovered the key.

Dripping wet, she climbed out. She was about a mile and a half from the central skyscrapers, the fortress still heading for them. She ran to an exit and pounded down the stairs beyond.

Eddie gave Macy the last set of ear defenders to shield her from the helicopter's clamour. He was about to resign himself to deafness when he saw the pilots react in surprise to something. Cheng, wearing headphones connected to the cabin intercom, also looked startled. 'What is it?' the Yorkshireman yelled.

'The fortress is moving!' the young man replied. 'It's heading for the city – and it's shot down two helicopters!'

'What, it's *armed*?'

'Some kind of qi energy blast, according to Major Wu. And Colonel Wu is dead!'

Eddie had little sympathy, but there were greater concerns. 'What about Nina?'

Even with the defenders, Macy still heard her mother's name. 'What's happened to Mom?'

'As far as I know, she's still inside the fortress,' Cheng told them. 'So is Zan.'

'How long before we get there?' Eddie demanded.

'A few minutes—' He paused, listening to his earphones. 'The pilot can see the fortress!' he reported. 'It's heading into the city. Major Wu has ordered the other helicopter to pick her up.'

'What about this one?'

'We've been told to observe the fortress from a safe distance.'

'How far is safe?'

Cheng grimaced. 'They, ah, don't know.'

'Great, so if its guns have a range of fifty miles, we're buggered!' Eddie held on to his daughter as the Z-20 banked towards the fortress.

★ ★ ★

Nina rushed out of the apartment block. The city centre had been to the south; she found the sun and got a rough bearing. No sign of the fortress – yet. She needed to get away from her landing site before it returned.

She ran across the park, ducking under trees for concealment. Down a flight of steps, through a gate and onto a street. A mixture of residential buildings and shops greeted her; the latter were all empty, some so newly built that tape crosses still adorned the windows. There were no people, no cars.

Shaking off the sensation that she had arrived late to the end of the world, she ran on. Tall cranes were visible to the west, one lazily turning. She headed for them: a construction site was still her best hope for rendering the key irretrievable.

The first proof that she was not alone came when she heard tyres screech about a block away. Considering the lack of traffic, it was less likely to be a near miss than someone seeing the huge flying dragon and skidding in disbelief. She hurried across the empty street to get under a long awning, then looked back—

A huge shadow swept over the apartment complex.

The sight, straight from an alien invasion movie, momentarily froze her. The fortress hove into view, its silence as unsettling as its size. It slowed, the fangs moving to point downwards—

The building with the swimming pool blew apart.

Nina screamed and ran as the pristine block disintegrated in a storm of shattered concrete, a seething grey dust cloud erupting like volcanic ash. Windows in neighbouring buildings shattered as hundreds of tons of rubble slammed to the ground.

'Oh my God . . .' she gasped, hoping the block had been as empty as the rest of the neighbourhood. Clutching the key, she kept running, trying to keep out of sight.

'Stop!' Gadreel roared as he saw the building crumble. 'She has the key – we need it undamaged!' A warrior at the altar passed on

360

his urgent command through the speaking crystal. He stared down through the window, looking for movement. The city was like nothing he had ever seen before, filled with colossal towers and enormous roads, but bizarrely, it seemed deserted. Where had the woman – *Wilde*, his new servant had reminded him – gone? She could not have got far . . .

Sidona had turned her attention to the machine at the central altar. She clicked her fingers to summon Zan. 'What is this?'

'It – it is called a qi tracker,' the Chinese told her. 'It shows us the lines of energy flowing through the world.' He seemed about to say more, but hesitated.

'And what else?' Sidona demanded. 'Speak! If you are of no use to me, I will have you cast down to the ground!'

Zan looked at the floor. 'It is . . . a weapon,' he mumbled.

Gadreel snapped around. 'A weapon? Why did you not tell me before?'

'I . . . It is a secret. I would be betraying my people . . .'

'You have already done that,' the Nephilim leader growled. He ordered his men to keep watch, then strode to the translator. 'How does it work – and what can it do?'

'It can send a surge of energy to any point in the world, and destroy whatever is there,' said Zan uncomfortably under the couple's intense gazes. 'But it has never been tried. We did not have anyone who could channel the energy. Wilde can, but she is not one of us. She is from an enemy tribe.' There was no direct translation for *country*. 'And we did not have any undamaged crystals.'

Husband and wife exchanged calculating looks. 'Now you have both,' Sidona told him coldly.

'Then it is time to test your weapon,' said Gadreel. 'You need an undamaged crystal? The entire *heart* of this fortress is a crystal!' He pointed to the mausoleum stairs. 'Do what you must to make it work.' A small smile at his wife. 'Sidona is the most powerful priestess of the Nephilim. She will channel the energy for you.' His expression became more predatory. 'And send it to a worthwhile target.'

'Ah . . . yes, yes,' Zan stammered. 'I will do all I can.'

'Good,' said Sidona. 'Then bring it.'

The translator looked in dismay at the heavy machine, then strained to pick it up. Sidona led the way to the stairs, Zan waddling after her.

'My lord!' called one of the warriors. 'There is a beast down there!'

Gadreel hurried to the window. At first he saw nothing but trees and strange buildings – then he glimpsed movement below the foliage. 'Did you see it?'

'Yes. A female.'

'What colour was her hair?'

'Red.'

'It is her!' Gadreel exclaimed. He looked beyond the trees to a structure with strange writing across its front. 'That building – destroy it! Block her way and force her into the open! But do not shoot her,' he added quickly. 'We will land – and hunt her down!'

32

Cheng peered into the cockpit – and let out an exclamation.
'What is it?' Eddie shouted over the helicopter's roar.

'I can see the fortress!' he replied.

'Macy, let me up,' the Yorkshireman told his daughter. She shifted so he could see for himself. Xinengyuan opened out before him, the endless sprawl of buildings and roads so new and clean and empty that the view seemed almost fake, as if a movie's visual effects team had run out of time and money before adding the details.

Even having seen the fortress on the video feed at the base, Eddie did a double take at his first sight of the real thing. 'Okay,' he said, regarding the UFO in astonishment, 'that goes straight to the top of my weirdest stuff list!'

Cheng nodded. 'What do we do now?'

Eddie watched the shimmering dragon glide slowly over the cityscape, turning as it moved away from a column of dust marking an apartment block's ruins. If it had been a normal aircraft, he would have said it was tracking something on the ground . . .

'It's after Nina!' he said with absolute certainty. 'She got out of it somehow – and she's taken something they need. Maybe that key.'

Cheng looked at him in surprise. 'How do you know?'

'If she hadn't, they wouldn't bother chasing her. And also, well – it's Nina! Getting into trouble and being chased by bad guys is kind of what she does. The archaeology's just an excuse. Although don't tell her I said that.'

'Then what— Aah!' The young Chinese jumped as another building exploded and collapsed, spewing out a dust cloud.

'Jesus!' Eddie growled. 'They're shooting at her!'

Nina hurried beneath a row of trees along the roadside. The hovering fortress was visible through the leaves behind her, but she hoped she was hidden from it—

A piercing roar – and a storefront exploded ahead, rubble and glass showering the sidewalk.

'Shit!' she gasped, shielding her face. They knew where she was – and her path was now blocked by fallen debris. Her only choices were to double back, bringing her closer to her pursuers, or run out into the open to reach an intersection. Neither appealed, but she couldn't stay where she was . . .

The key's weight helped her decide. If they blasted her directly, they would destroy the very object they were desperate to obtain. They would instead try to channel her, trap her – but if she kept moving, she might still escape.

She ran again, angling across the street. A glance back. The fortress loomed above the buildings – and was turning to follow.

Another earth energy bolt hit a six-storey office block on the corner. She swerved clear as it collapsed, then held her breath as she sprinted into the swelling dust cloud. Her eyes stung, but the nearby buildings were just discernible enough for her to reach the intersection and round it.

The air cleared. She coughed, powder caking her lips, but kept running. A road sign bore directions in both Mandarin and English. Straight ahead was Commercial Zone No. 4, which told her nothing, but heading left would bring her to something called Fair Rain Residential District. Again, the name was unhelpful – but she saw numerous tower cranes that way, suggesting construction was ongoing. It could be a good place to dispose of the key.

Where was the fortress? She looked over her shoulder – and was shocked to see it descending, slicing through the mushroom cloud rising from the destroyed apartment block towards the park.

It was landing. They were coming after her on foot.

The hunt had become even more dangerous.

Macy clutched at Eddie's jacket as another building blew apart. 'Daddy! We've got to help Mom!'

'We will, if I can figure out how!' he replied. The destruction had been preceded by a weird rippling distortion tearing through the air. 'Those things under its nose that look like fangs – I think they're guns. Cheng, you said those spears at the base were weapons, right? They must be bigger versions.'

'They could be,' said Cheng. 'But how does that help us?'

'They're underneath it – so they won't be able to point upwards! If we come in from behind and stay over it, your guys can blow the fu— the *flip*,' he corrected, remembering that Macy was in earshot, 'out of it with the miniguns and those rocket launchers.' He gestured at the tubular weapons carried by some of the soldiers. 'Tell the pilot to get above it!'

Cheng quickly relayed the suggestion. It was not met with enthusiasm. 'He says we have to wait for orders from Major Wu.'

'Nina could be dead by then! Tell him I'll lean out and fire at the bloody thing myself if I have to, but we need to shoot it down – or at least keep it occupied until she gets clear.'

Another hurried exchange – this time with more success. 'He'll take us in behind it,' Cheng reported as the pilot banked, bringing the Z-20 on an interception course. One of the gunners slid open a cabin door. Wind blasted in, Macy shrieking and shielding her face. The man hooked himself to a strap, then swung the minigun from its stowed position.

'Keep a tight hold, love,' Eddie told his daughter, before

looking back over the pilot's shoulder. The fortress had briefly landed, but now ascended again, resuming its hunt. To his alarm, he realised the helicopter was approaching the hovering dragon almost side-on rather than curving around to come in from astern. 'No, no! Get *behind* it – they can still shoot at us!'

But the Z-20 kept going, precious seconds lost as Cheng frantically translated the Englishman's words. One of the fangs swung towards the helicopter. 'Higher, go up, *up*!' Eddie shouted—

The gun fired.

There was no flash, no smoke – rather a ripple, as if the air was being torn by intense heat. The pilot threw his aircraft into a hard turn as the energy blast rushed at them—

It tore past with a crackle. The aircraft lurched as the bolt clipped it, a loud bang and a flash of sparks coming from the tail boom. Macy screamed, the soldiers yelling in fear. Alarms shrilled in the cockpit.

Eddie clung to the back of the pilot's seat. 'Jesus! Are we hit?'

The gunner shouted a frantic report. 'It's blown a hole in the tail!' said Cheng. 'He says something's leaking!'

Eddie couldn't guess whether it was fuel, oil or hydraulic fluid, but from the pilot's struggle to maintain control, it was something critical. Gleaming glass skyscrapers rolled into view through the cockpit windows. 'We've got to land before we crash—'

The gunner screamed a warning. The pilot slammed the stick hard over. The aircraft rolled, throwing the unprepared Englishman against the cabin wall as another energy bolt tore past.

He recovered and manoeuvred himself around the soldiers, all clinging desperately to their seats, to look through the open hatch. The dragon had turned to follow them.

The helicopter levelled out – and started to descend. Both fangs tracked it. 'No, *up*!' Eddie yelled. 'They'll keep shooting at us!'

Cheng hurriedly passed the alert to the pilot, getting a harried reply. 'He can't keep it in the air much longer!'

The skyscrapers reappeared ahead. Eddie's eyes locked on to a tall mirror-windowed tower with a matching but somewhat shorter neighbour. 'Go up, land on its roof!' he shouted, seeing the edge of what looked like a helipad above. 'If we go higher, they won't be able to bring their guns up, and we can get down in the lifts—'

He broke off as the minigun opened fire. Macy shrieked again, covering her ears. The gunner sent a blazing storm of metal at the pursuing fortress. The shimmering glow sheathing its hull flashed and rippled as hundreds of rounds hammered it.

The pilot was fully occupied with keeping the chopper airborne, but the co-pilot shouted into his mic. 'Major Wu's on the radio!' said Cheng. 'She says the fortress has a shield – but we can break through it with concentrated fire.'

'A shield? What is this, *Star Trek*? No, more like *Independence Day*,' Eddie corrected. 'But we still need to land! Tell him to get on that roof!'

Cheng did so, but the pilot was already gaining height. The two fangs tried to follow, only to be blocked by the hull above them. The minigun kept up its assault, hosing the fortress with fire. The gunner cried out in excitement. Eddie looked back. The flashes around the dragon's eyes weakened, and debris flew into the air. Then he lost sight of it as the helicopter turned.

The skyscraper's roof came into view; it did indeed have a helipad. The Z-20 slowed for a landing, but the pilot was now battling to maintain control, red lights flashing on his instrument panel. He extended the landing gear. 'Macy, hang on!' Eddie said, taking hold of her. Just a few more seconds . . .

A new noise reached Nina: the thud of rotor blades. She looked around, but couldn't see the helicopter past the buildings.

She saw the fortress, though. The shimmering dragon had dropped off warriors to pursue her on the ground, but was now airborne again – and once it spotted her, it would direct them to their target.

The construction site came into view as she rounded a bend, a dozen unfinished apartment blocks rising into the sky. A girder swung wildly from a tower crane. Its operator had seen the sinister UFO approaching and abandoned his post. Dozens more men in hard hats scurried in panic at ground level.

If she led the Nephilim to the site, innocent people would die. She had to find somewhere else.

Tiring, lungs aching, she reached a crossroads. Going right, northwards, looked too open; those aboard the fortress would spot her with ease. Left would take her towards the city's centre, where there were likely to be more people – but there were also more buildings, more cover. And everything had the almost fake, movie-set appearance of newly constructed properties. No goods in the store windows, no curtains in the apartments, no cars on the street.

Nobody to get hurt. She went left, quickly reaching the cover of another building—

The helicopter suddenly grew louder.

She looked up as it clattered overhead. It was in trouble, struggling to hold course. The Nephilim attack had caused damage – she saw something break loose from the fuselage and spin down towards the ground. It was not going down without a fight, though. Tracer fire blazed back at its attacker. The aircraft headed towards the city centre, disappearing behind an apartment block.

Nina ran after it. The fortress was not yet in sight behind her. Another intersection ahead – another chance to throw off the hunters. Keep going—

A siren's rising wail reached her. Maybe she was about to get some support . . .

A shout from behind.

The voice's inhuman echo warned her even before she turned that the Nephilim had found her. Two figures rounded the corner: giants in colourful yet aggressively decorated armour, bearing deadly spear weapons. Fear overcame fatigue, driving her onwards as fast as she could go.

It was not fast enough. The warriors were almost twice her size, their longer legs eating up the gap at a terrifying pace.

The wavering helicopter slid towards the pad, minigun still blasting fire down at the fortress. One of the throne room windows finally exploded under the relentless barrage. The gunner yelled in victory—

A loud crash of grinding metal as the tail rotor's gearbox ran dry, oil spurting from the damaged boom – and the chopper swung sharply around.

The tail rotor counteracted the main rotor's enormous torque; without it, the fuselage would spin like a top. Eddie threw himself over Macy to protect her, but he knew that if they didn't land in the next few seconds, they would both die—

The pilot shoved the collective control lever down hard. The Z-20 dropped – onto the pad.

The landing gear had lowered, but the impact was so fierce one of the hydraulic legs collapsed. The fuselage tipped sideways, belly screeching across the pad as it spun. The gunner was thrown out, swinging on his safety strap to slam against the helicopter's side – then was crushed beneath it as it rolled.

The main rotor blades smashed against the pad and disintegrated in an explosive blizzard of carbon fibre. Dozens of razor-sharp shards impaled the two soldiers closest to the open hatch. More debris ricocheted around the cabin, one piece slashing Cheng's cheek and another cutting the back of Eddie's head.

The fuselage lurched back upright. With the main rotor destroyed, it quickly ground to a stop. Macy sobbed quietly. 'Are you hurt?' Eddie asked. The response was a barely audible *no*. He raised his head, seeing the twitching, lacerated bodies of the soldiers by the open hatch.

Outside was nothing but empty space, the wrecked helicopter hanging over the tower's edge.

Nina ran, breath burning in her throat. But she couldn't outpace the Nephilim. The two warriors were rapidly gaining, about to catch her—

The approaching siren reached a crescendo – and a police car powered into the intersection.

It skidded to a halt as the driver saw the Nephilim and braked in shock. The two warriors also hesitated, unsure what to make of the wailing vehicle. Nina ran towards it as the cops scrambled out. 'Help! Help me!'

The sight of a panicked woman fleeing ten-foot armoured demons overcame any language barriers. Both men drew their guns. Nina hastily swerved from their firing line as they shouted commands at the invaders.

The Nephilim responded by bringing their barakas to bear. The cops opened up—

Bullets spanged from the armour, earth energy flaring. The two giants staggered – but didn't fall. The metal was not even dented. One recovered and angrily unleashed his weapon. A cop exploded in a bloody haze, spraying the car a sticky crimson.

His partner kept firing, hitting the attacker's helmet. The Nephilim's head snapped backwards, and he crashed to the ground. The cop switched his aim to the second warrior—

The baraka roared. The energy bolt exploded the officer's legs and most of his torso. What was left of his upper body slapped down on the car's hood.

Nina cried out at the carnage – but instinct sent her running to the car. She had ten seconds before either Nephilim could fire again. The driver's door was open. She leapt in. Three pedals; it was a manual. She stamped down on the clutch and jammed the stick into first, revving hard before releasing the pedal.

The tyres shrilled. The cop's remains slithered off the hood as she hauled hard on the wheel, powering away from the warriors—

Another burst of earth energy – and the back of the roof ripped open.

The car lurched and slewed around. Nina screamed, but managed to counter the spin. Into second, the car picking up speed. A look back. The roof's entire rear end was gone, along with the trunk lid, ragged fingers of twisted steel surrounding the new void.

The car had shielded her, taking the blast – but now she was exposed.

And the downed Nephilim sat up, raising his weapon—

She turned hard, wheels squalling over the asphalt. Another bolt clipped the vehicle's tail as it sped out of the intersection. The rear wing shredded like paper – but the car kept going.

Nina raced up through the gears, still accelerating. The Nephilim were lost to sight as she followed the curving road. The central skyscrapers rose before her. Smoke curled from the top of one of the towers; the stricken helicopter had landed on it.

Where was the fortress? She looked back. Her now-unobstructed view revealed it clearing some buildings – and turning to pursue her.

'There!' barked Gadreel. He had sent nine men to the ground, and a flurry of action told him some had found their prey. Colourful armour stood out clearly on a grey road, as did two bursts of blood – and something was moving quickly away from them. 'In that . . . chariot.' He frowned. A chariot without horses? 'Follow her!'

The fortress changed course to pursue the fleeing redhead.

Eddie cautiously rose. Wind blew in through the open hatch, the vertiginous cityscape far below. 'We've got to get out of the other side,' he said. The Z-20 rocked with the shift of weight. 'Macy, look at Cheng, okay? When we open the door, you go through.'

To his relief, his daughter did as she was told, not looking at the corpses. A surviving soldier pulled at the hatch on the opposite side of the cabin. It slid back – then stopped. He and a comrade strained harder, but it didn't move. The forced landing had buckled the runners. There was just enough room for the passengers to exit one at a time.

The closest man squeezed through to clear the way. The next gestured to Cheng and Macy. 'Get her out,' Eddie told the young Chinese. Cheng took Macy's hand and clambered to the hatch, letting her through first. The soldier already outside helped her down.

Metal creaked as the student hopped out after her. The soldiers started to follow, some in such a rush that they left their weapons. The fuselage rocked again. Eddie gripped a seat until the movement stopped, using the moment to look for their attacker. The fortress seemed to have resumed its search for Nina, advancing ominously over the city. Its guns still couldn't traverse high enough to target them. Maybe it was at its maximum altitude . . .

The minigun had definitely damaged it, one of the eye-like windows blown out. He briefly considered taking over the weapon to finish the job, but moving that far over might unbalance the chopper and send the whole thing plunging to the ground.

Instead he took weapons from the dead men. The first was a Type 95, the standard assault rifle of the People's Liberation Army. The second would be more use against the fortress: a Type 08 rocket launcher, an olive-green tube with a grip, a simple sight, a shoulder strap and very little else. It was a one-shot, disposable anti-armour weapon that could be used with little more training than knowing which way to point it. If a minigun could damage the fortress, a kilogram and a half of high explosive should cause it some real trouble.

If he got the chance to use it. His highest priority was getting Macy to safety. He crossed the cabin, one of the remaining soldiers letting him through the hatch.

'Daddy!' Macy cried as he emerged. 'Come on, quick!'

'I'm here, love,' he said, jumping down. The co-pilot climbed from the forward door, the pilot sliding across the cockpit after him. 'We need to get to the lifts and—'

The Z-20 shuddered again, battered underbelly rasping over the pad – and slipped over the edge.

Eddie grabbed the soldier behind him, yanking him through the hatch. 'Get out!' he shouted to the men still inside – but it was too late.

The helicopter tipped tail-downwards, throwing its remaining occupants to the back of the cabin. Fuselage panels were torn away as it slid over the building's side, but not even the shrill of tearing metal could drown out the screams of those inside.

'Shit!' Eddie roared, running to the edge in the hope that the Z-20 had caught on some lower balcony – but the tower dropped vertically all the way to the ground. The helicopter and its re-flection in the mirrored glass fell in tandem, shrinking, shrinking – then smashed like a dropped egg on the plaza below.

The Englishman stared helplessly at the wreckage before snapping his gaze back up to the fortress, still hovering menacingly a few blocks away. He felt the Type 08's weight on his shoulder, and almost unslung it – but family came before revenge. He ran back to Macy.

His daughter gazed wide-eyed at where the helicopter had been. 'There – there were still people in it . . .' she whispered.

'I know,' Eddie said, crouching to hug her – and turn her away. 'I know. But we've got to get out of here.' A stairwell led into the building's central core, some soldiers already heading down it. 'Let's get to the lifts.'

He took her hand and ran to the stairs, Cheng shouldering his pack and following. The other soldiers hurried along behind them. Into the tower, and they reached a bank of elevators. A man held one open, urgently beckoning them in. Eddie and Macy rushed into the car, Cheng and the rest behind them. The doors closed, and the lift started its descent.

33

Gadreel watched with satisfaction as the wrecked flying machine plummeted to the ground. Before he'd left on his fateful mission, there had not been a weapon in the world that could damage the vimana – but the humans had somehow found a way, piercing its shield and shattering one of the crystal windows. He narrowed his eyes against the gritty wind now blowing through it. All the machines sent against him had been destroyed, but the beasts had others . . .

They needed to be made afraid of the Nephilim, to deter them from attacking again.

He looked back up at the mirrored tower, just one of many gargantuan structures at the vast city's heart. He could not even imagine their purpose – but despite their size, he did not believe they were indestructible. Smaller buildings had been utterly obliterated by the fortress's weapons; now it was time to see their effect on their larger cousins.

He faced the men at the altars. They were still guiding the vimana after Wilde, but since its weapons could not be used directly against her, they should be turned against another target . . . 'The tower ahead of us, where the flying machine fell – charge the lightning spears and destroy it!'

'Yes, my lord,' one of the warriors replied. He relayed the order into the speaking crystal.

Gadreel returned to the window. The guns were hidden from his view by the vimana's prow, but it would take only moments for the gunners to aim them and fire—

Twin bolts of energy lanced out and slammed into the tower's side. Mirrored glass exploded into sparkling fragments . . . but the building remained standing.

The Nephilim leader frowned. He had expected to see stone or metal behind the surface, both of which would have been blasted to pieces, but instead, empty space was revealed beyond the gaping hole. A couple of floors were visible, but no supporting pillars. How was that possible?

'Fire again!' he ordered. A short wait for the weapons to recharge, then two more bolts struck their target. Another swathe of glass was ripped away, exposing more floors within – but the building didn't even shudder.

'My lord!' The oddly accented shout drew his attention away from the tower. The human, Zan, stood at the top of the mausoleum stairs. 'There is something Sidona says you must see.'

Another frown – even if it was at his wife's request, Gadreel did not like being summoned by a human, and he considered the beast both obsequious and cowardly – but he crossed the throne room. 'Keep firing!' he ordered, then descended into the chamber below, where the rest of his people still waited in their sarcophagi. He went straight to Sidona. The tracker was beside her, cables connected to the glowing crystal wall. 'What have you found?' he asked.

Her eyes shone with excitement – an almost predatory awe. 'I . . . I can *see* the whole world,' she said. 'When I touch it, I can see everything!'

'What do you mean?'

'I cannot explain it. But this thing, this machine – it shows me the flows of energy, everywhere. And I can guide them!'

Gadreel indicated Zan. 'He said it was a weapon. Can you make it work?'

'I think so. This picture,' she indicated the laptop's screen, 'is a map. The human showed me how it works, and chose a target

– and I could *feel* where it was. If I focus, I can direct the energy to that place, make it stronger and stronger . . . until it explodes.'

'That is what he told me,' Gadreel confirmed. A moment of thought, then: 'We will test it. I have a target – the tower in front of us. The beasts have forgotten the Nephilim. It is time to remind them of our power!'

Eddie watched the lift's floor counter tick down. The tower was eighty-three storeys high, which would have put it in the upper ranks of New York's skyscrapers. Sixty floors to go, and then he still had to find Nina before the Nephilim—

The elevator jolted. Macy gripped her father's hand. 'Daddy! What was that?'

'They're shooting at the bloody building!' Eddie cried as the car shook again. Its guide wheels squealed against the vertical tracks. 'We need to get out of this thing.'

'We're over fifty floors up!' Cheng protested as the Yorkshireman shouldered his way to the control panel. 'It'll take ages to get down the stairs!'

'Better than being trapped inside a metal box if it gets stuck – or falls.' Eddie checked the counter. Floor fifty-three, and still descending. He reached out to push the button for the fiftieth floor—

Another impact outside, more powerful – and the elevator car lurched as if struck. It stopped abruptly, emergency brakes shrieking against the tracks. Everyone staggered, an unprepared man falling. The display screen flashed up Mandarin warnings.

'What does it say?' Eddie demanded.

'An evacuation alert. It's telling us to get out at the next floor,' said Cheng.

'Well, I would if the bloody doors'd open!' The counter had just flicked past fifty-one, but the lift was now stationary. Eddie pushed the control to open the doors, to no avail. 'Must be between floors.' There was a red emergency button on the panel; he stabbed repeatedly at it, but nothing happened.

'Maybe there's an exit in the roof?' Cheng suggested.

'If there is, it'll be locked from outside. This isn't *Die Hard*.' He shoved his fingertips into the narrow gap between the doors, pulling with both hands. The space widened a little, but then the mechanism caught.

The soldiers quickly came to his assistance. With several pairs of hands hauling at them, and one man using his rifle's barrel as a makeshift crowbar, the doors finally surrendered. A concrete beam with the number *50* stencilled above a downward-pointing chevron greeted Eddie as they opened. Below was the shaft's blank wall – then the top of the doors to the level below.

He put down his weapons and reached into the gap between the car and the doors. A metal rod ran diagonally across the barrier: the release bar. He tugged at it. A clunk, and it shifted. He forced his hand into the gap and pulled. The doors slowly rumbled open.

Another boom shook the shaft. Eddie heard windows shatter. Right now it seemed the fortress's blasts were only hitting the tower's outer skin, but if they got through to the central core . . .

'Everyone out,' he barked. Even though he was not an officer, or even speaking the same language, the soldiers instinctively responded to his order, forming up behind Macy and Cheng. Eddie squeezed through the gap feet-first and dropped to the floor. 'Macy, come on,' he said, holding out his arms.

His daughter quickly emerged. He lowered her, then looked back up – to find Cheng holding out the rifle and rocket launcher. 'What're you doing?' he asked in surprise.

'You might need them,' the student replied.

'I *need* everyone out of the lift,' he said, impatiently, taking and shouldering the weapons. 'Move, quick!'

Cheng passed out his backpack, then clumsily worked himself

through. He got halfway – then stopped. 'Oh. Oh! I'm stuck!' He kicked and wriggled, trying to squeeze his midsection through the gap.

Eddie grabbed his feet and pulled, two soldiers shoving at his shoulders. 'Did you only eat bloody cheeseburgers since coming to America? Suck in that gut!' The young Chinese popped free with a yelp, falling to the floor. 'Okay, come on!'

The soldiers started to slip out of the lift. Eddie checked his surroundings. The fiftieth floor was apparently unoccupied, a wall directory devoid of any company names. That was a relief, meaning no civilian casualties; hopefully the other floors were just as empty—

A lightning-bolt crackle – and another burst of earth energy hit the tower.

More glass exploded, the shock wave ripping through the empty offices. A wall blew apart in an eruption of wood and plaster. Eddie reeled from a concussive blast, shielding Macy with his body as debris flew past. Everyone staggered, the floor shaking—

Metal screamed in the elevator shaft.

The whole building swayed – and the vertical tracks buckled as it twisted. Rivets burst from girders with the force of bullets. One punched through the elevator car's side, tearing a chunk of flesh from a soldier's thigh.

The man halfway through the gap gasped in fright as the car abruptly fell several inches. The jolt as the emergency brakes caught it pitched him out into the lobby. Eddie pulled him up. 'Everybody out, *now*!' he shouted at those still inside.

The co-pilot rolled fearfully through the now-wider opening. Two soldiers brought the wounded man to the doors. Eddie reached up to guide him through, another Chinese assisting him before moving the injured man clear as the Englishman went to aid the pair still inside—

A pounding *bang* of splitting steel from above.

The terrifying sound was followed by echoing clangs of metal striking metal – getting louder with each collision. Eddie realised with horror that a broken girder was plunging down the shaft. 'Get out!' he yelled at the last two soldiers, meeting their frightened eyes—

The elevator disappeared.

He leapt back as the girder hit it like a giant hammer, ripping it from its cables. The car came off its tracks, emergency brakes clamping uselessly around nothing as it plummeted down the shaft.

Macy screamed. Eddie picked her up – partly to comfort her, but also out of protective urgency. 'Where are the stairs?' he asked Cheng.

The young man was still stunned by the soldiers' fate. 'They . . . That way,' he said, pointing. A sign indicated a passage to one side of the elevator bank.

Eddie hurried to it, seeing a door marked with an exit sign. He opened it. A stairwell dropped towards infinity below. 'Can you run?' he asked Macy. She nodded. 'Okay, we've got to get to the ground as fast as we can!' He lowered her to the floor. She needed no more urging to start her descent. He followed, the rocket launcher's tube banging against his side as he led the remaining Chinese downwards.

Gadreel returned to the throne room to oversee the hunt for Wilde as Sidona worked. He looked ahead. A large bridge spanned the road between the woman's strange chariot and the tallest towers, a vast building of unknown purpose nearby. 'Destroy that bridge,' he ordered. 'Bring it down in front of her. She will have nowhere to run!'

Nina glimpsed movement on an overpass ahead, an eighteen-wheeler heading across it. But she was concerned only with what was at ground level. A large shopping mall rose to one side, an English sign beneath neon Mandarin proclaiming it as the Frozen Wonderland Leisure Experience. Giant posters of skiers and bobsledders reminded her that Cheng had said the city was home to an indoor ski run.

But she was already past its gate, dismissing it from her mind as she looked ahead—

The bridge blew apart.

Both the fortress's cannons fired simultaneously, enormous bolts of energy tearing into the overpass. The carriageway lurched, its supports giving way . . .

Then fell.

A section of roadway slammed to the ground with earthquake force directly ahead. The speeding police car was kicked into the air by the impact, landing hard enough to collapse a suspension strut.

Unrestrained, Nina was thrown from her seat. Her forehead struck the windscreen, leaving a smear of blood. Dizzied, she fell back, grabbing the wheel as the decelerating car swung across the road—

Something large plunged into the destruction ahead. She recognised it as the tanker truck from the overpass in the split second before it exploded.

A wall of seething flame erupted from the chaos. Nina screamed and jammed her foot on the accelerator. The police car mounted the high kerb with a bang and leapt across the sidewalk into an almost empty parking lot.

Flames gushed after her. She kept the pedal hard down, seeing a glass-walled atrium beyond one of the mall's entrances. A ten-foot fibreglass figure of a cartoon animal holding skis loomed in her path. She shrieked, demolishing the luckless creature, but held her course—

The car ploughed through one of the lobby's giant windows

– the fireball smashing the others a moment later. Flames boiled upwards as the tall atrium became a chimney. Nina ducked, driving blind as heat scoured the back of her neck.

Fire alarms wailed – then she simultaneously heard and felt a flat *thump* as glass ruptured a front tyre. The police car veered sharply. She raised her head to see turnstiles rushing at her—

She stamped on the brake. The car skidded into a spin, smashing sidelong through the barriers before pounding to an abrupt halt against a wall. The impact flung her across the cabin, the gearstick jabbing painfully into her thigh.

She blinked, stunned, before forcing herself to move. A black pump-action shotgun sat in a rack above the windshield; she pulled it free, grabbing a handful of shells from a box and stuffing them into her pockets. Checking she still had the resurrection key, she staggered out.

The fortress loomed through the smashed windows. It had tracked her here – and the warriors would soon catch up. She had to run.

A fearful face stared at her from a ticket booth. 'Stay down!' Nina shouted, gesturing for the young man to duck. He did so. The nearest exit was a set of glass doors, snowflake patterns etched on them. She hurried through.

Her surroundings changed from gleaming yet anonymous shopping mall to ersatz ski lodge, the walls clad with fibreglass logs. Long counters offered rentals of winter sports gear. Business was slow; there was only one man on duty. He dropped behind the counter when he saw her gun.

Through more doors – and freezing air hit her.

A snow-covered hillside stretched into the distance, its upper end shrouded in mist. The indoor ski run, illuminated by an endless grid of overhead lights, was as huge as Cheng had said – even if it was only the world's second biggest, it was still several hundred yards long. It was wide, too; as well as several broad lanes for skiers and snowboarders, there was even room for a bobsled run at one side. Five chair lifts and some shorter surface lifts serviced the slope.

All were empty, the entire cavernous space deserted. The combination of Xinengyuan's sparse population, its being a weekday and – Nina suspected from the numbers at the ticket office – high prices meant the complex was currently a gigantic white elephant.

That suited her – the fewer innocent civilians around, the better. But her own survival was paramount. Where to go?

A section of one long wall was glazed, looking into the sparsely occupied mall. No exits, though; anyone wanting to enter the winter wonderland had to pay. She saw a fire door far off in the opposite wall, but it would take her back into the sights of the fortress.

'Onwards and upwards,' she muttered. Shivering as cold seeped into her damp clothing, she tramped through the almost virgin snow to the nearest ski lift. If there was another emergency exit at the slope's top, she might be able to escape the vimana unseen.

She, Eddie and Macy had taken a skiing vacation two years prior; she boarded one of the moving chairs with ease. It quickly carried her up the hill.

Gadreel returned to the mausoleum in response to an urgent call from Zan. Sidona opened her eyes. 'I . . . I have done it,' she murmured. 'I have guided the flow of power, shaped it . . . It is rising inside the tower . . .'

Gadreel regarded her with concern. His wife always entered an almost dream-like state while channelling earth energy, but he had never seen her go so deeply. She had one hand on the chamber's crystal wall, the other touching the exposed piece inside the humans' machine. Both glowed, the light pulsing and shifting as if alive. 'Can you control it?'

'Yes. It is . . .' She smiled, the sadistic pleasure of a hunter who had just trapped her prey. 'Strong. Very strong. The larger the crystal, the stronger it becomes. Had I known I could use the power like this, we would never have needed to go into hiding. We could have defeated our enemies from half the world away!'

'The humans killed them for us – but now *they* are our enemies. If we are to save the rest of our people, we must defeat them first.'

'They murdered our son,' Sidona snarled. 'We must do more than *defeat* them. They must be *destroyed*. And with this,' she looked at the machine, 'I can do it.' Another cold smile, this time with bared teeth. 'I will show you. Go to the window and watch.'

He smiled back. 'Make them pay, my wife.'

She closed her eyes again, focusing her mind on the unseen world surrounding them.

'Come with me,' Gadreel ordered the nervous Zan, striding up the stairs. 'Let us see what your weapon can do!'

Ten floors down – but forty still to go. Eddie hurried down the stairs behind Macy, glad of the ten-year-old's energy. Whether it would hold out was another matter – and the same could be said of his own. He had done his best to keep himself in shape, but he was still half a century old, and even the fittest body had its limits.

He glanced back. The overweight Cheng was already struggling to keep up. The soldiers, on the other hand, were as fit as he would have expected – just as he had been at their age . . .

A moment of mental chastisement. It didn't matter how old he was – it was what he *did* that was important. And he would get everyone out of this mess, somehow—

Another jolt shook the stairs. Macy grabbed the banister. 'What was that?'

Eddie slowed. No explosions, so it wasn't another barrage

from the fortress. If anything, it seemed to have come from below. He looked down the stairwell, but saw nothing. 'I don't know, but we need to keep moving.' He caught up with her—

The lights went out.

Eddie swore under his breath, stopping and grabbing the banister with one hand as his other found Macy's shoulder. Thumps and gasps came from behind as the Chinese bumped into each other.

Illumination returned, but at a lower level, emergency lights kicking in. The tower shook again, hard enough to rattle the railings and produce ominous crunches from the joints of the cast-concrete stairs. A low rumble like an approaching subway train came from beneath them. Eddie looked down again. The descending flights no longer receded in perfect alignment; they were now swaying, twisting . . .

But it wasn't an earthquake.

A new light grew at the bottom of the shaft, a shimmering blue-white glow. Sparks crackled from the metal railings, lightning bolts lancing across the stairwell. The shuddering grew worse – and Macy shrieked as a crack suddenly split the wall beside her. Dust dropped from above . . .

Followed by larger debris.

A brick-sized chunk of concrete smashed on the steps. More pieces tumbled down the shaft. Eddie looked up to find their source—

And saw one of the higher flights of stairs tearing away from the wall.

Other sections cracked as he watched. 'Jesus! Get off the stairs!' he shouted. 'They're going to collapse!'

He and Macy leapt down to the next landing. He threw the door open and rushed into the access corridor. Cheng and a soldier were right behind them, the others stumbling as the stairs jolted. The first five recovered, piling through the doorway—

The last man was still in the stairwell when the weakened flight higher up broke loose – and fell.

It slammed onto the steps below, sending them plunging in a lethal domino effect. Another flight, then another, extra tons of concrete joining the cascade at each step. By the thirty-ninth floor it was as unstoppable as a runaway locomotive. A deafening bang, and both the landing and the trailing soldier were gone, leaving only swirling dust. More thunderous slams echoed up the stairwell as the flights below were demolished.

Eddie didn't even have time to be shocked by the soldier's death. The tower was now rocking, pitching him back and forth. Windows shattered as the entire building strained, battling to stay upright . . .

And failing.

A massive *boom* of disintegrating concrete from below – and the floor tilted.

Eddie pulled Macy to the side of the corridor. 'Hold on to me!' he cried, but there was nothing he could hold himself. He looked down the steepening slope. The offices on this floor were glass-walled, giving a view all the way to the exterior windows. The shorter tower was visible beyond, its mirrored face showing its neighbour. Broken glass ruined the infinite reflections intended by the architects, ragged black holes spattering the image—

The reflection changed.

The perspective of the building in the mirror shifted as the damaged structure tilted towards it. 'Jesus,' he gasped. 'The whole fucking tower's going to fall over!' Macy stared at him, shocked – but knowing he wouldn't have sworn in front of her unless something truly terrible was happening—

A flash at the reflection's foot, liquid lightning shooting from the skyscraper's base – and every window in the bottom twenty floors blew apart in a blast of seething energy. Huge chunks of concrete and pretzel-twisted girders flew out amongst the glittering debris . . .

And the tower started to fall.

Its back broke ten storeys up as the devastating release of earth energy tore apart its concrete core. Slowly, but with gradually increasing speed, its upper half toppled towards its smaller companion.

Eddie slipped, falling on his back. He dug his heels into the carpet to slow his descent, but couldn't find enough grip. 'Daddy!' Macy cried. He hoisted her onto his front as they skidded towards the offices.

The glass wall rushed at them. He jammed one foot down hard, knowing it wouldn't stop him – but it could still *steer* him. He swung sidelong to thump against a support pillar.

Cheng and one of the soldiers also managed to catch the framework – but the wounded man hit the glass. It shattered, bowling him over the frame as huge jagged shards fell on him. Screaming, trailing blood, he rolled onwards through the empty office – to hurtle helplessly through the broken exterior window into the void below.

Another soldier made a desperate snatch for the lower frame. He caught it, clinging on with one hand despite a glass dagger stabbing into his palm. The man behind him grabbed a pillar, but the co-pilot bounced off another with a crack of breaking ribs and fell to his death outside.

Eddie heard the rapidly fading screams, but could do nothing except grip Macy tightly as he fought to keep his hold. The ground at the other tower's base rolled into view through the windows, the skyscraper falling ever faster—

It hit the second building's roof.

An earthquake-force roar almost deafened him as the top quarter of the smaller tower was smashed into rubble by the toppling structure, the latter's uppermost floors shearing off and plunging into oblivion. But the remainder survived, the central core holding despite massive damage. The intact section between the tenth and fiftieth floors now formed a sagging bridge, sloping from the taller building's base across to the crushed summit of its neighbour.

Intact did not mean *secure*, though. The hanging section swayed sickeningly, overstressed girders squealing and screaming. The small number of unbroken windows shrank rapidly as the mirrored glass shattered.

Eddie drew in a fearful breath and took stock. He, Macy, Cheng and three soldiers were still alive. Beyond that . . .

'We're screwed,' he muttered. All the panes in the internal glass wall had broken. The floor was canted at a forty-five-degree angle, impossible to traverse. Any slip would send him helplessly out of the exterior windows – and despite the tower's slant, they were still over twenty floors up.

Macy clutched his chest. 'No, Daddy, we're not. We can't be! You always get us out of things like this. You can do it again!'

Eddie managed a smile. 'Thanks for the vote of confidence, love. Let's see what we've got to work with.' He looked around – and saw nothing. 'Okay . . . er . . .'

34

Gadreel almost laughed as the colossal tower fell. The beasts had built their weapon without knowing how to control it, blinded by their innate lust for destruction and violence . . . and now it had been turned against them.

Its first test was a success – but, he saw as the dust cleared, not a total one. The building had not been obliterated, instead caught by another tower behind it. An unexpected emotion at the sight: *annoyance*. He wanted to send a clear message, that the humans could not stand against the Nephilim, but the structure's partial survival seemed almost an insulting rebuke.

Sidona joined him at the unbroken window, Zan hanging back in shock. His wife appeared drained by her actions, but also satisfied by the devastation. 'We did it!' she exulted. 'We will make these animals pay for killing Turel.' She glanced across the room. Their son's body had been covered, but remained where he had fallen.

'We will. But you must finish what you started. We must make them *fear* us again.'

'And they shall.' She turned back towards the mausoleum—

'My lord!' shouted a warrior. 'There is something in the sky, coming towards us!'

Gadreel and Sidona scanned the vista. It took them a moment to spot a tiny dark, angular shape, high up. 'Another of their flying machines,' growled the Nephilim leader.

'There are two of them!' Sidona warned. A second trailed the first. 'What shall we do?'

He frowned, thinking. The People of the Tree had always known earth energy could be used to levitate objects, but only Nephilim ingenuity had applied that knowledge to a weapon; as a result, it had never been imagined that the fortress's lightning spears would be fired at anything other than ground targets. The smashed window and damaged hull proved that a costly oversight. And the approaching machines were flying far higher and faster than the ungainly, blade-spinning aircraft. The gunners would not be able to hit them . . .

'When you link with the energy flow through the machine,' he said as an idea formed, 'can you still sense the world around you?'

'Yes,' Sidona replied. 'Everything that is physical affects the flow, alive or not. I can feel it.'

'Even in the air?'

'Yes—' She stopped as she understood his meaning. 'I can bring them down,' she said, awed at the realisation that her powers no longer had limits. 'I can destroy them!'

'Go,' Gadreel ordered. She ran for the mausoleum as he watched the two aircraft close in.

The chair lift carried Nina up the slope. She looked back. No sign of her pursuers – yet. Through the glass wall she spotted a handful of people fleeing through the mall, heading away from her fiery entry point. The slope's top appeared through the haze. A fairy-tale castle stood at the summit, surrounded by fir trees draped with twinkling lights—

A bang from behind. She turned – and saw one of the armoured giants duck through the entrance. He looked around in confusion at the sudden climate change, then spotted the retreating figure on the lift.

His baraka came up – and fired.

Trapped on the chair, Nina shrieked – but the energy blast

missed, crackling past close enough for her to feel it sear the air. She fumbled the shells from her pockets and loaded the shotgun. Five cartridges slid into the tubular magazine, a sixth meeting resistance. She racked the slide with a menacing yet satisfying *ka-chak* to chamber a round, then pushed the last shell into the mag.

Below, the second warrior caught up with his companion and sent a blast of his own after her. The bolt missed by a wider margin than before, though it still made Nina flinch.

The lift had by now swept her halfway up the hill. Even if they ran after her, she had a huge head start, hopefully enough to reach an exit—

The first warrior fired again – at a new target.

The chair lift's bottom tower blew apart, the cable snapping. Nina screamed as she plunged towards the ground—

Even with over a foot of snow to cushion her, it was still a painful landing. She rolled clear as the whipping cable twanged down on her overturned chair.

She hurriedly recovered the shotgun, then waded upwards. The two warriors started after her. The snow came halfway up Nina's shins, but was only ankle-deep to the giants. Their ascent was much faster.

She pounded on, breath steaming out in increasingly hoarse gasps. A small rise lay ahead, a hump to give those descending the chance to catch some air. She dived behind it as a baraka came up. The blast hit the mound and showered her with snow. Even lying down, the shock wave still felt like a kick to her chest.

Anger joined fear. She rolled to the steaming bite taken out of the snow and fired the shotgun. The two Nephilim were sixty yards away – beyond her gun's effective lethal range, but still well within its maximum. They reacted with shock and pain as buckshot smacked against their armour, hot fragments stabbing through gaps between the plates. One cried out and tore off his helmet, clawing at a piece of searing metal buried just below his eye.

'Welcome to the twenty-first century, assholes!' Nina shouted, pumping the slide and firing again. The helmetless warrior screamed as more shot struck his head. Both Nephilim dropped, scrambling through the snow to find cover.

She ran uphill, staying low. The trees and castle rose into view as she neared the summit. A look back. The Nephilim were moving again. She fired a third time. The shot fell short, throwing up a spray of snow ahead of them, but was enough to force them down once more.

At the top of the wrecked ski lift was a platform where riders could dismount. She reached it, and searched for an exit. Ski tracks and footprints showed the attraction was in use, even if only by the staff. She followed a trail of boot prints through the trees towards the castle, now revealed as a café selling hot drinks and snacks – then halted as an idea came to her.

The helicopter that had collected Major Wu from the excavation site headed for the city. Wu herself was on the radio to the incoming fighter jets. Their report was not welcome. 'What do you mean, you can't attack it?' she demanded. 'It's huge!'

'We can't get a missile lock,' replied the lead pilot. 'It's not showing up on our radar.'

'Then use heat-seekers!'

'It isn't giving *off* any heat, Major. It doesn't have engines; there's nothing we can lock on to.'

Wu struggled to contain her anger. 'You have *eyes*, don't you? Use your guns! If you come in from behind, it won't be able to target you.'

'Yes, Major,' came the reply, faint contempt behind the pilot's professional calm. 'Moving in now.'

She watched as the two sleek J-20 jets made long, sweeping

curves over the city's outskirts to swing behind the fortress. 'Come on,' she muttered. 'Bring those bastards down!'

Sidona took her place beside the machine. She placed one hand upon the crystal inside it, then closed her eyes and laid the other against the chamber's glowing wall.

The world of light rose around her, her inner sense expanding to take in her surroundings on a different plane of perception. She had trained in reshaping the other world her whole life, and could affect the flow of the earth's power with more skill than anyone . . .

And now her own power had been increased.

The machine was a strange, unnatural interloper, jagged and harsh, disturbing the energy flowing through it. But however the humans had created it, it *worked*. With it, the boundaries of her perception increased enormously, letting her see the channels of power far beyond her past limits. And if she could see them, she could shape them. She didn't need to try to do so in order to know: it was a simple truth of the world of light.

She moved her mind's eye from the fortress, looking out-wards . . . and upwards. She sensed birds in the air, the towering buildings – and beyond them, something moving.

Something fast.

She focused. The two flying machines, bristling with a discordant power of their own. However they were kept in the sky, it was not the energy of the earth.

But now she could bring them down to it.

The leading pilot entered a shallow descent to line up his gun-sight reticule on the UFO. Whether or not it had been built by space aliens, he didn't know; what he *did* know was that being the first person ever to shoot one down would earn him a place in the history books, and hopefully money and fame besides . . .

The crosshairs found the dragon-like aircraft. It was stationary, hanging unnervingly over the city. The remains of the skyscraper it had just destroyed were nearby. The sight blew trivial thoughts of personal gain from his mind. This *thing* had attacked his country, killing who knew how many people. Whoever – or whatever – was inside was going to pay.

'Four thousand metres to target,' he reported. 'Closing at four-fifty knots.' He thumbed the weapon selector on his joystick. 'Guns hot.'

His wingman confirmed she was ready to fire. The city rolled past below as the fighter descended. 'Three thousand metres,' he continued. 'Two thousand.' His cannon had a maximum effective range of eighteen hundred metres, but he wanted to be close enough to damage the target; according to Major Wu, it had some kind of shield. It sounded like something from a superhero movie, but Wu did not seem the kind to imagine such things.

Besides, he was looking at a UFO! Who knew what it could do? 'Fifteen hundred, ready to fire.' His finger tightened on the trigger—

The air around the target seemed to ripple, a flash illuminating the ground around it – but there was no lightning. He hesitated, confused, but recovered. Less than a kilometre—

Another flash, brighter, closer – and a searing bolt of energy tore his fighter apart.

Major Wu stared intently at the two fighters as they closed on the fortress, waiting for them to unleash their weapons upon it. A flash, and she held her breath in anticipation, but it had not come from the jets. *What—*

A thick, weaving line of lightning lanced up from the ground – and hit the leading fighter. The J-20 disintegrated into a churning plume of liquid flame. She gasped in horror.

The second fighter sought vengeance, firing a stream of cannon rounds from its external gun pod. The shield shimmered – then the shells tore into the dark hull. 'Yes!' Wu cried—

Another lightning flash – and the J-20's wing blew apart as it swooped low over the dragon's back.

The crippled aircraft spun into a corkscrewing roll towards the ground—

It hit the base of the collapsed tower – and exploded.

Eddie's search for anything useful hit a blank – until he noticed a hatch set into the wall at the empty office's far end. He couldn't read the Mandarin on it, but the red-and-white graphic beneath was an international standard: a fire hose.

An idea formed. He didn't like it, but it was all he had. 'Okay, Macy,' he said, 'you stay here. Keep hold of this pillar.'

'Where are you going?' she asked, afraid. 'You can't leave me!'

'See that hatch? It's a fire hose. If it's long enough, we might be able to climb down it.' He was simplifying his still-fluid plan for her benefit, already certain the hose would be too short to reach the ground – but the other building might be a different matter. 'I'll go and—'

The tower shook.

This was not another shudder of straining steel and concrete. Something had hit it, the impact a sharp hammer blow – followed by the pounding roar of multiple explosions. The broken glass wall's framework rattled.

The soldier clinging on with one hand cried out, blood running down his wrist as the glass carved deeper into his palm. He flailed at the frame with his other hand, but couldn't quite reach—

He fell away down the steeply sloping floor. A last futile attempt to catch the outer window frame, then he was gone.

Macy pushed her face into her father's chest, crying. Eddie swore silently, realising the cause of the explosions. There had been a rising rumble of jet engines, but now everything was eerily quiet. One of the planes must have crashed into the tower, its ordnance blowing up with it.

He had to act now. 'Stay here,' he told Macy, carefully standing and bracing himself against the pillar.

'What are you doing?' called Cheng.

'Seeing if I can reach that hose.' He started across the tilted floor, using the glass wall's base as a precarious foothold.

'Wouldn't it be easier if you left your guns?'

The Type 95 and the rocket launcher were still slung from his shoulders. 'I might need the straps.'

A deep, strained moan from somewhere above. The central core was strong – it had to be to support a skyscraper's weight – but it had gone beyond its limits. The structure was succumbing to the impossible stresses upon it, and when it finally failed, it would do so in catastrophic fashion.

The thought quickened his pace. He reached the far wall; now he had to get to the hatch, ten feet below. 'Cheng!' he called out. 'I need help. The guy who's still got his rifle – tell him to get over here.'

The student passed on the request. The soldier in question gingerly made his way past Cheng and Macy to Eddie. By the time he arrived, the Yorkshireman had unfastened his rifle's strap. He gestured for the soldier to do the same with his own weapon, then examined the rocket launcher. Its strap was riveted to the launch tube; he would need a blade to cut it. The soldier might have one, but it would take time, and probably fray and weaken the fabric.

Instead he shouldered the launcher again and tied the two rifle straps together, making a tough canvas line almost six feet long. 'Okay, I need him to brace himself against the frame here, then lower me to the hose,' he said, resting his gun against the frame's upper side.

'Will you be able to reach it?' said Cheng dubiously.

'Bloody hope so, 'cause we've run out of rifle straps!' He waited for the young man to translate, getting a nod from the soldier. 'All right. Here we go . . .'

He looped one end of the strap around his left wrist and gripped it. The soldier took hold of the other end and wedged himself into the corner, then crouched. Eddie started to lower himself down.

The soldier let the strap out slowly. The knot creaked. Eddie gave it a worried look, but it held. The makeshift rope reached its full extension. The hatch was a few feet below him. He stretched out his free hand, but it was just out of reach. 'A little more, just a bit . . .'

The man above him grunted something. Eddie looked up – if the soldier bent any lower, he risked losing his balance and sending them both to their deaths. 'Okay, different approach,' he said. 'Tell him to hold on!'

He waited for Cheng to relay his message – then he swung and kicked the door as hard as he could.

Metal buckled, but the hatch remained closed. Another kick, then another. The door began to cave in.

The soldier let out a gasp of effort. Sweat beaded his face . . . and his hands.

The strap started to slip through his fingers.

Eddie redoubled his efforts, laying into the hatch like a football hooligan. The soldier groaned. The strap jerked, dropping by an inch—

A final kick – and the hatch rebounded open, revealing the red hose reel inside.

It was still beyond Eddie's reach, and the soldier's grip was failing. He would have to do something desperate—

'Tell him to brace himself!' he shouted, giving Cheng a moment to pass on the warning – then he let go.

He fell, feet hitting the open hatch. It tore from its hinges – but slowed him just enough to let him grab the hose reel with one hand as he dropped. It swung outwards on a heavy-duty pivot, stopping with a jolt. Eddie dangled from the reel as the broken hatch spun out of the window. Macy screamed.

He kicked at the floor, toes finding just enough purchase for him to bring his flailing hand to the red reel. He pulled himself up into the space where it had been stowed. 'I'm okay!' he shouted breathlessly to his daughter before checking the hose.

It was a tough plasticised fabric, flattened to allow the maximum length to be coiled around the reel. He pulled the nozzle. The reel turned, the hose coming away easily. He unfurled more, watching the flat snake jiggle to the windows below, then drop out.

How long was it? There was still a lot left on the reel. He spun it ever faster until its own weight started to pull it out. He let go as the reel whirled out of control – then banged to an abrupt halt.

Eddie assessed the situation. The hose was about fifty metres long, over a hundred and fifty feet. Roughly ten or eleven storeys. Not nearly enough to get to the ground . . . but it should reach the neighbouring tower.

'Okay!' he said. 'I'm going to swing across to the other building. If I make it, I'll secure it, then everyone else can use it like a zip-line.'

'*If* you make it?' said Cheng incredulously.

'All right, *when* I make it! Let's stay positive!'

'I did tell you about my vertigo, didn't I?'

'Well, if you stay here much longer, it'll be cured permanently! Tell your guys to use their equipment webbing as harnesses.' He addressed Macy. 'Once I'm across, you come here and the soldier'll lower you down. Then you can slide over to meet me.'

His forced casualness did not fool his daughter for a moment. 'Daddy, I'm scared!'

He dropped the pretence. 'I know, love. I am too. But,' he quickly went on, 'we're going to get down from here, and find your mum. Okay?'

'Mom,' she corrected, with a feeble smile.

Eddie grinned. 'That's my girl. Okay, I'll see you soon.'

He manoeuvred his legs to work the hose beneath the sole of one foot and up over the top of the other, bringing them together to trap it. He lowered himself slightly. The improvised step held his weight. It would act as a brake while he descended – as long as he could maintain his grip with his hands.

He took hold of the hose. 'Going down!' he announced, then started his descent.

The first part, over the sloping floor, was straightforward. It did not take him long to reach the windows.

Where his task became a lot harder.

He carefully brought his legs over the edge, wary of broken glass, then perched and looked down. He was over two hundred feet up, the end of the hose swinging far below. The space between the two towers was strewn with debris, young trees flattened by broken concrete and girders. But a fall was not the only danger.

Black smoke boiled from the toppled tower's base. The plane crash had started a fire, and it was growing fiercer. No way out that way – and the conflagration would weaken the skyscraper's remains. One way or another, it would soon come crashing down, killing anyone still inside.

He checked the smaller building. The upper floors of his own had mashed into it, merging the two structures together in a hideous snarl of twisted steel. Windows broke as he watched, mirrored fragments hailing down to earth. The tower's face was perhaps a hundred and twenty feet away. He should be able to reach it by swinging on the hose.

Getting *into* it would be another matter. Enough glass remained intact to pose a danger. Blow a hole in the windows with the rocket launcher? Maybe, but too many things could go wrong, any one of them likely to leave him as a gooey splat on the plaza far below . . .

Another option came to him. It wasn't much less insane than firing the Type 08 while swinging through the air over a hundred feet up, but the odds of success were still higher. Slightly.

Eddie readied himself, then slipped over the edge.

The wind immediately caught him, batting him about like a cat toy. Feet together, hands clenching the hose, he descended as quickly as he dared.

35

The Nephilim warriors warily reached the top of the ski slope. One held his baraka at the ready, the bloodied, helmetless man shouldering his own spear in favour of a trikan.

There was no sign of the woman, but tracks led towards a building. Their prey's footprints were smaller than most of the others, making them easy to pick out. They followed them through a gap in the trees towards the brightly lit little castle. She must have gone inside . . .

The first warrior raised his baraka – and fired. A tower blew apart, revealing not stone but wood and plaster behind the painted surface. The snow-covered roof crashed down into the wreckage. The second Nephilim spun his trikan, waiting for his quarry to flee the collapsing building—

'Hey!'

The shout came from *behind*. Both giants whirled—

Nina stepped out from the trees – she had backtracked along her own footprints before vaulting into her hiding place – and fired the shotgun.

The warriors were only twenty feet away. The helmetless man's head jerked back in a bloody spray as the tightly spread shot ripped the flesh from his face.

The other Nephilim's thumb jabbed the spear's trigger, but it had not yet recharged. Nina swung her gun at him and racked the slide—

It caught mid movement with a clunk. The smoking cartridge

had jammed in the ejection port, stopping the shotgun from cycling.

She tugged the slide again. It made no difference. The cartridge was still wedged tight. She didn't know how to clear it – and now the warrior's baraka had recharged.

He thumbed the trigger again—

Nina flung her useless gun at him as she dived sidelong. The spear's golden cover snapped open, rippling energy erupting – and hitting the shotgun at point-blank range.

The flying weapon blew apart. The gunpowder in the remaining cartridges detonated, blasting out buckshot like an exploding hand grenade. It tore through the gaps in the warrior's armour, lacerating his face and neck. He fell back with a scream, blinded and spitting blood from shredded lips.

Nina let out a cry of her own as shrapnel stabbed into her. She painfully sat up to see bloody rips in her trousers and shirt. The wounds were not deep, but they stung like hell. She scooped up snow and pushed it gently against the injuries to numb them, then stood. Her left leg, which had taken the brunt of the damage, quivered as she put weight on it, but held.

She wouldn't be sprinting for a while, though. Pain burned through her calf muscle. A clumsy jog was the best she could hope for.

And that would not be enough. Through the mist, she saw more towering figures hurrying up the hill.

She hobbled to the wounded Nephilim and snatched up his baraka. It occurred to her that she could use the weapon to finish him, but the moment she fired, the warriors below would home in on her.

Instead she went to the chamber's rear wall, which was painted to resemble a mountain range. There *had* to be a way out—

There was – behind the castle's wreckage. Doors below an emergency exit sign were blocked by debris. She could clear it, given a few minutes . . . but she didn't *have* a few minutes.

She looked around in desperation. If there were any other exits, she couldn't see them. The only way she could go was back down the hill.

Straight into the arms of her hunters.

The other Nephilim were moving quickly, following their comrades' tracks. Nina gripped the baraka, but it was seven against one. Fighting was not an option; she had to get past them. Somehow.

The ski lifts could carry people downhill as well as up, but she would be completely exposed. Skis or a snowboard would be faster, except there were none to hand. So how . . .

'No, nope,' she told herself, even as she started towards the bobsled run. 'I am *not* going to do that. I am *so* not doing that!'

But somehow she found herself crouched at its top. Several sleds waited beside a heavy-duty chain lift. She looked downhill. The limited space dedicated to the run meant it lacked the sweeping turns of an outdoor track, but it still snaked enough to give thrill-seekers some excitement on their ride.

Right now, that was the last thing she wanted, but it was the only way to get down without being caught. The leading Nephilim were more than halfway up the hill.

She frowned. They had clear line of sight across the slope, and the bobsled would make enough noise to draw their attention – and their fire. She needed to distract them, even if only for seconds.

Her gaze went to the ceiling. As well as lights, it supported a twisting maze of ductwork and pipes – the air-conditioning system, to keep the temperature below freezing, and fans to blow out an even covering of man-made snow. There was a lot of metal up there . . .

She hauled a one-person bobsled to the top of the run, seeing rings attached to the steering cables inside the streamlined fibreglass cowling. It was only then she realised there were no helmets; they would be rented from the counters below just like skiing gear. *It doesn't matter*, she thought; *I must already be missing plenty of brain cells just to be considering this . . .*

The rearmost Nephilim passed the halfway mark. That ought to be enough of a gap, and her distraction would hopefully delay them still further. She aimed the baraka at the ceiling – and fired.

The energy bolt's crackle instantly caused armoured heads to snap towards her. But by then the blast had hit its target. A hole blew open in the ceiling, sparks falling . . . followed by ducting and a heavy fan.

The last warrior looked up in surprise – only to be flattened by several hundred pounds of industrial air mover. Ductwork clanged into the snow around him. Another Nephilim was knocked down, others diving clear of the falling wreckage.

Nina took advantage of the chaos. She threw the spear into the bobsled, then propelled it into the icy half-pipe and leapt aboard.

The sledge immediately veered to one side. She yelped and grabbed the control cables to counter the turn. It straightened out, already picking up speed.

Flecks of ice spat up at her face. She narrowed her eyes and looked ahead. The course ran straight for a hundred feet before entering the first turn. She readied herself to steer into it, glancing sidelong.

The Nephilim had spotted her. Weapons came up—

A blast hit the edge of the run just ahead. She ducked as pulverised ice rained over her. Momentarily blinded, she shook off the freezing fragments – to see she was already at the turn.

The sled reeled, angling up the side of the pipe. She pulled frantically at the cables. The runners shrilled angrily against the ice, the vehicle shuddering as it ground along the lip of the course . . . then swung back down.

Her panic didn't subside. The bobsled cut across the centre line into the next turn, heading up the other side of the half-pipe at an even steeper angle. If she didn't regain control, she would vault right out – and crash into the ski run's wall.

She hauled at the other cable. The sled wasn't turning, runners skidding sidelong over the frozen surface—

They caught abruptly, cutting into the ice. The bob's nose jerked around. The sudden change of direction threw Nina sideways, harsh ice rushing past mere inches from her cheek. She gasped and pulled herself upright. The sledge veered back into the pipe, rocking violently – then steadying.

More energy bolts slammed into the ice and snow. She was partly protected by the track's walls, but she still leaned back as far as she dared, looking over the bobsled's nose to bring it into the next turn. It hurtled through, more or less holding course.

Nina didn't believe for an instant that that was down to any skill on her part – more like pure luck. The test would come in a moment. She rocketed towards a tighter turn, gaining speed. If she screwed up now, she would be launched into the air like a missile—

The bob shot into the turn, rolling almost perpendicular to the ground. She tugged the cables. It straightened, wavering as velocity and gravity battled – then angled back down, sweeping out of the bend into a longer straight.

Her relief was tempered with concern. The bobsled would now pick up even more speed . . . and the track's designers had probably saved the most challenging curves until last.

But she was past the Nephilim, more than halfway down. If she stayed on course, she would get her chance to escape . . .

A bend loomed ahead – and she knew in a flash of horrified realisation that she wouldn't make it.

Its upper edge curled back over the pipe, partially enclosing it. An expert rider at full speed would actually be inverted as they shot through. Nina wasn't even close to full speed – but nor was she an expert.

She pulled the cables, riding up the straight's side – then angling back down into the bend in the hope of cutting through it.

It didn't work.

The runner on the track's higher side dug into the ice, hard. It jerked around, yanking the handle from her grip.

Nina knew her ride was doomed. She threw herself out of the open rear – as the sled flipped over.

She slammed down on her back and slithered along behind the tumbling bob. The fibreglass cowling disintegrated, a broken panel barely missing her neck as it slashed over her. She didn't even have the breath to scream, desperately splaying her arms and legs wide to slow herself while trying to keep her head from rasping along the bumpy surface.

Both the sled and its former rider rounded the last corner. Nina dug her heels into the ice. The bob crossed a red line, a hooter echoing through the chamber. Her time flashed up on an illuminated sign: thirty-two seconds, a sad emoji telling her she hadn't broken any records.

All she cared about was that she hadn't broken any *bones*. She pushed her feet down harder, slowing as she crossed the line—

A crackling fusillade of earth energy flashed past.

She was not the target, nor the bobsled. The hunters were doing to her what she had done to them. The bolts blasted the ceiling, sending machinery plunging downwards—

It smashed straight through the floor. The overturned sled disappeared into the gaping pit, hitting something below with a fatal bang.

Now Nina screamed, feet scrabbling and hands clawing for grip that wasn't there. The hole swallowed her—

The fall was about five feet onto a sloping section of broken floor – not far, but still enough to deliver a jarring blow to her spine. She skidded down it, slamming to a stop against the boxy casing of a large fan. She lay still for a moment, dizzied and breathless. Broken ice showered over her. After a moment, she tried to move – only to cry out at a stabbing pain. The broken tip of a metal pole was buried in the side of her hip, blood oozing around it.

She had to get up. The Nephilim would soon be here. She braced herself – then slid sideways. The rod popped free, its last half-inch smeared with blood. She wailed, but dragged herself clear of the debris.

All she could do with the wound was press her hand against it to slow the bleeding. She stood, feeling stinging cuts up her back from her slide down the rough ice, and looked around. Beneath the ski run was a dimly lit service area, heavy girders supporting the slope and a huge network of pipes and ducts maintaining the low temperature. It was even colder than the huge room above, frost coating everything.

A green light not far away warmed her with relief. An emergency exit into the mall's lower levels. She could still keep the key from the Nephilim—

'Shit!' she gasped, realising that the artefact was no longer inside her clothing. It had fallen out somewhere along her wild ride – but where?

A frantic search. No sign of the golden disc. Either it had ended up under the fallen debris, or it was somewhere on the bobsled run. The baraka poked out of the mangled sled; she grabbed it—

Another energy blast above shook the ceiling and showered her with ice. Inhuman shouts told her she was outnumbered. One last futile sweep for the key, then she reluctantly limped to the emergency exit.

Shadows cut into the light lancing down through the hole.

The Nephilim had caught up. She ducked through the door and closed it behind her.

Blank-walled corridors stretched away to each side. She started in the direction of where she had entered the mall – back towards the fortress. The Nephilim would now almost certainly recover the resurrection key; she had to stop them from returning it to their leaders.

Arms straining, Eddie reached the bottom of the dangling fire hose.

He regarded the second tower. Some of the windows where he expected to land were broken, but it would be almost impossible to aim at them precisely enough to get through unscathed. Plan B it was, then . . .

He wound the hose around his left wrist before squeezing both legs over the brass nozzle. 'Let's get into the swing of things,' he said, then started to move.

Legs back, then forward, then back again, the length of his swing increasing each time. The wind whistled in his ears – but not loudly enough to drown out a bang from behind. Fires were now licking from the broken windows, the noise caused by a swathe of the facade shearing away. Hailstones of glass and broken concrete fell past him as he picked up speed.

Forward, and he came to within thirty feet of the other tower's fractured mirror before falling away. He would reach it next time – or *hit* it, if he didn't judge his sweep accurately. He unshouldered the rocket launcher, wrapping its strap around his other wrist, then held it on his thighs, pointing forward.

He slowed at the top of his reverse arc. Acrid smoke hit his nostrils. A momentary pause . . . then he swished forward again, extending his legs to gain momentum – and to support the rocket launcher.

Past the lowest point of the swing, narrowing his eyes against the slipstream, then he hurtled upwards. The tower rushed at him. He located the approaching point of impact. The windows were intact. He turned his feet, heels together but toes apart, and pushed the launcher's tube between them, bracing it in position with his outstretched arm.

His reflection grew ever larger. About to hit—

He buried his face against his arm to protect his eyes – and whipped his feet back beneath himself.

The launcher hit the glass like a battering ram. The window shattered – and Eddie hurtled through the falling pieces into the room beyond.

Sparkling debris showered over him, cutting the exposed skin of his hands and head. But he had to ignore the pain. The impact had robbed him of the speed he needed to complete the arc. He kicked away the Type 08 as he dropped—

And slammed down on his back. The pressure around his left wrist eased, but would return at any moment. The rest of the hose was about to fall back down – and would pull him with it.

Glass crunched beneath Eddie as he rolled to the neighbouring, undamaged window and flattened himself against the glass—

The hose's full weight suddenly yanked his arm against the frame, almost breaking his wrist. He yelled, but held on. A moment to recover, then he crawled from the window, dragging the hose with him and tying it around a pillar. It wouldn't come loose, unless the entire floor collapsed.

Which was now not an unlikely possibility.

Arm aching, he returned to the broken window and looked up, following the hose's pale line to its source. From this angle he couldn't see any of the people still in the other tower, but they would surely realise he had created an escape route. 'Come on, come *on*,' he muttered, picking glass from his hands.

★ ★ ★

'Here!' shouted one of the warriors, spotting the unmistakable gleam of orichalcum against the crash bags at the end of the bobsled run. He snatched up the key. 'I have it!'

A comrade looked into the broken hole, trikan at the ready. 'What about the beast? She fell down here.'

The first man shook his head. 'We have the key. That is all that matters. We need to bring it back to the vimana.' He took out a speaking crystal to tell Gadreel the good news.

The warrior at the edge of the pit peered into the shadows below, but saw no movement except wafting dust. Irked by his prey's escape, he followed the others from the frozen chamber.

'He made it!' Macy told Cheng. 'The hose isn't moving, look.'

The Chinese was less certain. 'What if it just got stuck on something?'

'This is my dad – he does this kind of stuff all the time! Well, not *exactly* like this,' she admitted. 'Although he did once tell me he and Mom escaped from a skyscraper before its top fell off . . . But whatever, he did it. We've got to go.' She carefully made her way to the waiting soldier.

He had retrieved the rifle straps, taking off his equipment webbing and the jacket of his combat fatigues. The latter was twisted and knotted into a crude rope, which he tied to the straps to increase their length. He held out the webbing to Macy with an encouraging smile. 'He's telling you to put the harness on, but not to fasten it yet,' Cheng translated. 'He'll lower you down. Once you reach the reel, fasten the harness around the hose to hold yourself, then put your legs over it and slide down.'

'If I've got his harness, how's *he* going to get down?' she asked.

The relayed question drew a chuckle from the soldier. 'He says not to worry,' Cheng told her. 'He's a tough guy, he can hold on.'

'Okay . . .' said Macy, unconvinced. But she let him help her don the harness, adjusting it to fit her much smaller frame, then nervously held the strap. He lowered her to the open hatch.

The journey, though nerve-racking, took only moments. She grabbed the reel with relief and stepped into the recess. From here, she could see the hose stretching away towards the other tower, though the ceiling blocked sight of its far end.

She leaned out and fumbled the harness around the hose. A heavy-duty plastic clip snapped shut with reassuring firmness. That done, she gripped the hose with both hands before wrapping her legs over it.

Fear returned. It was not the first time she had used a zip-line, nor climbed a rope; her father had made sure of that, and much more. But it *was* the first time she had done something where any mistake would kill her.

'Dad thinks I can do this,' she whispered. 'If he thinks I can . . . then I can.'

She started her descent.

After just a few feet, she cleared the floor, the taut hose lifting her as it angled towards the windows. Another surge of fear made her halt. She was now relying entirely on her own strength, and the plastic clip, to keep from falling. 'I can do this,' she said, forcing herself not to look down. 'Oh Jeez. I can do it. I can. I *can*!'

She set off again, reaching the windows. Wind gusted around her. Again she refused to look down, instead fixing her gaze on the hose's now-visible far end. It was about five storeys lower – and to her relief and joy, she saw her father waving from a broken window.

Filled with sudden hope, she headed across the gap, taking her hands off the hose to slide freely, at first for brief moments, then for longer and longer. She picked up speed, moving so fast that her hands almost couldn't keep up—

A new smell hit her nostrils. Not from the fires below, but a sharp scent, like melting plastic . . .

She looked up – and to her alarm saw smoke swirling from the nylon harness as it rasped over the hose. The friction was melting it!

'Oh no, *no*!' she squealed, grabbing the hose and clenching her legs together. She halted, but the smoke didn't stop. A *snap* as overstressed strands stretched and broke, then another—

'Macy!' Her father's voice, not far away. 'Keep going! You're almost here!'

'It's breaking!' she cried.

'Wrap your arms around the hose! Keep hold!'

'I'm scared!'

'I'll catch you! Just do it – trust me!'

She reluctantly let go with one hand. Her upper body swung, the harness taking her weight – and there was another terrifying crackle of breaking threads. She screamed, but pulled herself upwards and crossed both arms over the hose to let herself slide onwards.

Even through her clothing, the hose bit painfully at the bends of her elbows. She moaned, but kept her hold. The smaller tower's mirrored face rushed closer – and swallowed her as she slithered through the window.

Rough hands grabbed her. 'Got you!' said Eddie.

She burst into tears. 'Daddy!'

He hurriedly unfastened the harness clip and helped her down. 'I've got you, you're okay.' A hug, a kiss on her cheek, then he stood. 'But you've got to go. There are stairs through there.' He pointed at a door. 'Get down to the ground and *run*.'

'I don't want to leave you!'

'This place'll collapse any minute! Soon as everyone else is here, I'll follow. But you need to get clear. I saw a big park on the other side of a car park, that way.' Another jab of his finger. 'Wait for me there.' She didn't move. 'Macy, I mean it! *Go!*'

Despite the danger, she managed a full ten-year-old's pout. 'Buggeration and fuckery.'

Eddie's eyes went wide. 'Oh, your mum's going to kill me. If this bloody building doesn't kill us first!' He looked around as the hose shuddered. Cheng was making his descent. 'I don't have time to argue, Macy. I've got to help the others, then I'll come and find you.'

'Do you promise?'

'I promise. I always turn up in the end, don't I?' Another kiss, then he firmly pushed her away. 'Now go!'

With deep reluctance, she ran for the exit. Eddie watched her go, taking a few extra seconds to make sure she had actually left, then turned to observe Cheng's approach.

A warrior's voice echoed from the speaking crystal. 'We have the resurrection key, my lord!'

'Good,' Gadreel replied. 'What about the woman? Is she dead?'

Hesitation before the reply. 'She . . . escaped.'

The Nephilim leader scowled, but put his annoyance aside. They had the key, and that was all that mattered. He searched for somewhere large enough to set down the fortress. Beside the smaller of the two wrecked towers was a large grey building with a flat roof; past that was a wide-open swathe of grass and trees. He ordered the warrior piloting the vimana to land there, then told the men on the ground to head towards it.

The fortress silently glided towards the park. Gadreel returned his attention to the broken-backed ruins. Sidona would soon finish what she had started – and once the tower was reduced to rubble, the rest of the city would suffer the same fate.

Cheng slithered the last few metres into the office. Eddie caught him. 'Okay, I've got you.' He waited for the young Chinese to move, but he clung to the hose like a spider monkey, eyes tightly shut. 'Hey! Cheng! You made it, you're safe.' The floor shuddered, windows cracking. 'Well, not *safe* safe . . .'

Cheng opened one eye. 'I made it down?'

'No, you fell off and died; this is heaven and I'm God. Yes, you bloody made it!'

Like Macy, Cheng was attached to the hose by equipment webbing. Eddie popped the clasp. Cheng fell to the floor with a thud, his pack beneath him. 'Ow!'

'Sorry. But I need you to catch up with Macy. I told her to run downstairs and get to the park. I want you to stay with her until I get there.'

Cheng stood and headed for the door. 'I'll look after her, Eddie.'

'I know you will. Get going.'

The younger man hurried off. Eddie returned to the window. The first soldier was making a rapid descent. If the last man was as quick, they might all escape before both towers collapsed—

The fortress slid into view from behind the burning skyscraper, descending. Dismay as Eddie realised where it was going.

Towards the park – where he had just sent Macy.

He froze, torn between the urge to save his daughter and his duty to help the soldiers. They might be from an unfriendly nation, but right now, they all faced a common enemy. His mind found a reluctant compromise: wait for the man to arrive, *then* go after Macy while the soldier assisted his comrade.

Frustrated by the forced inaction, he waited for him to traverse the final stretch. The soldier soon arrived. Eddie helped him in. A hurried round of charades explained that the Englishman wanted to catch up with his daughter. The man nodded and smiled in understanding, waving for him to go. Eddie clapped him on the shoulder, then scooped up the rocket launcher and ran for the exit.

36

'M acy!'
Macy had just reached the fourth floor. She looked back up the debris-strewn stairwell to see Cheng several levels above, pounding breathlessly downwards. 'Are you okay?' she called out.

'I'm having several heart attacks at once, but yes!' he gasped. 'Your dad told me to get you out of here! No, don't stop,' he said as she halted. 'I'll catch up with you.'

'Only if I slow right down,' she warned, but she kept going. Three floors to go, two. She eased off to let him get closer. 'Come on! We're almost there!'

'I'm . . . so glad,' he panted as he caught up at the door.

Dust swirled in as she opened it, making them both cough. They saw why as they hurried into the lobby. The decapitated top of the larger tower had fallen outside, the main exit blocked by hundreds of tons of rubble. 'Over there,' said Macy, pointing. 'We can get out through the parking lot.'

Another set of doors led into an adjoining structure. 'Is it safe?' Cheng asked.

'I don't know,' she admitted. 'But if we stay in here much longer, we'll get squashed!'

'We definitely don't want that,' he agreed.

They both ran for the exit.

The vimana hovered over the park, turning so Gadreel could regard the two towers. His warriors were on the way with the key, but he warned them to give the broken-backed building a wide berth. When Sidona finally brought it down, the destruction would affect a large area . . .

The moment was coming. He saw lights in the tower's base – something more than the seething flames. The earth's power was rising again. More flashes, lightning bolts snaking into the air – and the whole ruin shuddered.

The toppled section sagged, every surviving window shattering in a dazzling mirrored cascade. Dust erupted from within as concrete crumbled.

The lights grew brighter – then another explosion blasted the lower floors apart.

With a fearsome roar, the entire structure started to fall.

The Chinese soldier watched his comrade descend the hose – then jumped in shock as strange lightning lanced from the bottom of the broken tower—

All the windows above burst apart. Tons of broken glass fell in a great wave towards the plaza below – sweeping the other soldier away with it.

The smaller tower lurched, earthquake-force tremors shaking it. He ran for the exit, barely able to keep his balance. Tiles and light fittings fell from the suspended ceiling, dust dropping from widening cracks in the concrete slabs above.

He swerved as a section of floor fell away, then sprinted for the door—

The ceiling pounded down on him like a sledgehammer.

Eddie was still nine storeys up when the tower shook. The wrecked skyscraper was about to come down – and take his building with it.

There was no way he would reach the ground floor in time. Instead he barged through the stairwell exit. He had only one chance of survival – and even that was slim.

He charged across empty offices. Wind blew in through broken windows ahead. Beyond them he saw the fortress settling over the park like a great dark bird. He had sent Macy towards it. The grim thought spurred him on. He had to save her, no matter what.

The car park came into view as he neared the windows. It was unfinished, a couple of large trucks, including a cement mixer, parked near a partially skimmed swathe of concrete surface at the far end. The workers had long since fled. The upper level was two storeys below him, a gap of fifteen feet separating it from the tower. The nearer end was strewn with fallen debris.

Eddie knew he could make the jump – but he would be falling nearly thirty feet onto a hard surface. However good his landing, he would almost certainly break bones.

But it was that or death. He looked for the clearest landing spot and ran at the window—

The floor dropped out from under him.

He stumbled to a stop just before the edge. Broken concrete and steel whooshed past the windows as debris shook loose from the upper floors.

Another lurch almost knocked him down. A huge, explosive crack of disintegrating concrete rolled up from below. The whole building dropped by a foot, the central core crumbling under the sheer weight of the toppled skyscraper. It was about to fall—

Eddie scrambled back across the room, then ran again.

The floor dropped once more . . . and this time did not stop.

The parking lot opened out before him. He reached the edge – and leapt into open air.

The gap rushed past below as he arced towards the concrete expanse. The tower's slow-motion collapse had eaten several feet out of his fall, but it would still be a hard landing—

His feet hit solid ground – and he rolled to absorb the impact.

Even so, it felt as if someone had whacked his ankles with a crowbar. But he couldn't stop. He dragged himself up, running painfully towards the trucks.

A terrifying crackle split the air behind him as both towers fell.

The precariously suspended section of skyscraper finally succumbed to its wounds and split at the middle. Both halves swung down, smashing through the faces of the structures at each end, and hit the plaza between them like a barrage of block-buster bombs.

The pounding shocks flung Eddie into the air. He landed hard on his side, the rocket launcher digging into his back as he rolled over it. Groaning, he looked up – to see the end of the parking structure drop away amidst a cloud of dust. Thousands of tons of falling debris had demolished its eastern end.

The collapse started a chain reaction. Huge concrete slabs flipped up like playing cards and disappeared into the maelstrom – each nearer to Eddie than the last. 'Arse chives!' he yelled, panic overpowering pain. He ran again, sections dropping behind his heels, getting closer—

The slab underfoot tipped backwards. He threw himself up the steepening slope, hitting its top at waist height. Flying rubble struck his shins and knees. He dragged himself over the edge, feeling the floor shuddering, about to collapse . . .

The vibrations faded.

Panting, he rose to his knees. Half the parking structure was gone, stubs of support pillars poking up through a swirling dust cloud. Beyond, where two gleaming skyscrapers had stood, was nothing but a vast, chaotic pile of smoking wreckage.

The two Chinese soldiers could not possibly have escaped. All he could hope was that Macy *had*. He ran to the side of the car park to look for her.

She and Cheng were nowhere in sight – but the fortress now

hovered over the park below, its closest point just metres away. It turned as it slowly descended, facing him. For a moment he thought it was going to finish the job and bring down the rest of the structure with its guns, but then it continued around, pointing back the way it had come, and halted, underbelly about ten feet above the ground.

Several Nephilim warriors in colourful armour ran towards it from the north. They headed for the hovering dragon's midsection, where part of the craft's edge curved down to just a few feet above the ground, forming steps up to the top of the hull where the open hatch awaited.

They were leaving. That meant they'd got whatever they were after—

Anger surged as he saw the leading warrior carrying something more than his weapons. The key! Nina *had* escaped with it . . . but now they'd got it back. He looked past the Nephilim. No sign of her. If they had killed her . . .

Even as the terrible thought came, he had already decided they weren't going any further. He unslung the launcher and swung its handgrip into firing position. From here, he could blast a rocket right through the broken throne room window and kill everyone inside—

Military pragmatism kept his finger off the trigger. The fortress itself was the threat, not whoever was inside its control room. If he killed them, others would take over. He needed to cripple the dragon, and with its shield still shimmering, he couldn't guarantee that. Not with a single shot. Even though the Type 08 was an anti-armour weapon, the fortress was a hell of a lot bigger than a tank.

He needed something more. But where would he find anything, trapped on top of a car park?

A low, churning rumble gave him the answer.

The abandoned concrete mixer stood not far away, its drum

still turning. The truck was relatively short, to let it navigate the car park's ramps, but it still had four axles. It was carrying a lot of weight . . .

He shouldered the launcher again as he ran to the truck and climbed into the cab. He had driven heavy vehicles during his army training; the controls were standard. Releasing the airbrakes with a hiss, he put the mixer into gear and slowly accelerated, making a turn.

The devastated ruins came into view. He drove towards the parking structure's ragged edge, getting as close as he dared before slowing. He felt the slabs beneath the wheels shiver, but he needed as much of a run-up as he could get.

A half-turn, and he straightened out and stopped. The fortress was now out of sight below the wall at the end of the deck. He pushed the driver's door open, then readied himself. Clutch pedal three-quarters down so as not to engage the clutch brake, into gear, then he revved the engine, the big diesel roaring in response.

The power built. He watched the rev counter rise towards the red zone – then released the clutch.

The truck leapt forward. A brief dip on the clutch to keep the engine from stalling as the revs plunged, then he re-engaged. A second lurch, but the diesel held firm. Accelerator hard down until the needle reached the red, up into the next gear, then again—

The wall rushed at him, the fortress coming into sight beyond. He kept going for another few seconds – then leapt from the cab.

Another hard landing on unyielding concrete. His elbow cracked painfully against it as he rolled, the launcher skidding away from him. The driverless concrete mixer roared on, engine note dropping sharply without his foot on the pedal, but still moving too fast to stop—

It smashed through the wall, sailing out from the parking structure's highest floor – and plunged towards the hovering fortress below.

From his vantage point at the broken window, Gadreel saw his warriors returning. They had the key; now he could not only revive his people here, but find the rest of them in their long-hidden prison . . .

A new noise reached him, mechanical – coming from above. Another flying machine? He looked up, seeing nothing in the sky, but it sounded very close—

The half-collapsed building's upper wall exploded as a huge, bizarrely shaped chariot burst through it.

It smashed down on to the fortress. Everyone within was thrown off their feet as the impact pounded the vimana's nose into the ground. The shrill and crunch of tearing metal echoed terrifyingly through the throne room.

Gadreel was flung against the wall, striking his head. He put a hand to it as he stood, feeling the sting of a cut. Zan lay sprawled nearby, the others in the room all dizzily recovering. The floor was still canted. 'Bring us level!' he ordered as he returned to the window.

To his shock, he saw the chariot embedded in the fortress's bow. The large drum it carried had split open, a thick grey slurry gushing across the hull and into the holes it had torn.

One of his men hurriedly retook the controls. Crystals glowed as more power flowed through them. The vimana struggled to rise, the chariot's weight straining its inner structure still further. More metal groaned – and he heard the sharp crack of crystal splitting apart below.

Sidona! She was in the mausoleum—

Gadreel ran to the stairs, calling his wife's name. He was halfway down them before a reply came. 'I . . . I am all right,' she said, sitting up unsteadily. 'What happened?'

'The humans dropped one of their chariots on top of the vimana!'

Sidona gasped as she saw a jagged crack in the crystalline wall. The chamber's glow now stopped short of the damaged area, as if it had been poisoned. 'The crystal is broken! It—'

They both clung to coffins as the floor shook. The fortress heaved itself clear of the ground, a huge crash coming from outside as the truck fell off. More moans and cracks around them – and a new light seeped through the translucent walls. Not the glow of the earth's power, but daylight. 'What has happened?' she said, alarmed.

'We have lost some of our armour,' Gadreel replied in grim realisation. The adamantium plating beneath the vimana's nose had been torn off, exposing what was shielded within.

'The crystal heart! If it is unprotected—'

'I know. And the humans' weapons may be able to damage it.' The crystal heart was the focus for all the earth energy powering the fortress. 'The key will soon be here.' He indicated the remaining sarcophagi. 'Be ready to use it!' He ran back to the throne room to oversee the impending battle.

Eddie got up, finding he had acquired a whole new layer of aches and bruises on top of those already there. He staggered to the broken wall to see the results of his handiwork.

The concrete mixer had smashed through the fortress's upper hull, leaking its load into the holes ripped in the metal. The aircraft's draconic snout was buried in the ground. 'How to *pain* your dragon,' he said, pleased by the damage he had caused. Even if it managed to get airborne again, it would be more vulnerable, even crippled.

The fortress shuddered and started to pull itself free, the truck noisily rolling off the hull. He turned to find the launcher. *Now* might be the time to put a rocket through its window—

Shouts from below. The warriors were no longer advancing in triumph, but had spread out, using the trees for cover as they ran towards him.

He ducked and ran as their spear weapons came up—

The wall and floor exploded behind him as he snatched up the Type 08, chunks of shattered masonry bouncing off his back. He kept running, clearing the blast zone, but he had nowhere to go. There was no way off the roof—

A fearsome *crack* – and the entire end of the structure where he had been standing fell in a storm of flying debris.

Gadreel looked on as his warriors blasted the building with their barakas. The chariot's driver had just shown himself, a bald human in a coat of dark leather, and the angry men below reacted accordingly.

The end of the structure collapsed, its upper floors falling and bringing those below cascading down. A large part of the strange building – he still could not fathom its function – remained standing, though.

It would not for long. 'Bring it all down!'

Eddie reached the upper floor's broken end and looked down. If he hung from the edge, he might be able to drop to the level below – but its surviving floor slabs were badly damaged. A safe landing was far from guaranteed, and even then he still had to get all the way to the ground.

Where he would be an easy target. More energy bolts slammed into the car park, concrete shattering explosively – and then a main gun on the fortress unleashed another devastating blast. A huge section of the top floor blew apart, tons of smashed concrete flying at him—

He dropped over the edge, hitting the slab below hard – and

scrambled backwards as a punishing grey hailstorm swept past in front of him.

No time for relief. More shots from the spears ripped into the concrete behind—

Another sizzling burst from one of the bizarre weapons – but further away. A moment later came screams as an explosion sent the Nephilim flying.

Nina pursued the warriors all the way from the mall, exhausted by the effort of keeping up with their greater pace, but refusing to surrender. She followed a road one block clear of the devastated remains of the skyscraper – *two* skyscrapers, she saw, praying they had been as empty as the rest of the city – to find the fortress hovering in a park . . . and the armoured group she was following opening fire on someone atop a parking lot beside it.

She instantly recognised their target. Eddie darted out of sight as explosions pulverised the wall. She gasped in fear, then saw an even greater danger as one of the fortress's fang-like guns swung around. A powerful blast of earth energy shot from it – and the structure's whole end crashed down like a house of cards.

'Jesus!' Nina cried. She ducked into the cover of a wall at the park's entrance, unsure what to do, before anger took over. Eddie wouldn't have left the Chinese base without Macy – and if he was in danger, so was she. She looked back out. The warriors were sprinting towards what remained of the parking structure, still attacking—

She aimed the baraka and fired.

The orichalcum cover snapped open, a bolt of energy bursting from the crystal within. It hit the ground amidst the running group. The explosion blew a crater from the turf, flinging warriors into the air. At least one was dead, his body torn in half, and another seriously wounded as he screamed and clutched at the stump of a missing leg.

But the others recovered quickly. Their own weapons came up—

Nina dived flat behind the wall. More blasts blew holes through it above her. Most of the debris was blown overhead, but she was still pummelled by broken brickwork. Clutching the spear, she crawled along until the fusillade halted, then leapt up and ran.

She reached a low building and hurried around behind it, heading along the edge of the park towards the parking structure – and her husband.

'Bring the key to the fortress!' Gadreel shouted into the speaking crystal. 'Now!' The urge for petty revenge had just cost him the life of at least one of his people, and wounded others – a mistake he should have known better than to make. 'Forget the beasts – we are leaving!'

The warriors on the ground started back towards the vimana, some with clear reluctance. They too wanted vengeance. But that would come once the resurrection key was safely in Sidona's hands and the fortress was in the air.

'Take flight as soon as everyone is aboard,' he shouted to the man at the central altar. 'Then we will destroy this entire city!'

Eddie dropped down through the car park's levels and leapt to the debris-strewn ground. The new attacker had drawn the Nephilim away from him. There was only one person it could be: Nina. Her Atlantean DNA had apparently powered up more than the UFO.

He hurried into the park to see the warriors climbing on to the fortress. No sign of Nina. Hopefully she was being sensible and hiding rather than running towards the fray looking for him—

'Yeah, right,' he muttered, knowing full well she would be doing the latter.

The last Nephilim clambered onto the fortress's hull, and it started to rise. The air trembled with the sheer energy flowing through it.

Eddie hurriedly brought up the launcher, but his firing angle through the broken window was already shrinking. He prepared to take the shot anyway. It was his last chance to bring the bastards down—

Something unexpected held his finger off the trigger.

Metal tore with an echoing screech. A large section of the lower hull broke loose from beneath the fortress's nose, torn armour plates dangling from buckled beams.

An unearthly light shone within the gaping wound. As the dragon rose higher, Eddie saw its source: a large pearl-like crystal set into its chin.

He didn't know what it did. But the armour had been there to protect it, so he knew what it *was* – his new target.

'Eat this, Smaug!' he yelled as he fixed the launcher's sights on the shining jewel – and fired.

The rocket shot from the tube, a small launch charge propelling it a few metres clear before the main booster ignited and blasted it onwards. It took only a split second to reach its target. The warhead's first stage detonated, punching through the crystal's skin – then the second, larger explosive charge exploded inside it.

The glowing sphere blew apart.

Jagged shards rained from the fortress, their glow fading as they fell. The light in the surviving crystals within the dragon's chin also flickered, then diminished. The hovering behemoth nevertheless kept climbing . . .

For a moment.

Then it wavered, losing height—

Heading for Eddie.

'Fuckeration!' he yelled, throwing down the empty launcher and running like hell. The fortress swept after him. The edge of its hull clipped the ruined car park – and smashed through the concrete as if it was cardboard.

Debris bombarded the park as the dragon swept overhead, trailing dust. Eddie dodged a hunk of slab tumbling past—

Another lump slammed into his back, knocking him down.

He bowled over the grass as more pieces fell around him. Dizzied, he looked up – to see a section of support pillar as big as a phone booth rushing at him—

Someone grabbed him.

He didn't even have time to see who it was. All he could do was force his legs into motion as he was hauled up. The pillar smashed into the earth behind him like a piledriver. He stumbled with his rescuer across the grass.

The hail of debris died away. Pained, exhausted, he flopped to the ground, looking up to see—

'Ay up,' said a familiar voice. Nina knelt over him, looking down with a relieved smile.

'Ay up,' he echoed wearily. 'Fancy meeting you here.'

'I wouldn't recommend the airline, but I'm glad I made it. Where's Macy?'

His daughter's name gave him the energy to sit up. 'With Cheng. I'm hoping they're well clear of all this.'

'We need to find her.'

'I know.' She helped him stand. 'How'd you get out of the fortress?'

'Long story, involving way too much falling from great heights and being shot at. I took the key – but they got it back.'

'Don't think they'll be doing much with it, though.'

'Why not?'

They moved clear of the drifting dust – and Nina was startled to see the fortress swaying drunkenly as it fought to stay airborne. It was fighting a losing battle, dropping slowly but inexorably back to earth. 'Turns out it had a glowing weak spot like something from a PlayStation game,' Eddie told her. 'So I blew it up with a rocket launcher. Job done.'

She grinned, but only briefly. 'They can still wake the rest of their people with the key – and they've got the Chinese earth energy weapon as well.'

Eddie frowned. 'What weapon?'

'That so-called tracker of theirs? It's more like a targeting system! Like the weapon DARPA built, but even more powerful. That must be how they blew up the skyscrapers.' She regarded the ruined towers. 'Gadreel made me wake his wife, Sidona – she's some sort of high priestess, and can control earth energy.'

'So can you.'

'She's better. A *lot* better. Colonel Wu said the tracker can use qi energy to blow up a target anywhere on the planet – and now the Nephilim have it. They've *used* it.'

'If their UFO's fucked, they won't be able to escape with it,' said Eddie – but then all concerns about the giants vanished as he saw two figures enter the park. '*Macy!*'

'Oh, thank God!' Nina cried, breaking into a run. Eddie followed at his best stagger. 'She's all right!'

'Mom!' Macy cried, leaving Cheng behind as she rushed to meet her parents. 'Dad! Are you okay?'

'We're fine,' Nina assured her, embracing her tightly. Eddie caught up to join in the reunion. 'What about you? Are you hurt?'

Macy shook her head. 'I got some bruises when the skyscraper fell over, but I'll be fine.'

Nina blinked. 'You were *in* the skyscraper?' She rounded on

Eddie. 'You took my daughter inside a *collapsing skyscraper*?'

'Like you said, long story,' he replied. 'I'll tell you later. We need to get out of here first, though. And I don't just mean this city,' he added as Cheng arrived. 'Getting out of *China* would be a very good idea. Before they blame all this on us.'

'I agree.' Nina looked back at the fortress. It weaved between skyscrapers, still losing height. 'But I don't think this is over . . .'

37

'What is happening?' roared Gadreel, clinging to an altar as the vimana rolled. 'Take us higher!'

'I can't, my lord!' the warrior at the controls protested. 'Something is wrong!'

Sidona hurried into the throne room. To Gadreel's shock, she had a bloody gash down the left side of her face. 'They destroyed the crystal heart! The mausoleum is also damaged. Some of the sarcophagi are broken!'

'How many?' he asked, appalled.

'I don't know – perhaps eight or nine?'

'The woman Wilde killed some of our warriors as well. We have lost too many people today.' A brief look, both grieving and angry, at Turel's body. 'The humans have become dangerous.'

'*Too* dangerous,' she snapped. 'There is only one way to deal with an infestation. Wipe them out!'

'And we shall. But first we must find the rest of our people.'

'They are imprisoned! We don't know where they are!'

His knowing expression changed her despair into hope. 'I do,' he told her. 'The humans' machine showed me a map of the whole world. And I saw where the lines of force meet at their strongest. I know how to find Tartarus! But the vimana is too damaged to take us there. Sidona, use the key and wake as many as you can, quickly. We will leave in the vimana-kal.'

Her gaze went to the golden clamshell behind the three thrones. 'It is too small to take us all!'

'We must make hard choices to survive.' He put his hands

firmly on her shoulders, eyes fixed on hers. 'But we *will* survive. Choose the strongest, the best.'

The weight of responsibility placed upon her was almost physical, her shoulders sagging, but she nodded. 'Yes, my lord. And . . . what of the others?'

'They must win us the time we need to escape.' He released her and went back to the window. The fortress was passing between towers, following a broad avenue into the city's heart. 'Can you go no higher?'

'No, my lord,' the pilot replied.

'The humans will send more flying machines against us. They came from the west . . .' He surveyed the vista ahead, then pointed at another park, with a low hill at one end. 'There! Land us with our weapons facing west – and the vimana's nose raised. When they come, we shall be ready for them. And if they attack our fortress on the ground . . .' His face twisted into a snarl. 'We will take a hundred of their worthless lives for every Nephilim who falls!'

To Major Wu's fury, the helicopter pilot hurriedly took his Z-20 well clear of the battle zone after the two jets were destroyed. He then orbited the city centre four kilometres out, giving those aboard a terrifying grandstand view of the sky-scraper's collapse. The loss of two fighters had deterred the officers at Cangliang from sending any more aircraft, angering her even more.

But now something had turned the tide. Through binoculars, Wu saw an explosion beneath the shimmering dragon's head – then the fortress went out of control, crashing into a parking lot before struggling back into the air.

There was no doubt that it was damaged. The multispectral ripple of its shield had gone, and it lost height as it fled deeper into the city. 'They've got it!' she cried. 'The men from the other chopper – some of them must have survived! They've taken it down!'

'It's still airborne,' the co-pilot cautioned.

'Not for long.' She switched her headset to communicate with the airbase. 'This is Major Wu! The UFO is crippled – I repeat, it's going down. I need ground troops to secure it and make sure none of the monsters escape. Get as many men here as you can, now!'

There was far less resistance to her orders this time. She switched back to the intercom. 'Take us in closer,' she told the pilot. 'And ready the guns!'

'We need to tell my mother what's happening,' said Cheng as his companions watched the fortress disappear behind more towers. He took the laptop from his backpack and unfolded the satellite link.

'Can't you just phone her?' Macy asked.

He shook his head. 'All civilian telecommunications will have been cut off. If Major Wu didn't order it, someone at the base will have.'

'Your government doesn't want videos of a UFO blowing up half the city all over the Chinese version of Twitter, I guess,' said Nina.

'Weibo, and no, it doesn't. They're kind of strict about state security. But this uses military channels, so it should still work.' He set up the antenna, then opened the laptop and started to type.

Eddie turned at the sound of a helicopter, seeing a distant Z-20 pursuing the fortress. 'That must be Major Wu. Christ, she's not going after that thing, is she? It's still dangerous.'

Cheng looked up briefly from the computer. 'If you blew up its power source, will the guns still work?'

'I don't know,' said Nina. 'It might depend who's using them.

Anything that requires care and precision and complex manipulation of the earth energy fields, that's a job for a woman. If it's just blam-blam blowing crap up, you only need a man.'

'Things haven't changed much in a hundred thousand years, have they?' Eddie said, grinning.

A voice came from the laptop's speakers: Dr Hui Ling. '*Mā!*' said Cheng, relieved.

His mother was equally happy. They had a heartfelt exchange in Mandarin, before Cheng switched to English so his companions could join in. 'Professor Wilde's here, and so are Mr Chase and Macy. They're all okay.'

'More or less,' said Eddie, stretching a sore leg.

'I'm so glad to hear that,' Hui said. The audio quality was low, glitchy; even using Chinese military channels, bandwidth had become limited now the armed forces were being mobilised. 'I am still at the hill; I have only received intermittent updates from the soldiers here. What has happened?'

'A lot of property destruction,' Nina told her. 'Potentially major civilian casualties. But the fortress has been damaged – it hasn't crashed yet, but it's only a matter of time. Eddie blew up the crystal it uses to focus earth energy.'

'Major Wu's chasing it in her helicopter,' Cheng added.

'I heard. I hope her anger does not get more people killed.'

'We need to get out of here before Wu and her superiors start looking for scapegoats,' said Nina. 'I doubt she's gonna let her father take the blame, so I have a horrible feeling we'll be at the top of her list.'

'I suspect we all will. The military always looks to the outside for blame before turning its eyes on itself.' Hui considered her next action. 'I will contact the base and have a helicopter pick me up – then I will collect you as well. Where are you?'

'Just look for the collapsed skyscrapers,' said Eddie. 'We're in the park next to them.'

'I will be there as soon as I can.'

'Thank you,' said Nina.

The call ended. She looked back across the city, seeing the helicopter pass out of sight as it followed the fortress into Xinengyuan's heart.

The Z-20 descended towards the city's streets. 'The UFO's landing!' said the pilot.

Wu saw the metal monster lower itself to the ground in a park, its chin on a grassy mound to bring its prow upwards. She realised immediately why. 'They're giving their guns a wider firing arc,' she said. 'Stay behind it so it can't target us.'

The pilot changed course. 'Do you want me to land?'

'Not yet,' she replied. 'We need to make sure it can't take off again.' A glance back; soldiers were ready on both miniguns. 'Prepare to fire!'

The fortress's touchdown was not gentle, sending the throne room's occupants staggering. Gadreel recovered and hurried to the mausoleum. 'Sidona! How many more have you woken?'

'About twenty-five so far,' his wife replied. 'The first are beginning to recover.'

The Nephilim leader performed rapid mental arithmetic. Inside the clamshell behind the three thrones was a smaller craft, the vimana-kal. Intended as a royal transport so that he could travel without moving the entire fortress, it had only limited space within. It could take perhaps twenty, twenty-two at the tightest squeeze – but it still needed room for the tracker and the annoying human, Zan.

'Then continue,' he told her. 'Those we cannot fit into the vimana-kal will defend the fortress until we can leave.'

'My lord!' shouted a man in the throne room. 'One of their machines is coming!'

'Destroy it!'

'It is behind us! We cannot bring the lightning spears to bear.'

Gadreel cursed. 'They are going to attack!' He picked out eight of the warriors in the throne room. 'You men, go outside. Find cover and shoot down the machine if you can. If the beasts reach the ground, kill them.' They ran from the chamber.

He went to the thrones. His seat at the centre had several stones and crystals inset into its arms. He touched his hand to one. To his relief, there was still enough earth energy flowing through the fortress to open the enclosure behind him. The clamshell slowly split apart.

Gold gleamed within. The vimana-kal was a flattened ovoid, its orichalcum skin polished to a near-mirror shine even after uncounted years. Three round crystal windows were spaced across its upper surface, an entrance hatch at the rear. It had been built to accommodate six travellers in comfort; how it would fare with almost four times that number remained to be seen.

But he would have to find out. He headed for the smaller craft's entrance – then paused as he passed his son's body. The wounded vimana's unsteady flight had slipped the robes from his face. The sight of the youth filled him once more with grief – and rage. 'I shall make them *pay*,' he promised, gently drawing the covering back over Turel's head before entering the vimana-kal.

The pilot brought his helicopter into a hover a hundred metres above the ground, facing the fortress's right rear quarter. 'Ready.'

Major Wu did not waste a moment. 'Open fire!'

Both gunners swung their weapons at the grounded dragon and pulled the triggers. The miniguns spat out a vicious barrage of gunfire. Wu felt a surge of angry triumph as the first rounds hit home; the fortress's shield was indeed down, bullets ripping into its hull. 'Aim for the window!' she ordered. 'If you see anyone, kill them!'

The gunners obeyed. Metal splintered, the storm of bullets hosing through the broken window—

'There!' cried the co-pilot, pointing. 'Someone's coming out!'

Wu saw several giant armoured figures rush from the open hatch. Most charged across the hull, but a couple dropped into cover behind the strakes and brought up their spear weapons. 'Incoming fire! Take evasive action!'

The pilot and gunners responded simultaneously, the former pitching the helicopter sideways. The latter briefly ceased firing as they found the threats – then opened up again. More rounds ripped through metal, and the men crouching behind it. Wu felt another surge of cruel satisfaction as bodies were flung backwards amidst flying shrapnel. Their fancy armour may have made the Nephilim invulnerable in ancient times, but it was useless against modern weaponry.

One gunner sent his stream of bullets after the other warriors, catching a giant in the back, but the rest leapt over the side to take cover beneath the fortress. The danger they posed had just risen hugely, Wu knew; the dragon was so large they could reappear from anywhere and shoot before the miniguns could target them. 'Pull back and land,' she barked. 'Ground troops, get ready!'

The Z-20 drew away from the fortress. As Wu had predicted, a warrior emerged from under its tail section and fired his weapon. The sizzling energy burst shot past, missing by a metre. Wu held on as the aircraft pulled up sharply to land behind a building, then threw open the main hatch. 'Move out!' she shouted, grabbing a rifle. 'Flanking positions, keep in cover – and if any of those monsters shows its head, blow it off!'

★ ★ ★

The hammer blows on the hull warned Gadreel he was running out of time. The humans were attacking from their flying machine; soon they would begin a ground assault.

He readied the vimana-kal as much as he could, but, like its parent craft, it needed the touch of a priestess and the resurrection key to bring the crystal at its heart fully back to life. He ran back into the throne room. Chaos greeted him. The clamorous assault had stopped, but the room had been devastated by the humans' weapons. One warrior had lost his legs, the wounded man moaning and twitching near the altars where he had crawled on a trail of blood. Gadreel could not spare him more than a pitying glance as he rushed to the mausoleum stairs, Zan following hesitantly.

Below, he saw the first of the newly woken Nephilim, bleary and confused from their revival. 'Sidona, I need you in the vimana-kal. How many more have you awoken?'

'Another ten,' his wife replied. 'I can still wake more—'

'It will have to do. Come, quickly! You, Zan – bring the tracker.'

Zan regarded the heavy machine with dismayed resignation. 'Yes, my lord.'

Sidona hurried to her husband, bearing the key. He led her towards the smaller craft. She gasped at the sight of the wounded man. 'Their weapons – they are too powerful! We cannot stand against them!'

'We can,' Gadreel growled. 'They are like everything human – crude and savage. But we have a power they do not, and we will use it to turn their own weapon against them!'

They entered the vimana-kal. Sidona quickly put the key in place and pressed her hand to it, her eyes going blank for a moment as she shaped the planet's invisible forces. More crystals around the room glowed brightly. The fortress was crippled, but its child was in perfect condition.

She withdrew. 'How will we know where to go?'

'There is a place where many lines of force meet,' Gadreel told her, 'a place of great power – it must be Tartarus. The tracker will guide us.'

'If you can trust the human.'

Beyond the windows, he saw Zan struggling to carry the machine across the throne room. 'If he wishes to stay alive, he will obey. He has betrayed his own people – there is nowhere else for him to go. Now, ready us to leave.'

He ran back out into the throne room to address his people from the central altar. 'The world has changed,' he said, raising his voice so those in the chamber below could hear. 'Our persecutors are gone – but they have been usurped by the beasts who bore us, the humans. They became powerful while we slept, but we can still defeat them!'

His words had the desired effect, rallying the warriors. 'We will reclaim our place and free our people,' he went on. 'But it will require sacrifice. The fortress is crippled. Our only hope is to use the vimana-kal to reach the hidden prison – but it is too small to take us all. Some must remain here. I am sorry.' He briefly bowed his head, then continued: 'Defend the fortress to the last. Your lives will not be wasted. We will free our daughters and sons, our sisters and brothers, all those who were taken from us by the People of the Tree. They will remember you for a thousand generations!'

Some of the newly woken entered during his speech, listening with excitement – or alarm, wondering if they would be the ones asked to give their lives. He made eye contact with each of them, reassuring them that he had not taken this decision lightly. 'We have little time left. We must make good use of it. Lady Sidona and I will give each of you your tasks. Then,' his voice rose to a crescendo, 'we will take back the world that is rightfully ours!'

The throne room erupted with cheers. Gadreel granted himself a moment to bask in the long-missed adulation of his people, then gestured for silence, ready to begin the difficult task of choosing who would escape – and who would be left to fight to the death.

Major Wu's team split into two groups, flanking the fortress. Those heading left had the more dangerous approach, as they would be within the firing arc of one of the big guns at its front.

Wu led the other group, going right. It was not out of cowardice, she told herself; she wanted to be the one to kill Gadreel for murdering her father. That meant fighting her way to the entrance, and if she had to shoot every giant in her path, so be it . . .

They ran across the park. Everything had gone unnervingly quiet, but that would not last—

Movement in the shadows beneath the fortress. 'Cover!' she barked, diving flat at the foot of a tree. Her men followed suit, using planters and benches for protection as they brought up their rifles. A towering figure rose under the dragon's tail, golden spear in his hands.

Wu shot first, sending three rapid rounds at her target. As a special forces operative, marksmanship was not only an expected skill, but demanded. Her shots were true, striking the Nephilim's chest – but his armour flared like the fortress's hull, shielded. Her Type 95 had neither the stopping power nor the sheer rate of fire of a minigun. By the time she realised he was unharmed, he had recovered—

Rippling energy crackled from his spear – and the man to Wu's left exploded in a shower of blood and shredded flesh. A hot wetness splattered her cheek.

Fighting shock, she flicked the rifle's fire selector to full auto and pulled the trigger again. This time, half the magazine hit her target. A scarlet burst from the giant's neck told her she had found a gap in his armour. He fell backwards.

Other dark shapes moved beneath the fortress. 'Grenades!' she shouted. 'Clear those scum out!'

Two of her remaining men had grenade launchers beneath their rifle barrels. Wu and the others ducked as a pair of forty-millimetre fragmentation charges were unleashed. Explosions and razor-sharp shrapnel tore through the space under the fortress. Shrill screams replaced the echoes of the detonations.

Wu jumped up and sprinted towards the downed aircraft. 'Move in! Kill them all!'

She ducked under the hull. The warrior she had shot lay on his back, clutching his throat as he gargled blood. She fired a single shot into his eye, then moved on. Another giant had been torn practically in half by a grenade, a second bloodied Nephilim on hands and knees several metres away. Wu ran up to him and jammed her rifle's muzzle against the exposed nape of his neck, then fired. The huge figure flopped to the ground.

Chattering gunfire to her left. The other group was engaging the warriors—

An ear-splitting crackle from the main gun – and a huge blast tore a crater out of the park. Wu whipped her head around to see pieces of her soldiers tumbling back to earth.

But her way to the hatch was now clear – and she heard the thud of rotor blades. The support she had called in from Cangliang was finally here.

Sensing victory, she advanced into the open to find the way into the ship. The Nephilim were now trapped like rats—

The fortress shuddered.

Wu reacted in alarm, but it was not trying to take off. Something had moved inside it, shifting its weight . . .

She looked up – and saw the dragon's head split open.

A section of hull behind the windows swung upwards. Gold

shone within. She realised where it was in relation to the rest of the chamber – the enclosure behind the thrones. The Nephilim had hidden something inside it—

Wu stared in surprise as a golden object, a flattened egg as long as a truck's trailer, silently levitated from its nest. The sight of windows made her realise what it was – another aircraft, some sort of shuttle or escape pod. They were trying to get away!

She whipped up her rifle and emptied her magazine at it. The rounds twanged off, the golden skin shimmering with iridescent energy. It too had a shield. The UFO kept climbing, turning southwards – then, without a sound, whisked away into the distance.

'No!' Wu shouted, rapidly reloading and sending another futile burst after it. She somehow knew Gadreel was aboard. And now he was escaping, denying her revenge – and taking the secrets of the Nephilim with him.

Not caring if any Nephilim still posed a threat beneath the fortress, she ran back the way she had come. 'Chopper pilot, this is Major Wu!' she shouted into her headset. 'Pick me up, now! They're escaping – we have to go after them!'

'Look!' shouted Macy, pointing. The others turned to see a golden pod-like craft flash between the skyscrapers.

'What the hell's that?' said Eddie.

'It's another vimana,' Nina realised. 'A smaller one – it must have been stored inside the fortress!'

'What is this, *Pimp My UFO*?' He tracked the object as it headed south. 'It's not hanging about, whatever it is.'

'It's got to be Gadreel and Sidona. The fortress is wrecked, so they're bugging out.'

'Going where?' asked Cheng.

'To find their people – to find Tartarus.' The golden craft shrank into the distance. 'We need to follow it! They've got the resurrection key – so if they find the prison, they can wake up their people. All of them.'

Cheng looked pensive. 'But we don't know where they're going.'

'Gadreel knew where the prison was,' she told him. 'Or at least he had a good idea. When he looked at the map on the tracker, he was very interested in part of it.'

'Which part?' said Eddie.

'I'm not sure. Somewhere in the southern hemisphere. We know the Veteres have been there, because they went through Indonesia and Australia all the way to Antarctica. So somewhere along the way, they found a place to site their prison – at a major confluence point of earth energy. We need to find it.'

'The tracker!' Cheng said excitedly. 'It has a wireless connection to the computers at the research centre. Everything it does is recorded – so there'll be a copy of whatever Gadreel saw!'

'Then we've got to get back there,' said Nina. 'Fast.' She looked around as Hui's helicopter came in to land, ready to ferry them to the base.

The vimana-kal's interior was overcrowded beyond the point of mere discomfort, but all those aboard knew they would have to endure it. They had greater concerns.

Sidona had made Zan connect the tracker to the craft's crystal heart. Even though it was much smaller than its counterpart in the crippled fortress, she soon discovered the machine gave her every bit as much power and control over the earth's energies. Her first priority had been to locate Tartarus, guiding their craft towards it.

Next came vengeance.

'The beasts cannot be allowed to claim the vimana,' Gadreel growled. 'We must destroy it to keep it from them.'

'My lord,' Sidona said quietly, 'the warriors who remained with it . . .'

He closed his eyes. 'I know.' A breath, then he opened them again, his expression stone. 'They will not be forgotten.' The other Nephilim crushed together in the cabin expressed silent appreciation for their sacrifice. 'Now. Begin.'

Sidona bowed her head, then turned to Zan. 'The vimana. Show it to me.'

'Yes, my lady,' the translator replied nervously. He zoomed the laptop's map in on Xinengyuan. 'It is here.'

'Target it,' ordered Gadreel. Zan hesitantly did so, the crosshairs locking on the park. 'What you did to the tower,' the Nephilim leader continued to his wife, 'do so again. Except . . . how great a devastation can you bring?'

'I do not know,' she replied. Her face hardened. 'But for Turel, for all our people who died at the hands of the beasts, I will find out.'

She closed her eyes, then touched her hands to the qi tracker's core – and the vimana-kal's crystal heart.

The helicopter landed. Major Wu sprinted to it, vaulting through the hatch and crouching behind the pilot. 'It went south!' she shouted as the Z-20 took off again. 'Get after it, full speed!'

The aircraft came about, the city dropping away. 'There!' said the co-pilot, pointing. A golden dot was visible in the sky.

'It's a long way ahead,' the pilot warned.

'Follow it,' Wu snapped, hiding her worry. The smaller UFO was travelling at the speed of a plane rather than a helicopter. But if it had the same radar immunity as its parent, she couldn't allow it to be lost to sight.

The Z-20 picked up speed, Xinengyuan sweeping past below. But it became clear after a couple of minutes that her quarry was outpacing her. The dot shrank, becoming fainter. She cursed—

A flash, buildings casting new shadows for a split second. 'Shit!' said the pilot. 'Major, they're shooting at us – they'll blow us up just like the jets!'

'It's not us,' she said. The burst of light had come from behind them. She scrambled to the hatch and looked back towards the city's centre. Were more fighters under attack?

None were in sight – but the realisation of what was happening was even more terrifying.

Another flash came from amongst the skyscrapers, then a third. Bolts of unnatural lightning squirmed and writhed between the towers. Even from this distance, she saw the walls of mirrored glass shatter. Dust rose as buildings shook, more and more bursts of light erupting amongst them—

A dazzling, silent flare. She jerked back into the cabin, shielding her eyes. For a moment, even the helicopter's clamour seemed to fade to nothingness . . .

A monstrous roar – and the Z-20 lurched as a shock wave pounded it.

Wu clung desperately to the seats as the aircraft spun. Her ears popped: it was falling, fast. She opened her eyes, seeing the city whirl past, getting ever closer—

The helicopter swayed sickeningly . . . then stabilised.

Panting, Wu looked out at Xinengyuan as the Z-20's turn slowed. Its centre came back into view.

Or rather, it *would* have . . . had it still been there.

Where glass towers had stretched towards the sky, now she saw nothing but a hideous, boiling mass of dust and smoke. At the city's heart was a crater at least a kilometre wide. Buildings far beyond it had been scythed into rubble. Countless fires burned amongst the wreckage.

She stared at the appalling sight, speechless. The qi weapon worked, exactly as predicted . . . but it had been turned against its creators. Xinengyuan had been devastated. Even though the city's population was only a fraction of its potential, thousands must have been killed.

She turned to look through the opposite window. The tiny golden mote of the Nephilim craft shrank to nothing amongst the haze on the distant horizon. 'You bastards,' she hissed after it. 'You *bastards*. I'll kill you all . . .'

The same shock wave also struck Nina and Eddie's helicopter. They were farther from ground zero than Wu, but the impact was still terrifying, their Z-20 falling several hundred feet before the pilots regained control.

'Oh my God,' Nina gasped, seeing the destruction behind them. 'They blew up the city!' Macy, too frightened to speak, clung tightly to her.

Eddie regarded the sight with grim dismay. 'Jesus. Knocking down some skyscrapers was bad enough, but *that*? The Chinese'll kick someone's arse in revenge. Terminally.'

'Let's make sure it's not ours,' said Nina.

Dr Hui nodded. 'We must get you out of here as quickly as possible.' She spoke to the pilot.

He increased power, the helicopter gaining speed as it fled the cataclysm.

38

Dr Hui led the group into the research facility. They were met by a young lieutenant, who it quickly became clear was the senior officer present; most of the other soldiers had been recalled to face the threat in the city. He reacted in nervous bewilderment to the civilian director's arrival. Hui gave him a brisk, firm explanation. The young man was clearly unsure how to take it, but settled for accepting the word of an authority figure, letting them pass.

'He doesn't know what has been going on,' she told Nina and Eddie as they headed for the control centre. 'The military is in confusion after Colonel Wu's death.'

'What about *Major* Wu?' asked Eddie. 'She'll cause us the most trouble when she gets back.'

'He said she is still in the city. But I do not think she will stay there for long. We will have to act quickly.'

They arrived at the control centre. The scientists hurried to greet Hui, both in relief that she was safe and to bombard her with questions, but after giving rapid reassurances, she waved them off and went to a workstation. 'I will access the records of the qi tracker.'

It did not take long to find what she was after. 'That's what Gadreel saw,' said Nina as the screen flashed up a world map overlaid with a complex network of red lines.

'The flows of qi around the earth,' Hui said. 'Where was he looking?'

'Down here.' The redhead indicated the lower right corner.

Southeast Asia, the great sweep of the Indonesian archipelago, Australia, New Zealand . . . and down at the very bottom, Antarctica.

'Lot of ground to cover,' Eddie noted. 'And a lot of earth energy lines over it.'

'It's not the lines that matter,' Nina told him. 'It's where they *meet*. We're here.' She indicated a spot in northern China where several thicker lines intersected. 'They hid the fortress here because it had enough power to keep them in suspended animation. But the Veteres would have put their prison in the place with the *most* power, to keep the Nephilim trapped in Tartarus for eternity. So that would be . . .' Her finger hovered over the screen, then tapped a specific point. 'Here.'

It was in central Australia. Eddie frowned. 'That's a long way from where we found their settlement on the west coast. Australia's nearly as big as the States – it'd be like walking from LA to Dallas.'

'They travelled all the way from Africa to Antarctica,' Nina reminded him, 'and they had much longer lifespans than us.' She took a closer look at the lines. 'And to get that much power, they were probably pretty motivated. It must be one of the strongest confluences in the world.'

Macy also examined the screen. 'I know where it is,' she piped up. 'It's Uluru!'

'You mean Ayers Rock?' said Eddie.

She shook her head with more than a little condescension. '*No*, Daddy. It's not called that any more. Uluru is the name the Aboriginal people gave it.'

Nina laughed. 'You just got schooled in post-colonialist nomenclature by a ten-year-old, darling.'

Eddie shrugged. 'I didn't understand half those words, so I'm not surprised. But if Macy says that's the proper name, then Uluru it is.'

'Are you sure it's the right spot?' Nina asked Macy. 'Like your dad said, it's a big country.'

'It is,' Macy insisted. 'I remember the maps from when I was reading about lost underground civilisations.'

Her mother adopted a fixed smile. '*That's* the stuff you remember? Not, y'know, actual archaeology?'

It was Eddie's turn to be mockingly patronising. 'We just saw a spaceship full of frozen demons from the Bible blow up a city with death rays. I don't think we need to worry about scientific accuracy any more.'

'It wasn't a spaceship,' Nina huffed, but she took his point. 'Okay. So Gadreel and his warriors are on their way to Uluru. We need to follow them – and warn people.'

'You won't be able to contact anyone until you are well clear of here,' said Hui. 'All civilian communications are blocked. But,' she picked up a phone, 'I can *get* you clear. The jet that brought you here is still on the runway. I can use my authority to arrange a flight to Australia. With luck, you will be out of Chinese airspace before anyone realises you are gone. It should take about two hours to cross the southern border. And,' a knowing look at Eddie, 'should an order to turn back come through, I am sure you will be able to persuade the pilots to disobey it.'

He nodded, clenching his fists. 'I'm sure I will.'

'I will make the arrangements.' She started to dial.

'Okay, so we get out of here – hopefully – and go to Australia,' said Eddie. 'Then what?'

'Tell the Australians they're going to have some unexpected visitors, I guess,' Nina replied. 'I should be able to use my United Nations contacts to reach someone in their government.'

'What can they do?' said Cheng. 'They won't be able to intercept that ship. If it's like the fortress, it won't show up on radar.'

'What, it's got stealth as well as a shield?' Eddie said incredulously.

'I listened to the helicopter crew on the way back. They said the fighter jets couldn't use their missiles because they couldn't lock on to it.'

'The shield might be what makes it stealthy,' Nina mused, before turning her mind to more immediate concerns. 'Anyway, we have to get the Aussies to close off Uluru. There could be hundreds, even thousands of tourists there.'

'And Aboriginal people live there too,' Macy was quick to point out.

'We're trying to protect everyone – and not just at Uluru,' said Nina. 'The Nephilim can now destroy entire cities.'

'They won't know where they are,' Cheng said.

'Zan will. He's helping them. He realised the only way he could save himself from being executed as a traitor was to throw his lot in with the Nephilim – and from what I saw, he's turned into Gadreel's own Renfield.' Blank looks. 'Dracula's lackey? No?'

'*I* know who you meant, Mom,' said Macy.

'Thanks, honey.'

Hui finished her call. 'Professor Wilde? The plane will be ready to leave in twenty minutes, although it will need to refuel on the way to Australia. I will try to get you anything you need.'

'Thank you,' said Nina.

Cheng spoke to his mother, drawing a look of surprise, then dismay from her. She shook her head as she replied.

'What's wrong?' Eddie asked.

'I want to come with you,' Cheng announced. 'Mom is . . . not happy.'

'I don't blame her!' said Nina. 'She only just got you back safely, and you want to go right back out and face the Nephilim again?'

'I can help you! I know their language – not as well as Zan, but good enough. If I can talk to them, we might be able to stop all of this before anyone else gets hurt. And if there really is a Shangdi site there, I'll be able to read any texts we find.'

Nina reluctantly nodded. 'I'm afraid he has a point, Dr Hui. Being able to talk to Gadreel directly – and not through Zan – might be the only way to stop this from turning into all-out war.'

Hui looked stricken. 'Cheng, it could be very dangerous. Are you sure?'

'I have to do it,' he told her. 'A lot of this, it . . . it's my fault. People have died. If I hadn't told Professor Wilde about the key, they'd still be alive.'

'It was our plan, not yours! If anyone is to blame, it is me,' she said, shoulders slumping. 'I should never have let you become involved.'

'But I said yes. I made the decision to do it.' Cheng put a gentle hand on her shoulder. 'Mom, I have to set things right.' A glance at Nina. 'I broke all of Professor Wilde's rules of archae-ology. And,' he added with forced levity, 'you wouldn't want her to give me a bad grade, would you?'

Hui smiled sadly. 'Very well. But,' she added, raising a finger in motherly warning, 'keep yourself safe.'

He nodded. 'I will, Mom. Don't worry.'

'Worrying about my child is my job.'

'Ain't that the truth,' Nina said to Eddie.

He made an *mm-hmm* sound in response.

Hui hugged her son, then kissed him softly on the cheek. She said something that caused him to blush, then released him. 'Go to the lifts, I will join you in a minute.'

Cheng collected his belongings and headed for the exit. Nina, Eddie and Macy started after him, only for Hui to hold Nina by her arm. 'Please take care of him,' she whispered.

'I'll do everything I can,' Nina assured her.

'Thank you. I do not want him to go, but . . . I think he may be as safe with you as he would be here.' A moment to let the ominous meaning sink in, then she went on: 'Now, go, quickly. I will catch up.'

Cheng had paused at the door to wait for them. 'What did Mom say to you?' he asked.

'She just wants us to keep you safe,' said Nina, dissembling a little. 'Come on. Let's get out of here.'

Twenty minutes later, the Longitude taxied into take-off position. Despite the frenzied military activity at the base, the seemingly civilian plane was granted immediate clearance to depart. It powered into the sky, turning south.

Nearly another hour passed before a helicopter landed at the bunker. Major Wu Shun climbed out, exhausted. The sun was only just setting, but she felt as if she had been awake for days. She composed herself, straightening both her body and her mind. Grief and pain and rage had to be put aside. There was too much to do.

All trace of the golden pod had been lost once it was out of sight. Like its parent craft, it was invisible to radar, slipping through China's defences like a ghost. It could be going anywhere – but she had a shrewd idea of who could narrow down the possibilities. Nina Wilde, she had learned, had somehow escaped from the fortress and been brought back to the base. Whatever she knew, Wu was going to find out.

The moment she entered the control centre, she sensed something was wrong. It was not merely because of the city's destruction; the scientists reacted to her appearance with nervousness, even fear. 'Where is Dr Hui?' she demanded.

'In . . . in her office,' one of the team replied.

'And the American? Professor Wilde?'

The man couldn't hold her gaze. 'I don't know.'

Wu gave him a hard glare. He shrank into his seat, but said nothing. Anger rising, she strode to Hui's office and entered without knocking.

The former director was alone at her desk, drinking tea. The scene's casual appearance was belied by her hand's slight tremble as she raised the cup. Wu knew from Hui's medical records that she had no debilitating illnesses. She was as afraid as the rest of her team.

The major stood before her, hands held imperiously behind her back. 'Where is Professor Wilde?'

'Welcome back, Major,' said Hui, putting down the cup. Its base rattled faintly as her hand shook again. 'I'm glad you're okay. My . . . my condolences.'

Wu had no time for fake pleasantries. 'Something's going on. Where is she?'

'I don't know.'

An almost subconscious flicker of Hui's eyes towards the clock in the corner of her computer's screen told Wu she was stalling for time. 'This isn't the day to test me, *Doctor*,' she snarled. 'Tell me where she is, or I will have you arrested – and then I will *make* you tell me.'

Hui drew in a slow, deep breath, summoning courage. Even before she spoke, Wu knew she would have to get the information the hard way. 'I'm afraid I can't help you, Major.'

'Your choice.' She swept items on the desk aside to reach the phone, and called the security station. 'This is Major Wu. I need armed guards to Dr Hui's office, immediately. She is under arrest for treason!'

39

India

'So let me get this straight,' said Australian Prime Minister Bruce Sainsbury, voice thick with sarcasm. 'You're telling me there's a UFO full of fallen angels on its way to Uluru?'

Nina gritted her teeth. 'Well, when you put it that way, of course it sounds ridiculous!'

The plane was three hours into its flight, now clear of China and crossing eastern India. The first two had been the most tense; while the jet was still in Chinese airspace, it could be intercepted and forced to turn back. The passengers' worries had not eased once they crossed the Indian border. Even though Dr Hui had given Eddie a pistol, he was far from certain he would be able to force the pilots to disobey orders to return to Cangliang.

But the plane continued southwards. The pilots left the cockpit door open at Cheng's request, ostensibly so he could watch the plane's operations, but in reality so the compass was visible and any radio exchanges could be overheard. All so far had been mundane dialogues with air traffic controllers.

Nina held off from using the jet's satellite phone until they were out of China, partly because she didn't want to alert eavesdroppers from Chinese spy agencies to their escape, and partly to plan the best way to warn the Australian government what they were facing. Unfortunately, when boiled down to the basics, her story did indeed sound less than plausible. 'But I'm telling the truth,' she pressed on. 'The Chinese woke the Nephilim, and it was not a successful first meeting. You only have to look at what's left of Xinengyuan to see that!'

'I'm looking at my computer right now,' drawled Sainsbury, 'and the only news out of that part of China is that a gas main blew up and wrecked some buildings. Lucky for them, it was one of those ghost cities in the middle of nowhere, so nobody was in them. There's even a picture. No UFOs hovering over it, though.' That last was said with a little chuckle.

Nina struggled to control her irritation. 'They imposed a media blackout, and made up a cover story. The last thing they want is for the world to know they've not only woken up an ancient threat, but also let the Nephilim escape with their new superweapon!'

'A superweapon?' She could almost see his smile widening even over the phone line. 'Now, this isn't all some publicity stunt for another of your movies, is it?'

'I wish it was, but I'm deadly serious, literally. People have died – and if the Nephilim reach Uluru, there might be more deaths in *your* country. You need to evacuate the area and get the army to cordon it off.'

His tone changed as he lost patience. 'Cordon it off? Now listen, *Professor*, I don't think you appreciate just how big Uluru is! We'd need *thousands* of men to do that, and do you know how many soldiers I've got sitting around in the desert? Here's a hint: none! Now, if there really is a UFO heading for our airspace, we'll either force it to land or shoot it down. Anyone who gets out, we'll deal with them like we do any illegal immigrant: lock 'em up, then send 'em back.'

'Okay, well, I can tell I'm not going to convince you,' Nina said, exasperated. 'Thank you for your time, Prime Minister. But remember: I *did* warn you. I'm recording this call, so if the shit

454

hits the fan, everyone will know you ignored me. G'day.' She hung up before Sainsbury could reply.

Macy stared at her with wide eyes. 'Mom. You just swore at the prime minister of Australia!'

'It didn't go well?' Eddie asked.

'He didn't believe me – and I can't entirely blame him,' Nina sighed. 'But he wouldn't even lift a finger to close off Uluru. I'll have to contact someone with authority actually in the area and hope they're more willing to act.'

'I'll call Matt in Sydney and get him to find out who to speak to,' he suggested.

'Thanks.' Nina leaned back in her seat, annoyance giving way to concern. The Nephilim had departed Xinengyuan as fast as a jet five hours ago, giving them a considerable head start. If Sidona used the qi tracker to guide them, they would probably reach Uluru before dawn. And that was when hundreds of tourists would be at the rock to watch the sunrise – innocents who could find themselves targets for Gadreel's wrath . . .

But there was nothing more she could do. Even after escaping China, she was still trapped, helpless.

Three hours later, they landed at Melaka airport, south of the Malaysian capital Kuala Lumpur. Refuelling had been arranged in advance, a tanker truck pulling up alongside the jet almost as soon as it stopped. 'How long before we take off again?' Eddie asked.

Cheng conferred with the pilots. 'About forty minutes.'

Nina struggled out of a half-sleep, Macy dozing against her. 'What about the next leg of the flight?'

'About five and a half hours.' He spoke to the co-pilot, who gave him a quizzical look but opened the main cabin hatch. Hot, muggy air with the sharp tang of aviation fuel wafted in.

'We're not getting out, are we?' said Eddie. 'We don't need to be messing about with customs checks. Especially not with *hmm-hmm* aboard.' He glanced pointedly at his leather jacket; the gun was inside. By necessity, international pilots spoke at least some English, and he didn't want to warn them he was armed.

'No, no,' the young man assured him. 'But I've got to find out what's happening at Cangliang, and the satellite link won't work through a window.' He started to set up the antenna in the open hatch.

'Did you reach Matt?' Nina asked her husband.

He nodded. 'Got a contact number for the ranger station at Uluru. Tried to ring it, but nobody answered. Must be closed at this time of night.'

'We'll have to try again in a few hours.' She looked at her watch; it had been a long time since she last ate. 'God, I'm hungry.'

'There's some food back there,' he said, gesturing aft.

Nina gently shifted Macy off her. The sight of the compartments at the cabin's rear used as cells during their flight from New Zealand reminded her of their former occupants. 'What do you think happened to the Millers?'

'Not sure I want to know. I doubt they're going to give 'em tickets back home.'

'I would say it couldn't happen to nicer people, but . . . I just feel we should do *something*.'

'What *can* we do?' Eddie asked with a rhetorical shrug. 'They got taken out of New Zealand on a black-bag flight – the Chinese'll deny knowing anything about them.'

The truth of his statement did not make Nina any happier. She tried to take her mind off the grim thought by finding food. The pre-packaged meals she discovered were only marginally more appetising than the typical airline fare, but they were all that was on offer.

By the time she returned to her seat, Cheng had connected to the research facility – and she saw at once that something bad had happened. She put down her meal and went to him. 'What is it?' she asked, concerned. Eddie joined her.

'I . . . I tried to contact my mom, but she didn't answer,' Cheng said in a low voice, lips tight. 'So I messaged someone else on the team. He told me, uh . . .' He blinked, eyes brimming. 'She was arrested. Major Wu's . . . interrogating her, to find out where we are.'

Eddie gave the cockpit a wary look. 'Think I'll keep an eye on things in there. Make sure there aren't any unexpected radio calls.' A sympathetic hand on Cheng's shoulder, then he engaged the pilots in mock-casual conversation.

Nina stayed with her student. 'My God. Cheng, I'm so sorry . . .'

He put on a brave front. 'I don't think she's told her anything yet. Otherwise someone would have ordered us back to China. But . . .' The tears broke free, rolling down his cheeks. 'When they say "interrogate", they mean "torture"! They're torturing my mom!'

'She hasn't told them anything yet because . . . because she's protecting you,' said Nina, trying to provide some comfort, however small. 'She's protecting *all* of us. She's doing something unbelievably courageous to give us a chance to stop the Nephilim.'

He jumped up. 'And that's supposed to make me feel *better*?' he shouted in sudden anger, the outburst making Macy jerk awake. He turned towards the exit, but with the plane's steps still raised, there was nowhere to go. Instead, he stormed to the cabin's rear, dropping heavily into a seat.

'I'm sorry,' Nina said again, but to no response.

Macy looked after him in concern. 'What's wrong? Why's Cheng so upset?'

'He got some bad news, honey. About his mom.'

'Is she okay?'

'I don't know,' was the only answer Nina could give.

The refuelling took less time than predicted; the plane took off after thirty-five minutes. Eddie moved to the seat nearest the cockpit door, paying even closer attention to the activity within. Sure enough, thirty minutes after departing, both pilots reacted in surprise to a radio message. 'Cheng, I need you,' he called out. '*Now.*' This was not a time for empathy: he needed to know exactly what was happening.

Cheng reluctantly walked up the aisle, giving Nina an angry look as he passed. By now, Eddie had returned to the cockpit door. 'There a problem, guys?' he said loudly, hand slipping inside his jacket.

The pilot looked back at him. 'We have been ordered to return to Cangliang.'

'Oh yeah? Why?'

He and the co-pilot exchanged worried glances. 'You, ah . . . they said you are not supposed to be on this flight.'

Eddie gave him a humourless grin. 'Well, we're more than halfway through now, so we might as well finish it.' He indicated a spare set of headphones. 'Cheng, put those on and tell me what the radio's saying.'

The sudden tension overcame Cheng's recalcitrance. He squeezed past Eddie and donned the headphones, sitting on a folding jump seat behind the pilot. 'It's someone at Cangliang,' he whispered. 'He's waiting for an answer.'

The Yorkshireman could tell from the pilot's brief lick of the lips that he wanted to respond. He drew the gun. Both officers reacted in shock. 'Yeah, let's keep quiet for now, eh?'

'If you kill us, you won't be able to land the plane!' the co-pilot gabbled.

Eddie shrugged. 'I've had flying lessons.' He opted not to mention that they had been in a helicopter, there had only been three, and on the last he had crashed into a New York skyscraper.

'But I'm lazy, so just keep going and I won't have to do anything drastic.'

Cheng signalled for silence. 'He's talking again . . . "I repeat, you must return to Cangliang immediately. Your passengers are spies who have committed espionage against the People's Republic of China." We're not spies!' he protested to the pilots.

'No, we're not,' Eddie added. 'You think we'd bring our little girl with us if we were doing some James Bond crap? Besides, we'd have had to work bloody fast. You brought us to the country in the first place, remember!'

'Yes, we did,' the pilot grudgingly agreed. 'But I must still turn back.'

'No. You mustn't. After you've flown us to Uluru, you can tell 'em I had you at gunpoint the whole time. Which I will if I have to.'

He scowled, but gave Eddie a small nod. 'We will take you there. If you promise you will not hurt us.'

'Take us there without any trouble, and I won't need to. Deal?' Another nod. 'Okay. Now, I'm not daft, despite what a lot of people say, so I'll be keeping an eye on things.' He indicated the control panel. 'So long as that compass keeps pointing south, I'll be happy. Cheng, you listen to the radio. Make sure they're not getting any sneaky messages – or sending any.'

He returned to his seat. 'I think everything's under control,' he told Nina. 'Just got to make sure one of us is always awake so they don't do a one-eighty while we're having a nap.'

She nodded, then said quietly: 'Is Cheng okay?'

'I think so. Probably good to give him something to do to keep his mind off what's happened, at least for now.'

'Yeah,' Nina replied sadly. In a way, the news Cheng had received was worse than being told his mother was dead: not only did he have the awful knowledge that she was suffering, but he would almost certainly never see her again even if she survived. She looked over to Macy. What if her daughter had to endure the same one day?

That she had already, and more than once, almost put Macy through exactly that torment because of her own obsessions was a piece of self-realisation she did not want – was *afraid* – to face. She turned away, looking out at the darkness beyond the window as the plane continued its journey.

Major Wu stood at the shoulder of the nervous communications officer. 'Well?' she snapped. 'Have they turned around?'

The computer at his station was running a flight tracking program, showing the positions of numerous aircraft over the Java Sea. 'No, Major,' he replied. 'I explained the situation, but since then they haven't responded.' He indicated one of the dots, the Longitude's tail number beside it. 'They're still holding course for Australia.'

'Hui gave Chase a weapon,' growled Wu. 'He's probably got them at gunpoint.' Her face darkened at the thought of the traitorous scientist. Hui had held out for hours of interrogation, to the younger woman's surprise and anger, before finally giving up the information she had been protecting. She had used her authority as head of the research facility to put Wilde and Chase – and her son – on the same plane that had brought them to Cangliang, now on its way to the Nephilim's destination: the great red rock of Uluru in Australia.

Wu had been disgusted – both at the scale of Hui's treachery, and at her own failure to realise the significance of the jet's absence. Her father's death had affected her judgement. She should stand down.

But she couldn't bring herself to do that. The Nephilim had to pay – not just for his murder, but for declaring war on her country. They were a threat to China – with the stolen qi weapon, to the whole *world* . . .

That thought suddenly changed her entire perspective. Recapturing Wilde and Chase was no longer important. If anything, they might actually help – by leading her to the last of the Nephilim. From what Hui told her, the Shangdi had imprisoned hundreds, even thousands, of the giants in suspended animation. If Gadreel freed them, an army of monsters would emerge to attack humanity.

But she had a chance to stop them; to exterminate the entire nest . . .

She turned to another officer. 'Get me the Central Military Commission in Beijing. I need to speak to the head of special operations forces. And also,' she added, face set and grim, 'the commander of the tactical nuclear division.'

40

Uluru, Australia

Dawn was still a couple of hours away, but Rosie Tapaya was already at work. The park ranger guided her white Land Cruiser around the long road circumnavigating the great sacred rock of Uluru, the curves of both as intimately familiar to her as a lover's, then turned off the asphalt, heading north-east into open desert.

The 4x4's banks of spotlights cut through the darkness to illuminate the rust-red terrain. Normally she would have taken it slowly – even knowing the track, it was still a bumpy ride – but tonight, lives could be at stake.

Whose lives, she had no idea. When she was first stirred from sleep by a call from her boss, Sandra Piddock, she'd thought it was a joke. A UFO landing in the park? Sounded like, as she'd politely put it, a load of 'roo poo.

But a quick check of the news on her phone told her *something* weird was going on. Sightings of strange lights in the sky from the northern coast down through Western Australia and into the Northern Territory – and now somebody on the road to Yulara, the tourist town twelve kilometres north of Uluru itself, had reported something coming down in the desert. The airport had seen nothing on radar, but the caller was adamant.

So now Rosie was scouring the outback for signs of a plane crash. She stopped the off-roader at the top of a rise and got out.

Ignoring the bugs swarming around the spotlights, she surveyed the plains ahead. The distant lights of Yulara were off to her left, a lone vehicle on the empty desert road further north. But there was nothing else in sight . . .

She started to turn back to the truck – then glimpsed something. As she looked directly at it, though, it vanished. She frowned, then reached into the Toyota and closed her eyes before switching off its lights.

The spots' intense glare vanished. She opened her eyes again, letting them adjust to the darkness. It didn't take long. It was a clear night, and the sky was bright with stars, the glowing band of the Milky Way cutting across it. She looked back at the desert.

There: a softly shimmering bluish light. Chemical glowsticks? There was a shape that she at first took to be a tent, before realising it would be a really big one – it was well over a kilometre distant.

There was definitely someone there, though – and she had a good idea what they were doing. She got back into the Land Cruiser and picked up the radio handset. 'Hey, Sandra, are you there? It's Rosie.'

'I'm here,' came the reply. 'Have you found anything?'

'Yeah, but it's no UFO – no plane crash, either. I think we've got some illegal campers.'

'You sure? The bloke who called was sure he saw something come down from the sky.'

'I'm going to have a look. Pretty sure it's just some penny-pinchers who don't want to pay for a hotel room, though. I'll call back soon.'

'Okey-dokey. You need any help, Barney and I can get out to you.'

'I'll let you know.' She restarted the engine. Camping inside Uluru national park was prohibited, and there was no shortage of signs to make that clear. Bloody tourists! She set off again.

The terrain was tricky, but she was an expert off-road driver. She travelled over a kilometre before halting at a dry riverbed. Its sides were too steep even for the Toyota to traverse, but she was not far from her goal. She switched off the engine and lights, then collected a torch and set out on foot.

The journey to her final destination did not take long. She climbed another rise – and stopped in surprise.

Maybe it *was* a UFO. Something as big as a truck, part buried in the sand a hundred metres ahead. It was the odd light's source, but it wasn't coming from any bulbs; rather, the whole thing seemed to be faintly aglow. Silhouetted figures moved around it.

Rosie felt a chill as she realised they were not human.

They were giants, three metres tall, some even bigger. Too many to count in the darkness, but at least twenty.

And they knew she was there, heads turning towards her torch. She froze. What the hell was she going to do?

Her job, she decided, overcoming her shock. Whoever – whatever – they were, they were visitors to her land, and as both a park ranger and a representative of the local Anangu peoples, she ought to greet them. She started down the slope. 'G'day!' she called out, cringing inwardly – the first word said to a bunch of space aliens, and it couldn't have been any more stereotypically Australian! 'My name's Rosie, and, ah . . . I'd like to welcome you to Uluru.'

One of the towering figures strode towards her. He wore robes, and was carrying some kind of golden staff. The leader? She raised her light to see his face. The pale being flinched, narrowing his wide, slanted eyes. Another shiver ran through her at the sight of his features. Tribal stories she had been told as a child came back to her, ancient legends of gods who shaped the world before people ever walked it. Something about the giant felt almost familiar . . .

being woken up in the night, but today I was already up. And when you called, I figured your problem might have something to do with *our* problem.'

'What problem?' Eddie asked.

Sandra gestured for them to enter the terminal building. The air conditioning was a relief even after mere minutes in the sun. 'Somebody called and said they saw a plane going down near Uluru, so I sent Rosie Tapaya, one of my park rangers, to investigate – she lives in Mutitjulu, right by the rock. She radioed in to say she thought it was just campers, which is illegal but happens all the time. Except . . .'

'She never came back?' Nina offered.

Sandra gave her a grim nod. 'Rosie's an Aboriginal, she knows what she's doing in the desert—'

'An Aboriginal *person*,' Macy corrected.

'Yeah, that's what I said,' was the Australian's airy response, before she continued. 'And she's a tough girl, your typical tourist wouldn't mess with her. So when you called me, I was already a bit worried – then once the sun rose and there was still no sign of her, I knew there was something wrong.'

'Did you call the police?' Eddie asked.

'I did, but this isn't exactly Sydney. We only have a handful of cops to cover about a hundred kilometres in each direction. They're looking for her, but I haven't heard from them yet.' The two customs officers gave her brusque farewells and headed away. Sandra waited for them to go, then lowered her voice conspiratorially. 'So what's going on, Professor Wilde? I know you by reputation – and your reputation is that whenever you get involved with an archaeological thing, it means some nut's trying to take over the world! We've had UFO reports, then one of my rangers disappears . . . and now you turn up. After phoning me from a plane in the middle of the night and asking me to close the entire park, at that. What's it all about?'

'*Have* you closed the park?' said Nina.

'No. I only have the authority to do that if there's an immediate danger to life, like flash floods or brush fires.'

'What about a murder?'

Sandra twitched in surprise. 'What *about* a murder?'

'Your ranger's dead. If she found the people we're after, they'll have killed her.'

'Macy, let's go over here for a minute,' said Eddie, ushering his protesting daughter out of earshot.

'What people?' Sandra demanded.

'It's hard to explain – and to be honest, if I came straight out and told you, you'd think I was crazy. Let's just say that they're here, they're dangerous – and there's something they want at Uluru. Closing the park is the best way to make sure nobody else gets hurt.'

The ranger regarded Nina in silence for a long moment. Then: 'You're sure Rosie is dead?'

'I'm afraid so, yes.'

Another lengthy pause, then Sandra took out a phone and dialled. 'Dougie, are you busy right now? Okay, can you do me a huge favour? I'm at the airport, with four other people. Can you pick us up and fly us to the rock? Yeah, it's serious – I wouldn't ask otherwise. Okay, thanks.' She looked back at Nina. 'A mate of mine owns a helicopter for tourist flights around the rock. He'll take us there so we can search from the air.'

'Thank you,' Nina replied.

Eddie and Macy came back. 'Oh great,' grumbled the Yorkshireman. 'Another helicopter.'

'You don't like helicopters?' asked Sandra.

'Our last flight didn't end very well,' said Cheng.

'Hopefully this one'll be better. Come on,' she said, leading them through the terminal.

★ ★ ★

The promised helicopter arrived fifteen minutes later, a Jet Ranger painted in the colours of the Australian flag. Sandra ushered everyone else into the cabin's rear, then took the co-pilot's seat. The chopper quickly took off and headed south-east. 'All right,' she said once they had all donned headphones, 'Rosie went looking for this plane somewhere north-east of the rock. It's off the tourist flight path, so even if there was something there, probably nobody would have noticed it.'

'Why not?' Cheng asked.

The pilot, a middle-aged man with deeply tanned and wrinkled skin, pointed ahead with a chuckle. 'They'd be looking at *that*, mate!' All eyes went to the great red rock of Uluru, rising with almost startling suddenness from the desert plain. Even from a distance it dominated the landscape, a towering sandstone iceberg in an empty orange sea.

'Wow,' said Nina. 'Now that *is* impressive.'

Eddie nodded. 'That bloke Ayer must've had an ego even bigger than the rock to name it after himself. How big is it?'

'Over three and a half kilometres long and almost two and a half at its widest,' Sandra announced. 'Three hundred and forty-eight metres tall at the highest point.'

'How far underground does it go?' Nina asked thoughtfully.

'Underground? I don't actually know. Three or four kilometres, I think, although some people reckon it could be more. Why?'

'What these people are after might be *inside* the rock.'

She shook her head. 'You can't *get* inside. There are caves, sure, but they've all been explored, and none of them are very deep. If there was anything there, the Aboriginals – the Aboriginal *people*,' she corrected, with a patronising smile at Macy, 'would have found them.'

'The entrance might have been hidden.'

'By *who*?'

Nina said nothing. Sandra made an annoyed sound, then turned to watch the russet landscape speed past. 'Okay, we just crossed the highway, which is the only road in or out,' she said. 'The bloke who reported a plane going down was driving along it, so it's somewhere south of here. Rosie came out of Mutitjulu, which is by the rock,' she pointed at the huge landmark's eastern end, 'and came north. So we've got an area of about seventy square kilometres to cover.'

'What was she driving?' Eddie asked.

'A Land Cruiser, one of our ranger trucks. It's white, so it should stand out.'

'There's some binoculars in the back,' the pilot chipped in.

Nina passed a set to Sandra, then she and Eddie began their own sweep of the plain. While dry, it was far from dead, dotted with desert trees and scrub. Green against red – so anything else would stand out clearly, whether white . . . or gold.

'I see something,' said Eddie after a few minutes. 'There's a truck down there.'

Sandra found it north of the rock. 'It's moving – it must be Barney. Another ranger, he's looking for Rosie.' She used the radio to contact the man on the ground. 'He hasn't seen anything yet,' she reported.

Nina lowered her binoculars. The ranger's truck was a clear white dot against the endless red, so the missing woman's vehicle ought to stand out equally well. She looked further out from Uluru. The desert stretched away to the hazy horizon. Earth tones, as far as the eye could see . . .

'There's something!' she cried, snapping up the binoculars for a closer look. 'It's white . . . it's another truck!'

Sandra looked for herself. 'Jesus, it's rolled over! Dougie, get us down there, quick. She could be hurt.' The pilot changed course as she radioed again. 'Barney, we've found her jeep. We're going to land – follow us in.'

The helicopter closed on its destination. A dry riverbed weaved snake-like across the plain. The vehicle Nina had seen was indeed lying inverted at its south bank, but it had been damaged by more than a rollover. 'Christ!' said Dougie. 'Looks like it got blown up by dynamite!' The Land Cruiser was a mangled wreck, torn in half with shredded debris scattered around it.

Eddie gave Nina an unhappy look. 'One of those bloody spear guns,' he whispered.

She nodded. 'I can see its tracks. It came from the rock, then stopped here because it couldn't get across the riverbed . . . so where was it going?' Her eyes followed its path northwards—

A shock of fear. 'Eddie!' she hissed. 'It's there, look!'

The golden vimana was about two hundred metres beyond the dry river. It was half buried in the red sand; whether it had augered into the dirt in a hard landing, or its occupants had tried to hide it, she couldn't tell.

Said occupants were nowhere in sight – but that didn't mean they weren't there. 'We need to land right now and get out,' Eddie said with commanding urgency. 'Then take the chopper well clear.'

Sandra turned in alarm. 'What's wrong?'

'The people we warned you about are definitely here,' said Nina. 'They blew up that truck – and they might blow up this helicopter.'

'You *what*?' squawked the pilot.

'Just get us down, fast,' Eddie ordered.

Dougie reluctantly landed on level ground a hundred metres from the wrecked truck, keeping the rotors just below take-off revolutions as his passengers hurriedly disembarked. As soon as they were clear, he took off again in a blinding flurry of dust. 'Jesus!' Nina coughed. 'He could have let us get farther away!'

'Can't really blame him,' said Eddie, shielding Macy's face as they waited for the whirlwind to subside.

Sandra hurried towards the riverbed. 'Rosie! Can you hear me?'

The others followed. 'I can't see anyone,' said Eddie as they reached the bank. Metallic debris was scattered around them; the 4x4 had been parked here when the baraka's bolt blasted it apart. There was no sign of a body, or even remains.

Nina slithered down the bank and crossed the dry river, seeing tracks where someone had climbed up the far side. 'She went this way. Macy, wait there with Cheng.'

'But *Mom*—'

'Just do it, Macy,' Eddie told her curtly as he followed his wife.

Sandra hurried after them. 'All right. What the hell's going on?'

'You'll see in a second,' Nina told her as she picked her way through the scrub. 'But the short version is that the Chinese found a fortress that had been buried for a hundred thousand years. The people preserved in it . . . weren't human.' The Australian stopped, her expression a picture of disbelief. Nina faced her. 'Do you know your Old Testament at all?'

'A bit. Wouldn't call myself a Bible-thumper, though. Why?'

'There was a race that existed before humans developed civilisation. Some of them interbred with humans, and their offspring were a hybrid of both species. They called themselves the Nephilim.'

Sandra frowned. 'I've heard the name.'

'In the Bible, they're considered to be fallen angels, who were imprisoned for eternity beneath the earth. They're not angels, that was just how ancient humans saw them because of their advanced technology, but some of them really were imprisoned.' She looked back at the towering monolith of Uluru. 'Here.'

The ranger's instinctive response was a sharp laugh. 'What, you reckon they're inside the *rock*?'

'I don't know – but it's what the Nephilim think. The Chinese found them in a kind of suspended animation, and woke them up.'

'Not their brightest move,' said Eddie.

'They thought they could use Nephilim technology to create a weapon,' Nina went on. 'Which they did – except it was used against them! The Nephilim escaped and came to find the rest of their people.' She set off again, cautiously ascending a low rise. 'They came in . . . a ship, I suppose. It's over here.'

'Just call it a UFO and be done with it, love,' said her husband.

She gave him a mocking smile, then dropped low as she reached the crest. Eddie hunched down beside her.

The sand-shrouded vimana was a hundred metres away. Sandra gasped. 'Oh my God. It really is! It's a flying saucer!'

'So where are Gadreel and his goon platoon?' Eddie wondered, surveying the area. 'They definitely got out, I can see a lot of tracks around the UFO . . .' He trailed off.

Nina saw why. 'Oh no.'

Between their position and the vimana was a darker patch in the sand. Flies swarmed over it, the ground thick with scavenging insects. 'What is it?' asked Sandra, confused.

'It . . . it's your missing ranger,' Nina told her, grim-faced. 'I'm sorry.'

'What? I don't understand. There's no body, there's no—'

'There wouldn't be,' said Eddie. 'The weapon that blew up the truck? It does the same thing to people. I'm sorry too, but . . . she's dead.'

'No, that can't—' The Australian regarded the bloody patch – then jumped up and ran towards it.

'No, wait!' Nina shouted after her. 'They might still be there!'

But nobody emerged from the downed craft, no blasts of earth energy tore across the sand. Sandra reached the spot, holding a hand over her mouth and nose to shield them from insects – and block out the unmistakable stench of death. 'Oh God,' she whispered. Dried blood splattered the ground, shredded scraps of clothing amongst it. 'Rosie . . .'

'Wait there!' Eddie shouted to Macy and Cheng – despite the warnings, they had started across the riverbed – before running after Sandra. He was fully prepared to tackle her into cover, but to his relief, the area remained devoid of threats. 'This is why you need to close the park,' he said on reaching the ranger, who was staring silently at the remains. 'These arseholes are still here somewhere – and they're dangerous. You've got to get everyone out.'

Sandra looked up at him, tears rolling down her cheeks. 'There are hundreds of tourists here . . .'

'There'll be hundreds of *corpses* if you don't do something.'

Nina joined them. 'The Nephilim think we're animals – *pests*. They won't hesitate to kill anyone they meet.'

The Australian wiped her face. 'Okay. Okay. I'll close the park.' She took a radio from her belt.

Eddie cautiously approached the grounded vimana. A hatch was open; he peered inside. 'It's empty,' he reported. 'A lot of footprints, though. The thing must have been packed.' He saw a smaller set of prints. 'Zan's still with them.'

'They need him to work the tracker,' said Nina. She turned back to Sandra as she finished her urgent call. 'I know this is hard, but we need your help. Are you up to it?'

Sandra clenched her lips, then nodded. 'Yeah. Yeah, I am.'

Eddie spotted more footprints in the dirt. 'They went towards the rock.'

'Then let's go find these bastards.' She set off, Nina and Eddie exchanging concerned looks before following.

They collected Cheng and Macy at the dry river and continued across the desert landscape. Before long, a rising plume of orange dust signalled a vehicle's imminent arrival. Sandra climbed a mound and waved. A white Land Cruiser pulled up and a paunchy middle-aged Anangu man in a ranger's uniform climbed out, donning a cowboy-style hat. 'Heard you on the radio,' he told Sandra with alarm. 'Rosie's *dead*?'

'Yeah,' was her terse reply.

'Where's her body? Her family'll want to—'

'There isn't a body. There's nothing left.' She went past him to the truck. 'You got your rifle?' He nodded.

'You're armed?' asked Nina, surprised.

'We get dingoes out here, and kangaroos can mess you up if they're in a bad mood,' said the new arrival. 'Better to be safe. Who're you?'

She made the introductions. The ranger, whose name was Barney Jungala, was not impressed. 'An archaeologist? What's that got to do with one of my mates being killed?'

'She thinks there's some kind of ancient prison buried under the rock,' said Sandra, returning with a hunting rifle. 'I didn't believe her at first, but then we found a flying saucer, so now I don't know what the hell to think.'

Barney regarded her with a fixed expression. 'A flying saucer,' he said flatly.

'I wish I was joking. But whoever or whatever came out of it killed Rosie, then headed for the rock – so I want a rocket up the arse of every single tourist to get them out of the park, fast. We'll bring in outside help as quick as we can, but it'll take a while for anyone to get here, so for now it's up to us to keep everyone safe.' She inserted the rifle's small magazine and chambered a round.

The ranger shook his head. 'This is a load of *Pine Gap* conspiracy crap, Sandra. I don't know what you found, but it can't be a flying saucer! There's not a single bit of proof that space aliens are real.'

'Actually, there is,' Macy piped up.

Everyone looked at her. 'What do you mean?' asked Nina.

'There's a carving of a giant alien skull on Uluru's side,' she said. 'I saw it in one of my para-archaeology videos!'

'By *para*-archaeology, you mean *pseudo*-archaeology,' her mother said with a deep sigh. 'I keep telling you, Macy, just because you see something on YouTube doesn't mean it's real! People will believe any old nonsense, even without a scrap of evidence to support it.'

'Actually,' Barney said, 'there *is* a big skull on the side of the rock.'

Eddie grinned. 'High five,' he fake-whispered to his daughter, who clapped her hand against his.

Nina glowered at them, then turned back to Barney. 'You know what she's talking about?'

'Yeah. It's right over there.' He pointed at the rock. 'You can't see it from here, there are trees in the way, but it's pretty well known.'

'Does it have a name? In the indigenous language, I mean.'

'Sure. We call it "the head".'

Nina couldn't tell if he was being sarcastic, but decided not to ask. Instead, she said, 'Can you take us to it?'

The Land Cruiser brought the group across the desert to a road. Rather than turn onto it, Barney went straight across towards the base of Uluru. 'Is this an airstrip?' Eddie asked as they crossed a suspiciously straight stretch of flat ground.

'Used to be,' said Sandra. 'Until the Anangu decided, "Hey, we don't actually want tourists landing right on our sacred land." So we built the airport on the other side of Yulara.'

'Still named it after bloody Ayer,' muttered Barney, rounding some trees. 'Here's the head.'

He stopped. Everyone got out and looked up at the rock. 'Well, yep,' said Eddie. 'That's *definitely* an alien skull.'

Nina was forced to admit he was right. A long swathe of the monolith's northern face was a near-sheer cliff, worn smooth by aeons of wind and rain – but set into it as if carved by giants were numerous shapes, rough and striated in sharp contrast to their surroundings. Most seemed natural, the result of erosion . . .

But one was very familiar.

About halfway up was what she could only see as a giant skull, side-on, lower jaw agape as if shouting. The head was unnaturally elongated, resembling the popular image of an alien – or the proportionately larger cranium of the Nephilim and their parent species. It was almost identical to the image of the skull set into the resurrection key. 'Okay,' she said, 'why has nobody ever shown me *this* before? I would have realised it was modelled on the Veteres the moment I saw it!'

Macy let out an all-too-teenage *ughhh* of exasperation. 'I *did* show it to you, Mom. You just never paid any attention!'

Cheng was also entranced – but he was looking beyond the skull itself. 'The other markings . . .'

'What about them?' Nina asked.

'They're distorted, they've been eroded . . . but they look like words. *Nephilim* words. Just a moment.' He removed his pack and took out his laptop.

'You won't get any Wi-Fi here, mate,' said Barney.

The young Chinese was too absorbed to recognise the mockery. 'I don't need it, the files are on the hard drive.' He sat, balancing the machine on his thighs as he worked. 'Yes! I was right. They *are* words.'

Nina looked up at the indistinct shapes. 'What do they say?'

'They're a warning. I can't read the whole thing, but my guess would be "Stay away, there are Nephilim inside."'

Macy gave her mother a smug smile. 'See? I was right.'

'Yeah, that's enough of that,' Nina sighed. 'Okay, this is the place. So where are the Nephilim?'

'Who?' asked Barney.

Eddie beat her to an explanation. 'Ancient race of bad guys. They were frozen, they woke up, they're not happy – and they think their mates are inside the rock.'

'Frozen?' The idea appeared to trigger some memory for the ranger.

'If the warning is here, the entrance must be here as well,' Cheng suggested.

'Good point,' said Nina. 'If we can find their tracks, we'll be able to see where they went.'

Finding the footprints of over twenty giants, even after several hours, was not difficult. The oversized tracks led to a small cave almost directly beneath the giant skull. 'Okay, they went in,' said Eddie, 'but they didn't come back out.'

Nina checked the cave. It did not take long; it was barely ten feet deep. 'Secret entrance, maybe?'

Barney made a sarcastic sound. 'We've lived here for thousands of years. We know every centimetre of the rock. But I suppose another great white explorer's going to find something we missed?'

'This isn't the time for that, Barney,' chided Sandra.

He grudgingly acknowledged her words, but still muttered, 'She'll probably name it after herself.'

'Cultural imperialism bad, that's Archaeology 101 – at least in my classes,' said Nina, taking a closer look at the cave walls. 'But right now, all I care about is stopping the Nephilim. They came in here, and since they can't walk through solid rock, there must be another exit.' She put her palms flat on the stone in the hope of feeling some connection to whatever had brought Gadreel's people here, but there was nothing.

Then where had they gone? The cave was shallow enough that sunlight reached the back wall, exposing every detail. There was nothing that could be an opening, a keyhole . . .

Some instinct made her look up. The ceiling was naturally in shadow, and at first glance it seemed to be made of the same vivid sandstone. But a crack ran to join a larger one angling all the way down the edge of the rear wall. She gazed at it. There appeared to be a piece of darker stone *in* the crack above. 'Eddie, can you pick me up?'

'You're a beautiful, intelligent woman,' he replied.

'What? *Ohh*,' she groaned, getting the joke. 'No, I meant literally. I need a closer look at the ceiling.'

The cave's roof was about twelve feet high. Eddie crouched to grab Nina around her lower legs with one arm and support her with the other, then hoisted her upwards. 'Bloody hell,' he complained, 'I used to be able to lift a full-sized bloke *and* all his gear with no trouble. Getting old is a load of arse.'

'But think of how much you save on haircuts!' she replied, rubbing his bald head before looking up. At full stretch she could reach the crack, but first she needed to see what was inside it. She fumbled out her phone and switched on its light.

A dark purple stone was revealed. Set into it was a crystal splinter . . .

'I think I've found how they got in,' she said with excitement – and trepidation. She extended a finger, brushing its tip against the inset stone—

A crack of energy made her jerk away. 'Whoa, shit!' she gasped, arms whirling as she overbalanced. Eddie dropped, rolling backwards to catch her. She landed on top of him with an undignified squawk.

Macy ran to them. 'Mom! Dad! Are you okay?'

Nina struggled off her husband. 'Yeah, I think so. Eddie?'

He half grinned, half grimaced. 'I'm okay. Who needs ribs anyway?' He sat up. 'So, did it do anyth—'

A deep, grinding thud echoed through the cave.

The two rangers drew back in alarm. 'What was that?' said Barney.

'I think,' Nina replied, helping Eddie to his feet, 'it's a secret entrance.'

Dust and sandstone flakes spat from the rear wall – and the vertical crack widened as the whole section of rock slowly swung back to expose a dark passage. 'Wow!' Macy gasped.

She was about to take a closer look, but Eddie stopped her. 'Let's make sure it's safe,' he said, turning to the rangers. 'I need that gun.'

Sandra shook her head. 'I can't let a civilian have it.'

'I'm ex-SAS, I know what I'm doing. And I know what we're *facing* – you don't. If one of the ten-foot-tall bastards who killed your friend comes charging out of that tunnel, you might hesitate. I won't.'

She unhappily handed the weapon to him, and he checked it over. It was a basic wooden-stocked Beretta bolt-action hunting rifle, its magazine holding six .223-calibre rounds. Deadly enough – if the first shot was on target. If the iron sights were off, the moment needed to cycle the bolt and reload could be enough to bring retaliatory fire upon him. 'Right, everyone back up.' He waited for the others to retreat into daylight before going to the opening, aiming the rifle inside.

The tall passage sloped down into Uluru's heart. It looked like a natural cleft that had been widened by hand. No movement in the shadows. Gun raised, he cautiously moved deeper and took out his own phone. Its light revealed only red rock as the tunnel snaked into darkness.

'Looks safe,' he told the others. 'Don't know what we'll find further in, though.'

'We have to look,' said Nina. 'If the Veteres prison really is down there, hundreds more Nephilim could come back up this tunnel any minute.'

'Maybe we should just blow it up and seal 'em inside.' The suggestion drew shocked disapproval from the two Australians. 'Yeah, thought not. So I guess we've got to go in.'

'Not you,' Nina said firmly as Macy started towards the cave. 'It's far too dangerous.' She addressed the rangers. 'Can one of you stay here with her?'

Sandra and Barney exchanged looks. 'Go into a dark tunnel with a white guy with a gun, chasing after giants who'll try to kill me – or look after someone else's kid?' rumbled the latter. 'I'll take the tunnel.'

'It's no wonder you're single, Barney,' Sandra said. 'Okay, Macy? Sorry, darling, but you'll have to stay with me.'

'Aw, Mom!' Macy protested.

'Go on, love,' Eddie told her. 'We'll be back. Soon, I hope.'

'And in one piece,' Nina added under her breath.

Macy reluctantly went to Sandra. 'There's sunblock in the jeep,' the Australian said. 'Come on, let's put some on you. You don't even have a hat!' She led Macy towards the Land Cruiser. 'I'll bring you guys some torches.'

Nina turned back to her companions. 'We ready?'

Cheng peered nervously into the tunnel. 'Not really, but . . . I guess I'll have to be.'

'You'll do fine,' Eddie told him. 'You've managed all right so far.'

The young Chinese looked uncertainly at Nina. 'From him, that's a compliment,' she assured him, before facing the dark opening. 'Okay. Let's see what's down there.'

41

The group carefully descended the sloping tunnel. Sandra had provided two flashlights, Nina taking one and Barney the other. Cheng concentrated on keeping his balance while carrying his backpack, and Eddie led with the rifle.

The passage was originally a natural feature, but it was clear that the Veteres had worked hard to enlarge it. The walls were at least four feet apart at all times. The dimensions rang a bell for Nina. 'Y'know, if they brought one of their sarcophagi down here, this tunnel is just big enough to fit it,' she mused.

'You think that's how they got them to the prison?' asked Eddie.

'They couldn't have flown here, only the Nephilim had the technology. They would have had to transport their prisoners the hard way – by sea, then across land.'

'Australia as a dumping ground for someone else's criminals?' groused Barney. 'Sounds familiar.'

'They didn't want them to die in transit; they considered themselves far too *civilised* for that,' Nina went on, with scathing sarcasm for the race that used primitive humans as slaves. 'So putting them in stasis was the best way to keep them alive.'

'Saves on food and water an' all, I suppose.' Eddie glanced back at Cheng. 'You okay?'

'Yes,' Cheng replied, though he was breathing heavily with exertion. They had come quite some distance down the winding tunnel. 'At least it's cooler than outside.'

As Nina gave him a reassuring look, Barney caught her

attention. The Anangu appeared nervous, understandable as the group descended into the unknown – but there was also something pensive about his expression. 'What is it?' she asked.

'You say these . . . *beings* were asleep for a long time, frozen, and then were woken up?' he said. She nodded. 'We have legends about things like that. Like the Ninya, the ice men – they're asleep under a lake a few days' walk from here.'

'The legends could be based on reality,' said Nina. 'I know there's an Australian tribe with a legend of a fire demon that fell to earth, and scientists found evidence of a four-thousand-year-old meteorite impact in their territory.'

'The Luritja,' he confirmed. 'But I always knew all our stories were true, if you understand the way they're told. I didn't expect *this*, though.' He gestured down the tunnel.

'If it makes any difference, nor did I.' She gave him a small smile, which to her surprise was returned.

Eddie held up a hand. 'Everyone stop,' he warned quietly. 'Turn your lights out.'

'We won't be able to see anything,' Cheng said.

'And nothing'll be able to see *us*,' replied Nina. She switched off her flashlight, Barney doing the same.

Darkness swallowed them. They stood statue still, listening. Faint echoes reached them: dripping water. 'I can see something,' she whispered. A faint greenish light became discernible down the tunnel.

'Is it them?' said Cheng.

'Dunno,' Eddie replied. One hand against the wall for guidance, he slowly picked his way onwards. The dim glow revealed a sharp bend in the passage ahead. Whatever the light's source, it was constant, unmoving. 'It's not firelight, and it's not like earth energy. It's . . .'

Unexpectedly, he laughed.

'What?' Nina demanded. 'What is it?'

'Come down and see. Turn your light back on until we get to the turn.'

She switched on the flashlight, and they made their way to the corner. 'Okay, now switch off,' said Eddie. 'Close your eyes first, it'll help 'em adapt.'

'Are you sure it's safe?' asked Cheng.

'I don't think it's the Nephilim. But you'll see in a second.'

Nina gave the Chinese a shrug, then shut her eyes and switched off her light. Barney followed suit. She waited for several seconds, then looked again. The glow was now sufficiently bright to let her see the shadowy forms of her companions.

'Okay, come through here,' said Eddie, advancing cautiously. 'Careful, there's a drop.'

Nina followed him into what turned out to be a large cave. A path had been carved along one sloping side. Below was a dark expanse: a pool of water, stretching the cavern's length. Its surface shimmered as droplets fell from the ceiling with almost musical *plips* and *plops* . . .

Wait – how could she even *see* the surface?

She looked up – and gasped.

The entire ceiling was alight with a galaxy of tiny blue-green stars. 'What are they?' Cheng asked, awed.

'Glow-worms,' said Eddie. 'Saw some once when I went caving – when I was still in the army, long time before I met you,' he added to Nina. 'These are a lot more impressive, though.'

'Never seen anything like this before,' said Barney, also amazed. 'There aren't any glow-worms in this part of the country.'

'There are now,' Nina said. 'It could be a new species. Maybe they'll name it after you.'

'*Miserablus gittus*,' Eddie whispered to her. She tried not to laugh. 'Must be cracks in the rock to let water down here – and for bugs to get in so the worms can catch them. But this is a pretty big pool, and it smells fresh. Maybe whoever built the tunnels used it as a reservoir.'

'It'd make sense,' said Nina. 'But as beautiful as this is . . .' She aimed her light at the water and reluctantly clicked it on. The cavern appeared around her, but the spectacular display above instantly vanished, even a single flashlight overpowering it. 'We need to keep going.'

Barney turned on his own torch. 'Over there.' The path continued to an opening in the far wall.

Nina led the way. They were still on the Nephilim's trail; there had been no side passages large enough to fit even a human, never mind the giants. Beyond the cave, the tunnel resumed its downward course. She paused, listening for activity below. All she heard was the music of the pool. She resumed her descent towards whatever lay at the heart of Uluru.

A hundred miles to the north, a commercial air freighter powered through the sky at thirty-six thousand feet. Cargo China International flight IV283 was on a regularly scheduled journey from Guangzhou in southern China to Sydney, having stopped at Singapore to unload some of its cargo.

This time, though, the Boeing 777F had a last-minute change of manifest before starting its voyage. This came as an unwelcome shock to its crew, who knew they would be endangering their careers, their freedom – they would be arrested on landing – and the aircraft itself. But their orders had come from the very highest levels of government, and even the biggest Chinese corporations existed entirely at the whim of the Communist Party. Failure to obey, the airline's senior executives were told, would result in their arrests on any number of charges of crimes against the state before the day was over.

So with a heavy heart and a sickening ball of nausea boiling in his stomach, the captain disengaged the autopilot and brought his plane into a long turn southwards.

The response from air traffic control was immediate. Even over the outback's vast emptiness, Australia still had radar coverage: the military base at Pine Gap, a hundred and twenty miles from Uluru, was a vital part of the United States' global communications and intelligence network, and as such was well monitored. 'IV283, you got a problem up there?' drawled an Australian voice.

'Don't answer him,' ordered the woman standing behind the captain: Major Wu Shun. 'Take us down to ten thousand feet.'

The captain did as he was told. The jet straightened, now on a direct heading for Uluru. At its current speed, it would take just over ten minutes to reach its destination.

Wu listened to the increasingly concerned radio messages, but there was nothing the controllers could do. Australia's air defences were concentrated around its long coastline; no military jets were stationed close enough to intercept the rogue aircraft before it reached its target. Five minutes to go, the 777 now at ten thousand feet – and Uluru itself became visible, a red bump rising above the horizon.

'Slow to one-twenty knots at ten kilometres out,' she said, turning to leave. 'Signal me at one kilometre.'

'Major,' the pilot said, 'the cargo door isn't designed to be opened in flight! It could seriously affect the handling, even damage the plane—'

'You're a trained pilot,' she cut in. 'Adapt.' She exited the cockpit.

Crowded into the small crew section behind it were twelve men. All were members of Wu's special forces unit. Considering the team's racial make-up, entirely Han Chinese, China would inevitably be the prime suspect in the highly illegal operation – but proving it had been made as difficult as possible. Their dark clothing was devoid of any insignia or identifying marks; even the tags had been removed. The only forms of identification they carried were – exceptionally good – counterfeit US passports, and all spoke fluent English. If they were captured, it would take the most extreme torture to break them, and all would give their life to protect their country long before that happened.

'It's time,' said Wu. The group went through a hatch into the main hold. It would normally have been packed tightly with cargo containers, but at considerable expense to the plane's operator, the first two rows had been left empty to give the soldiers clear access – and provide storage space for their equipment. They all rapidly donned low-profile parachutes, then armed up. Even the team's weapons were the product of American or European manufacturers, bought through a long and complex chain of intermediaries and shorn of serial numbers.

There was one weapon whose origins would be impossible to disguise. But that would only matter if it were captured, and Wu had no intention of letting that happen.

She climbed up on top of the containers, quickly crawling to the hold's rear along the gap beneath the crown of the curving cabin roof. Her men followed. Another space had been left beside the main hatch. The last weapon waited there, its protective crate attached to a parachute of its own.

Wu double-checked that the chute was set to open automatically at the correct height, then switched on a tracking device. They would be landing in the desert, and she didn't want to waste time recovering the weapon. She donned a helmet and lowered its visor, the men doing the same.

The engine note changed, the shrill of the two huge turbofans dropping as the pilot reduced speed. Ten kilometres from Uluru, just minutes from the drop. 'Everyone get ready,' she said, going to the hatch controls. An interlock system was meant to prevent it from being opened in flight, but she had been instructed how to override it. She quickly did so, then pushed a button.

Warning lights flashed and a siren wailed as the door hinged upwards, but the noise was almost immediately drowned by the scream of wind and the engines' thunder. If not for her helmet's protection, Wu was sure she would have been deafened. She held on as the hurricane-force gale blasted into the hold. The plane trembled as its aerodynamics were disrupted.

The door reached its limit with a thud. Wu cautiously leaned out. The wind hit her head with sledgehammer force, but she saw the great rock of Uluru straight ahead, only a few kilometres away.

She pulled back. 'Ready to jump!' The others lined up beside the hatch. They would leap from the plane's aft main door for two reasons: the first was because several men could jump through at once, keeping them in close proximity. The second was pure pragmatism – going out of either crew door at the front risked the soldiers smashing into the wing or being sucked into an engine.

The last two men lifted the crate, ready to fling it out before leaping. Wu took up position behind them. The weapon was the most important part of the entire mission, and she wanted to follow its progress all the way to the ground.

Everyone waited, tension rising—

The pilot's voice came through Wu's earpiece. 'One kilometre.'

Her response was immediate. *'Jump!'*

The first five men threw themselves from the hatch, a second group following two seconds later. The last pair hurled the crate out into the slipstream, then dived after it. Wu waited for them to get clear before following.

The Boeing hurtled away as she hit the wall of air. She tumbled, land and sky swapping places, then spread her limbs to bring herself under control. The world righted itself. Uluru swelled ahead, the team arcing towards its northern face.

From ten thousand feet, a free fall to the ground took under sixty seconds. She glanced at the crate. Its parachute was set to open at three thousand feet. Her team would release their own at two thousand, to keep them well clear of its unguided descent. Any second . . .

A spring-loaded cap popped from the crate's parachute pack, a small pilot chute firing out into the airstream and pulling the black main canopy after it. She shot past it as it opened. A glance upwards to make sure the parachute had deployed correctly, then she looked back at her men. They had spread out to ensure nobody collided.

The ground rushed at them. Two thousand feet—

Wu pulled her ripcord as more dark shapes blossomed below. She took hold of the control lines to guide herself in for a landing.

Now that she had slowed, there was time to check the area below. A road wound around the rock, but there was no traffic on it. A single white vehicle sat stationary on what looked like an abandoned airstrip. Park rangers, probably – but were they already helping Wilde and Chase?

She angled towards the dirt runway. Her men did the same. The crate continued on its original course; it would touch down west of their landing zone.

Trees took on three-dimensional form as she neared the ground. Another tug on the cords to avoid them, guiding herself to her target. A hundred feet, fifty—

She pulled to slow herself, making a perfect landing and quickly collapsing the canopy. Her men touched down just as expertly. She looked back. The crate's parachute dropped out of sight behind the trees about a kilometre away.

Wu shrugged off the empty pack. There was no point wasting

time gathering and burying the chutes; like all their other gear, they had no markings that could link them directly to China. Instead she unholstered her sidearm, a compact Heckler & Koch MP7 personal defence weapon, and signalled the others to head for the vehicle.

Macy looked up at the sound of a plane thundering overhead – and saw a jet pass directly over the rock. 'Wow! That's coming in low.'

Sandra, crouching to show her an insect nest, watched the airliner pass with concern. 'It *is* low. And it's completely missed the airport. Maybe it's in trouble.' She stood, looking back the way it had come – and gasped. 'Crikey!'

Macy saw a line of black parachutes dropping swiftly towards the earth. 'Oh no,' she said, horrified. 'We have to get out of here!'

'What is it? Who are they?'

'They're from China, they must be! They've followed us! Come on!' She tugged the woman's sleeve. 'We've got to get to the jeep!'

'Barney's still inside the rock,' Sandra protested. 'And so are your mum and dad.'

'They'd want us to go, trust me. Come *on*!' Macy pulled at her arm again, desperate.

The parachutes disappeared behind trees. Sandra broke through her indecision and took Macy's hand, hurrying with her through the scrub. The Land Cruiser came into view—

As did the parachutists.

The black-clad figures had discarded their chutes and were heading towards them. Sandra froze when she saw they were armed. 'Oh my God! They've got guns – get back!'

But it was too late. They had been spotted. One of the new arrivals – a woman – shouted as they ducked back into the bushes.

'Go into the cave!' Macy cried. 'It's the only place we can hide from them!'

'We don't know what's down there,' warned Sandra.

'We know what's *not* down there – those guys!'

'Not a bad point for a sprog,' the Australian admitted. 'Okay, get over there, quick – but keep your head down!'

They scurried through the undergrowth. 'We can make it!' Macy said. 'We just have to get across here.' The cave was not far ahead – but open ground lay before it.

'You go first,' Sandra said, pushing Macy ahead as they came to the end of the scrub. 'I'll be right with you. Run!'

Heart pounding, Macy raced out into the open, Sandra behind her. Thirty feet to safety—

A man shouted. She glanced sideways, seeing a black-clad figure pointing at her.

Fear drove her to run faster. Almost there—

Red dust exploded from the sandstone. She shrieked, jumping back and shielding her face from spitting shrapnel. Sandra stumbled to a stop behind her. Macy recovered – but before she could run again, another bullet blasted a chunk from the cave mouth. 'Don't move!' the black-clad woman shouted.

Macy felt another surge of terror as she saw a familiar face. Wu Shun marched towards her, gun raised, expression cold and hard.

A last desperate look at the opening, but Macy knew she wouldn't reach it in time. 'No, don't shoot!' she cried, holding up her hands.

'She's just a kid!' Sandra shouted, moving to protect her. 'Leave her alone!'

Wu reached the pair, her men forming up alongside her. 'Hello, Miss Wilde,' she said, the greeting devoid of friendliness. 'If you are here, your parents must be here as well.' She looked towards the cave. 'In there?' Macy said nothing, glowering. 'I will take that as a yes. What about the Nephilim?'

'They killed one of my rangers,' Sandra told her. 'We're not your enemies. Let Macy go, and I'll contact the authorities in Canberra. We can work together to deal with these things.'

Wu shook her head. 'They declared war on us – so we will end it ourselves.' She spoke to two of her men, handing one a phone-sized device. They ran to the Land Cruiser.

'What are you doing?' Macy asked as the 4x4 set off, heading west. It was Wu's turn not to answer. Telling her team to watch the prisoners, she investigated the opening, shining a flashlight down the tunnel.

The Land Cruiser returned after a few minutes, stopping outside the cave. The two men opened its rear to lift out the crate, now stripped of its parachute.

'What's that?' asked Sandra.

'The end of this war,' was Wu's cryptic answer as she came back outside. She switched off the tracking device and opened the crate. A check of its contents, then she called to the larger of the two men: 'Liu!'

With some effort, Liu pulled out what Macy at first thought from its straps was a large backpack. But as he put it on, she saw that the canvas-shrouded object was shaped like a squat barrel, about two and a half feet tall. A box, also hidden inside a custom-fitted canvas cover, protruded from its rear.

'I don't like the look of that,' muttered Sandra.

'Nor do I,' Macy replied. 'What is it? A bomb?'

'You are very perceptive,' the major replied. 'Yes, it is a bomb. Specifically, a sixty-kiloton tactical nuclear device.'

Macy gasped.

'A – a *nuke*?' said Sandra, appalled. 'You've brought a bloody *nuke* to Uluru? Are you crazy?'

'The Nephilim are a threat not only to my country, but to the entire world,' said Wu. 'They must be destroyed. We do not know exactly what is beneath the rock, or how many more

Nephilim are down there. There could be thousands, and they have weapons of immense power.' Her expression somehow became even harder. 'But so do we. Whatever is down there will be completely destroyed.'

'But my mom and dad are down there too!' Macy shouted.

'We are not on a suicide mission. If they cooperate, they will have the chance to leave with us before the bomb goes off. As will you.'

The ten-year-old stared at her. 'I don't trust you,' she finally said.

'I don't care,' was the blunt reply. 'Now, you will come with us – or I will shoot you both.'

'We don't have a choice, do we?' Sandra said bitterly.

'No. You do not.'

The Australian took Macy's hand as the group headed for the entrance. Torches and tactical lights on their weapons were switched on. Wu took the lead, the man with the bomb at the rear – and Macy and Sandra sandwiched helplessly in the middle as they descended.

Nina led the way deeper. It was hard to judge exactly how far down they had gone, but she estimated several hundred feet. The route became more tricky to follow as side passages branched off it, but the job of navigating the labyrinth had been done for them. The dust of ages on the floor had been stirred up by the Nephilim, who had faced the same decisions: which tunnel to take? 'The one with the most footprints,' Barney observed acerbically.

They followed the trail downwards. In places the slope had been carved into steps as it became too steep to traverse, each foothold sized for a giant. Nina came down a flight, then paused at the bottom. 'Hold on,' she whispered.

'What is it?' asked Eddie.

'I can feel a breeze.'

'All the way down here?' But he sensed it too, a faint warm draught blowing up the passage.

Cheng looked past the couple. 'Turn out the torches,' he said. 'I think there's something ahead.'

Barney and Nina did so. As their eyes adjusted, the group saw there was indeed a low light.

'More glow-worms?' Nina wondered.

'If it is, they're a different colour,' said Eddie. 'And they're flickering.'

'Disco worms?' she said with a half-smile. 'I think we're almost there.'

They advanced more cautiously. The light grew brighter as they approached a bend, carved steps dropping sharply as the tunnel turned almost back on itself. The breeze became stronger. 'It's coming through there,' Nina said, seeing a ragged opening in the wall.

She climbed onto a ledge to reach the gap. Broken stones were scattered over it; the hole had opened up long after the tunnel's builders finished their work. More oversized footprints told her the Nephilim had done what she was about to do: look through the cleft to see whatever lay beyond.

The sight took her breath away.

The light's source was beyond anything she had imagined. She stared at it, then almost unwillingly retreated. 'You *have* to see this.'

Eddie took her place. 'Bloody hell,' he said, astonished. 'Dunno what I expected to find down here, but it definitely wasn't *that*.'

Beyond the hole was a gigantic shaft within the red sandstone, dropping almost vertically into the unseen depths below. A colossal pillar of crystal over fifty feet thick rose at its centre, disappearing into the red rock ceiling a hundred-plus feet above. The whole thing was aglow in an ever-shifting spectrum of colours, the shimmering light of earth energy coursing slowly through it.

Nina returned to the opening and peered down. The crystal pillar dropped towards infinity below. 'It must be *miles* deep.'

Cheng and Barney took their turns to look, both reacting with amazement. The Australian, though, was more than simply awed by the sight. 'The Rainbow Serpent . . .' he whispered.

'What's that?' Nina asked.

'One of our stories – well, the *first* story. It's how everything began. The Rainbow Serpent brought life to the whole world from underground. This looks like it, a great snake digging down into the earth.'

She nodded. 'More truth in ancient legends.'

'Seems to be a theme with you,' Eddie noted with amusement.

'I've kinda built a career on it, yes.' She looked down again. 'There are some bridges crossing the shaft to the pillar— Whoa!' She instinctively drew back as she saw movement below. 'I can see the Nephilim!'

Several figures stood before the pillar at the far end of a wide bridge made of red stone. One raised her head and called out, her voice echoing up the shaft. Nina realised that a narrow walkway spiralled around the crystalline tower. At its top, about a hundred feet below her position, was a smaller crossing, an opening at its end leading *inside* the pillar—

Again she drew back in alarm as a figure emerged from it – one she recognised. 'It's Gadreel!' she hissed. Gold glinted upon the head of the robed Nephilim leader as he surveyed the activity below, then started down the spiral pathway, holding a baraka like a staff.

'We've found them – so what do we do now?' asked Cheng.

'If their people are here,' Nina replied, 'we have to stop them from waking them. If we can get the key off Sidona, throwing it down that very, very big hole would be as good a way as any.'

'Except we have to *get* the key off Sidona,' Eddie pointed out.

'Just because she's nine feet tall doesn't make her invincible. They're giants, not superhumans. If we can catch her alone and off guard . . .'

He raised the rifle. 'Let's see if we can, then.'

They resumed their trek down the tunnel, moving with even greater caution as they neared their enemies.

42

Gadreel reached the bottom of the spiral walkway. From here, a broad stone bridge crossed the chasm to a large chamber where most of his forces were resting – but the most important of his people was here.

Sidona stood before a wide portal in the great crystal pillar's side, the opening blocked by a translucent door. Hints of what lay beyond were dimly visible, shadowy forms picked out by the ever-shifting light running through the enormous column.

His people, imprisoned within.

The Nephilim leader had been as amazed as his followers by what lay within the giant red rock – Zan told him the humans called it Uluru – but forced himself to overcome his awe. The People of the Tree had discovered this wonder . . . and corrupted it, turning it into a place of torment and despair.

Sidona had made contact with the glowing spire when they first crossed the higher bridge, her inner senses exploring it – and finding over a thousand souls trapped in an unending nightmare. It was the same ordeal Gadreel and the others had experienced themselves, but they had *chosen* to endure it. Those here were prisoners, left to suffer for all eternity, their persecutors too cowardly to kill them.

But now eternity was over.

He gently touched his wife's shoulder. She twitched, surprised; one hand was against the crystal wall, her mind fixed upon things beyond the physical realm. 'My love,' he said. 'Is all well?'

She turned, revealing tear-stained cheeks. 'Yes, my lord,' she said, composing herself. 'I was . . . with our people.'

'They will *all* soon be with us.' He glanced up to the spiral's top. 'Zan is preparing the machine – under guard, of course. I do not trust him.'

'A traitor can never be trusted,' she agreed. 'I will be glad when we no longer need him.'

'As will I. Is everything prepared here?'

'It is.' She indicated a shallow recess beside the portal. 'The resurrection key will open the door – once the gas inside has been removed. Come, look.' She led him to the ledge's side. 'Down there – do you see the pools?' Light shimmered off pockets of water lower down the red cliffs. 'The gas will flow down through lead pipes into the water and become harmless. When it has all gone, the door will open.'

Gadreel turned back to the entrance. 'Our persecutors were very clever,' he mused. 'If they had applied that cleverness to weapons, they might still be here.'

'But we would not.' Sidona returned to the portal, producing the key from her robes. 'Be thankful they considered themselves too civilised for war.'

He smiled. 'Indeed. Then begin. Bring our people back to life!'

She placed the key into the recess. It clung to the glassy surface as if magnetised. She closed her eyes and placed her palm upon it.

A low rumble slowly rose in volume. 'It begins,' Sidona proclaimed. 'The gas is being drawn from the chamber.'

Gadreel turned to the portal. There was a faint yellow tinge to what lay beyond; the room was filled with the same gas as the sarcophagi. As he watched, the colour gradually disappeared, as if draining out through the floor.

Before long, it was gone. 'It is safe,' said Sidona. 'I can open the door.'

She did nothing physically, but Gadreel knew she was reaching out with her mind. The rumbling faded – then the door started to open, slowly rising upwards.

He pulled her back as residual wisps of gas curled from the widening gap, but they dispersed in moments. The barrier continued to rise. Gadreel held his breath, waiting for his first view of what awaited within . . .

Both he and Sidona were left briefly speechless by the terrible yet incredible sight. Finally, he spoke. 'We have found them. They are here!'

His wife took the key. 'I will wake them.'

'Wait.' She stared at him, demanding an explanation. 'Summon Maseen – any priestess can bring them from their sleep. I need you for something more.' He looked up the spiralling walkway. 'Our enemies of old are gone. But we have new ones – powerful ones.' His expression turned cold. 'Come. We will use the humans' machine to destroy them!'

'There's another split coming up,' said Nina. 'Which way do we go?'

The main passage continued its descent, but another angled off it, heading slightly upwards. Eddie and Barney examined scuffed dust on the floor. 'Most of them went down,' said the Australian.

'Only most of them?' Cheng said, regarding the other tunnel nervously.

'A few went up and didn't come back. The man went with them.' He pointed out the tread of Zan's shoes.

Eddie nodded. 'I'd say they sent scouts to check the side tunnel. They came back, told Gadreel what they'd found, and he sent Zan up there. Maybe he even went with him.'

Nina thought back to what she had seen of the shaft. 'It could be the way to the higher bridge. If it is, then Gadreel's probably not there any more – he went down that spiral pathway.'

'So Zan's alone with the qi tracker?' said Cheng.

Barney shook his head. 'A couple of those bigfoot fellas went with him. Even if one's gone somewhere else, he's still got company.'

'Sidona will have the resurrection key,' said Nina. 'We need to find her first.'

'She might have gone with Gadreel and Zan,' Eddie suggested.

She nodded. 'And if she did . . . right now she could be alone with Zan! We can get the key *and* the tracker at the same time. So we need to go that way.' She indicated the upper tunnel.

Eddie readied the rifle. 'Let's do it.'

They proceeded cautiously up the new passage. Like the main route, it appeared to have been carved from a natural fault, but this one was not as wide. Nina guessed the Veteres had not needed to bring sarcophagi through it – which in turn suggested the prison of Tartarus was somewhere below.

Before long they reached another junction – and heard noises. 'Lights out,' Eddie growled.

A new passage to their left sloped steeply downwards. A glow was visible at its end – the same multispectral shimmer as the crystal pillar. Signalling for Cheng and Barney to stay put, Nina and Eddie crept down it. 'Must be something big,' Nina whispered. 'It's lit up like a football stadium!'

They reached the bottom, finding themselves on a balcony overlooking a huge cathedral-like chamber. The pair ducked behind the stone parapet when they saw numerous Nephilim below. Most were warriors, wearing their bizarre, brightly coloured armour, but to the couple's relief, they did not seem to be expecting battle. They had divided into smaller groups amongst broken boulders scattered across the floor; parts of the ceiling that had fallen over the untold millennia. 'Looks like they've made camp,' Eddie murmured. 'I count . . . about eighteen.'

'And they all squeezed into that little ship?' said Nina. 'Damn, and I bet it didn't even have a bathroom.'

A brief smile, then they surveyed the chamber. A high vaulted ceiling, great vertical columns carved into the red walls. The bases of many had crumbled into rubble over time. Giant heads between them stared sternly down at those below. The stone faces were not human.

Nina recognised the features immediately: the same as those of the mummified corpses she had discovered in the Garden of Eden. 'The Veteres *did* build this place . . .'

Eddie's attention was elsewhere. The long path from the surface ended at a tall gateway to his left; at the great space's opposite end was an even bigger and more ornate arch. The crystal pillar's glow came from beyond it, reflected by numerous large metal mirrors to illuminate the chamber. 'What do you think this is? A church?'

'Something a bit less spiritual.' Her gaze traced a path from the room's entrance to the archway. The fallen rocks had damaged several areas, but there was a clearly defined route through it – and one area contained the remains of cages. 'It's a *processing centre*. The Veteres brought their prisoners down here in the sarcophagi, woke them up, then took them through there,' she indicated the towering exit, 'to the actual prison.'

'Why not just leave 'em in the coffins? It's not like they could get out.'

'They must have had another way of . . . storing them.' She went back to the tunnel. 'We can't get through there. We'll have to keep going.'

They rejoined the two men, then continued up the passage. Before long, it opened out into the colossal crystal-lit shaft, leading to the narrow bridge Nina had seen from above. She dropped to a crouch at the tunnel's mouth, looking across the gap.

At the bridge's far end was an entrance to a chamber within

the pillar. She couldn't tell if it was natural or had been carved out, but she could see people inside.

Zan. Sidona. And Gadreel, the Nephilim leader having returned. The qi tracker was with them, guarded by a towering armoured warrior. Both he and Gadreel were armed with the deadly spear weapons. 'Balls,' Eddie muttered, lowering the rifle. 'No way I can take 'em all out fast enough with this.'

Barney's first sight of the giants left him staring in shock. 'What . . . what are they doing?'

Sidona had her hands on both the crystal inside the tracker and the chamber's glowing inner wall.

'Nothing good,' was Nina's ominous reply.

Gadreel gazed at his wife as she shaped the power flowing around her – and far beyond. It was almost gloriously ironic that the bestial inferior race had built a weapon that used the world's near-infinite forces for destruction, while being almost incapable of operating it themselves . . . and even more so now it was being turned against them.

They still had to rely on one human, however – for the moment. Zan was their only source of knowledge about the world the beasts had built. Typically for animals, Gadreel had learned from him, they had broken up into countless antagonistic packs selfishly battling for supremacy rather than uniting for the common good. 'And which . . . *tribe*,' the Nephilim leader asked, barely containing his contempt, 'is the greatest danger to us?'

'A tribe called America,' Zan replied. The name sounded odd and unappealing to Gadreel's ears. 'It has the most weapons, the most powerful armies. It is my tribe's greatest enemy.'

'Your tribe is also our enemy. Perhaps I should ally with this America?' The Chinese looked decidedly unhappy, until Gadreel let out a mocking laugh. 'All human tribes are a danger to us. For my people to reclaim this world, we must remove such threats.' He pointed at the tracker's screen. 'Show them to me.'

Zan brought the map to North America. 'Here, my lord.'

The Nephilim leader hid his concern. Seemingly arbitrary lines across land marked tribal territories; the one Zan indicated was huge, stretching from one coast of the unknown continent to the other. A single tribe controlled such a vast area? And while America was the most powerful, there were others on the world map as big, or bigger. The enormity of the challenge he faced started to become plain.

But it was one he would accept; that he *had* to accept. The humans had wiped out the People of the Tree, their capacity for raw violence outmatching their masters' lofty intentions, and he was sure they would attempt to do the same to his own people even when faced with the superior weapons of the Nephilim – perhaps *especially* when faced with them. There was no animal more dangerous and vicious than a cornered one . . .

A statement had to be made, a display of power so great it would shock the humans into surrender. 'Where is their largest city?'

Zan zoomed in on the east coast. 'It is called New York.'

He pointed. Gadreel couldn't read the text, but assumed the sprawl of grey where two rivers met in a bay marked the city's boundaries. Several red lines ran close to it. 'Then that is our target.'

He waited for Zan to fix the crosshairs, then went to his wife. She was in a fugue state, barely aware of the real world. 'Sidona. Can you hear me?'

'I can, my lord,' she replied, voice distant.

'There is a target in the machine. Can you sense it?'

'Yes.' Her expression became one of discomfort, that of someone with a small but sharp stone trapped in their sandal. However the tracker marked its target, it felt unpleasant to those with the gift. 'It is a long way from here, but I will reach out.' She closed her eyes, concentrating – then gasped.

'What is it?' he asked.

'So many beasts,' came the whispered reply. 'They are so many! The city, it is huge. The one we saw is nothing to it. The buildings, they . . . I cannot even count them. Tower after tower after tower, stretching to the sky . . .'

'No tower stands for ever,' he said firmly. 'Can you bring them down?'

'Yes. I can shape the power, even from so far away. I can destroy them.'

'Then do so.'

Sidona became still, concentrating. Zan watched the display anxiously. 'The power is growing,' he said as numbers flashed up in secondary windows.

'How long until it will be released?' asked Gadreel.

He examined a shifting graph. 'Fifteen minutes.'

The Nephilim did not know the human unit of time, but guessed from Zan's tone that it was not long. And after so many centuries, he could wait a little more . . .

Sidona gasped again. Gadreel hurriedly crouched beside her. 'What is wrong?'

'Nothing,' she whispered, a look of near-delight dawning. 'I have just realised – this machine is more than a weapon. It . . . it is a focus for my power, it increases it.'

'It *increases* your power? How?'

'I do not know. But I know what it can do.' She gripped his hand, eyes shining. 'The larger the crystal, the greater my power becomes. I can use the key to wake our people. Not one at a time – *all* of them! All at once!'

Gadreel could not reply for a moment, absorbing the magnitude of her discovery. He had thought reviving all the imprisoned Nephilim would take days, but now he could have his entire army before sunset! 'What about the attack that is under way? Will moving the machine affect it?'

'No. Now that it has begun, even without me the power will continue to build until it cannot be contained.' She proved her point by withdrawing her hands from the crystals.

'She is correct, my lord,' Zan said, checking the screen.

Gadreel helped Sidona stand, rising to his full height. 'Then it is time to free our people. Every one of them!'

Nina drew back into cover as Gadreel and Sidona emerged hand-in-hand from the crystal chamber and started down the spiral. 'What are they doing?'

'Dunno, but they look far too happy about it,' said Eddie. He watched them disappear around the glowing pillar, then looked back. 'Ay up. Zan's doing summat with the tracker.'

The group watched as the translator closed the laptop and bundled up the machine's cables, then strained to lift it. He spoke to the warrior, who glowered disdainfully at him. 'I think he was asking him to help carry it,' said Cheng.

'Looks like he got told to piss off,' said the Yorkshireman. Zan hauled the tracker from the floor and carried it to the entrance in an undignified waddle. Eddie brought the rifle back up. 'If I shoot him and the tracker goes over the side, that's one problem sorted.'

'We still have to find the key, though,' Nina reminded him.

Barney had other concerns. 'You're just going to *shoot* him? That's murder!'

'He's a traitor,' Cheng said, with surprising vehemence. 'Because of him, thousands of people have died – including your friend.'

'That thing he's carrying is a weapon,' Nina added. 'The Nephilim used it to destroy a city in China. They'll use it again. They consider this their world – they think we're animals, vermin. They want to wipe us out.'

'And that arsehole's helping them to save his own skin,' said Eddie. He lined up the sights on Zan's head as he lugged the tracker to the top of the spiral—

A noise from behind them.

'Shit!' Nina hissed. 'Someone's coming!'

There was nowhere to hide; they would be seen by Zan or his guard if they exited the tunnel's mouth. Eddie looked back the way they had come. A light washed over the walls, its source hidden past a bend in the passage – but it was getting closer. Muffled footsteps reached them. Three people, more . . .

'They're going!' Nina whispered. Zan descended the walkway, the armoured giant following. They rounded the pillar, backs turning towards her—

'Come on!' She ducked and scurried across the bridge. Eddie hesitated, then followed, Cheng and Barney behind him.

The guard passed out of sight. Nina increased her pace and ran into the empty chamber inside the pillar. The others darted after her. Eddie peered out . . .

The lights became visible in the tunnel. Not the shimmering glow of earth energy, but the steady beams of several torches – so it wasn't just Sandra and Macy. 'Who's that?' said Barney, concerned. 'Sandra wouldn't have let anyone down here.'

The answer came a moment later.

Wu Shun appeared in the tunnel mouth. Cheng jerked back into hiding with an involuntary gasp of fear.

'What the *fuck* is she doing here?' Eddie growled.

She was not alone. A Chinese man in the same dark clothing emerged behind her – then it was Barney's turn to be shocked by another arrival. 'It's Sandra!'

A freezing hand clutched Nina's heart. 'Oh my God. Macy was with her!'

Eddie's face became a mask of cold rage, hands tightening around the rifle. 'If those fuckers have hurt her—'

But he didn't move. If he showed himself, he would be dead in moments – the Chinese special ops team were all armed and ready. Instead he forced himself to observe, and wait.

Torch beams swept through the opening, glinting off the crystalline walls – then suddenly they clicked off, the intruders ducking back. Faint footsteps and Zan's grunts told Eddie why: the translator and his escort had come around the spiral, and the tunnel was in their line of sight. Fortunately – or otherwise – both were concentrating on where they put their feet rather than looking up.

The two men continued round the pillar, passing from sight again. Wu reappeared, looking down the seemingly infinite shaft before staring across at the entrance to Nina and Eddie's hiding place . . . then cocking her head at a message through an earpiece. She gave an order. Her companions turned to retreat—

A sweep of light caught a figure smaller than the others: Macy. It took all Eddie's willpower not to call out her name. 'They've got Macy too,' he rumbled, unable to keep the fury from his voice.

Even expecting the grim news, Nina felt as if the blood was draining from her body. She put a hand against the wall to steady herself—

And was slammed into another reality.

The crystal pillar was inconceivably huge, the power flowing through it beyond imagination – and the full force of both hit her so hard that her consciousness was almost swept away. Somehow she clung on, overcoming the shock of contact with the earth's strange energies . . .

She sensed others in the maelstrom with her.

Tiny points of awareness, diamond hard, trapped and tormented. The rest of the Nephilim. The captives of the Veteres, 'benevolently' imprisoned rather than killed for their crimes of birth, were here.

All of them. So many, she couldn't even count. They were somewhere below her, inside the pillar itself.

But there was something else, outside the pillar – beyond Uluru, the entire *country*. A seething discord, growing in strength with every passing moment. Somehow, she knew Sidona had set it in motion. Another attack, on a far greater scale than the destruction in Xinengyuan. Nina tried to reach out to reshape it, but it was too big, too powerful—

The real world snapped back into place. Eddie's worried face filled her vision. 'Nina!' he said. 'Are you okay?'

'Yeah, yeah, I . . .' she said, confused, before recovering. 'Eddie, they've used the tracker to start another attack – I don't know where, but it's big. The power's building up already.'

'Can you stop it?'

'No – not without the tracker, and maybe the key as well.'

'Then we have to catch Zan!' said Cheng.

'We've got to rescue Macy,' Eddie countered. 'The only reason Wu would have come here with a special forces team is to kill the Nephilim – and us.'

'There's something else,' said Nina. 'I felt it when I touched the crystal. The other Nephilim really *are* imprisoned, somewhere below us. And there are *hundreds* of them, thousands.'

'What? Jesus Christ, Gadreel's going to end up with an *army*!'

'No, he isn't,' she said, desperately trying to explain. 'Yes, some of them might be warriors – but most of them aren't. There are *children* imprisoned here, for God's sake! If Wu and her team kill them all, it won't just be murder – it'll be genocide. We can't let her do it.'

'So what are we supposed to do? Let Gadreel wake 'em up so both sides can fight it out?'

'I think the best thing would be to leave them where they are. If they're resurrected, they'll all be killed, one way or another. Humans exterminated the Veteres, just like the Neanderthals;

you think we'd let another potential rival survive?'

'But if you leave them trapped,' Cheng reminded her, 'it'll be like torturing them for eternity.' A fearful look crossed his face at the reminder of what had almost certainly happened to his mother.

'It's better than being dead,' she replied. 'And they survived all this time down here. They might survive another hundred thousand years, and eventually wake up. The Veteres are gone, and we probably will be too by then. Maybe they'll finally get the chance to live that they've never had.'

'Let's worry about the present before the future,' said Eddie impatiently. 'What are we going to do?'

'I *have* to get to the tracker,' said Nina. 'I'm the only one who can stop Gadreel's attack – and maybe prevent a genocide.'

'I'm going to get Macy,' Eddie said firmly. 'We need to split up.'

'Yeah, because that always goes so well, huh?' They shared a resigned smile. 'Okay, Cheng, you come with me. I might need your help with the Nephilim language – and the Chinese, for that matter. I can't read the text on the tracker.'

Barney looked askance at Eddie. 'So I guess I'm coming with you to take on a heavily armed commando team?'

'You want to take on the army of giants whose guns make people explode?' the Englishman shot back.

The Australian was not happy. 'Sounds like I'm screwed either way. And I thought *tourists* were a pain in the arse.'

Flashlights were shared between the two groups. 'Okay,' Eddie said to Nina. 'I'll save Macy, you save the world.'

'I don't know which is going to be harder,' she said. 'Let's . . . let's get her home safely, huh?'

'Yeah. With both of us.' He embraced and kissed her, then let go. 'Let's *all* get home safe,' he said to the two other men, before looking back across the bridge. 'Okay, it's clear.'

'Good luck,' said Cheng.

'You too.' A last touch of Nina's hand, then he started across the narrow bridge, Barney behind him. He glanced down. Gadreel and Sidona were at the bottom of the spiral, the female Nephilim entering another chamber inside the crystal pillar while her husband crossed the larger bridge to the cathedral-like room. Higher up, Zan was still struggling to carry the heavy tracker down the walkway—

The Chinese slipped, reeling towards the edge before lurching back against the crystal with a frightened yell.

The noise draw Gadreel's attention. He looked up, spotting the panting translator on the spiral—

And the unexpected figure on the higher crossing.

Eddie hurriedly pulled back, but it was too late. A commanding shout echoed up the shaft. 'Buggeration!' he barked, readying the rifle as he looked down again. It was a long shot, but if he could take out the Nephilim leader before he organised his forces—

The warrior behind Zan was already responding to Gadreel's command. His baraka came up – and fired.

The bolt of energy hit the bridge's underside, red stone exploding beneath Eddie and Barney. The ranger staggered, then slipped over the edge as a section of the crossing fell away—

Eddie lunged, catching his wrist. The big man's weight almost dragged him into the abyss. He strained to haul him back up, but felt his hold slipping. Tossing the rifle aside, he clapped his other hand around the Australian's arm.

The bridge shuddered. A chunk fell away just beyond Barney, splitting the crossing in half. Eddie finally found his grip and dragged him onto the dusty surface. He felt the bridge shifting under his feet – with the supporting arch broken, the crossing's separate halves would soon collapse—

Another sizzling bolt of earth energy slammed into the bridge's far side. Gadreel had fired his own weapon. Pulverised fragments struck Eddie and Barney – and the weakened structure gave way.

Nina and Cheng jumped back into the chamber as the section of bridge before them sheared from the pillar, smashing through part of the spiral walkway lower down before spinning out into the chasm. Gadreel ran for cover as debris fell past him.

Half the bridge had gone – and the other half was about to follow. 'Run!' Eddie shouted, pulling the winded Barney to his feet and hurrying for the tunnel. The rifle was balanced precariously on the crossing's edge. He bent to snatch it up as he passed – but another jolt pitched the gun over just before his hand reached it.

No time even to curse. Still towing the Australian, he dived into the tunnel just as the rest of the bridge broke from the cliff behind them.

The panting ranger said something in what Eddie assumed was a local language. 'If that means "buggeration and fuckery", I'm with you,' he muttered.

He risked a quick look down the shaft. The petrified Zan was being forced to continue downwards by his guard. Gadreel shouted more orders on the lower bridge, Nephilim spilling from the cathedral behind him. The Yorkshireman looked across at Nina in alarm. Her expression matched his. She and Cheng were trapped on the far side of the abyss—

An explosion came from below.

43

Major Wu and her team returned to the main passage in response to a scout's radio message. He had located a Nephilim force in a large chamber below, some eighteen men. Considering the size of the craft that had escaped from Xinengyuan, that was probably most if not all of the survivors.

Her unit had the advantage of surprise, and more powerful weapons. Their MP7s fired high-velocity armour-piercing rounds; even shielded, the warriors' gaudy suits would provide little protection. The team also had explosive and stun grenades, smoke bombs and thermal sights – more than enough to counteract their enemies' greater numbers.

And if all else failed . . . there was the nuke.

Leaving Liu, the man bearing the bomb, to guard Macy and Sandra at the junction, Wu led the rest of her team to the bottom of the tunnel. 'They aren't expecting trouble,' the waiting scout whispered.

Wu checked for herself. The Nephilim were in several groups, but relatively close together. 'That balcony's accessible from the other tunnel,' she said, indicating it. 'If we position some men up there, we can attack from two angles simultaneously—'

A shout from beyond the towering chamber – then the crackle of a Nephilim spear weapon. A moment later, an explosion echoed down the shaft.

Whatever had just happened, the warriors were unprepared for it. Several jumped up, looking towards the huge shaft in confusion – before grabbing their own weapons.

No time now for carefully coordinated ambushes. 'We attack now!' Wu hissed, raising her weapon. 'Move in! Wipe them out!'

She took the lead as her team rushed into the cathedral, splitting up to use the fallen boulders for cover. Another qigun shot tore up the shaft, several warriors running through the giant arch—

She snatched the pin from a hand grenade and lobbed it into one of the groups of Nephilim. The metallic *smack* as it hit the ground made some of them turn. Inhuman shouts of alarm as they saw the intruders—

The grenade exploded, blast and shrapnel tearing the closest giants apart.

Other grenades arced through the chamber, killing and wounding more warriors. Wu felt no pity, focused completely on extermination. She opened fire on a monster bringing up his qigun. His armour sparked with unnatural light as the rounds hit home, but the earth energy shielding it was not enough to withstand the assault. He fell backwards, holes torn through his chest.

More guns chattered, warriors falling, but now they had overcome their surprise. They dropped into cover – and fired back.

Macy and Sandra reacted in shock at the sound of battle below. Liu also responded with alarm. The hulking guard turned, moving a few steps to look down the sloping tunnel—

'*Run!*' Sandra cried. She grabbed the girl by her arm and raced back up the narrow side passage.

Liu yelled for them to stop, then lumbered in pursuit. The weight of the nuclear bomb on his back slowed him. Sandra rounded a corner, towing Macy after her. They passed into darkness—

The Australian stumbled over a protruding stone.

Macy ran into her from behind – and fell. Sandra lost her hold. She stopped, grabbing at her charge, but Liu was already gaining. 'Sandra, *run!*' Macy yelled as the Chinese soldier came around the corner, his light pinning her.

She tried to stand, but his weapon rose—

The sound of gunfire in the confined space was deafening. Macy screamed, dropping flat and covering her ringing ears. The noise stopped. Before she could recover, Liu was upon her, seizing her roughly and dragging her back to the intersection.

'Sandra!' Macy screamed. 'Sandra, keep running!'

But she heard no reply as her hearing returned. Nor did she hear any rapidly retreating footsteps. The tunnel was silent and still.

The Nephilim blasted energy bolts back across the cathedral at their attackers. Most hit stone, shattering the fallen rocks with explosive force, but that was enough to knock down the Chinese soldiers behind them. One man made a dash for better protection as his hiding place blew apart—

Another bolt caught him mid stride. He burst into a wet red haze.

The horrific sight filled Wu with fury. 'Smoke!' she shouted, readying another grenade, this one cylindrical. She threw it to land slightly short of the Nephilim front line. A sickly orange fog gushed from it, obscuring everything beyond. More canisters clanked down. The swirling curtain cut the chamber in half.

The qigun barrage slowed, but did not cease, some Nephilim still firing blind through the smoke. Wu sent shots of her own at their source, then gave another order. Two men responded, bringing up weapons much larger than the MP7s.

M2010 sniper rifles – equipped with thermal sights.

The scopes cut through the obscuring mist, revealing what lay beyond in stark digital white and grey against cold black. The guns had an effective maximum range of twelve hundred metres; this close, it was a turkey shoot. Heads exploded, blood sprayed from gaping exit wounds as rounds punched straight through armour. The two snipers maintained an even fire, the sharp retorts of their weapons echoing deafeningly around the chamber. Find target, shoot, confirm it was down, find another—

The Nephilim finally overcame their shock and dropped behind whatever cover they could find. 'They've ducked!' shouted one sniper, sweeping his scope from side to side and finding nothing.

'Finish them off with grenades!' Wu called back, readying another of her own. The chamber was large enough that the enemies near the far exit would be beyond the reach of a thrown bomb. She signalled to a man unshouldering a new weapon: a Chinese-made but untraceable copy of the American China Lake pump-action launcher that could fire forty-millimetre grenades over hundreds of metres.

Another barrage of hand grenades flew over the smoke as the soldier rapidly swept the China Lake's four rounds at the room's far end. Three of the charges hit the end wall and sent deadly debris over those hiding near it.

The fourth shot straight through the archway onto the bridge. It whipped past Gadreel and the warriors who had left the cathedral, glancing off the floor without triggering its detonator and angling back upwards—

Into the towering crystal space within the pillar.

Sidona had climbed higher inside it, but the priestess Gadreel had summoned was still at its foot. The grenade exploded just behind her, tearing her apart.

The thrown grenades all exploded a moment later. More warriors in the cathedral were dismembered by razor-sharp steel fragments.

But not all the Nephilim were dead. One warrior, sheltered between boulders, raised his baraka in response to a human's cry of pain from a balcony above. A beast staggered with a bloody wound to his arm, another jumping up from behind the parapet to help him.

The Nephilim took aim – and fired.

Eddie and Barney hurried back through the tunnel. Gunfire echoed up the side passage. 'Down here,' said the Yorkshireman.

'They might be on the balcony!' Barney protested.

'That's all coming from floor level. Hurry up!' He descended, the ranger reluctantly following.

The piercing crackle grew louder as he reached the balcony, dropping low to peer over the parapet. Wu's team had come in from the main passage to the left, the Nephilim mostly on his right and clearly caught by surprise. Several were already dead or wounded. But they had recovered enough to fight back, a grotesque red burst showing where a soldier had taken a baraka's full force.

Orange smoke erupted almost directly below – then a pair of snipers equipped with what Eddie guessed were thermal sights opened up. He had a ringside view as more Nephilim were cut down with pinpoint precision. The survivors flattened themselves behind debris and the room's carved fixtures – only for Wu to shout an order.

Grenades sailed over the fog bank as another man unleashed several rapid shots from a forty-millimetre launcher. Three of his rounds exploded devastatingly in the chamber, a fourth hurtling through the archway onto the bridge. The sound of its detonation reached Eddie just as the hand grenades went off below.

He ducked as shrapnel filled the air. Barney was not so quick to react. Steel shards slashed into his forearm. He screamed.

Eddie sprang back up to pull him into cover – only to see a spear swing towards them—

An earth energy blast ripped into the balcony. It collapsed under the two men.

Eddie was thrown clear as the falling slab hit a pile of rubble, landing hard and tumbling down the broken debris. He came to a painful stop on the floor, smoke swirling around him. Despite being winded, he held his breath – coughing would give away his position.

He heard Barney groan nearby and crawled towards him, moving clear of the smoke to find the Australian sprawled against a stone-walled booth; some part of the processing centre. Whatever it was, it was keeping them out of sight of the Chinese – for now. But if they advanced, the pair would be sitting ducks . . .

'Keep quiet,' he whispered, dragging the wounded man into the booth as Wu shouted commands. 'We're stuck between both sides! Stay here.'

'Where are you going?' Barney asked through pain-clenched teeth.

'I've got to get past them to find Macy. Fuck knows how, since I don't have a gun – or even a stick.'

'Hey, hey.' The ranger pointed at his belt. 'I've got something.' He popped open a leather sheath and took out a gleaming steel Leatherman multi-tool.

Eddie accepted it, unfolding the largest blade with a snick. It was only four inches long, but the point and edge were clean and extremely sharp. 'Ripper, mate,' he said in an attempt at an Australian accent.

Barney frowned. 'Don't do that.'

'Sorry. But thanks anyway.' The blade ready in his hand, he moved back to their hiding place's entrance. The wall of smoke roiled at him, drawn towards the tunnel by the air flowing up to the surface. 'Don't breathe this stuff in,' he warned. Barney took several deep breaths before clamping a hand over his mouth and nose. Eddie held his own breath again as the dirty cloud reached him, the acrid gas stinging his nostrils.

He squinted into the mist. No sign of any Nephilim, but he briefly glimpsed one of Wu's men cautiously advancing through the scattered obstacles about sixty feet away, an MP7 raised.

Could he use the thickening smoke to sneak up on the Chinese and take his weapon? Too far, too risky. Once he was unsighted, he might miss his target by twenty feet—

A boot scuffed *less* than twenty feet away.

Eddie looked for the source, but saw only a vague shadow before the orange haze wiped out all detail. That sighting was enough, though. One of the snipers, rifle raised so he could use the thermal sight to see through the smoke. He would pick out any Nephilim who raised their heads as clearly as if they were lit by spotlights; the Englishman would be just as visible . . .

Which, he suddenly realised, might work to his advantage.

He clenched his fists, ready for action – and stepped out into the open.

Nina and Cheng cautiously picked their way down the spiral walkway. It was adamantium, the same dark grey material the Nephilim used in their vimanas; the Veteres had presumably had the same knowledge of metallurgy. The path had survived the ages intact, only to be damaged within minutes of her arrival. 'I am *not* to blame,' she grumbled. 'I have *not* trashed another archaeological site!'

'What?' said Cheng from behind her. The young man's shoulder was pressed against the pillar, eyes fixed firmly on his feet.

'Nothing!' She paused as her corkscrewing descent brought the bridge and the great archway back into view. The fierce battle between the Chinese and the Nephilim had spread, a grenade exploding inside the pillar itself. Conflict was still ongoing, but she now heard more modern weapons than baraka fire. Wu's team seemed to be winning.

Gadreel lurked at the side of the arch with a couple of his men. All were armed, but they were hanging back from the fight. Nina saw why as one warrior peered through the opening – only to fall backwards when a sniper's bullet punched straight through him with an explosive spout of blood. Cheng swore in Chinese. 'What's that English saying about frying pans?' he asked.

'Getting out of them into the fire?'

'Yes – except the fire is also surrounded by men with machine guns!'

'We've *got* to get past them somehow,' Nina said firmly. 'It's the only way out of here – and Macy's over there.'

'We still have to get down this path first.' He looked over the edge – only to hurriedly pull back with a gasp.

'Vertigo?'

'Yes, yes.' He wiped his sweating brow. 'Somehow I forgot I had it. My brain reminded me!'

'Just stay on the inside and don't look down.' She promptly ignored her own advice to see what lay below. Zan was nowhere in sight; he had presumably reached the bottom of the spiral and entered the lower chamber. His armoured chaperone ran across the bridge to join Gadreel.

'Zan made it down,' she reported before continuing. 'He must have taken the tracker to Sidona.'

'Why does she need it?' he asked. 'She's already started the attack.'

'Maybe they can use it to revive the rest of their people more quickly.' She made another turn around the spiral – then abruptly halted. 'Oh, crap!'

'What is it?' Cheng asked.

'There's a big-ass hole in the walkway!'

A chunk of the path had been torn away by the fallen bridge, only twisted stubs of the support struts remaining. The gap was over ten feet wide. Cheng paled. 'How are we going to get across?'

'Either jump, or climb down.' She went to the ragged edge. The next leg of the spiral was more than fifteen feet below. Lowering herself as far as she could before letting go would cut the fall to eight or nine feet – manageable, but any stumble on landing could send her over. On the other hand, the path's curvature around the pillar provided a very limited landing area if she jumped the gap.

She didn't like either option, but the first seemed marginally less risky. 'I'm going to drop down.'

'Are you sure?'

'You'd rather jump?'

'No! I . . . I don't want to do either.'

'Nor do I, but I've got to stop Sidona.' Nina lowered herself over the edge. A glance down to check she was lined up with her landing site – then she let go.

She dropped, the crystal pillar flashing past her—

Her feet hit the metal floor with a jarring bang. She gasped, reeling towards the endless drop below – before throwing herself back at the pillar. 'Professor!' cried Cheng. 'Are you okay?'

'Yeah,' she said, straightening shakily. 'Okay, your turn.'

Panic crossed Cheng's face. 'I . . . I can't,' he whispered. 'I want to, I know I have to, but – I can't!' The last was almost a gasp. 'I'm . . . I'm scared.'

Nina felt both sympathy and impatience. 'I know, and I understand – but I can't wait for you to pluck up the courage. If you drop down, I'll catch you, but you've got to do it *now*.'

His wide-eyed gaze flicked between her and the chasm. 'I – I'm sorry, Professor. I can't do it!' He screwed up his eyes.

'Okay, it's okay,' she assured him. 'You come down when you feel ready. But I've got to go.' She turned to resume her descent.

'I'm sorry,' he said again, before adding with strained humour: 'This won't affect my grades, will it?'

'I think you've already earned an A,' she said with a smile.

He managed to return it, just. 'Good luck.'

She continued down the spiral. A crowbar-sized length of metal lay upon it, one of the broken support struts. On impulse she picked it up. As a weapon it was no match for a baraka, but at the very least, it might crack a giant's kneecap . . .

Her confidence slightly bolstered, she resumed her descent.

The Chinese sniper moved carefully into the smoke, panning his weapon. Nothing on the thermal scope, but it wouldn't be long before the surviving Nephilim ran out of places to hide . . .

A white flare against the black. He snapped the rifle towards it. Another of the monsters who'd left the chamber just before the attack peered through the archway.

His crosshair intercepted the ghostly shape – and blood sprayed in a hot glowing fountain as he put a .300-calibre Winchester Magnum round through the towering Nephilim's skull. Target down, and he brought the rifle around to search for more—

Footsteps, worryingly close.

The sniper whirled to see another inverse silhouette just metres away. His finger tightened on the trigger—

And eased. It was no giant. One of his comrades had been disoriented by the fog. 'Hey, over here,' he said. The glowing figure came towards him. He lowered the gun, seeing the approaching man take on form through the smoke—

He wasn't Chinese.

★ ★ ★

Eddie stepped up to the startled sniper and stabbed the four-inch blade into his throat.

It punctured his windpipe. The man let out a choked gasp, unable to scream a warning. The Englishman forced the blade across his neck, severing his trachea and slashing a carotid artery. The soldier dropped like a wet sack, blood gushing from the wound. Eddie dragged him back to the stone booth. It took all of Barney's willpower not to yell in shock as the twitching body was dumped before him. The Yorkshireman held up the bloodied multi-tool. 'Want this back?'

The ranger recoiled. 'You keep it, mate!'

Eddie grinned darkly and pocketed it.

A rapid search of the Chinese gave him both the M2010 and an MP7, as well as a couple of hand grenades. He looked between the two guns, then unlocked the thermal sight from the larger weapon's Picatinny accessory rail and slotted the device into place on the compact MP7's matching mount. There was no way to test that the sights were correctly centred, but at close range it wouldn't matter. He collected an extra magazine, then moved back into the smoke.

The other sniper's rifle boomed. He had spotted another Nephilim – but also given away his position. Eddie snapped up the MP7 and looked through the scope. The shooter stood out clearly, his M2010's barrel glowing hot white. A sweep revealed the other soldiers, clustered in two groups flanking the sniper as they advanced.

He quickly turned to check nobody was coming up behind him. Two figures were holding position; one was Major Wu, the only female team member. Neither had thermal sights, meaning they couldn't see him.

Another rifle shot, then a third. An inhuman scream from the mist. If the Nephilim hadn't yet been wiped out, there could only be a few left in the cathedral.

Eddie located the other soldiers again, then rapidly shouldered the MP7 and hefted both grenades. He pulled the pin from the first with his teeth and lobbed it in a high arc at the nearer of the two groups, then armed and threw the second at the further before ducking.

The first grenade bounced off the stone floor about ten feet from the Chinese. They whirled, knowing instantly what it was, but couldn't find cover in the smoke—

The bomb went off. Razor-edged steel blasted outwards at supersonic speeds, tearing bodies apart. The second grenade detonated a moment later. Men were hurled screaming into the air.

Eddie jumped up. The sniper had been caught between the two explosions, staggering. The Yorkshireman snapped his gun's fire selector to single shot for precision and sent a round at his head. It hit slightly below the crosshairs, but the result was still lethal. A chunk of the man's lower jaw spun away amidst a spray of white, and he fell.

Eddie clicked the MP7 to full auto and swung it towards the nearer group. Only two were still moving. Brief bursts of fire corrected that. He found the other squad. More had survived the second explosion. They did not live long enough to be grateful.

The magazine ran dry. He ejected it and slapped in the replacement as he spun back towards Wu and her companion. Macy and Sandra weren't with them, so there was at least one more soldier somewhere . . .

Wu ran for the tunnel. Eddie tracked her, but just as he fired, her bright blur vanished behind an obstacle. The bullets cracked against stone.

He followed her path to catch her as she reappeared – but then her companion flashed through his sights, his own gun coming up. Eddie unleashed another burst. The soldier fell. Where was Wu? He swung the MP7 towards the exit—

She reappeared. He fired again – but she disappeared into the tunnel, the rounds blasting shrapnel from the sandstone. 'Shit!' he barked, running in pursuit.

He quickly cleared the smoke. The cathedral was now in a sickly half-light, the orange fog tainting the crystal pillar's glow. He hurried to the tunnel's mouth. Wu was gone. He raced after her.

44

The bridge came back into sight below as Nina completed another circuit of the pillar. There had been another couple of explosions and several bursts of gunfire as she descended, but now the chasm had fallen eerily silent. Who had won the battle?

More loops around the pulsing pillar, and she neared the walkway's foot. She slowed. Zan was down here somewhere, and she had no idea where the rest of the Nephilim might be.

The living ones, at least. She looked across the bridge. Nephilim corpses littered its other end. Gadreel was not amongst them – but he could now have few, if any, surviving followers.

Nobody was in sight within the cathedral, though, human or otherwise. She took that as a good sign and hurried down to the broad stone platform at the bridge's end.

A wide opening had been carved into the pillar. She went towards it—

Some instinct made her halt. The glowing crystal wall was translucent enough to reveal a shadowy shape inside. A standing figure. It wasn't large enough to be Nephilim . . .

Zan. The translator lurked in the chamber's entrance.

She quietly moved to the side of the opening. The Chinese hadn't yet realised she was there. She hefted the strut. A brief hesitation – what she was about to do could easily have fatal results – but then decided: *fuck him*. Zan's treachery had caused enormous destruction and death, to say nothing of the peril she and her family had faced.

She readied herself, then whipped around the corner – and swung the spar at Zan's head.

He heard the movement and started to turn – only for the metal bar to strike his skull with a flat crack. The blow dropped him instantly. Nina quickly dragged him out, pulling him under the foot of the walkway, where he would hopefully be out of sight. He was still alive, but would have a hell of a headache, if not a concussion, when he awoke.

It was the least he deserved. She returned to the entrance, stepping through it . . .

And stopped in amazement.

The sight greeting her was mind-blowing: a crystal-walled chamber resembling the mausoleum inside the Nephilim flying fortress, but on an infinitely grander scale. It was cone-shaped, widening as it rose, and stretched upwards for well over a hundred feet. Another spiral path, this one hewn from the glowing surface and paved with adamantium plates, circled the inner wall almost to the vaulted summit. Glassy stalagmites stabbed upwards from the edge of its lowest turns.

All around the chamber, held upside down in recesses within the walls as if cocooned by crystalline spiders, were the rest of the Nephilim.

Nina stared in shock at the unmoving figures. There were hundreds of them, entwined in the same glassy tendrils she had seen when Gadreel's sarcophagus first opened. A legion of grey faces, trapped in the eternal sleep of the damned.

She had found Tartarus, the inescapable underground prison from Greek and Roman mythology – which also entombed the half-angelic Watchers from biblical apocrypha. Once again, a truth from before the dawn of known history, when *Homo sapiens* were little more than the animalistic slaves of the Veteres, had been mutated by time into part of human religion. The fallen angels were real.

And they were about to awaken.

Blood and torn flesh disfigured the luminous walls where a Nephilim woman had been blown apart by a grenade. The frozen figures around her were similarly mutilated, dead in their crystal cocoons. The priestess – not Sidona, Nina could tell from the remains of her clothing – had been standing before one of them. The glassy strands around the warrior's corpse had withdrawn into the wall. The glow of the crystal around him was different from the others, turquoise in tint. Again, she had seen the same thing with Gadreel's sarcophagus. The priestess had been watching the warrior's revival when the grenade killed them both.

So where was the resurrection key?

She looked up, following the spiral to its top. Dark shapes were visible through a crystalline ledge protruding out to beneath the centre of the chamber's ceiling. The qi tracker – and Sidona.

The high priestess hadn't heard Zan falling. Too far away – or was she in a trance? It didn't matter. She wasn't yet aware of Nina's presence.

The redhead ran up the spiral. The Veteres had had space for many more prisoners, empty recesses dotted between the occupied. She passed another warrior whose resurrection had begun, the gossamer strands partially reabsorbed. Based on her experience, it would take a few minutes for him to wake. He was not a threat – yet.

She kept going. The inverted figures flicked past her. Disturbingly, many of the sleepers were frozen mid scream as if the process had been both rapid and terrifying, faces twisted in torment. Men, women – and children, ranging from near adulthood to toddlers. She felt a surge of disgust towards the Veteres. If their idea of civilisation was imprisoning babies for no crime other than being born, the world was better off without them.

She shook off her anger. The Veteres were long gone. It was

the Nephilim, their bastard outcast offspring, who now posed a danger. Hate had begat hate, Gadreel and Sidona about to take it out on the race they considered the inferior side of their genetic heritage.

Unless she could stop them.

Halfway up. What to do when she reached Sidona? Proving Gadreel's beliefs about humans true would, ironically, be the best approach: resorting to violence. Even if she could speak the Nephilim language, Nina doubted she could persuade the high priestess to embrace peace.

She neared the top. Sidona came into view. She sat cross-legged, one hand raised to hold something against a large, spiky node protruding from the ceiling, the other touching the crystal inside the tracker's toroidal case. The machine was linked by cables to the wall – to the entire pillar. The colossal spire was a confluence for vast amounts of earth energy . . .

And Sidona now controlled it all.

Not for long, Nina vowed. If the Nephilim could influence the flow of power across the world, so could she. Deal with Sidona, and she could stop the attack.

She clutched the spar more tightly as she passed the final prisoners to reach the ledge. Sidona still had not registered her presence, entirely focused on the other world beyond the physical. Again Nina hesitated. She was about to club down a completely helpless, unaware woman. Even though she knew the stakes, it still felt wrong—

Something changed.

The light coursing through the crystal shifted in hue, a turquoise glow flowing through the chamber's walls like dye in clear water. She looked down. One place was unaffected – because it already *was* the new colour.

Where the warrior was awakening.

'Oh shit . . .' Nina whispered. She saw what Sidona was

holding against the node: the resurrection key. The qi tracker was again amplifying her control of the earth energy flow, weaponising it – to wake *all* the Nephilim simultaneously.

She wouldn't just be facing one revived warrior. She would be confronting *hundreds*, emerging from their long imprisonment confused, angry . . . and with Gadreel and Sidona to lead them against their enemies.

Gadreel, at least. His wife could be taken out of the equation right now. Nina hefted the bar and hurried towards the sitting giant—

Sidona gasped – and her eyes opened.

Wu reached the intersection and rounded the corner. Liu had put his torch on the floor, shining it up at the ceiling to act as a makeshift lantern. He only had one prisoner: the girl, tears streaking her face. 'Where's the woman?' she demanded.

He gestured up the side tunnel. 'Dead. She tried to run.'

'Chase is coming. Put down the bomb and help me kill him.'

'Where are the others?' he asked as he started to unfasten his heavy cargo.

'He's killed *them*. Move, quick!' She grabbed Macy and pulled her close.

'Get off me!' Macy cried, struggling and kicking as Wu forcibly manoeuvred her into position as a human shield.

'Shut up!' She aimed her gun at the intersection, tactical light illuminating it. Running footsteps grew louder – then slowed.

'Daddy!' shrieked Macy. 'She's got me! There's another man—'

Wu angrily clamped a hand over her mouth. Macy writhed, driving her elbow into the Chinese woman's stomach. The major grunted – the blow was surprisingly painful. She retaliated by cracking her MP7's grip against the girl's skull. Macy let out a muffled shriek.

Liu finally released his harness and carefully swung the bomb to the floor, then raised his weapon. Wu watched the intersection intently. The tunnel had gone silent. 'Chase!' she shouted in English. 'I know you are there! I have your daughter. Show yourself.'

'Let Macy go or I'll kill you,' came the blunt reply.

'Show yourself or I will kill *her*!' Wu placed the muzzle of her gun against Macy's head – but frowned. Something wasn't right, Chase's voice sounding . . . odd.

It didn't matter. He was no more than five metres away, almost impossible to miss at such close range. 'Turn your light out,' she told Liu in muttered Mandarin. He obeyed, collecting and switching off the torch. 'Countdown from three – I'll turn mine out on one. On zero, fire a sweep around the corner. Move into position.'

The soldier crept forward. Macy tried to shout a warning, but only stifled moans escaped from behind Wu's hand. 'Three,' the major began. 'Two . . .'

At one, Wu switched off her light, plunging the passage into darkness – and a moment later, Liu whipped around the corner and sent a deafening blaze of fire down the tunnel, bullets ricocheting from both walls.

The MP7's thirty-round magazine fell empty. Liu switched his torch back on and shone it down the tunnel, expecting to see the Englishman lying dead on the floor.

He *was* on the floor – but still very much alive.

Eddie knew that rounding the corner to face two enemies would be suicide – but he also knew the Chinese would act very soon, the urgency of Wu's orders a giveaway. He advanced to just short of the junction and silently lay flat on his chest. Gun aimed up at the corner, he waited for the inevitable attack – which went right over his head. The MP7's muzzle flash obscured him from the soldier's sight . . . until it was too late.

Three armour-piercing rounds punched up through Liu's stomach into his chest. He crashed to the red stone floor, his torch rolling away down the incline to wedge against a wall.

Eddie jumped up. Wu hadn't yet turned on her light. He raised the MP7 and whirled around the corner. The sight flared as it found hot targets against cold stone—

An object was starkly silhouetted against the woman and the girl's bright conjoined shapes. A gun – pointed at Macy's head.

With his sights not zeroed, Eddie couldn't risk taking a shot at Wu. He sidestepped for a better angle—

Too late. Wu's tactical light clicked back on, illuminating the side of Macy's face. The Chinese agent turned to pull her between them. 'Drop the gun!' she snarled.

'Kill her and I kill you,' he growled back.

'And then you will kill yourself,' she sneered. 'Knowing you had let your only child die? You could not live with that.'

His lips curled in anger – and she responded with a small, cruel smile. 'Where's Sandra?' he demanded.

'Dead,' came the cold reply.

'She tried to run!' said Macy, crying. 'That man shot her!'

A desperate plan started to form. 'Macy, everything's going to be okay,' said Eddie, fully aware that he had no way to guarantee that. He surreptitiously clicked the fire selector to single shot for maximum accuracy. 'Just . . . *think fast.*'

Macy's eyes widened in understanding – and she dropped—

Eddie fired. The bullet hit Wu's right shoulder, knocking her backwards. She screamed. Macy broke from her hold. 'Down!' he yelled as the gun swung towards him. He fired again, but only clipped the woman's upper arm—

Both he and Macy dived as Wu's MP7 blazed. The Yorkshireman rolled down the sloping tunnel as bullets pounded the wall behind him.

The gunfire stopped. Eddie darted back to the corner, resetting his weapon to full auto. 'Macy! To me!' He lunged out to cover his daughter's approach, finding his opponent—

Wu had retreated, dropping down behind a large barrel-shaped backpack on the floor. It wasn't big enough to give her full cover. He grabbed Macy and pushed her around the corner, then fired a burst at Wu as he withdrew. The rounds cracked off rock and metal, but not flesh—

'*Daddy!*' Macy shrieked. 'Don't shoot! It's a bomb!'

He froze. The pack must be some sort of demolition charge; it was big enough to contain several dozen kilograms of high explosive. That would reduce himself, Macy and Wu to their component atoms and blast a big hole in Uluru's innards if it went off . . .

If it went off. Modern explosives were specifically designed for stability – C4 could be dropped into burning petrol or blasted with a shotgun and still not detonate. If one bullet hadn't set it off, more wouldn't either.

It was safe – which meant Wu wasn't. He moved to take another shot—

'No, Daddy!' Macy cried, desperately grabbing his gun hand. 'A *nuclear* bomb!'

That made him pull back. 'You *what?*'

'She is right,' Wu said, voice strained. 'A sixty-kiloton nuclear demolition charge. And . . . I have just activated it.'

'Well, that was pretty bloody stupid,' said Eddie. Was she telling the truth? She sounded sincere. 'Because you'll be next to it when it goes off.'

'There was always a chance that we would not return from this mission. We accepted that. It was worth it to wipe out those *creatures.*' She almost spat the word. 'Which will happen in . . . twenty-nine minutes.'

'Oh great, a ticking clock,' he said sarcastically, trying to hide his concern. 'You just got shot twice, and you must be losing blood – think you can stay conscious for that long?'

'Only I can stop the countdown. And there is no torture you can use to make me. But if you try anything and I am still awake, I will detonate it manually.'

He caught himself before saying, 'So what's stopping you?' There *was* nothing stopping her – and if she had to, she *would* push the button. He had to neutralise her. But how, without being gunned down himself?

Blindly hosing the tunnel with automatic fire wouldn't work. He had to be certain of killing her—

The dead man. If he had grenades, the stand-off would be over in moments. Wu would be killed, but nuclear bombs were precision instruments. Even a grenade explosion was more likely to damage than detonate.

'Macy,' he whispered, pointing to the dead man's flashlight, 'grab that torch. Then go down into the room at the bottom and find Barney. He's hurt, but he should be able to look after you. He's near the wall on the right about halfway along.'

'What about the bad guys?' she said.

'They're all dead.' She made a frightened sound. 'Just . . . try not to look at them,' he said in a feeble attempt at reassurance.

It didn't work. 'Where's Mom?' Macy asked, even more afraid.

'Other side of the shaft. She's okay – I hope. Now, get the light and find Barney.'

'What about the bomb?'

'I'll sort out the bomb. Go on!'

He squeezed her hand. She reluctantly descended and picked up the torch, giving him a last look before continuing.

He waited for her to get clear, then searched the fallen soldier. 'Arse!' A spare mag, but no explosives. The nuke had obviously been more than enough.

No weapons – but maybe the Chinese could provide a *defence* . . .

Nina overcame her shock at the Nephilim's recovery and swung the spar—

Sidona whipped up an arm to intercept it.

The metal rang with the impact, the priestess screaming and scrabbling backwards. Damn it! Her expanded senses had felt the life within the pillar – and warned her the intruder was there. Nina swung at her again, catching her shoulder. The key clanked to the floor.

Sidona jumped up, towering over her attacker. Her physical presence alone made Nina waver, but she swept her weapon at the Nephilim's knee. Sidona twisted away, the strike only glancing, but enough to cut her skin.

The giant's mouth curled into a pained snarl. She charged at her opponent. Nina tried to dodge, but Sidona used her sheer reach to backhand her hard in the face – then grab her ponytail.

Nina shrieked as she was hauled off the floor by her hair. She felt strands snapping, her own weight tearing hard at her scalp. She flailed the bar at her attacker's arm. It hit her elbow, drawing blood – but too late to stop Sidona from hurling her off the ledge.

She screamed as she fell—

Her cry was cut off as she slammed down on the spiralling path fifteen feet below.

But she was not safe. Her legs were over the edge, tipping her into another fall—

She dropped to a lower turn of the pathway. Her left knee hit the crystal with hammer-blow force. Another scream, but she managed to roll against the wall beneath one of the frozen figures.

An angry exclamation from above – and Sidona started down the spiral to finish the job.

Nina looked around. Where was her weapon?

An echoing clang gave her the answer. The spar had fallen all the way to the bottom of the chamber.

'God damn it,' she snarled, tasting blood. Pain coursed through her knee, and the back of her head burned where her ponytail had almost been ripped from her skull. But she forced herself back to her feet. She had no choice. If she didn't fight, Sidona would kill her.

But how could she defeat a foe almost twice her size?

Memories rushed back: Eddie training her in martial arts, many years previously. After her experiences in the hunt for Atlantis, where she had been forced into cooperation by more physically powerful adversaries, the lingering humiliation had made her want to protect herself. She was far short of Eddie's combat prowess, and had not actively trained for some time, but could still deliver a bloody nose to anyone who underestimated her.

The problem was, she couldn't even *reach* Sidona's nose . . .

She clenched her fists, then straightened, facing up the slope. The priestess pounded down it. Nina started towards her. Bad idea. Her knee flared again. She could hardly walk, never mind run . . .

Let her come to you. Let her think you can't *fight* . . .

She let out a loud gasp, stumbling on her aching leg. It was an exaggeration, though not by much. Sidona seemed taken in, however. A cruel half-smile came to the Nephilim's face as she rounded the spiral and charged at the smaller woman—

Nina threw herself at the giant's feet.

Sidona was too close and moving too quickly to draw either leg back into a kick. All she could do was jump awkwardly over the unexpected obstacle, stumbling as her feet came down behind her opponent.

Nina swung around. She *did* have the chance to kick – and

drove her boot's toecap against Sidona's ankle.

Giant or not, Nephilim anatomy matched a human's, the same spots just as vulnerable. Sidona shrieked, staggering – and Nina sprang up and body-slammed her at hip height.

Sidona sailed over the edge with a scream—

She hit the path thirty feet below, her right leg folding with a hideous crack of breaking bone. The impact flung her away from the chamber's inner wall – and she plummeted all the way to its floor. Her terrified cry ended sharply as her skull burst against the unyielding crystal.

Panting, Nina looked down. The crimson spray around Sidona's body told her the high priestess was no longer a threat. But the events she had set in motion were still a colossal danger. They had to be stopped.

She limped back up the slope – seeing to her alarm that the resurrection was well under way. The crystalline threads holding every entombed Nephilim were starting to shrink. She only had minutes before facing an entire army . . .

Leg throbbing, she finally reached the ledge. The key lay on the floor near the tracker. The device's laptop displayed the world map, the lines of earth energy flowing through the planet—

And the Chinese weapon's target.

Her breath froze in her throat. The Mandarin was unreadable, but the crosshairs were fixed upon a location she recognised instantly. The eastern seaboard of North America, a third of the way down the United States from the Canadian border . . .

New York. Her home.

The pain in Wu's shoulder and arm almost overwhelmed her, and Chase was right: she was losing blood. But she refused to submit. Even if it cost her her life, she would carry out her self-appointed mission – to burn every last one of the Nephilim monsters from the earth.

She heard rustling noises. Was the Englishman searching Liu's body? He hadn't been carrying any grenades, but Chase could still use his gun to double his firepower. Could she withstand an attack?

If she couldn't . . . her mission might fail. Maybe she *should* detonate the bomb manually, while she still could . . .

She shifted position to see the control panel. It was set into the boxy protrusion, a twenty-button keypad glowing softly beside the main activation switch. A small LED display showed the timer. It flicked down to twenty-eight minutes. The two minutes already gone had felt like an eternity. Again, maddeningly, Chase was right. She wouldn't stay conscious until the end.

So the end would have to come sooner.

A six-digit code was needed to switch the detonator from the timer to manual control. Once correctly entered, all she had to do was flick the switch. She started to tap it into the keypad—

Noise from the tunnel. Chase was moving.

Two digits left, but she didn't have time to put them in. A figure lunged around the corner into her spotlight—

She fired – but it wasn't Chase.

Eddie hauled the dead man from the floor, awkwardly holding the corpse in front of his body. 'Come on, Bernie,' he muttered as he brought his ungainly cargo to the corner – and swung out into the open.

Wu's MP7 fired. Bullets smacked into the human shield's torso, making it twitch and flail – but some of the armour-piercing rounds penetrated to hit the man behind.

Eddie cried out as he felt searing metal tear into his chest. He lurched back – but saw the glaring tactical light over the corpse's shoulder. He aimed his gun to the side of the dazzling spot and held down the trigger—

A scream, abruptly cut off – and Wu's fire stopped. The light reeled away from him and clattered to the floor.

His gun fell silent. He dropped the body and staggered forward. The Chinese woman lay on her back behind the bomb. Blood covered her neck and chin. She was not dead, red bubbles swelling and bursting in her mouth with each wheezing breath.

He kicked Wu's weapon clear of her twitching hand. His furious burst of fire had stitched a line diagonally across her chest, blood flowing from ragged wounds. She would not be alive for long without medical help – which he had no intention of giving.

Instead he crouched to examine the weapon. A display showed the timer ticking down. Below it was an illuminated keypad . . . with every key blank.

'You're fucking *kidding* me,' he growled. Without knowing the function of each button, all he could do was tap in random codes, running the risk of triggering an anti-tampering system – and detonating the bomb. 'How do I stop it?'

'You . . . can't,' Wu gurgled.

'You can, though.'

'But I will . . . not.'

'Let's try again.' He jammed his thumb into one of her bullet wounds. She screamed, squirming. '*How* do I stop the bomb?'

Her reply came in strained, venomous Mandarin. He didn't need to understand the language to know she was not being cooperative. He withdrew. She gasped, spitting blood.

The special forces operative had been trained to resist torture, as he had. It was impossible to hold out for ever – sooner or later, everyone broke – but he doubted he could bring her to that point in just twenty-seven minutes, even if she lived that long.

He straightened for another look at the panel, only to wince at the pain in his own chest. At least three rounds had hit him. Their journey through the soldier's body had robbed them of most of their energy, but they had still had enough force to tear into his flesh. His clothing felt sticky – he was bleeding. He needed to see how badly he had been hurt; he couldn't afford to pass out halfway through disarming the nuke. He turned towards the light—

Wu stabbed at the keypad. A bleep as her finger hit a button. She tried to enter the last digit – only for Eddie to crack his empty gun against her forehead so hard it slammed her into an unconsciousness from which she would never emerge. 'That's for hitting my little girl, you fucking bitch.'

He dropped his weapon and retrieved hers, using its light to examine his wounds. Three bullet hits; two were painful but relatively superficial, buried in his pectoral muscles. The third was deeper, having tunnelled into the flesh at the left side of his chest beneath his arm. Every movement produced a sharp, burning pain.

All he could do for now was endure it. He squeezed his arm against the injury to compress it, grimacing as nerve endings flared, then turned back to the cylinder. Bomb defusal – including various nuclear devices – had been part of his SAS training, and it wasn't the first time he had been face to face with a live nuke. He still had a large scar from the crude but effective method he'd used to prevent another from exploding: jamming his arm into the explosive-propelled piston acting as a detonator.

He pulled away the canvas. That approach wouldn't work this time. He didn't recognise the bomb type, and the drum containing the warhead was sealed by heavy-duty bolts and screws with special star-shaped slots that a normal screwdriver would be unable to turn. The only apparent weak point was the detonator itself, the box on the cylinder's side. It too was attached by nonstandard screws – but there was a narrow gap where its case was not quite flush against the bomb.

He shone the light inside. A skein of wires was visible a

couple of inches in, entering a small hole in the bomb casing. Could he cut them?

He took out the Leatherman and unfolded the blades. He was not after the longest this time, but the thinnest. It was just over two inches long – barely enough to reach the wires.

Eddie was all too aware that cutting them could trip a booby trap. But he had little choice. In twenty-six minutes, the bomb would explode no matter what. 'Okay,' he said. 'Live nuke. No pressure . . .'

He slipped the narrow blade into the gap, wincing at a stab of pain from his chest, then probed deeper. The blade's tip brushed the wires. There was less than a centimetre of play before the Leatherman's grip would jam against the bomb casing. Did he have enough room to cut them?

He moved the knife above the wires, then forced it in as far as it would go. If he brought it downwards, it would hopefully catch the skein – and cut through it.

And then he would know if the bomb was booby-trapped. Although possibly only for a millisecond . . .

He took a deep breath, steadying his hand – and brought the blade down.

It caught on the wires. He kept pulling until they drew taut. The moment of truth. Any more pressure would cut the first wire.

He applied it.

A faint metallic *tink* – and the blade was through.

Eddie exhaled. One down. He pushed again. A second wire was severed, then a third. He was still here, along with everything around him. Keep going—

Another *tink* – followed immediately by a shrill bleep from the control panel.

'Shit!' His hands froze, eyes darting to the display. Still twenty-five minutes to go—

The timer changed. *Fifteen* minutes.

He didn't know if it was an anti-tamper system or a glitch. Either way, ten minutes of his safety margin had just vanished. He withdrew the blade—

It brushed the severed wires – shorting them out.

Bleep!

Five minutes remaining.

Eddie stared in horror as the numbers remorselessly ticked down. 'Buggeration and fuckery!'

45

'Oh my God,' Nina gasped, staring at the laptop screen. The Chinese qi weapon was locked on to Manhattan. Zan's doing, it had to be – the Nephilim had asked him to choose a target that would deliver the maximum shock and awe. He had in turn picked the city that both embodied modern human civilisation and represented the cultural capital of America. Even as a traitor to China, he had not selected his own country for destruction.

She collected the key, then moved to where Sidona had sat, stretching her arms so she could both hold the key against the nexus above and reach the crystal within the tracker. Touching the pillar had been almost overwhelming; with the device boosting its power, she had no idea what to expect . . .

Her mind exploded into another dimension.

It felt as if some great force was thrusting her up, up, through the rock and out of Uluru and high into the sky. The entire world spread out before her. She travelled with the flow, surfing the coursing channels of earth energy at the speed of thought. Everything was visible, felt more than seen . . .

Something raw rubbed at her psyche. The tracker. The Chinese scientists had created a machine that could interact with the currents of qi, but there was no grace or finesse to it, the device instead stabbing a hook into the other world to cling on like a parasite. Nina brought her attention to the unpleasant interloper. Could she use it to *will* the impending disaster to stop?

No. The machine might now be part of the network of energy, but it did not control it. Even with the boost it provided, it could only reshape what was already there.

But she could sense what *was* there: the ever-building eruption Sidona had brought into being, directing several flows into a single spot as she had in Xinengyuan, but on a far greater scale.

Sidona had built it – so now Nina had to tear it down.

If she could.

She reached into the flow, imaginary hands sweeping one line of energy away from the confluence, then another. Even with the tracker's aid, it was almost a physical strain, her entire mind focused upon the task. What little perception remained of her immediate surroundings vanished. All she could now see was the churning, seething mass of power rising up beneath her home. Little by little, she redirected the channels of force feeding it . . .

She couldn't do it fast enough. The confluence had reached critical mass, becoming a black hole that drew more and more energy into its vortex.

She couldn't stop the approaching cataclysm.

Below her, the crystal chamber was silent – until a gasp cut through the air.

Eyes closed for millennia snapped open. The warrior whose resurrection had begun earlier drew air into his long-unused lungs. His stasis had left him perfectly preserved, not a single cell decayed since the People of the Tree had forced him into his crystal prison. His last waking memory was still fresh, his captors watching impassively as darkness swallowed him. He looked around in anger. Where were they?

Nobody was there. Only his people, now greater in number, trapped as he had been.

He clumsily freed himself from the recess. What was going on? Why was he awake, and no one else? He slowly stood—

And saw bodies upon the floor of the great chamber.

A woman had been torn apart by some force more savage than a baraka. A priestess? More captives nearby had suffered the same fate, their tormented sleep brought to a cruel and abrupt end.

But there was another woman there – one he knew.

Sidona.

The high priestess, the queen of the Nephilim, was dead. She had fallen – or been thrown – from somewhere on high, her skull smashed like an egg. But her features were intact enough for him to recognise her. Rage quickly replaced shock. Her blood was still wet. Who had done this?

He looked up. A shadowy form was discernible on a crystal ledge at the summit of the chamber. Sidona's murderer.

He had no weapons other than his hands – but they were all he needed. Fists clenched so tightly his tendons strained, he hurried up the spiral path.

Nina almost released the crystals in despair. She couldn't stop the earth energy surge from exploding . . .

But, she suddenly realised, she could *move* it.

The focal point was beneath Lower Manhattan. She knew her hometown well enough almost to pinpoint the block, in Tribeca – but it was less than a mile from the waters surrounding the island. She brought her illusory hands back into the flow, now not so much trying to dam as divert it. Sweep the maelstrom clear, a little at a time . . .

Sidona had forced the channels of energy away from their natural paths to create the confluence. Some seemed almost eager to return to where they belonged, pulling the seething force with them. Nina followed the path of least resistance, even though this drew it roughly southwards over land rather than directly towards the Hudson River.

She could *feel* the people around it – all the lives that would end if she failed. And they now knew that something was happening. The enormous power swelling beneath the earth was affecting the city above, buildings shaking, static discharges crackling through the air. Panic spread through the streets.

Her streets. She had lived in Lower Manhattan for the first three decades of her life. Now she was the only person who could save it.

Even with the Chinese machine expanding the limits of the possible, it felt like trying to redirect a tornado with a hand fan. Her actions were having an effect, but frustratingly slowly. Everything she did brought it that little bit closer to the water, though. *Keep moving—*

A warning at the back of her mind. Something had happened – not halfway around the globe, but close by. Inside Uluru. A change in the energy within the crystal pillar, a life resuming . . .

She couldn't afford to withdraw from her task to investigate. The confluence was at bursting point. Appallingly, she realised it was near the site of the former World Trade Center: Ground Zero, now a memorial garden that had left her in tears on more than one visit. *Not again*, she swore. It was *not* going to happen again!

Her determination strengthened her grasp on the intangible. She guided it clear of the park, beneath buildings, towards the waterfront. The pent-up energy started to escape; bolts lanced up into the sky, a display heralding the approaching destruction. Almost at the river, almost there—

It reached water, but she couldn't stop. She had to get the confluence as far from land as possible – but the Hudson and Upper Bay were swarming with water traffic, commercial vessels and tourist boats rounding Manhattan's photogenic southern tip. There would be casualties, no matter what. Her only hope was that any captain seeing the unnatural display would turn away at full speed . . .

She guided the disturbance onwards. It was now roughly equidistant between Manhattan and Liberty Island, in open water but still less than a mile from either. She tried to force it south-wards into the wider bay, but she was out of time—

Nina used every remaining ounce of her willpower to hold the confluence in check, desperately trying to prevent the inevitable for a few more seconds.

It wasn't enough.

Ten and a half thousand miles away, the planet's raw power finally erupted in a massive burst. The effect was like the detonation of a nuclear device at the bottom of the Hudson.

Unimaginable energies flashed water to steam, blinding bolts of impossibly coloured lightning stabbing skywards as the blast kicked up a huge circular wall of water. It rushed outwards, consuming boats before smashing into land.

The flat, mostly artificial Ellis Island was all but obliterated, visitors to the Museum of Immigration suffering horrific casual-ties as waves demolished the historic building. Tourists on Liberty Island were also swept screaming into the bay, though the Statue of Liberty itself, high on its plinth, took only minor damage.

The same could not be said for New York, or Jersey City across the Hudson. The towering wave pounded both cities, overwhelming tidal defences and sending deadly tsunamis across parks and down streets. People were carried away by the force of the water, cars and buses and trucks dragged from the roads, subway lines and road tunnels flooded.

Then the cataclysmic release of earth energy faded to nothing, spent. The waves slowed, fell, retreated . . .

Leaving devastation in their wake.

★ ★ ★

The explosive release hit Nina almost like a physical blow, knocking her backwards – and cutting her link to the nether-world. She sat stunned for a moment, before scrambling back to the machine. What had happened to New York? She had to know . . .

She put her hands back against the crystals, re-entering the parallel world. It was instantly clear that the eruption had taken place: the *pressure*, the feeling of unimaginable forces straining to burst loose, was gone. She followed the paths back around the world to her hometown . . .

It was bad. The explosion had left a deep scar, severing the earth energy flows in a way that might take months or years to recover. Bringing her alternate senses closer, she found that in places where there had been life, now there was little, or none. A chill ran through her. She had failed. Hundreds of people had died, thousands injured . . .

But far fewer than Gadreel and Sidona had planned. They had meant to obliterate the entire city, killing *millions*. And now Sidona was dead – and with her, any hopes her husband had of using her powers against the rest of humanity.

Except that Sidona's last act had been to begin the resurrection of her people. There were women amongst the imprisoned Nephilim; if any were priestesses, they would have the same ability to control earth energy. Nina snapped her mind's eye with dizzying speed back to Uluru. She had to stop the process – or reverse it, returning the giants to their eternal sleep.

The chamber took on ethereal form around her. Throughout it, she sensed the tiny jewels of frozen consciousnesses – but now they were starting to thaw as the prisoners crept towards wakefulness—

One had already awoken.

And was right behind her.

★ ★ ★

Macy fearfully picked her way through the huge cathedral-like chamber. Her father's warning had been true: the bad guys, on both sides, were indeed all dead. She tried to follow his advice by not looking at the bodies, but they were scattered everywhere. The only way not to see them was to look down at her feet, and change direction if anything bad came into view.

Smoke wafted through the space, stinking like rotten eggs. Light from the giant crystal pillar came through a big archway, but the haze turned it the sickly shade of orange soda. She knew she shouldn't go towards it; she had to find Mr Jungala.

On the right, halfway along, Dad had said. She angled in that direction, raising her gaze. No sign of him – but she did see a dead Nephilim, sprawled against a rock. She cringed in revulsion and looked down again.

Something glinted on the floor. She recognised it – a trikan. The Nephilim must have dropped it. Conflicting feelings ran through her: leave it alone, or take it? There was the ick factor that it had come from a dead man, but on the other hand, it would make her feel safer. Even though it was much larger than the Atlantean one, sized for someone ten feet tall, she still felt confident she could handle it.

She hesitated, then picked it up. The handgrip was so large she could barely close her fingers around it, and the whole weapon weighed several pounds. But she felt an odd sense of *connection*, as if she knew exactly what it would do if she threw it – or rather, it would know what she *wanted* it to do.

Whatever; it really *did* make her feel safer. A little. Her confidence boosted, she moved on.

Drifting smoke wafted past, making her cough and obscuring the view ahead. But she was not far from the chamber's right wall, and nearly halfway along. Still no sign of the ranger. Dad had said he was hurt; maybe he'd passed out?

If he had, she needed to help him. 'Mr Jungala?' she called softly.

No answer. She advanced, repeating his name—

A low voice from the fog ahead. 'Hey! Is that you, girl?'

'Yeah, it's me, Macy!' she replied with relief. 'Where are you? I can't see much. Are you okay?'

'I'm good. What about you?'

'I'm fine – but Dad needs your help.'

A pained chuckle. 'I don't think I'm in any state to—'

The whooshing crackle of a Nephilim spear weapon cut him off – followed an instant later by a wet, explosive thump.

Macy froze, petrified. 'M-Mr Jungala?'

A figure emerged from the smoke. But it wasn't the Australian.

Gadreel stepped into the open, a qigun in his hands. He looked down at her, almost expressionless, as if he couldn't even be bothered to feel contempt.

She stared back, a bird hypnotised by a cobra – then remembered she was not helpless. The trikan was heavy in her hand. She swung it back, feeling the bladed disc start to spin inside its guard, then whipped up her arm to send it at the Nephilim—

The spear thrust at her. Its ovoid head caught the trikan just as it left the handgrip, knocking it to the floor. Before she could recover, Gadreel struck again, hitting her wrist and jolting the grip from her hand. She cried out, clutching her arm.

The giant said something she didn't understand, but she knew the tone: he was mocking her. She turned and tried to run, but had barely gone two steps before he grabbed her shoulder. She tried to pull free, but he was too strong.

He regarded her with a calculating expression, then shouldered his qigun and bent to collect the fallen trikan. A flick of his wrist, and the weapon snapped back into place inside the handgrip. He hauled her arm above her head as he rose to his full height, then pulled her towards the archway.

★ ★ ★

Nina was torn out of contact with the crystal pillar before she could react to the Nephilim warrior's appearance. The key flew from her hand and fell from the ledge as he threw her to the floor.

Dazed, she tried to get clear. The naked giant was too fast, catching her arm in his huge hand and flinging her across the ledge. She bowled towards the drop—

She slapped her splayed palms against the smooth crystal surface, halting herself right on the precipice. The contact for an instant linked her with the other world, but she forced herself back to reality.

It had *seemed* like an instant to her. But it had been a second, or more. The Nephilim suddenly skip-framed closer as he charged at her—

And kicked her over the edge.

Nina fell, landing hard on the spiral below. She caromed off it and tumbled down again, and again, each touchdown like being trampled by a football team. All she could do was try to protect her head as she fell past the ranks of reviving prisoners—

She slammed down on her back. The pain was so intense she almost passed out. The chamber swam around her. She was about thirty feet above the entrance, Sidona and the other dead Nephilim below.

She also spotted the key. It had landed not far from her, perched at the edge of the path.

Nina knew she had to keep it from Gadreel – but she also needed to use it first. The sleepers had to be returned to their endless night. But she couldn't reach the tracker, not with the warrior in her way—

She didn't *need* to reach the tracker. The realisation was as clear and sharp as ice water. The device was connected to the great crystal pillar, now part of the network of earth energy – and

550

when she used the resurrection key, she would be too. She would be able to amplify her ability to manipulate the power without being in direct contact with the machine.

She hoped.

A look up. The warrior stared back at her from on high. He saw she was not dead, and started to run down the spiral.

Nina crawled down the slope. Pain crackled through her spine, one leg blazing as if someone had driven a chisel into the bone. Blood ran from her nose. Rippling darkness encroached on her vision. She forced herself onwards. She had to reach the key, or she would die – and before long, all the Nephilim survivors, including the innocents, would suffer the same fate at the hands of the frightened human race.

The warrior continued his looping descent. Much closer, she saw the crystalline tendrils holding a Nephilim child start to melt away. The prisoners would soon recover – and once they did, there was nothing she could do to stop them.

The key was almost in reach. She dragged herself closer—

Got it.

Not knowing what to do next, she acted on instinct, pressing it with her palm against the crystal wall beneath the child.

The hidden dimension of energy surrounded her. She was still firmly connected to reality, though; her pain did not lessen. She forced herself to push through the torment of cracked bones and torn muscles to concentrate on her task.

She had to reverse the resurrection process. But how?

The thought alone was enough. She *willed* it, and it happened. Energy flowed through the web of crystal fibres surrounding each Nephilim captive, suspending every cell in their bodies in a state of perfect stasis – but that flow's force had been fading to nothing. Now, as she redirected the currents, it began to rise again.

She held the thought, feeling the pricklings of consciousness around her sink back into sleep. It was working – the resurrection had been reversed. But there was something else she had to do. What was it?

A memory of Gadreel's sarcophagus came to her. The gas. Somehow, she sensed a source of the toxic yellow miasma above her, produced within Uluru itself by a process she didn't understand or have time to think about. All she knew was that she had to release it—

It happened. The energy flow shifted, tripping some Veteres-made mechanism – and the gas began to gush into the top of the chamber.

The mechanism was linked to another. The large door at the chamber's entrance began to lower, starting to seal it off from the rest of the chasm.

And she was still inside.

The thought snapped her back to reality. She withdrew the key and struggled to stand. The door inched shut. She had to get to it before it closed – or the gas reached her.

She looked up. A vile yellow cloud roiled downwards, already past the top ledge and swallowing the uppermost ranks of prisoners. The running warrior reacted in surprise as he saw it—

The fog reached him. He gasped, staggering – and fell over the edge.

He hit the side of the path two orbits below, neck snapping with a horrific crack. His limp body rebounded into the chamber's open centre, falling another thirty feet before smashing down on the spiral – right above Nina.

She tried to run, but her battered body was slow to respond. The Nephilim's broken corpse tumbled over the side – straight at her—

The punishing impact swept her from the ledge. She fell – on to a glassy stalagmite on the lower turn.

It stabbed through her left calf like a spear. She screamed –

then her breath was pounded out as the dead warrior landed on top of her. Another spike punched through his torso, pinning him in place.

Nina gasped for air. His weight bore down relentlessly on her chest. She pushed, but he didn't move. Darkness closed in again.

The door was still lowering, the gas drifting downwards. She turned her head towards the entrance, hoping against hope that Eddie or Cheng would appear to help her—

Instead, she saw Gadreel marching across the bridge.

The horror of utter defeat hit her. He was not alone.

He had Macy, gripping her raised wrist. His baraka was slung over one shoulder, a trikan in his other hand. Shock crossed his face as he saw his wife's body – then rage as he spotted Nina.

His march became a run, dragging Macy with him.

Nina tried again to move, but only managed a breathless scream as her wounded leg muscles strained and tore. The dead Nephilim still trapped her. Panicked, she tried to focus. How could she stop Gadreel – and save herself?

She belatedly realised that she was still clutching the resurrection key, forgotten in her agony.

She looked back at the entrance. To either side of the bridge was a sheer drop to infinity. If she threw the key over the edge, Gadreel would have no way to revive his people.

She drew back her arm as far as she could. No choice but to endure the pain as the movement twisted her impaled leg. Line up, and – *throw*!

The key arced through the opening. Even in her weakened state, she had lobbed it far enough to clear the ledge. It dropped towards the void—

Gadreel released Macy and swung his own arm at lightning speed. The trikan flashed from its grip, spinning across the bridge . . .

And swerving in mid-air.

It swooped out from the crossing to intercept the falling key. A *clang* as metal struck metal – and the key was knocked back onto the ledge. The trikan returned to its owner, clanking into the handguard.

Nina stared in disbelief at the ancient weapon's impossible manoeuvre. Macy had been right all along. The trikan really *could* be controlled by someone capable of channelling earth energy, steered by the unseen force levitating it. She owed her daughter an apology . . .

If she survived long enough to offer it.

The door was now almost halfway closed, the gas still rolling down towards it. In less than a minute, Nina would be entombed – and suffocated. But even with the key, Gadreel could not stop the process himself.

Which meant he had to use her instead. And with Macy as his hostage, she would have no choice but to obey.

46

Gadreel hurried across the bridge towards the crystal chamber. He dropped the trikan and unshouldered his spear, then retrieved the key and released Macy. Key in one hand, baraka in the other, he went to the foot of the metal walkway and shouted. Zan responded, dazed; Nina had forgotten the translator was there. The Nephilim impatiently pulled the Chinese man with him under the slowly descending door. He noted the gas with concern, then stood before Nina, weapon aimed up at her as he spoke.

Still unsteady, Zan translated for him. 'Lord Gadreel orders you to use the resurrection key to wake his people.'

'Tell Lord Gadreel that he can go fuck himself,' Nina growled back.

Zan didn't need to relay her words; her attitude was enough for Gadreel to understand. He scowled, then tossed the key beside Nina and aimed his spear through the doorway at the terrified Macy. Again, Zan's translation skills were unnecessary.

'You son of a bitch,' Nina spat.

The Nephilim leader spoke: a single sharp word at a time. A countdown.

Zan hurriedly caught up. 'He will kill her in three, two—'

She snatched up the key. The action made her moan in pain, but it was not merely physical. She had gambled and lost, and now she was out of options.

Except . . .

Nina looked back up at Gadreel, suddenly determined – then placed the key firmly against the floor. The parallel world of earth energy swallowed her.

'Mom!' Macy cried as her wounded mother went into a trance. 'Don't do it! You can't let him win!'

But Nina didn't respond. The ten-year-old stared helplessly at the scene, watching the door edge down and guessing from Zan's nervous upwards glances that there was some other danger coming closer. She wanted to run, but was too scared – Gadreel was still pointing his spear at her.

Her gaze found the abandoned trikan. Only feet away – but she didn't dare move towards it. If Gadreel was distracted, she might be able to reach the weapon, but right now, she was trapped—

She flinched at a flash inside the chamber. Gadreel and Zan also reacted with surprise. Another burst of light, and this time she saw the source: what looked like a tiny lightning bolt crackling across the crystal wall. Another followed, larger, then another – this one *outside* the pillar.

The Nephilim barked a command to Zan. The translator stammered a reply, then started towards Macy. 'Professor Wilde!' he said. 'If you don't stop whatever you're doing, Lord Gadreel has told me to – to throw your daughter into the pit!'

Macy wanted to run, but Gadreel's spear was still raised. Zan emerged from the chamber and advanced on her—

A frantic howl from above – and Cheng leapt down from the walkway at his countryman.

He hit Zan feet-first, kicking him hard in the back. The student landed heavily, but the translator's own touchdown would be far harder. The blow propelled him over the edge, sending him shrieking into the unseen depths kilometres below.

Cheng's unexpected appearance caught Gadreel by surprise. He whipped his weapon towards the new arrival – then saw Macy lunge for the fallen trikan. He swept the spear after her, thumb poised over the trigger crystal—

Liquid energy flashed across the chamber right in front of him. He jerked back – then whirled to face Nina. Shocked realisation crossed his face: she was doing here what Sidona had done to a whole city, creating a surge of earth energy that would build to an explosive release.

His baraka came up at her—

Macy flung the trikan with a yell of pure protective rage.

The bladed disc sliced through the air, curving beneath the chamber's still-closing door . . . then angling back up as she *willed* it to save her mother.

It homed in – and hit.

Gadreel roared as the trikan, blades glowing with earth energy, hacked his hand off at the wrist in a spray of blood. The spear clanked to the floor, his fist still clenched around it. He staggered back, clutching at the spouting stump—

The walls came alive with seething, roiling power – then a bolt as thick as a tree trunk lanced out from beneath Nina and blasted the Nephilim leader in the chest.

The impact's explosive force sent him hurtling out through the opening and over the precipice beyond. His entire body wreathed in flames, he plummeted into the void with a long, echoing scream of defeat.

Macy stared after him in shock – then dropped the trikan and ran into the pillar. 'Mom!' she cried. 'Cheng, help me!'

He limped after her around the spiral's first leg. She saw the gas cloud falling towards them. 'What *is* that?'

'Bad!' Cheng replied. The toxic yellow miasma would reach Nina in seconds. They got to her first. He saw the spike through her leg – and the dead giant pinning her in place. 'We've got to move him off her!'

'Oh God,' Macy moaned, cringing – but she still strained to help him lift the impaled corpse.

Nina released the key, gasping in pain – then saw the young pair and reacted in horror. 'No! What are you doing? Get out, get *out*!'

'I'm not leaving you, Mom!' cried Macy. She tugged desperately at the Nephilim's arm as Cheng crouched to lever his body upwards. Blood gushed from the body's wounds, flowing over the glowing surface underfoot. 'Come on!'

'You've got to leave me! There isn't time – you'll die as well!'

'You're *not going to die*!' Macy shouted back. Her voice was nothing like her father's, but to Nina she had never sounded more like him. The gas cloud reached the level above, sickly tendrils wisping downwards as if clutching for their prey. 'We can do it!'

Her daughter's utter conviction and determination sparked Nina's own. Despite the pain, she pushed at the giant with all her remaining strength. All three of them gasped and growled, straining – then the Nephilim came free, his dead weight sending him slithering over the bloodied edge to land with a crack of bones below.

'This is going to hurt, sorry!' said Cheng. Before Nina could respond, he pulled her wounded leg sharply from the spike. She screamed. He and Macy tried to support her – but like the warrior, her own weight dragged her over the slick side.

She fell, screaming again – and landed hard on the Nephilim's corpse.

'Mom!' Macy cried, running down the crystalline ramp to her. 'Are you okay?'

'No, I'm – fricking not!' Nina managed to gasp. She crawled off the dead giant, Macy taking her arm to help her. The gap under the door was now only three feet high and shrinking every second. 'Go on, go – get out!'

'Not without you!' Macy dragged her mother across the floor. 'Cheng, come on!'

Cheng moved to jump down – then swayed as his vertigo returned, stepping back—

He slipped on the Nephilim's blood – and tumbled down the slope.

His flailing ankle struck a jagged crystal spike. The *snap* of fracturing bone was clear even across the chamber.

'Cheng!' cried Macy. She shoved Nina through the shrinking opening, then started to run back to him—

Nina grabbed her. 'No! You won't reach him – you'll *both* die!'

'Mom, no!' She tried to break free. 'We can save him! We can—'

'Macy!' Nina pulled her daughter forcefully to her. 'You. Will. *Die*. I won't let that happen. Never.'

'No!' Macy wailed again – but she knew her mother was right.

They both stared helplessly as Cheng tried to stand, only for his injured leg to give way. The gas cloud passed the ledge where Nina had been trapped, a vaporous hammer about to crush him . . .

Then, unexpectedly, he looked back at them – face alight with hope. He dragged himself to an empty recess. 'What are you doing?' Nina shouted.

'I can put myself into stasis!' Cheng called back, excitement plain even through the pain in his voice.

'You're crazy! You don't even know if it'll work!' The gap shrank to a foot, then inches.

'You started the process, so it should keep going – but I don't have much choice now, do I?' He dropped back against the glowing crystal. 'And . . . I really *am* going to become a part of history!'

'Cheng, no!' Nina cried – but then door met floor with a sonorous thud. The light filtering through the crystal wall took on a yellow tinge as the gas finally filled the chamber.

Macy gazed wide-eyed at the barrier. 'Oh no. Oh no,' she whispered. 'Is . . . is he dead?'

'I don't know,' Nina answered truthfully. 'But maybe some day, a long time from now . . . somebody will find out.'

A noise behind them. She looked around in alarm – was it Nephilim survivors, or the Chinese special forces team? But relief flooded through her when she saw Eddie lumbering across the bridge, a sub-machine gun with a tactical light held awkwardly in one hand as he carried a heavy barrel-like object in both arms. 'Eddie! Oh thank God, you're okay!'

He carefully put down the cylinder and hurried to his family. 'Been better. Jesus, though – so have you!' he added on seeing her leg wound. 'Macy, put pressure on it, both sides. Try to stop the bleeding.'

Macy did so, though she still had time for sarcasm. '*Hi*, Dad.'

A faint smile. 'Sorry, love. Been a bit busy. Are you okay?' His face grew grim. 'I'm guessing you didn't find Barney.'

'No . . . Gadreel caught me.' She didn't need to say more to explain the Australian's fate.

Eddie muttered a curse. 'Where *is* Gadreel – and where's Cheng? What happened?'

'Cheng's . . . in there,' said Nina, gesturing at the now-sealed door. 'I don't know if he's alive or not – and it might be another hundred thousand years before anyone finds out. Gadreel's dead, though.' She pointed down the shaft. 'So's Zan. Well, they might not be – I don't know if they've hit bottom yet.'

'The deeper it is, the better,' he rumbled.

'What do you mean?'

He quickly returned to his erstwhile cargo. 'Major Wu

brought the Nephilim a little present to celebrate getting out of prison – a nuke.'

Nina's eyes popped wide. '*What?*'

'It's on a timer, and it's got . . . buggeration, two minutes left!'

'Can't you defuse it?'

'I tried. Didn't go well – it should have had *twenty*-two.'

'Oh, that's just super-fine! So now what do we do?'

He strained to lift the heavy bomb again. 'Chuck it down the hole and run like fuck! Sorry, Macy,' he added.

'Totally forgiven,' his suddenly pale-faced daughter assured him.

'What do you mean, chuck it down the hole?' said Nina. 'It'll still blow up! And even if I *could* run, which I can't, we can't outrun a nuclear explosion!'

'We'll have a couple of miles' head start by the look of it,' he replied, peering down to the great glowing pillar's vanishing point far below. 'And if we're lucky, the thing'll smash to bits when it hits the bottom!' He swung the nuke around – and before Nina or Macy could protest further, heaved it over the edge.

Nina stared after it in stunned dismay. 'I'm glad you're so confident about that.'

Macy was equally appalled, but for different reasons. 'Dad, you . . . you just threw a nuke into the middle of Uluru! It's a sacred site! The bomb'll have radioactive stuff in it – you'll poison the whole desert!'

'It'd be a lot more poisoned if it went off here rather than all the way down there,' Eddie pointed out. 'And since it's a sacred site, maybe the local spirits'll be good to us. But we don't have time to stand around arguing about it. We need to move.'

He returned to Nina and picked her up. She moaned as Macy released her hold on the wound. Eddie gave it a quick but practised look. 'The jeep should have a first-aid kit. I'll be able to patch it up until we can get you to a hospital.'

'If we can *get* to the jeep,' she countered.

'We'll know in about a minute and a half! Macy, come on.'

They started across the bridge as quickly as they could. Nina looked back as they reached the archway. The stunning secret of Uluru lay behind them: an enormous crystal pillar acting as a focal point for the earth's mysterious energy field, containing the last of a long-lost race, the fallen angels of biblical myth, trapped in suspended animation. They had survived undisturbed for hundreds of millennia; if the bomb did not destroy them, they might continue for at least as long again, perhaps one day awakening into a world she couldn't even imagine.

And now there would be a human with them, an unexpected hitchhiker on their journey through the ages. Based on *Homo sapiens'* seemingly relentless race towards self-destruction, she couldn't help feeling he would also be the *last* human – though at the same time she refused to be so pessimistic as to believe Cheng was already dead. She had to give him a chance, even if only in her mind. 'Goodbye, Cheng,' she whispered. 'A-plus from me, no question.'

Eddie entered the steep tunnel, blocking her view of the hidden wonder. She looked ahead as he used the gun's light to illuminate their way. 'How long have we got?'

He checked his watch. 'About forty seconds.' A pause, then he continued, with uncharacteristically exposed emotion: 'If it goes off, we . . . we won't have too long to worry about it. But I want you both to know, well . . .' A crooked grin at Nina. 'Ever since I first met you, all those years back? You've caused nowt but trouble.'

'Gee, thanks.' But she knew he was joking. Her eyes started to well with tears.

'You changed my life,' he went on. 'For the better. I've seen things nobody ever imagined, done things I never dreamed of doing – saved the world a few times an' all. I couldn't have done it without you. And I wouldn't have had the most amazing daughter in history either.'

'Aw, Dad,' said Macy, blushing despite the tension.

'Well, yeah, I kind of had to be involved in that part,' Nina said, smiling. 'And y'know, you changed my life too. If I hadn't met you – well, I'd have died seventeen years ago, so there's that! But . . .' She looked him in the eye, pulling herself a little closer. 'I don't need to tell you how I feel about you, do I? You already know.'

His own smile widened. 'Yeah, I know.'

'Plus,' she went on, more quickly, 'there's a limit to how many times I can say "I love you" in the next ten seconds!' She turned towards her daughter. 'But Macy, however long I had, I couldn't say it often enough. So just once'll have to do. I love you. I love you *both*, so much.'

Macy halted, grabbing them in as big an embrace as she could manage. 'I love you both too!' She squeezed her face against them, muttering under her breath, 'We're *not* gonna die, we're *not* gonna die, we're *not* . . .'

Eddie kissed Nina, the couple in a moment reliving every other they had ever shared. Then they closed their eyes, holding their daughter to them—

Nothing happened.

Seconds passed. Eddie cautiously opened an eye and peered at his watch. 'We're five seconds past . . . ten seconds . . .' He looked back, listening for any sounds echoing up the tunnel. Only silence reached his ears. 'The conventional explosives didn't go off . . .'

Macy nervously detached herself from her parents. 'What does that mean?'

'Nukes use normal explosives to trigger the main bomb. If they'd blown up, we would have heard it – which means the bomb really did smash to bits.' He sighed in relief.

'So . . . we're safe?' Nina asked.

'From getting blown up, yeah. We still need to get you to hospital, though. Actually, I think we *all* need to get to hospital!' He set off again, bearing his wounded wife up the long tunnel with their daughter beside them.

They were roughly halfway back to the surface when Macy gave Nina a sly smile that again reminded her of Eddie. 'So, Mom . . . I was right, wasn't I?'

'About what, honey?'

'About the trikan. Back on the ship, three years ago – I *told* you I could steer it just by thinking about it! You didn't believe me, but I was right!'

'Yes,' Nina told her through a wide fake smile. 'You were.'

Eddie chuckled.

'*And* I was right about the skull on the side of Uluru. I bet all those other things I told you about that you said were garbage are true as well—'

'Okay, *yes*, you win, I suck at archaeology!' said Nina, exasperated.

Her husband laughed. 'Never thought I'd hear you say that.'

'It's poetic justice, I'm sure. I spent my whole career showing the archaeological establishment they were wrong by proving that ancient legends were real, and now my little girl's doing the same thing to me. Damn, I must have been insufferable.'

Eddie smirked. 'I'm saying nothing.'

She narrowed her eyes. 'Don't make me regret saying that I love you. Now, can we go home?'

His only reply was another laugh.

They continued up the steep slope. After what seemed like an age, a faint sheen of daylight became discernible ahead. 'Finally,' muttered Eddie. 'Just a bit further, and we're done.'

'Not quite,' said his wife. 'There's one more thing we need to do.'

'What?' Macy asked.

'We're now the only people in the world who know what's hidden inside Uluru. I think it should stay that way. Once we're outside, we need to close the entrance. Nobody should ever find the Nephilim again – so they won't try to wipe us out, and we won't try to wipe *them* out. Let them sleep. Maybe their time will come in another hundred millennia.'

'Bit hard on Sandra and Barney's families,' said Eddie. 'We can't tell them what happened.'

'I know. But . . . what's the alternative?'

He sighed. 'No. You're right. But we'll have to come up with some way of explaining it to them.'

'We'll have to explain a lot of things, I suspect. But let's not worry about that right now. Let's just get out of here.'

'Yeah, totally,' Macy agreed vigorously.

They finally emerged into daylight. The sun was by now low on the horizon, long shadows stretching across the rust-red desert. Nobody was in sight, the Land Cruiser parked a short distance away. Nina looked up at the little crack concealing the crystal lock. 'Let's close it.'

'How're you going to reach it?' Eddie asked as he tossed the gun back through the opening. 'You can't stand up, not on that leg.'

'Macy'll have to do it.'

'Me?' said Macy, surprised.

'You're my daughter,' Nina said, 'which means you're a descendant of the Atlanteans – and apparently the Nephilim too – just like me. So when it comes to earth energy, you can do anything I can. Probably more. I can't do your yo-yo tricks, for a start!'

Eddie peered at the recess. 'Think you can reach it if you stand on my shoulders, love?'

'Uh . . . I guess.' Macy sounded less than confident. 'You *will* hold on tight, won't you?'

He smiled. 'I won't let go of you, don't worry. Not ever.' She smiled back.

Eddie took Nina to the car and carefully lowered her into the front passenger seat, finding the first-aid kit and bandaging her leg, then returned to the cave with Macy. He picked her up and helped her stand on his shoulders.

'Okay,' Nina called. 'You can do it, Macy.'

'I *can* do it,' Macy echoed, stretching up as far as she could. Her fingertips brushed the red rock, straining to make contact – then Eddie hoisted her up off his shoulders and her probing finger found the crystal inside the gap. She yelped as a *snap* of energy made her flinch, but her father managed to keep her upright. She quickly jumped back down to the sand.

Behind them, the hidden door ground shut, closing off the tunnel into the heart of Uluru, and sealed with a final, decisive *boom*.

Nina stared at it for a long moment, wondering if it would ever be opened again . . . before deciding she did not want to know the answer. Her gaze went to Eddie and Macy. There were more important things in life.

'Come on, then,' she said as her family approached the truck. 'We're done. Let's go home.'

Eddie gave her a smile as he got into the driving seat, Macy climbing in behind him. 'We need a break. Couple of years sound good?'

Nina smiled back, unfastening her ponytail and letting her hair fall loose. 'At least!'

They all laughed, and he started the engine. Safely reunited at last, they drove off into the sunset.

If you loved *The Resurrection Key* . . .

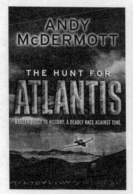

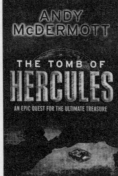

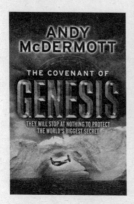

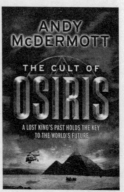

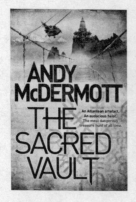

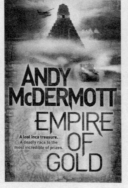

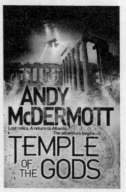

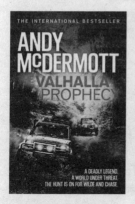
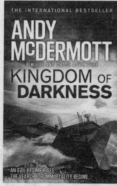

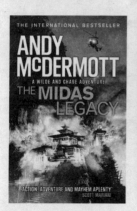
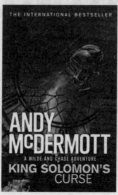
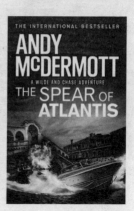